Janet McNulty

Book 1 in the Enchained Trilogy

Enchained
Copyright © 2018 Janet McNulty

ISBN-10: 1-941488-81-1 (MMP Publishing)
ISBN-13: 978-1-941488-81-2

Library of Congress Control Number: 2018905178

Printed in the United States of America

First Edition

This book is dedicated to all those who actually read the dedication page. I mean, who actually reads the dedication page? If you do, you are a rarity and deserve to have a book dedicated to you. I mean that with sincerity.

This book **is not** for the easily offended. If you are part of this group, you probably shouldn't bother reading—period.

As for the critics, I do not care what you think. I am certain that you will point out everything that is wrong with this book as though your opinion is the only one that matters, but I didn't write this book for you. I wrote the book the way it needed to be and best told Noni's story, not to please you.

Contents

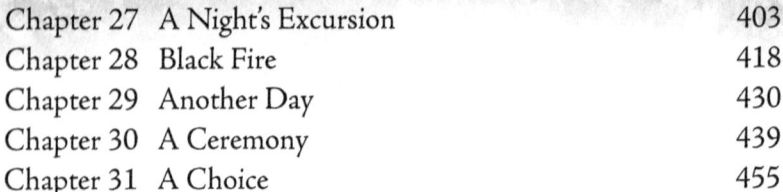

Chapter 1

The Gauntlet

I have trained for this day my entire life: the day I become a member of the Martial Diplomatic Corps and earn my uniform as an arbiter. Only the strongest, the fittest, and the smartest are allowed to be a part of this honored service. I passed the written exams, but today is the day I must pass the gauntlet. Failure means death.

I never knew my birth parents—a fleeting thought that races through my mind as I approach the starting line—and as far as I am concerned, I never had any. On the day of my birth, men came and took me from my mother's arms as she screamed, or so the whispers of others have said. It doesn't matter. The officers around me are the only parental units I have ever known. Every year, the Martial Diplomatic Corps visits the maternity wards and does an evaluation of the healthiest pregnant women in the region, taking their children upon birth. Those infants are taken to a bunker, where they learn not love, care, or guidance, but how to be strong, self-disciplined, and the need for eradicating one's emotions, but above all, to learn the law.

I stand in front of the starting line, surrounded by others like me, all 18 years in age, all dark-skinned, all dressed in black jackets and pants that hug every curvature of our bodies, and all expecting to win. I spot Faya, my only friend in this place, not that we ever speak of it as friendships are discouraged, and we lock eyes a moment before she nods in the direction of Trevors. My eyes roam over to him, taking in the muscles that he has built within the last year and the extra foot he has grown as well, making him over six feet tall. I hope I do not have to go up against him in a one-on-one competition. He is arrogant and enamored with the idea of having authority over others, and he loathes me, a feeling that is mutual.

"This is your final test," says Molers, our commanding officer, head of the training center, and overseer of the gauntlet. His rank is Master Arbiter, and by his lack of gray hair, you would never guess that he is 57. His boots echo with each purposeful and steady step that he takes, breaking through the buzzing silence within my ears, making certain that he has our full attention and that we all know he is in charge. "The gauntlet is a five-mile obstacle course. Not all of you will survive."

A few murmurs rise from those who refuse to believe that the officers of the training facility would allow recruits to die. I scoff at their stupidity, having witnessed their ferociousness before.

Molers' harsh eyes glare at those who laughed at his speech and ringing silence fills the hangar we are in once again.

"Some of you will not survive," Molers reiterates, his bass voice sending chills down my back. A part of me dreads this final test, but I shake it off. "Those of you who do will take your place among the elite, a special group of people charged with and dedicated to maintaining peace and order within our society. If you survive, you will be responsible for ensuring the security of the citizens of Arel. You"—he stops in front of me and I shrink before his unforgiving gaze as the man has always frightened me—"are our future."

He walks away to the sidelines and joins others of his rank and station, my superiors. They each bear the same hardened expressions and lined eyes as they scrutinize the line of recruits. I watch as he picks up the gun on the pedestal covered in a blood-red cloth and lean forward, ready to sprint the moment it sounds.

"Recruits, I wish you luck!"

The gun fires.

I race forward, leaving the ones standing next to me behind as I sprint for the first phase of the gauntlet. I do not have to go far before I reach it. Just before the double doors to the hangar that lead to the city outside, huge flames shoot out of the floor, reaching the ceiling and leaving fresh burn marks that cover the ones from the previous year. I skid to a halt, my heart racing and pushing its way past my esophagus in an effort to escape what could very well be my death. The fires disappear.

Unsure of whether I should proceed, I wait, while others who had stopped when the flames first appeared sprint forward. It is a mistake. Fire erupts from the floor a second time, consuming those who had tried to continue through; their tortured screams fill my ears and I want to block it out, but cannot. I knew that death awaits in the gauntlet; everyone did, but did not want to believe it at first. My first failure. Death is everywhere.

The flames disappear again, but another set shoots out from the walls further down, before vanishing, only to be replaced by another series of fiery bursts. As I study them, I realize that there is a pattern to their madness, but there are certain areas where the fires do not reach. The first set of flames erupt once more; I start counting until they cease and begin my count again until the next set appears. Ten seconds. I glance back at the starting line where Molers and the other superior officers sit and scrutinize the recruits. They will move to the observation area soon to finish watching the recruits on the viewing screens, after which they will take a shuttle, also known as a railcar, to the finish line to welcome the survivors.

I turn back to the first phase and begin my count again, ignoring those who go too early and their anguished cries when their bodies are burned until they are charcoal. The first fires appear again and I begin my count.

One... two... three... four... five... six... seven... eight... nine... ten.

The flames vanish and I run while counting in my head.

One... two... three...

Sweat drips down the sides of my temples from the heat that fills the metallic tomb.

Four... five... six...

Almost there. I stretch my long legs, focusing on the safe zone ahead when someone rams into me, sending me flying sideways toward the wall where the next series of fires will erupt from. I crash against the metal wall and an echoing bang fills the area. I look up. Trevors sneers at me before racing away. That bastard! I do not have time to be angry, having lost a couple of seconds. A low rumble vibrates the wall next to me. I know that at any second the second series of flames will spring forth.

I jump to my feet, stumbling a little as I regain my sense of balance, and flee. I have gone eight steps when the fires burst from the holes in the hangar walls, the heat searing my skin and singeing my jacket. I dive for the safe area I had spotted earlier and hit the ground, wrapping my arms around my head to protect my face from the intense heat, my ears begging for relief from the thundering roar that surrounds me. Cold air hits my skin, followed by silence, and I know the flames are gone—for now. I jump to my feet, my boots slamming the ground with their hollow sound, and spring forward, starting my count once again.

One... two... three... four...

My eyes spot a charred body that had been a recruit only moments before. A part of me thinks that I should feel pity for him, but my training and will to survive ignores it.

Five... six... seven...

I stomp on a smoldering sleeve of someone's jacket as I focus on where I need to be in order to avoid the third set of flames.

Eight... nine...

I push myself, running so fast that I almost trip as my feet threaten to entangle themselves.

Ten!

I reach the safe zone and skid to a stop just as fire erupts around me, surrounding me, threatening to cook me alive. I smell charred smoke and realize that my jacket has caught fire. I tear it off, throwing it to the floor and stomping on it to put the flames out before straightening up and staring at the fire in front of me. My black skin glistens in the dancing light from the sweat that has formed, running down my arms in streaks.

The inferno dissipates. I rush forward, recounting the seconds before the last set of flames show themselves. To my dismay, I spot Trevors. He has already reached the end of phase one and turns and waves at me as his disappointed look turns to a sneer. I want to wipe that smug expression off his face, but have to concentrate on what lies ahead.

Five... six....

The last safe zone is not far. Someone comes up beside me. I recognize his face and his wavy hair, but cannot recall his name. He trips and crashes to the ground, landing in front of me, forcing me to leap over him.

Nine.... ten!

I reach the last safe zone, but the other recruit's screams fill my ears when the inferno begins again, and chills run down my spine. I spot Faya through the licking flames and the name of the fallen recruit that I had just passed hits me: Jonas. Two days ago, Faya had pointed him out to me, saying that she liked him; that is why his face was familiar. Sadness fills me for a moment, because if we both survive, I will have to tell her that the first boy she had ever shown romantic interest in is dead.

The fires vanish. I race forward, restarting the count. If I reach the end, I will be safe, for the moment, until I reach phase two of the gauntlet. My heart beats against my chest as I shoot forward, pushing myself with all the strength that I have.

Two... three...

I glance to my left and notice Faya on the ground, struggling against something. I stop. Her right foot is caught in a snare. I am so close to the end of phase one, so close to escaping the flames, but if I continue, she dies, my only friend. Ever since we were first bunkmates, we have been friends. We would stay up after lights out, talking about our day, the latest recruits, whom we liked and didn't like, whispering so as not to wake the others, or get into trouble. Though attachments are forbidden, everyone, including the officers, know that people form their circles, gravitating toward those they like and relate to while staying away from others they consider enemies. As I stand there watching Faya struggle with the snare, I know that I must make a choice.

I hear the rumble as the tubes get ready to spew more of their wrath and change course, sprinting for Faya, dodging others who wish only to get away from what they know is coming. I shove others out of my way, garnering angry shouts and curses, but I do not care. I refuse to allow my friend to die. I squat on the ground when I reach Faya and her surprised face informs me that she had not expected anyone to help her.

"What are you doing?" she asks, the fear in her voice masking my own trepidation.

"Can you move it?" I reply, ignoring her question.

"It's some sort of rope. You will need a knife or something to cut it. I feel so stupid. I should have known…"

I pull on the rope, but cannot tear it apart. The rumble grows louder and I know we are out of time. I pull on the rope again and it stretches, having untangled itself, but still remains firm around Faya's ankle. We are next to one of the vents that the fire will erupt from and I get an idea, though I know that Faya will not like it. I grab her by the shoulders and drag her, pulling the rope around her ankle across the smoking vent until it is taut.

"What are you doing?" She struggles against me, but my grip remains firm.

"Just trust me!"

"We'll both die!"

It does not matter. There is no time for me to make a run for the end and I refuse to leave her. Before she or I have a chance to say anything else, fire bursts from the vent, vaporizing the rope that holds her while we both throw our arms in front of our faces to shield them. They vanish. We both grin at one another before we realize that her boot is on fire. As she shakes her foot in an attempt to put out the flames, her wiry hair bobbing up and down with each movement, I put all my weight on her leg to hold it down and tear off her boot, thrusting it aside before lifting her off the ground. By now, I have lost my count and have no idea when the next series of flames will appear; all I know is that we need to get out of here.

I take off for where I know the last set of flames will erupt from, but if we make it past them, then we will have passed phase one. I hang back a little so as not to leave Faya behind as she hobbles, her movements unsteady now that she is without a boot. We hurry past the smoldering vents as they threaten to spew more of their furious inferno on us, Faya hobbling, weaving side to side, mimicking a seesaw, as I push her onward. Either we both make it, or we both die.

The rumble begins again. Three more recruits appear next to us (one of them my bunkmate), their mouths wide open as they suck in air in an effort to push themselves and avoid what we all know is coming. It grows louder, and an orange glow fills the metal tubes of the vents. We are just yards away from safety. I seize Faya's shirt and push her across the ledge marking the end of phase one and leap over it myself, rolling across the ground just as a wall of fire explodes from the vents. I glance at Faya. Her chest still heaves as she tries to control her breathing. I turn to look for the three who had been running beside us. One did not make it.

Though we survived phase one, we do not have time to rest or congratulate ourselves. Faya and I stand up while other recruits run past us.

"Go," she says.

"But…"

"Go on. I'll catch up."

I look up at the drones hovering around us, capturing us on their cameras, and know that the officers are probably frowning at my actions. The gauntlet is supposed to be a test of an individual recruit's strength and endurance, and I risked everything to save a friend. I take one last look at Faya, still hunched over, catching her breath before hurrying away, passing through the hangar doors and into the outside world.

My eyes hurt and I squint as they adjust to the bright sunshine after having been enclosed in a darkened cave that had almost become my tomb. The road lights up with images of Arel's insignia dotting the center, marking the path we are to follow. People walk by me, giving me odd glances and keeping their heads low. The only ones who stand proud are those who are dark-skinned like me— they are the noble class. I realize I have wasted precious moments looking around and jog down the road, following the marked path to phase two. I just hope phase two is easier than phase one, but know that it will be just as unpleasant, if not more so.

Someone yanks my ponytail and jerks me back. I fall to the ground, landing on my butt, my neck aching from the sudden tug on it, and watch as another recruit races ahead of me. Sabotaging the others in an effort to win is the norm, but it still incenses me. It is cheating in the end.

"You win by any means necessary," I hear Molers' commanding voice in my head and I have no doubt that he killed any who got in his way when he had to run the gauntlet at my age.

I spring to my feet and run down the road, following the lighted marks, keeping my eyes focused on the one who had pulled me back. If this is how he wants to play, then I will show him what it means to be cast aside. I increase my speed, running faster to catch up, lining up behind him, and positioning myself so that I can shove him into the electric fence that lines the path, placed there just for this occasion. Almost there. My breaths are in short gasps as I close the distance between us.

The ground drops beneath us and I find myself in a state of freefall as my momentum propels me forward, but I am no longer on solid ground. I slam into something sharp and reach out, grabbing onto anything to stop me from falling further, until I am left with my feet dangling in the air. I have managed to reach the edge of the hole. I realize that the recruit who had flung me to the ground by my ponytail is no longer with me. I look down into the hole and see spikes on the bottom with his mangled body upon them, and his vacant eyes staring at me. My earlier wish to get even with him vanishes and I regret ever thinking of such a thing.

I turn back to my own predicament and heave myself up over the ledge and onto solid ground, just as the trap doors shut and the path looks solid once more. Tunnels run beneath the city with trap doors placed in certain areas so as to make it easier to send military personnel and supplies, should Arel be attacked by the neighboring city state of Kition, but it seems that those in charge of the gauntlet decided to use those same tunnels as a test of our resolve. Someone lands beside me, having jumped over the opening. I take a deep breath and pull myself to my feet, only to be forced to turn around when the screams of an unlucky recruit pierce my ears. Looking down, I see one of my bunkmates hanging from a spike, facedown.

I have no time to waste and continue onward. If I fail to reach the end of the gauntlet, I will be killed. I race ahead, trailing after two more who leap over the dark opening, desperate to get ahead. Another trap door opens and I jump to the right to avoid it, skipping across the narrow pavement that keeps me from falling through the hole or slamming into the electrified fence. Another trap door starts to open and I leap across it, landing on the slanted doorway, but before it drops, I jump back onto solid ground.

A blur races past me and I dodge it, turning away as someone crashes into the electric fence, pushed into it by another recruit, and sparks fly from him as the 10,000 volts go right through his shaking body. There is no time to gawk at him or pity him. I must continue. A final trap door opens, but I avoid it by jerking to the left and running along its edge before jumping over the ever expanding space. Phase two is now complete.

An incline forms and my breathing becomes more labored as I race up the steep hill, following the lighted markers, continuing my trek through the gauntlet. My pace slows. I cannot allow myself to lose because losing means death—it means I am a failure. The thought of failing gnaws at me and my pride spurs me onward. I quicken my pace, forcing myself to climb the hill leading to the reservoir of Arel, where phase three must begin.

Another recruit passes me. By the strained look on her face, I know that she is using every ounce of strength she has to make it up the hill. I realize that we are the only two here and think it strange that there are no citizens. One can usually spot a person or two on the road to the reservoir and there are always at least three people monitoring the city's water supply, but the area is empty. I glance at her, but she refuses my gaze, not bothering to acknowledge my presence. Only one thing is on her mind: completing the gauntlet. I let her go. It is best to reserve my energy. I will need it for whatever phase three holds.

An explosion jolts the area and its force knocks me down while bits of dirt and flesh rain down upon me. I remain still until I calm my nerves and look up to see a bloodied hand, the other recruit's hand, on the ground in front of me. Now I know why no one is here. The makers of the gauntlet have laced this area with landmines and must have warned people to stay away, making this phase three.

I take my time standing up and survey the area. The positions of some of the landmines are obvious, with the dirt turned up and gleaming in the sunlight, but it could be a trick. Phase three is meant to test our ability to reason and to think. Footsteps sound behind me and I whirl around. It's Trevors. Did he get held up with the traps in phase two? When I last saw him, he was well ahead of me. I watch as he continues running and notice that he is heading straight for the field of landmines. I contemplate letting him go. Maybe he will step on a mine and that would be the end of his taunting and constant attacks, but such a thought seems cold and spiteful. There is no logical reason to let him die, not when it is within my power to save him.

I spot a rock, scoop it up, and race for him, running as fast as I can. My feet slip on the dirt, but I manage to retain my balance. Trevors never sees me coming. I plow into him, tackling him and forcing him to the ground, and we roll across it for a few feet.

"What the hell, Noni?" he yells at me, but my answer is to throw the rock I have. It lands on a mine, triggering it, and the earsplitting explosion stops his rage while he stares at the dirt that shoots into the air before pelting the ground around us.

I look at him, but he says nothing. I just saved your life, jerk; the least you can do is thank me. I do not tell him what I am thinking, but anger swells within me at his unappreciative actions. I jump up, looking around for anything I can use to prod the ground with. I spot a fallen branch at the base of a nearby tree, just the right size to use as a walking stick and snatch it. After testing it, I notice that it is brittle, so I will have to be careful. I jog back to the mine field and ease the stick into the ground at an angle and toward the side of an upturned mound of dirt. Nothing. I prod at it a bit more and realize that the mound was put there to fake us out. I step on it. Trevors is right behind me, no doubt thinking it more prudent to just follow me and let me be the one to set off any mines.

I push my stick into the ground again, being careful to not make any sudden movements and to keep it at an angle. It hits something hard. Knowing that I have just found a mine, I ease the stick underneath the solid object and pry it up, my slow movements masking the anxiousness within me. The mine pops out of the ground and I scoot it to the side. Since the mine itself is activated by a change in pressure, or when someone steps on it, I can move it without worry, so long as I don't touch the plate. I step where the mine was and take a deep breath, glad that I have avoided death, for the moment.

Again, I ease my stick into the ground at a shallow angle and touch the base of another mine. Trevors breathes down my neck as he stands behind me, watching my movements, his usual bravado gone. After I work that mine out and push it aside, I look behind me in an effort to ease the crick forming in my neck and see that a line has built up with me in the lead. Others had arrived, and having seen me picking my way through the field with Trevors trailing behind, they have decided to line up behind him.

I turn back to the task at hand, not sure how much farther I have to go, but I spot the lighted markers and guess that they must be marking the boundary. I shove my stick back into the dirt, using the same gentle motions as before. Nothing. I take one more step forward. Again, I ease my stick in at a 25-degree angle and feel a light jolt as it hits something. Another mine. No one speaks as I pry the mine out of the ground and flip it to one side. Minutes tick by, as my mind concentrates on what I am doing, blocking out all distractions. After taking a few steps and finding no more mines, I know I have reached the end of phase three. Trevors senses it too, since before I get very far, he shoves me aside, and my knee rams into the ground and burns as gravel rips through my pants leg and into my skin. Maybe I should not have saved him, I think to myself, as I watch him speed off with the others behind him.

An explosion rocks the air and I turn to watch as the remains of an unlucky recruit litters the earth. He should have paid more attention. I pull myself to my feet and start running again, jumping over rocks and another recruit who has tripped and fallen in front of me. My lungs burn for relief, but I refuse to give it to them. I need to get to the top of the hill before the others as phase four of the gauntlet awaits.

I skid to a halt when I reach the top and the edge of the reservoir.

Other recruits stand next to me, not liking what they see, and I soon discover why. The dam had been opened just a little, enough to allow some of the water to pour into the canal system, which circles through the city and empties back into the reservoir. On the surface, it does not seem like such a big deal, but I know that once in the water, I will have to watch out for the current that has been created. If I get caught in it, I risk drowning. The lighted markers are on the other side and I know that we are supposed to swim across, but how will I get through that undercurrent?

Someone runs and jumps in. I watch as his head pokes through the surface and he bobs as he takes a breath before he stretches his arms and starts to swim across. We all stare at this brave recruit, and for a moment, it looks as though he might make it. He lifts his arm out and strokes the water and... he disappears. The current created by the opened dam captures him and drags him under. We all watch, helpless, as the recruit struggles to break free of the current, but is sucked under as he is washed away through the opened dam and into the canal system. No one speaks. We all know that he has died.

Trevors dives into the water and speeds across it, passing through the undertow with ease. He always was a strong swimmer. Others jump in. Some make it. Some do not. I do not like my options. I am not that strong of a swimmer. It was the one thing I struggled at during training, but I know that I cannot stay here, and my superiors are watching, as the hover drone reminds me.

I look up and down the reservoir and notice that the surrounding wall of it borders onto the inner wall that surrounds Arel. I think back to the schematics of the city that I had to memorize for the written exam. A protective wall surrounds Arel, but it is really a double wall. There is the outer wall that outsiders see, and it borders onto the wildlands, but there is also the inner wall, which serves as another layer of protection. The reservoir borders onto the inner wall. I wonder why the architect of the city would do such a thing as it does not seem safe, but perhaps it was at the time. Arel is old, or so I have always been told, and as I look out at the city below, I see that Arel has grown around the reservoir, forming a bit of a 'W' around it. I also spot two mountains where Kition is supposed to be, a constant threat. The official history is that Kition and Arel were once allies, having formed during the time of Great Upheaval, but something happened, and for the last 150 years, the two have been bitter enemies. I wonder if they are watching us now as we try to pass this final test.

I pull myself from my fleeting thoughts and back to what I must do. I run to the edge of the reservoir and notice that there is a gap between it and the inner wall. If I can jump it, I can bypass the current, though I will have to swim the rest of the way. I risk it. Splashing water sounds behind me as I run to the reservoir's eastern edge and take a running leap across, grunting as the wind is knocked out of me when I land on the other side and a metal bar slams into my stomach. I grip the bar, relieved to have made it. Wild barking forces me to look down into the gap between the reservoir and the inner wall. Spikes await at the bottom, and falling would have meant my death, but darting around those spikes are wild dogs, kept there in case anyone survives the fall. They are kept in a state of constant hunger, turning them into man-eating animals, and best avoided.

I turn around so that my back is pressed against the bars that line the top of the wall and I am facing the reservoir. I watch as recruits swim across: some disappear beneath the water, others make it to the other side. A clink sounds above me. I look up at one of the towers and a masked face stares down at me. Idiot that I am. I forgot about the guard towers and the watchmen that are there with orders to shoot anyone who dares to cross the wall, even if they are trying to leave. I sometimes wondered if the wall around Arel was meant more to keep people in than to keep danger out. I stare at the watchman. Why hasn't he shot me yet? Could he have orders not to shoot the recruits as they run the gauntlet?

I have no time to worry about it. The more I stand here, the more I risk being the last one to finish. I scoot across the top of the inner wall, my toes poking out over the edge, and my heart skips several beats as the dogs follow my movements, their incessant barking shattering what nerves I have left. My foot slips and I flail my arms, seizing the bar with my sweaty palm as they threaten to let go, my feet dangling in the air. The dogs gather around below me, deafening me with their excited and hopeful barking. Calming myself, I pull myself up, relief flooding through me when I place my feet back on the edge of the wall.

I have no time to rejoice. I am falling behind and must catch up. Inch by inch, I scoot sideways, clinging to the bar, my shoulders hurting from the odd angle I am keeping them at, and make my way over the spillway of the dam. A scream catches my attention, followed by the detonation of a landmine. Another unlucky recruit has failed. I crawl over the dam opening and make it to the other side, away from the powerful current. If I go any further along the wall, I will end up away from the reservoir and where I need to go. I must jump back across.

I gauge the distance, but will not have the advantage of a running start. The dogs below me circle around with saliva dripping from their fangs as their mouths hang open in anticipation. More recruits jump into the water. Regulating my breathing, I balance on the edge of the wall and jump across. Air whistles past me and my stomach leaps into my throat as I sail through the air and free-fall. I miss my mark. I smash into the side of the reservoir wall and scramble to grab hold of something before I fall. My descent stops. Ignoring the burning pain within my arms and hands, I heave myself upward, placing my feet against the side of the wall and pushing with my legs. I reach the top and roll onto my back, staring up at the clouds in the sky, wondering how many times I will cheat death today. The disappointment of the dogs meets my ears. I lean over and glare at them as I pick up a rock and chuck it at them. Stupid animals. Remembering that I still have to swim across the remainder of the reservoir, I haul myself to my feet and dive in.

I gasp as the cold water hits me, shocking my unsuspecting body, and gag because water slips into my mouth and chokes me. Kicking, I burst through the surface, coughing, while trying to inhale at the same time. It only results in more ragged coughs. I turn my head around, spotting where I need to go, and kick my feet to propel myself through the water. My swim is uneventful, and I think that perhaps I will make it to the other side with no interruptions, but strong hands seize me from behind and shove me under the water. I kick and swing my arms, causing white bubbles to surge around me in frenzied circles that block my vision as I struggle to break free from my attacker's grasp, but a fist rams into the base of my neck, stunning me.

I notice he has a knife shoved in his boot, an illegal item as well, since recruits are not supposed to have any weapons on them while within the gauntlet; they are supposed to rely on their stamina and wits, but I am not surprised that some cheat. I snatch the knife from his boot and stab him in the ankle with it. Blood pools around us, darkening the water. His grip loosens and I tear myself away, twisting around and elbowing him in the jaw twice. While he rears back, stunned, I bring my feet up and kick him hard in the chest before swimming for the surface. Crisp air attacks my face and I breathe deep, glad to have air in my lungs again. Something bumps into me. It's the recruit who had tried to drown me, floating in the water facedown. I should leave and let him die. He did try to kill me.

I start to swim away, but stop. I do not know why I stop, but something in the pit of my stomach tells me that I cannot just leave him there to drown. I move toward him, flip him onto his back, and wrap an arm under his left shoulder, while using my other arm and legs to propel us to the embankment. I reach the sandy bank out of breath and exhausted, but I drag the recruit onto the ground, out of the water. Wiping the water from my face, I take a deep breath and continue on. If the recruit wakes up, he can finish the gauntlet on his own, but at least he won't drown.

Phase four is over.

I pull myself back to my feet, stuffing the knife into my own boot, and stagger on. My muscles are tired, but I have trained for this, and I will them to continue—to obey my command. Sand sticks to my soaked pants legs, falling in chunks as I move. The whine of a drone tickles my ears. I refuse to look at it as it follows after me, capturing my small moment of triumph, relaying every detail back to the viewing area for the Corps' instructors. I wonder what they think of me saving the one recruit who had tried to drown me. I shake off such a thought. It does not matter.

My boots stomp the ground, beating it with their incessant stride as I run to catch up to the others who are far ahead of me. I find the path and speed up, flying across the ground, steadying my breathing as I hurry, and not paying attention to the lack of everyday sounds as I enter a small clearing in the city, but I realize that there are no people, no carts, no open stores, or conversations. It is still. I pass it off as perhaps people were told to stay indoors until the gauntlet is over, so that they do not interfere. I quicken my pace. It could be that…

A bit of wind rushes by my face and my cheek burns, as the concrete pavement forms a dent, causing me to fling myself to the left and hug the ground. Another bullet strikes near my side. I scramble to the edge of a building and hide behind a corner in the shadows. I turn my head, searching for the sniper, and stop. Slumped in the corner with a round hole in his chest is another recruit. This must be phase five.

Another bullet strikes the wall, its clink snapping me back to attention. I dive to my right and back into the clearing, running across the paved stone and heading for the truck-sized planters on the other end. Nothing but dead plants spill over the edges, killed by an unusual frost. I skid across the ground as I duck behind the planters just as another bullet grazes it, sending chips of stone to the ground. I pick them and study them, recognizing the pattern. I have been trained in the use of a sniper's weapon, though I am not as skilled as a true sniper who spends an extra three years in training if he passes the gauntlet.

I search for the sniper, but he is well concealed and I cannot stay where I am. I toss the stone bits from the planter a few feet away. Within seconds, another bullet strikes the ground next to it, but I use the small amount of time to search for the sniper. I spot him. Just a flicker of movement, and his camouflaged clothing hides him well, but I notice the small shift in the bricks that make up the side of the building. Got him.

Before he realizes that he has been tricked, I dart from behind the planter and hurry to the side of another building, a butcher shop, and hunker behind a sign. The doors open, activated by the motion sensors that picked up my movement. Damn it! I should have known better. I flee to another area while the shattering of glass reminds me of how close I came to being struck by the sniper's weapon.

Footsteps come from my left and I glance over, watching as an unsuspecting recruit rushes up to the small city square. He falters and plummets to the ground as a bullet strikes his left leg. I race to him, seizing him around the shoulders and drag him to cover, and it is then that I recognize his face: he is the one who had tried to drown me and I have saved his life for a second time.

"You idiot!" he screams at me, but I ignore him as I peek around a corner, searching for the sniper.

Another bullet pelts the side of the store and I smile. Now I know where he is.

"That's my knife," says the recruit, noticing the hilt poking over the top of my boot.

"Not anymore," I reply, scooping up a shard of glass and running off. I dart behind another sign, clinging to the shadows, glad that my skin matched them, making me more difficult to see.

A scream shatters the silence. I turn and see a small boy, a plebeian, wandering in the square. His white skin provides a stark contrast against the dark pavement. The scream sounds again as a woman rushes for the boy, sweat gleaming from the brand on her right forearm (a sign of her status), while the legs of her pants swished together from her frantic movements. Two shots permeate the air and both woman and child lie on the concrete. I seize this chance to hurry across the square, staying near the edge and out of the sun. My foot presses into the thin stream of blood that runs from the boy and toward me, and I curse about the prints that will be left on the ground because of it. In my attempt to scrape the blood off my boots as I walk, my eyes focus on the boy laying on the ground. He was just one plebeian. Others will replace him.

I hurry away and hunker under the low hanging balcony that the sniper is hiding on. Another recruit runs up and stops when he sees the two dead plebeians before him, diving behind a motorcar just as two more shots ring out. Knowing this is my only chance, I jump up, grasping the lower edge of the balcony, and pull myself up, taking the shard of glass I had tucked in my waistband and tossing it away from me as a distraction. As the sniper whirls around to see what had made the sound, I fling myself over the railing and kick him in the back. He crashes into the rail, but recovers quicker than I had expected. He swings the butt of his weapon at me, but I duck and tackle him, forcing him to the floor while I grab his weapon with both my hands and straddle him as I try to pin him to the ground. He head-butts me. Though a bit stunned, I wrestle the rifle from him and hit him in the head with it, knocking him unconscious, and dismantle his weapon, throwing the bullets away so that he cannot harm any more recruits that will pass through.

When I jump off the balcony and land on the pavement, I notice that the other recruits have left. I have no time to waste and start running again, following the lighted markers as I head for phase six, leaving the two bodies in the square. Sanitation will clean them up.

The markers lead me to a wall, which seemed to have been built just for this occasion, with little hand and footholds on it, at uneven intervals. A line runs from above the wall and to the other side, and my guess is that it leads further into the city where phase seven awaits. I jump at the wall and cling to the handholds that are there. Before I have a chance to climb any further, rough hands seize my shoulders and rip me away, throwing me to the hard ground, where I land with a grunt. My left elbow throbs where it smashed into the cement and I feel the beginnings of a bruise form; the swelling is unmistakable.

One of the female recruits bears down upon me, glaring at me, her unnatural blue eyes filled with hatred. Grelyn. I should have known. She and Trevors were close—more than close. If unions were allowed in the Martial Diplomatic Corps, they would have applied and been granted it. The two were the same, each trying to outdo the other in ruthlessness, and like Trevors, Grelyn detested my very existence. She must have seen me and decided to take advantage of the situation.

Her blue eyes were made that way after she underwent a procedure so that she could see in the dark the way nocturnal animals do. Upon our 17th year, each recruit is offered a chance to undergo the operation, but most refuse since it is dangerous and not everyone comes out of it unharmed. One of the side effects on those whose bodies reject the implants is permanent blindness, but on Grelyn, her body not only accepted the implants, but it was also as though she was meant to have them. Right now, I wish that she had suffered from the side effects. It would have saved me the trouble.

I kick at her knee, but she is waiting for me and swerves out of the way, bringing her foot up to my stomach. Gasping for air, I clutch my abdomen as I breathe in, trying to ignore the sharp pain. A blur of motion heads for my head. I roll out of the way, forcing her to hit air. I tackle her. We roll across the ground, and for a moment, I think I have the upper hand when she grabs my right arm, kicks me in the chest with her knee, and flips me onto my stomach, with my arm wrenched behind my back. I feel the tendons in my shoulder threaten to tear as she pulls it back and shoves my face into the ground. Dirt fills my mouth and nose and I cough, but coughing only forces me to choke even more, while her sneering laugh fills my ears, filling me with rage. My left hand flails across the ground and I squeeze my fingers together, scooping up a handful of dirt. I throw it behind me and into her face. I'm free.

Before she has a chance to pin me again, I roll onto my back and see her about ready to jump on me when a single shot shatters the silence around us. From the sound, I know it is not a sniper's weapon, but a handheld pistol, and means that the first recruits have finished the gauntlet. Neither Grelyn, nor I, have time to waste on our eternal squabble. Grelyn kicks more dirt into my face and runs to the wall, jumping on it and climbing it like as spider. Despite my own hatred for her, I could not deny her skills.

I wipe my face, coughing twice more and hauling myself to my feet with my elbow, shoulder, and stomach all in pain. I push through. I have to push through it. Pain is a sign of weakness and weakness will not be tolerated. Only the strong survive. Only the strong can protect Arel.

I charge the wall, leaping into the air and gripping the handholds that have been placed there. Sweat drips from my face onto my chest, while more forms between the skin of my palms and the smooth wood. I pull myself up, bracing the balls of my feet against the flattened areas of the wall while pushing with my legs. My grip slips, and for a moment, I fear that I will fall, but I manage to regain my hold on the wall as my moist breath forms mist on its exterior. I look up. Grelyn has already reached the top. Her balance wavers for a second as she stands upon the ledge of the wall beneath the zip lines, and a part of me hopes she will fall, but she doesn't. She grasps the remaining harnesses of the zip lines and looks down at me, grinning, before shoving them down the line while keeping one for herself.

That bitch.

I climb faster, grabbing another handhold and propelling myself upwards, refusing to stop until I reach the top of the wall. My hands find the ledge, and I heave myself upon it, but Grelyn has gone. I lay on my side, catching my breath, and glace toward the lower part of Arel, while a dark shape grows smaller in the distance.

What am I going to do? Without the harnesses, I cannot ride the zip line down to the next stage of the gauntlet. A small portion of my brain reminds me that neither can anyone else.

I stare at the three lines above me. Something pokes my shin and—I am such a fool! I still had the knife and I could have stabbed Grelyn with it! Cursing my own forgetfulness, I push such regrets aside as none of it will help me off this wall, but perhaps the knife will have another use. I rise to my feet, not daring to look at the ground, but keep my eyes focused on the lines above me. I touch one with my hand and, if I'm lucky, I may be able to cut through it and use it to slide down the zip line to the next phase.

I find the bolts holding it into the wall and use my knife to pry them loose. After so much use by all the recruits—not that these bolts were meant to last for very long anyway, and I think they have been designed to become loose after a certain amount of usage—they pop free and fall to the ground where they disappear. I wrap the end of the line around my hand and stretch it out, placing the blade of my knife over it and hack at it. At first, nothing happens and I fear that I may fail to pass the gauntlet, but, without warning, it frays. As I continue to saw at it, more strands of the line break apart and snap free. The piece of cable goes limp in my grasp and dangles in the wind, swaying in the chill breeze. I hear running footsteps, but do not care as I ignore them, flinging the cable over the zip line and wrapping the ends around my hands. I push off.

My stomach leaps into my throat as the sudden loss of a solid surface leaves my feet and I hang in the air, careening over Arel, past towers, and over the tops of buildings. My eyes water and sting from the cold air that blasts my face, causing my cheeks to burn, but all of that is cancelled out by the cord cutting into my flesh as it bears my weight. I watch as the city zips past below me, having never seen it from this angle before. My admiring mind freezes. How am I going to stop? I am going so fast, that I have no idea how I will stop. My small moment of triumph may mean my death because of my own shortsightedness.

My answer comes the moment worry threatens to take over my mind when I look ahead again. In front of me is a massive canvass trampoline, but hanging vertical from a crisscross mesh of ropes, and the zip line veers off so that anyone in the harness would be sideways when they hit it, not head on. Though I might survive, I know it will hurt. I let go. The momentum flings me into the hanging trampoline, and I curl into a ball, wrapping my arms around my head to protect it, and I feel the canvass wrap around my body before chucking me back out and I drop. I open an eye to peek and see a net hurling for me. I squeeze my eyes shut again and plow into the netting. As it absorbs the impact, it breaks away, and I fall into another net below it, before it, too, breaks away, allowing me to land into a third net, which remains intact, and I bounce up and down a bit before stopping. Laying on my back, I look up, marveling, and relieved, that I am still alive. Plebeians scurry up ladders and ropes to refasten the nets and make them ready for the next recruit.

I roll over and crawl out of the mesh, dropping over the side and landing on the muddy ground on my hands and knees. Slime fills the gaps between my fingers, and before I can stand up, a staff strikes the slick ground next to me, jolting me. I fling myself away from it, rolling on my side, getting covered in the oozing mud. I look up just in time to see a plebeian charge me, thrusting his staff through the air in an attempt to stab me with it, his hardened and emotionless eyes betraying his wish to vanquish his enemy: me.

This must be phase seven, a test of our skills in hand to hand combat, and what better way to test them than against those trained to fight for sport?

I rear up, my knees planted into the ground, and grab the staff, but he must have expected it because he kicks me in the face and jerks the staff away from me. I fly backwards, landing in the mud, dazed, and it forms a mold around my body. The man charges again, but I roll to my right and swing my legs around and knock him off his feet. I jump on top of him and punch him in the face. I go for the staff again, but he throws me off him and, in a second, my opponent is on top of me, using his staff to force me deeper into the mud. I bring up my right leg, placing my foot firm on the ground, and use all of my strength to roll over onto my side, knocking the man off balance. Before he has time to recover, I jump to my feet and ready myself for his attack, remembering the years of training I have been through.

He rushes me. I block him and step out of the way. The lines on his face betray his frustration. He attacks again, and again, I step aside, allowing him to strike nothing but air. He turns around and charges me, but I lean into the attack, seize the staff, and fling him over my back. He crashes into the slick mud and I leer over him, the staff poised to strike. The high-pitched hum of a drone hurts my ears as it lowers and hovers next to me, no doubt those watching are waiting for me to make the final move. I could do it. All it takes is one jab in his windpipe and he would die. I think back to the two plebeians who died in phase five: a woman and a child. I did not think about them when their lives were taken, nor did I care, but they were killed by the sniper, not me. If I strike this man before me, then…

I swing the staff and hit him on the head, knocking him out. There is no logic in killing him. He is just obeying orders like a plebeian should. The drone still hovers beside me, annoying me, and I know what Molers and the others are thinking. In one swift move, I knock the drone into the mud with the staff and toss it aside where it sinks into the black ooze, and hurry away. There is one more phase: the final push to the finish line.

I reach the edge of the mud pit and step over a recruit who was not so lucky and a plebeian who had met the same fate. Mud drips from my pants and shirt as I run, following the lighted markers on the ground, and as it dries, my movements are constricted. The markers take me to another hill and I follow. Though my legs are tired, I know that I can do this. I breathe deep and pace myself, conserving my energy as I jog uphill, hoping to use what I have left to bolt down the other side once I pass the crest and allow gravity to assist me. Pounding steps echo around me, telling me that I am not alone as other recruits near the end along with me. A few go by me and I curse for not being able to prevent their actions.

I reach the top of the hill. At the bottom, the markers end, and a white, luminescent strip marks the finish line, the end of the gauntlet. I push harder. My legs threaten to give out on me, having turned to rubber, but I refuse to finish last. Another recruit threatens to pass me. Determined to not fall behind another, I use the tactic of many of the recruits, one that has been deemed acceptable by the makers of the gauntlet: I veer to the side and ram into her, forcing her off her feet. She lands face first into the ground and I know I have created another enemy, but I do not care. The finish line is so close.

I give it all I've got and run so fast that my feet feel as though they are flying over the ground and am breathing so hard that my lungs ache for relief. Just a few more yards. I am almost there. I push harder. There are no cheers, no applause, when I cross the finish line, but I do not care. I have finished. I have passed the gauntlet. I am not a failure.

Relieved to have made it, I hunch over, allowing myself the chance to catch my breath, inhaling gulps of air, while controlling their release. Once my breathing has slowed, I stand up, refusing to show weakness, and to await the last of the recruits to finish as well. My eyes scan the line of people and find Faya standing among them, still missing her boot, and I smile, pleased that she has made it. She waves at me and I wave back. Trevors and Grelyn are there as well, which does not surprise me. They were born for this life.

A rail car pulls up and stops, allowing Molers and the other officers to get off. We all stand at attention as they walk to the front of the line, their faces as grim as they were on my first day of training. Heavy footsteps break the still atmosphere. Some of us turn and watch as a lone recruit, the same one who had tried to drown me, the same one whom I saved, the last of all of us, approaches, his haggard demeanor betraying his exhaustion. The white line flashes as he crosses through it, finishing the gauntlet, and he takes his place in line, his chest heaving from his exertion.

"Congratulations to all of you," Molers says. His bellowing voice could be heard in any corner of Arel. "You have passed the gauntlet and have proven your worth, your strength, and your fortitude. You have proven yourselves worthy to be part of the Martial Diplomatic Corps, to be the arbiters and peacekeepers of Arel."

Molers stalks over to the recruit who has finished last. "Except for you," he says to him and the fear on the recruit's face is unmistakable.

I close my eyes and look away as Molers pulls out his pistol and shoots the recruit in the head, a reminder of what failure means.

"Failure is not an option in Arel. Finishing last means you are weak, and weakness will not be tolerated. We are the leaders of Arel, superior to all. We have been chosen over our lighter-skinned compatriots to keep harmony in our society, and it is because of us that we survived the chaotic wars of the past. All of you are a testament to that strength. Strength in—"

"—our kind!" we finish, and I repeat it with the same conviction as everyone else. It is the motto of Arel and we are taught it from the moment we can crawl. "Strength in numbers! Strength over weakness! Weakness is failure! Failure is death!"

We finish the chant and I feel invigorated as the realization that I have passed the gauntlet sinks in and that my 18 years of training have paid off. I am part of an elite group and will be responsible for keeping Arel safe.

"You will all go back to the barracks and hit the showers," Molers orders us. "Tonight, there will be a banquet to honor you in your moment of triumph. There, you will receive your commissions. Dismissed."

I follow the others as we disperse and head back to the bunkers. My eyes pass over the one recruit who had made it to the end, but was unlucky enough to be the last one to finish, and, for a fleeting moment, I pity him, but shove it aside. Such thoughts are not tolerated.

Weakness is failure and failure is death.

Chapter 2

The Banquet

I turn off the lukewarm water to the shower and grab my towel, patting my skin dry, glad to have the sweat, dirt, and blood washed off me. I am alone in the showers area, having been the last one to get in, and I am glad that no one is there. I like my solitude.

I toss my towel away and grab my clean clothes. I snatch a comb from the counter and run it through my long, silky, black hair, exposing the tattoo on the back of my neck. Every recruit has one. It is the crest of Arel, and our service number—mine is N27461—is tattooed on the back our necks when we are infants, along with the first initial of our name, when we are first brought to the Martial Diplomatic Corps.

After I pull up my skintight pants, black in accordance with regulations, I pause, realizing that I am standing in front of the floor-length mirrors on the locker room walls. I observe my body, my flat stomach, toned muscles, all signs of my physical training, and I stop when I see the mark; it looks more like a pin-prick, on my lower abdomen. When they reach the age of 13, all recruits, male and female, are forced to undergo sterilization. The boys receive a vasectomy while the girls get a hysterectomy, thus ensuring that we are unable to reproduce, as children are forbidden in the Martial Diplomatic Corps. Breeders are set up who give birth to the infants that become future recruits. Or as Molers puts it, "An arbiter's function is to provide stability, safety, and security to Arel, not child rearing."

I brush the tips of my fingers over the tiny scar, a part of me wondering if there is merit in being able to have children, but shove such thoughts aside. I am an arbiter. This is my role, my duty, and children would just get in the way. We function just fine in Arel. The Maternity Ward is where the children are born, and each child is sent to its approved parental units or the place where it's needed. That is the structure of my city and its order must be maintained, or we will all die.

The hinges of a door squeaks, ripping me from my reverie. I tug my shirt over my head and put on my tailored jacket, the maroon emblem of Arel sewn onto both sleeves and the collar. I must get to the mess hall where the banquet will be held. Tardiness is not acceptable.

When I arrive at the mess hall, I am bombarded by noise, not the standard conversations that take place between recruits, but an excited and jubilant fare greets me. I do not recognize the room. Its long tables are missing and the stainless-steel walls have been covered with shimmering maroon, silver, and powder-blue drapery with an emerald trim braided along the edges, giving off a more inviting and warm atmosphere, compared to the cold reminder of my profession. I stop in the entryway, staring at the pale yellow lanterns that hang from the ceiling; their homey glow makes me think that I have just stepped into another world.

I step through the entranceway and stop again. Instead of hearing my boots clack on the hard cement floor, they make no noise and sink into a soft layer. Looking down, I see carpeting and am puzzled. Why would they have carpet in here? The banquet is only for one night. I drop to my knees and pry up a section of the thin carpet and see that it has only been tacked down; this way, it can be removed the moment the celebration ends. Three recruits walk past me and I jump back up to my feet, smoothing out my jacket, pretending that I had not been interested in the new decorations as arbiters are discouraged from liking fancy things. We are charged with keeping the peace and enforcing the laws. The acknowledgement of luxury is best left to the council.

I walk into the room and spot a passing plebeian with a silver tray full of finger food, stuff that is not normally served in the mess hall. Most days, we had just 15 minutes to eat before being shuffled off to our next stage of training. Our diet consists of beans, meat, eggs, anything that is high in protein, steamed vegetables or fresh leafy greens; water is all that is allowed as a beverage, and bread is only served at dinner. The food is not bad as the plebeians who cooked it must have known how to make it taste delicious, though anything less would have resulted in their punishment. The marbled, lime green mousse on a cracker is new and I have never tasted it before, so I snatch one from the tray and shove it in my mouth. My taste buds are oversaturated from the sweetness which is broken up by the crunchiness of the cracker.

It is clear why we are not allowed to eat such foods on a regular basis: we would all be fat, and for an arbiter, physical fitness isn't just a requirement, but a necessity. I grab three more of the sweet treats from the tray as the plebeian tries to walk away, much to his ire, but he remains silent; they are not to speak unless spoken to.

I wander the room, strolling past circular tables covered in lacy tablecloths, their edges swaying a little from the breeze produced by the ventilation system. I study the design that worms its way along the edges of the tablecloth, entranced by its delicate pattern and the bit of character it gives a basic table. I spot the buffet table and my stomach grumbles, reminding me that I have not eaten since breakfast, and after running the gauntlet, I am famished. I stride over to it and look at all the food that is upon it with its array of six different kinds of meat (ham, herbed chicken, roast beef, lobster, bacon-wrapped pork chops, and braised turkey legs), surrounded by platters of vegetables which have been steamed, roasted, sautéed, or just served raw. I am not surprised. Even though this is a celebration to honor the recruits who have passed the gauntlet, we are still expected to maintain our high protein diet. Splashing grasps my attention. Behind the buffet table is a five-tiered fountain with the most luscious and reddish liquid I have ever seen spilling over the edges. Lights in the bottom give it a golden glow. Mesmerized, I stand there, gawking at it.

"Fascinating, isn't it?" Faya walks up to me, her curls bobbing with each movement she makes.

I smile at her. "I've never seen such a thing."

"You can drink it."

"Drink it?" I had thought it was colored water, nothing more.

"Yeah, here." Faya walks to a table where stacks of drinking glasses form a pyramid and grabs two, placing them both in the red liquid, allowing it to slosh over the sides—some of it drips onto her new shiny boots—and hands one to me.

I sip it. Within seconds, my mouth is overloaded with a mixture that is both tart and sweet. I do not know what this drink is called, but I like it.

"It's good, isn't it?"

"What is this stuff?"

"They call it cranberry juice. It's too bad we are not allowed to have this stuff more often. And you need to visit the dessert table." Faya points it out to me as it is hidden behind the fountain of cranberry juice.

My eyes widen. It is another long table, overflowing with serving tiers of brownies (and different flavors, such as peanut butter, the standard chocolate, and marshmallow crème), ten different cakes (some are fluffy and moist, while others are more creamy), platters upon platters of cookies, and…

"Ice cream?" I ask Faya, and she nods.

"I've already had two dishes of it."

I have only had ice cream once and will admit that it is best if I am not allowed near it; otherwise, I will be as round as Chief Councilor Weston. His name is Troy Weston and he is the head of Arel's governing council, but still answers to our two presidents. It is rumored that he eats nothing but sweets and his 700-pound body proves it. It takes 12 plebeians to carry him to and from his home to the council chambers.

"What's the matter, Noni?" mocks Trevors as he approaches us. "You've never seen a table full of food before?"

"Not this sort of food, and neither have you," I spit.

"OOOOH, such animosity," he jokes.

"I think your girlfriend is missing you," says Faya, pointing at Grelyn, who had decided to turn her short hair into spikes for the banquet. In the morning, she will have to smooth it out, but tonight, we are allowed to forgo a few regulations, as my flowing hair demonstrates, since I did not bother to put it up, but wear it down instead.

Grelyn looks at us, her unnatural blue eyes unnerving me like they always do in this sea of black and brown. I hope I never have to fight her in the dark. I would certainly lose. I look from her to Trevors, and judging by the irate look on his face, I know that Faya has hit a nerve. Though relationships are forbidden among arbiters, everyone knows that they happen, and it is no secret that Trevors and Grelyn are more than just friends.

"You watch your mouth," hisses Trevors, closing the distance between him and Faya.

I step between them. "She didn't mean anything by it. Just get what you wanted and go."

"Stay out of this, Noni."

"What's going on over here?"

We all break up and take a few steps away from each other as Mandi, one of our superiors, walks up, trying not to meet the others' gaze.

"Answer me."

"Nothing," replies Trevors, but the look on Mandi's face shows that she does not believe him.

"If you have differences, resolve them in the arena where that sort of thing belongs."

Trevors grunts.

The arena is what we call the place recruits who have arguments go to fight it out. It is a 12-foot by 12-foot space that it marked off by ropes. Any recruits who wish to prove they are better than another go in there and fight, hand to hand, until one gives up. Fighting to the death is not allowed, but that does not mean that some are not sent to the hospital ward afterward. I always thought it a bit strange that, while in training, recruits are not allowed to harm one another, but in the gauntlet, those rules do not apply, which must be what makes it the ultimate test of our abilities.

"What was that?" Mandi notices Trevors' lack of respect. "Should I bring Molers over?"

Trevors' demeanor changes. He straightens up, salutes her, replying, "No, ma'am."

"Then, get what you came for and go."

Trevors hurries away, grabbing two plates and piling whatever desserts he can fit on them before running back to Grelyn. He fears Molers. I think Molers is the only person whom Trevors fears more than death.

There was an incident, two years ago, where another recruit had challenged Trevors in the arena and Trevors detests being challenged. The rule in the ring is that you can injure, but you cannot maim or permanently disable, but Trevors went too far. He had penned the poor recruit down and did not stop when Molers had blown his whistle. I remember watching as Trevors bashed the boy's face into the floor until blood pooled around them, covering his bare feet. Molers had to enter the ring to break them up. He seized Trevors by the neck and threw him to the ground. For the next five minutes, we all watched as Molers beat Trevors so bad that he spent the next three weeks in the hospital ward, but the recruit who had been foolish enough to challenge Trevors was not so lucky and had died, and Trevors avoided Molers ever since.

Mandi turns to Faya and me. "Are you two enjoying yourselves?"

"Yes," we both reply.

I have always liked Mandi. She is kind, which is unusual for an arbiter, but fair. She never flaunts her authority, nor does she take any nonsense from others, and she never allows Molers to intimidate her. I hope to be like her someday: strong-willed, fair, and an upholder of the law.

"You should both get some ice cream before it disappears," says Mandi, "even though I know it will be your third helping, Faya."

Faya grins, her guilty expression proving that Mandi is right.

A clatter sounds across the room, followed by Molers' angry shouts and a plebeian being thrown across the room. She looks to be no more than ten and the room watches as she cowers under Molers' wrath, but she should have known better than to anger him. Molers pulls off his belt and smacks her with it while she cries, doing her best to cover her head from the blows.

Motion makes me jerk my head and I notice that another plebeian, about my age, clenches his fists together and starts to move toward the girl, but another stops him, shaking his head, holding onto his arm. Mandi shifts in the same manner as the one plebeian and I do not know why, but anger and disappointment clouds her face. Why is she upset at Molers' actions? I turn back to the scene with Molers. The girl huddles on the floor, begging him to stop and another superior officer walks up to Molers and places a hand on the belt.

"That is enough," he says; his firm tone commands obedience.

Molers glares at the other officer, but says nothing, since the man outranks him, and stalks off, heading toward the front of the room.

As the commotion ends, music and conversations resume as though nothing has happened, but I remain where I am and watch as Mandi whispers into another plebeian's ear. The servant hurries to the girl and helps her up, taking her out of the room. I motion to Faya that we should go to the dessert table. She agrees. I think she is as addicted to ice cream as I am, and we both fill up a bowl with the frozen strawberry banana swirl custard.

"Recruits, I welcome you!"

Molers' voice spills over the speakers and he stands in the front of the room with a microphone. The time for the congratulatory speech has arrived. Every one quiets down and the room stills as though what had taken place a few minutes prior is ancient history.

"You all have passed the gauntlet, demonstrating your strength, your fortitude, and willingness to overcome obstacles. You have proven yourselves worthy of being arbiters for Arel, upholders of our laws. Strength in our kind! Strength in numbers! Strength over weakness! Weakness is failure! Failure is death!"

The rest of the room recites the motto with Molers, our resolute voices echoing off the walls and high ceiling. My eyes survey the room and I notice that Mandi's lips just seem to be moving as though she does not believe in the mantra—something I have never noticed before. Should I report her? Dissent cannot be tolerated as it leads to chaos. Though, I could just be imagining it, since Mandi has never given any indication that she disagrees with our way of life.

"By the end of this night, you will all receive your commissions and your first assignments as arbiters and members of the Martial Diplomatic Corps. And to commemorate this momentous moment, we have a special gift for you all tonight. It is my duty and my privilege to announce the presidents of Arel: Kumi and Tapiwa."

Applause goes up and two people enter the stage, shaking hands with Molers while waving at everyone. Kumi and Tapiwa are brother and sister, fraternal twins in fact, and co-presidents of Arel. When their father died, he refused to name just one successor, and chose to name both. They rule Arel together and it is rumored that they are closer than siblings should be and their relationship is more incestuous. No one speaks of it, not publicly anyway, but rumors have a way of getting around, and judging by the way Kumi has his arm around Tapiwa's waist, I would say it is more than mere rumor. No one cares though. So long as they perform their duties as president and adhere to the council, they can do as they wish. Besides, the last person who questioned their relationship disappeared and his body was found days later, torn apart by the wild dogs that guard the wall.

"Thank you," Tapiwa says into the microphone; her wide smile exposes teeth that are so white, they sparkle in the light. "Kumi and I are pleased to be here with all of you on this momentous day. You have all done well and proven yourselves worthy of the faith that Arel has placed in you. Congratulations!"

She steps back and claps her hands. The room follows by erupting into applause again and I join them, thrilled that the presidents believe in us—in me.

Kumi hugs his sister and approaches the microphone, preparing for his speech. It is customary for both to say something when the current year's recruits pass the gauntlet. He waves and has the same glittering smile as his sister.

"Arel could not be more proud of you all."

Everyone in the room straightens, including me. We have pleased them.

"Your fortitude in the gauntlet," he continues, "has proven that Arel's future is in good hands. We have survived the tests of time. When the world fell, and darkness consumed everything, nation fought against nation, brother against brother, and chaos reigned everywhere, yet we survived. Arel rose from the ashes. We withstood the attacks by outsiders and freed ourselves of the tyranny of the fair-skinned, ridding ourselves of their scourge. Now all are in their rightful place."

Murmurs of agreement flow through the room as Kumi recites the accepted history of Arel.

We are taught from the moment we can walk that a great war

overtook the world. Most of the nations fell and were destroyed by weapons so destructive, that entire cities were eradicated. Such weapons were created by the fair-skinned, people who had no conscience, but only thought of ways to murder any they deemed unworthy of life. Despite their efforts, they failed. Some managed to escape the terror, and when the great war ended, probably because most everyone was dead and there was no one left to fight, much less care, those survivors formed a city state, a new society, a better one: Arel.

Those deemed responsible for the outbreak of war were punished. Many survivors came to Arel, and the leaders of the time chose to show kindness on the fair-skinned, even though they deserved far worse. They were provided shelter and security in exchange that they work. It was a fair bargain. Over the years, irrigation and sewer systems were repaired. Homes and businesses were rebuilt, and the council was established with a president as its head. The outside world crumbled, but we survived, growing stronger. Those like me, the dark-skinned, have achieved justice and equality.

This is the accepted history of Arel and no one questions it.

There is a story that one man did question the official history of Arel. It was before my time. The man was said to have been antisocial, a loner, someone who preferred the company of books, and contraband books at that, over the company of people. He wrote his own history of Arel, one that collaborated some of what is taught to us, but it also challenged other aspects of the official record of events. The man was arrested—Professor Gareth I believe was his name—and branded a traitor. Evidence was produced, proving that he worked for Kition, and he was hung. His body was burned on live television for everyone within Arel to see.

"The tyrants have become our servants," continues Kumi, "and those worthy of leadership have risen to their rightful place. We have had peace and prosperity since we, the noble race, have taken our birthright. You are now guardians of our way of life, of our future. You all are our future. Embrace it and protect it."

Kumi steps back from the microphone, and once again, the room erupts into thunderous applause as we all cheer him. I join in, clapping my hands so hard that they sting from the impact, though I refuse to whistle and jump in place the way Faya is. I glance at Mandi. For the second time that night, I notice that she claps, but there is no vigor to her movements, and though her face remains impassive, her eyes possess a mixture of sadness and anger.

The plebeians in the room appear frightened. I wonder why they are. They are in their rightful place. Have we not protected them all these years? Have we not clothed them and fed them? Is it too much to ask that they repay such kindness? They should learn to not be frightened and to appreciate what we have given them. Fear has no place in Arel, only loyalty.

Molers shakes hands with Kumi and Tapiwa again and they exchange more pleasantries before he takes the microphone.

A plebeian approaches me with a tray full of treats and I take one. As I raise it to my mouth, he trips and falls back into me, knocking me off my feet and causing me to lose my treat. I am furious. I stand back up and backhand the man. "You idiot!"

The force of my hand sends him to the floor and he stares at me with wide, frightened eyes as I raise my hand a second time. The scene causes everyone in the room to watch me and I lower my fist. My eyes find Molers, who looks at me with a pleased smile—I have been taught well—before I see Mandi and the pity in her eyes. Why does she pity the servant?

"Get back to your duties," I snarl at the plebeian and he snatches his tray and scrambles to his feet, hurrying away before I can change my mind.

"One by one," Molers says as though nothing has happened, "you will be called up to receive your badges and your first assignments."

A woman steps forward with a tablet that has a list of our names. "Jamal."

A recruit walks up, the pride on his face lights up the room, and shakes Kumi's, Tapewa's, and Molers' hands while a badge is pinned to his jacket. We all watch as we are each called to the stage, each of us shaking the hands of our presidents and Molers and standing proud as a badge is pinned to the left breast pocket of our jackets.

"Faya," says the woman reading the list of names.

Faya beams and we share a look—I know how much this means to her as her excitement matches my own, and it was all she talked about for the last several days—as she marches up to the stage and accepts her badge.

Two more recruits are called before I hear my name.

"Noni."

My heart pounds in my chest as I realize what this moment means and how my life is to change after tonight. I step toward the stage, straightening my jacket, which always seems to form a wrinkle or two when I am nervous, and pick at the edges of my sleeves, before wringing my hands and placing them by my side in an effort to calm my nerves. I walk up to Molers first and shake his hand and he holds mine in that firm grip of his for a moment.

"You did well back there," he whispers to me. "Sometimes they need a firm hand."

He glances at the plebeian that I had struck a few minutes before and smiles. He is pleased. At least I am on his good side, for now.

Molers releases my hand and I walk over to Kumi and Tapiwa, shaking both of their extended hands before placing mine back by my side and standing tall as Tapiwa places a badge, the arbiter's shield, on my jacket above my left breast, while Kumi hands me a thin, translucent, and pliable disk, rolled and tied with a gold ribbon. I do my best to remain serious, but judging by the pleased smile on Tapiwa's face, I know that I have allowed my pride to seep through. It doesn't matter. I should be proud. I am now an arbiter. Once the badge is fixed on my jacket, I salute the three of them on the stage and turn around, striding back to my place in the room.

The festivities continue well into the night before we are all dismissed and sent back to our rooms. When I enter my barracks, Faya and my two other surviving bunkmates are asleep. It is just as well. I do not feel like staying up late and talking with them as I yawn and realize just how tired I am. I unbutton my jacket and pull it off, taking a moment to rub my thumbs over the shiny arbiter's shield, admiring the curvature of the raised emblem upon it: the crest of Arel. As I place my jacket on a hanger and hang it up in my locker so that it will not wrinkle, unlike my bunkmates, who just threw theirs on the sides of their bed, I glance at the one empty bed in the room, the one that had once belonged to my fourth bunkmate who had died in the gauntlet. I think back to the look on her face when she knew that her moment had come: acceptance. I shake my head, refusing to think about it. She was weak; that is why she died.

A light from outside the window catches my attention and I move closer, covering the lamp in the room for a better look. A shape moves from the barracks to the edge of the compound. I cannot make out the face. After a few more minutes of staring out the window, I decide it is useless to try and discern who it is I saw and it probably doesn't matter. Some of the dignitaries and superior officers have stayed late and it might have been one of them I saw. Minding your own business is also prudent at times.

I uncover the lamp and pull out the thin disk that serves as my commission papers, which I had received earlier, remove the gold ribbon, placing it on the desk as I unroll the flexible diskette. I place it against the wall, which is a computer monitor, and it lights up, as an official note appears on the screen. I am to report to the eastern sector of Arel where Commander Vye will be my mentor and provide the on-hands training that is required of every recruit who passes the gauntlet.

Though I am officially an arbiter, the training received within the compound only provides us with the physical training as well as schooling, but real-life experience is another matter. For that, every newly commissioned arbiter is to be apprenticed to another of superior rank where they will receive on the job training for one year. After that year is up, they are assigned there on a permanent basis, becoming part of the group, part of that family. How well that person performs determines if they remain as one of the many arbiters who patrol the city, but always have to report in, or if they are trained for something else, something of more prestige. I do not know much about Commander Vye, other than she is a real hard-ass, which is good; it means that by the end of the year, I will be well-prepared to perform my duties as an arbiter and to protect Arel.

Another yawn reminds me of my exhaustion and I strip off my shirt and pants and crawl into my bunk. Tomorrow, my new life begins.

Chapter 3

Morning

I awake before the sun peeks over the horizon, having always been one who loves the morning over the night, and stroll over to the window, taking in the warm glow of the sunlight. I snatch my pants, shirt, and jacket from the night before and tiptoe to the wall monitor (it is a touchscreen computer that takes up the entire west wall of the room) and press my index finger against it, bringing it to life. The words "awaiting your command" flash across the screen.

"Shuttle schedules," I say.

The day's schedule for the shuttles appears and I scan through them, looking for the one that I need to take to get to my assignment. The 13th line is the one I need and it leaves in three hours, but the first shuttle that goes from the Diplomatic Martial Corps to the shuttle hub leaves in 85 minutes. I am pleased. At least I have not overslept. Arriving late is not only bad form, but unacceptable and would lead to questions about my commitment to my duties, and such doubts could haunt me for months or years afterward. A soft knock sounds at the door and I shut off the wall monitor and answer it. Before me stands a plebeian.

"Yes," I say in a harsher tone than is necessary.

"Your bands, ma'am," he replies and hands me a small, silver box.

I snatch it from him, knowing what they must be and toss him my clothes. "I want these washed and pressed and returned to me before the hour is up."

"But, it will take a minimum of thirty minutes before the washers are…"

My glare stops him.

"Yes, ma'am. Washed and pressed before the end of the hour." He bows, squeezing my clothes in his arms and hurries off.

Closing the door, I open the box and find four bracelets, each the thickness of a necklace chain, but made from a metal that is virtually indestructible. I place the box on the desk and touch each of the bands, pulling the one out that flashes green, informing me that it is mine and has been coded to my biometric signature and…

Faya's snores disrupt me. I walk over to her bed and kick the corner, jolting her awake.

"Wha—?"

"It's morning."

"Come back when it's actually time to get up," she says through a yawn and pulls the blanket over her head.

I kick her bed again. "It is time to get up."

"MMMPPHHH." She buries herself further under her blanket.

I kick the corner of her bunk again, which jerks the person in the bunk above her awake.

"Geez, Noni," says the girl above Faya, "do you have to make so much noise?"

"It's time to get up, or you will all miss the first shuttle."

I grab my towel and hurry out the door, annoyed that they won't listen to me, and head toward the showers just as the morning alarm blares overhead, signaling that it is time to wake up. The showers are crowded when I get there and I realize that I am not the only one who had wanted to get an early start. The other graduates, no doubt, do not want to be late to their first assignment either. I sling my towel over my shoulder and stroll over to the women's section of the showers, picking a stall and stripping off my underclothes.

The moment I turn the knob, hot water spills from the faucet, covering me in its heat and filling the area with steam. I snatch a bar of soap from the shelf that is built into the wall of the stall— recruits do not get their own bar of soap; they use what is provided and it's shared—and run it through my hair and over my skin, washing away the sweat from last night and the sleep my body still craved. After seven minutes, I turn off the water and snatch my towel, wrapping it around me as I step out of the shower stall and into the main walkway.

Someone rams into me, stopping me. "Give me your soap."

I glare at Grelyn. Do we have to do this now? Every day, either she or Trevors taunted me. I don't remember what I did to infuriate them, but they had fixated on me for some reason and I had become a constant target. "There are plenty of bars over there." I point at the shelf with ten bars of soap lined up.

"I want yours." Grelyn pushes me.

I do not have time for this. I toss the soap to her, but it slips from her grasp as she tries to catch it and lands on the wet tile floor. Before I know what is happening, she charges me, dropping her towel and knocking me backward into a wall. I knee her in the stomach and she grunts, but it does little to deter her and fuels her anger. She grabs my shoulders—by now I have lost my towel—and flings me to the floor where I land face first and my jaw hits the hard tile. Cringing from the pain that reels through my jawbone and up the left side of my face, I do not see the kick that she thrusts my way and plants in my side.

The other recruits in the shower room back away, not wanting to get involved, yet they stick close by enough to watch and learn the outcome of our fight. I take a sharp breath, refusing to give in and roll on my back just as she tries to stomp on me. Her foot crashes into the tile, cracking one, but before she can recover from missing me, I swing my feet, catching them behind her ankle and pull it out from under her. She loses her balance. I seize my chance and kick the side of her knee on her other leg, forcing her to fall down, landing on her side, and the pain evident on her face gives me a small amount of satisfaction.

As she writhes on the tile, I jump to my feet and wrap my left arm around her neck, placing her in a headlock, while I snatch the bar of soap from the floor with my right hand and shove it in her mouth.

"You wanted this bar of soap," I whisper in her ear through gritted teeth, "then, eat it, bitch."

The banging of batons on the wall and counters echo throughout the shower area and those who had gathered to watch our fight run. Some manage to get away. Some do not. Arbiters, our superiors, storm into the room; the fury on their faces could have frozen lava. One snatches me by the arms and yanks me off Grelyn. The look on her face tells me that she wants to kick me in retaliation, but thinks better of it as more arbiters enter the room and one hauls her to her feet.

"Ten lashes each," says the commanding arbiter. "The rest of you will watch." She paces the room, glaring at each of those who had watched the fight.

Grelyn and I are lined up against the wall, face first and naked, while two arbiters, one for each of us, and each with a switch, stand behind us.

"Begin!" orders the commanding arbiter.

The sting of the switch burns my skin as it strikes my back, but I refuse to show any weakness, determined to appear stronger than Grelyn, whose face remains more emotionless than the statue in the square. Another burning sting attacks my back, and a small tear escapes my eye. I cannot reach up to wipe it. If I do, it will be considered an act of disobedience and more lashes will be added to my punishment. I let it fall and hope that no one notices it as the

switch strikes my back for a third and fourth time. My teeth grind
together as the remaining lashes are completed and we are allowed
to turn back around. I know we deserve the punishment. Fighting
is not allowed among recruits outside the arena, which is only done
when a formal challenge is made, and we have disobeyed that rule.
Disobedience is not tolerated.

"If you have finished your showers," the commanding arbiter
says to everyone in the room, "then report for your duties."

The other recruits scurry away, not wanting to be on the receiving end of such punishment.

"As for you two,"—the commanding arbiter turns toward Grelyn and me—"break the rules again and you will receive far worse
than lashes. Now, get out."

Grelyn finds her towel and wraps it around herself, trying to
cover the marks on her back and hurries away.

Someone hands me a towel. I stare at it for a moment, wondering why I should bother, and angry that now I am covered in sweat
and blood again and do not have time for a second shower to clean
myself up. Reporting for my first assignment like this is not a good
first impression, and I know this mark has already been placed on
my record when I notice another with a computer pad typing away.
I snatch the towel and fling it by my side, stalking out of the room
naked, refusing to show shame for what I have done.

I pass a group of male recruits on my way back to my room.
At first, they stare and chuckle, but stop the moment they see the
marks on my body and face forward, jogging to get far away from
me. I reach the door to my room. Just as it slides open, the plebeian
whom I had ordered to clean my clothes runs up to me. He stops
short, surprised by my lack of embarrassment for being naked in
the corridor.

"Yes?" I snap at him.

"Your clothes, ma'am." He holds them out to me.

I take them from him, and for a moment, I consider slapping

him, but change my mind, reminding myself that he did follow my orders and it wouldn't be right, nor would it make me feel any better.

"You're dismissed," I tell him and go into my room.

"Noni!" Faya eyes me with a curious expression as I enter the room, still naked.

My other two bunkmates stare at me as well, but when they see the marks on my back, they grab their stuff and leave.

"What..." Faya begins.

"Grelyn," I say, cutting her off.

Her mouth sets in a firm line, and I know that I do not need to say anything more as she understands, and can probably picture, what has happened.

I set my uniform on my bunk, taking care not to crease it, and yank open the door to my locker, grabbing some underclothes and put them on. As my undershirt touches my back, I wince.

"Here." Faya grabs some rubbing alcohol, a roll of bandages, and medical tape, something most recruits smuggles into their rooms in case they need it, which seems to be often. "Take off your shirt."

I do and turn my back toward her. The alcohol hurts worse than the lashes when it touches the wounds on my back and I gasp from the pain.

"Sorry," says Faya.

"It's not your fault."

With gentle hands, she places strips of the bandages over each lash mark and tapes it there. "There, that should hold."

I put my undershirt back on. "Thanks."

Faya smiles, trying to comfort me, and places her duffel bag on her shoulder and walks out of the room.

Knowing that I have wasted enough time, I pull on my pants, put on my uniform shirt, cursing when wrinkles appear, which always happened no matter how hard I tried to be careful, and run my hands over them to smooth them out before putting on my jacket. I snatch a hair tie from the top shelf of my locker and put my hair up in a tight bun, glancing in the mirror, and grimace as a black and blue bruise forms on the left side of my chin, covering it. Great. Now I will have to explain it the moment I report for duty with Commander Vye.

I pack my bag, shoving everything in there, zip it closed, and start to head out the door when I remember my arbiter's band that still sits on the desk. I leap across the room, grab it, place it around my wrist, and run out the door, speeding through the corridor to the mess hall, hoping that I can grab a quick meal before I head to the shuttle station. When I reach the entrance to the mess hall, I stop. All of the special decorations and tables of luxurious food have been taken down, turning the eating area back into its usual, and familiar, gray and gloomy demeanor.

Faya stands by the entrance with two hard boiled eggs in her hand, while still chewing her own breakfast.

"This was all I could get."

"Thanks." I take the eggs and shove one in my mouth, chewing while we hurry down the corridor to the main stairwell, race down the steps, and burst out the metal doors into the courtyard. As we jog past the statue of the first president of Arel, I ram the other egg into my mouth.

"Where is your first assignment?" I ask through a mouthful of egg yolk, doing my best to not choke on it.

"The business sector where the economic planning and shops are."

"That is a good assignment."

A part of me is a little jealous. The business section is a nice area, always clean, always quiet. Everyone who had ever been stationed there moved up in the ranks quicker than anyone else, and afterward, they could have their choice of assignment.

We hurry past a group of recruits, who are in their 10th year of training, practicing drills until we exit through the gates and run down the paved road that leads into the city, our heavy boots pounding the solid ground. I spot the long stairwell that leads to the shuttle station and veer for it with Faya right behind me. We stomp down the concrete stairs; some of them are split from the winter storms that have harassed us over the years and the moisture from all that rain had seeped in through the porous steps, causing cracks. Sweat from my exertion streams down my face—the humidity is terrible today—and heavy breathing sneaks up from behind. I turn to see who it is, but I find myself knocked into the railing as a recruit shoves Faya and me out of his way and continues down the steps. I cling to the metal railing to avoid falling down the stairs as I regain my footing and glance at Faya who does the same. She has a disgusted look on her face.

I hear the whine of the shuttle and curse. Despite my efforts to be on time, I am running late because this is the one time the shuttle decides to arrive ten minutes early. Of all the days for it to do this. Three more recruits push past us, ramming us into the metal bars of the stairwell. We won't make it if we continue down the stairs. I look around for some way Faya and I can get to the station on time before remembering that an open drainage pipe is just a few yards away from us. It allows water to drain from the compound and into the aqueduct just below us, which takes the water to the treatment center before dispersing it to the rest of the city. Eight years ago, during our allotted free time on a hot and humid summer day, some of us used that drainage pipe as a water slide. I tap Faya on the shoulder and point to it.

"Are you kidding me?"

"Do you want to be late?" I look through the trees and see a glint of light, warning me that the shuttle is not far away.

Faya shakes her head and hops over the railing with me by her side. Some other recruits give us quizzical stares as they charge down the steps. We find the open drainage pipe and I breathe a sigh of relief that enough water runs down it to provide a slick surface for us to slide down.

"You first," I say to her.

Faya shakes her head at me. "Not this time."

I remain silent. That time some of us used this as a waterslide eight years ago, Faya was with me. There is a bar at the bottom that you have to catch; otherwise, you will go right into the open aqueduct below and drown, and Faya missed it when she slid down, but there had been another recruit there who had managed to grab her before she went over. She has never come here since, and, now, I am asking her to face one of her fears.

I jump in the open pipe first. Maybe I can grab her if she misses the bar again. A dull pain attacks my butt as it slams into the metal pipe, intensifying with each passing second as I slide down it. Water sloshes around me, soaking my pants and the bottom of my jacket. I do not like the idea of reporting to my first assignment drenched, but it is better than being tardy. Harsh echoes circle around me as my boots bump into the sides of the rusty, metal pipe and I cling to my bag, not wanting to lose it.

I see a light ahead. I near the end and prepare myself to grab the bar. Water propels me downward and my body is moved up the sides a bit before dropping back down. There it is! Surrounded by bits of light and water vapor, I see the bar and gauge how much time I have until it will be too late. I reach up and bend my knees, holding my feet above the water so that I balance and slide on my butt. Just a little bit closer. Now! I slam my feet into the metal pipe and jump up, seizing the bar with my hands and cling to it as I haul myself up.

"I've made it!" I yell up the pipe.

A tremendous bang pounds my ears and I know that Faya has jumped in. Precious seconds tick by and my hands hurt from gripping the bar while my knuckles turn white. The muscles in my arms strain from supporting my weight, but I refuse to go any further until I know that Faya has made it. A shadow dances on the sides and I hear her muffled screams. I see her. Shifting my grip, I hang onto the bar with one hand and reach down with my other. Faya spots me. Her fearful face turns to hope. She positions herself like

I had and jumps up just as she reaches me. I grab her wrist and pull her up so that she can grasp the bar.

"That wasn't hard, now was it?" I joke.

I reach for the rungs of a ladder that is just above us and built into the sides of a manhole, leading up to the outside world. Faya is right behind me. We climb in silence and I open the manhole cover, crawling out of the pipe and onto much appreciated solid ground.

The whine of the shuttle is closer and we haven't much time. I tap Faya on the shoulder as she crawls out of the manhole and she nods, understanding my message: she hears the shuttle too. We both spring to our feet and run for the station, which I can now see. The shuttle pulls in. Damn! We are going to miss it. I push myself harder, steadying my breathing and focusing on the shuttle doors as they open. My feet find themselves on the hard surface of concrete, instead of the softer greenery surrounding us. I look behind. Faya is with me.

We reach the back of the crowd as other recruits, like us, shove their way onto the shuttle. One tries to get on the shuttle, but keeps getting pushed aside as others cram onto the transport. I maneuver over to him. He tries to get on the railcar once more, but another forces him aside. An alarm sounds, warning us that the doors will close soon. I elbow another out of my way and seize the poor recruit by his pack, hauling him onto the shuttle with me just as the doors slide shut, forming a pressurized seal, and we are off.

"Thanks," he says.

I just smile in response and look around for Faya, spotting her next to a pole, put there for people to hang onto. I let out a slow exhale, relieved that I have made my transport, despite the fact that my water soaked pants garner a few odd glances and cause goosebumps to form on my legs from the chilly, recycled air that blasts from the vents.

The streamlined, tarnished-white shuttle glides over the rails, weaving its way through Arel, and I look out the tinted windows, getting a view of the city that I have never seen before. The morning glow of the sun on the roofs and sides of the buildings form a bit of a halo around them, setting them apart from the vast, flat grassland that morphs into a mangled mess of trees in the background with their white tips, which mesmerizes me. My city is beautiful—a beacon of light in a dark world. We pass through the tunnel and the inside takes on an artificial glow as the transport's inside lights flicker on, until we reach the end and enter into daylight again.

I see the first stop. The shuttle slows down, pivoting us forward as the change in momentum affects us and I cling to the bar I am next to. When we stop, the doors slide open with a harsh ding and people scramble off. I find myself being jostled around as they bump into me in their eagerness to get off, forcing their way past those that are trying to board in the 15 seconds before the doors close. Another harsh ding sounds and the doors seal shut just as two people try to get on, forcing them to take a step back before the shuttle speeds off. The smooth acceleration is different from the sudden stops, but I continue to hold onto the rail for safety's sake.

I glance at Faya again, but she does not look in my direction as her eyes are focused on the tops of the buildings we pass over. My center of gravity shifts as the shuttle climbs upward, heading to the upper levels of the city where the business district is, the district that Faya has been assigned to. A bit of jealousy passes over me, but I try to push it away. I should be happy for her. She is my friend and, perhaps if I work hard, I can get reassigned there.

We follow the tracks over some mansions with green lawns, lush gardens, water fountains, and gazebos before entering the business district. Once again, the shuttle slows to a stop and the doors slide open, followed by the rush of passengers trying to get off while others attempt to board. I watch as Faya disembarks, shifting her duffel on her left shoulder before turning and waving at me. I wave back.

The doors close and the shuttle speeds up again, diving downwards, before plateauing out as it heads for a transparent building with platforms spread throughout as rail lines swarm in, each going to their own station, before heading away: the central hub. I watch as railcars pull in, passing underneath marbled archways as they stop at their designated station, allowing passengers on and off before speeding away to their new destinations. Shadows cross over us as we turn and head for the central hub, the shuttle's speed decreasing the closer we get.

A final rectangular shadow stretches over us as we glide through an opening and into the transparent building that is the central hub. People gather around on the platform we head for, squishing together, preparing to force their way on. I clutch my duffel even closer. This is where I get off and must catch my connecting shuttle to the eastern sector, and I cannot afford to miss it.

The shuttle stops and the doors open. Mayhem strikes as people force their way off, with me caught in the middle, clinging to my bag, while others ram their way on, not wanting to miss their transport. I shove my way through the mass of people, and once my feet touch the platform, I run, hurrying through the wave of people going in the opposite direction, while working my way to the edge where a walkway is. Once freed from the chaos, I charge down the loggia and to a map, which illustrates each of the rail lines and where they go. I tap the monitor screen once I reach it.

"Destination?"

"The eastern sector," I reply.

"Go one level up and take the thirteenth line. It departs in seven minutes."

Seven minutes? Does every shuttle have to be leaving early today? I scramble away from the map station, bumping into someone as I dodge around a pole, and careen down another stoa to an escalator, ignoring the angry shouts that I receive. The escalator is packed when I arrive there, and I do not have time to wait in line in order to get on, so I jump over the side of the rail and land on the black moving stairs, kicking someone in the shin by accident and knocking her bag on its side, spilling its contents, and almost dropping my own as well.

"Young lady, that is completely…"

I regard the woman whose bag I knocked over, standing in her orange pantsuit, which contrasts well with her dark complexion, with a matching headband holding her wavy hair back away from her plump face. She stops midsentence, glancing at my arbiter's badge, and chokes back the rest of her recriminatory words as she swallows and looks ahead. A nagging feeling that I should apologize for my behavior nibbles at me as I watch her scramble to retrieve her lost items, but I find it difficult to push the words out. Saying you are sorry in the Martial Diplomatic Corps is considered a sign of weakness, something Molers always reminded us, and weakness is never tolerated, but at the same time, I feel as though I do owe her an apology for kicking over her bag and dumping its contents.

"Sorry." My voice sounds mechanical, and even I cringe at the lack of genuineness behind the single word I managed to mutter. I imagine Molers' irate face, knowing just what he would say to me if he learned that I have apologized to someone.

"You are arbiters," he told us recruits once, "and arbiters never apologize. Admitting you are wrong is a sign of weakness and…"

That session ended with all of us reciting the mantra of Arel, much like every training session did. I allow the memory to fade and bend down to scoop up a tablet when the woman stops me.

"No need," she says, through a forced smile, which makes me wonder if she was also constipated, in addition to being angry with me.

Before I have a chance to say or do anything, the escalator reaches the upper level and I realize that I need to leave. I snatch the tablet from the step, thrusting it in her hand, and shove my way past the line of people stepping off the escalator, moving in a zigzag fashion as I ram my way to the 13th line. A harsh chime sounds, and I know the doors are about to close. I pick up my pace, clutching my duffel bag and pressing it into my side so that it doesn't cause any drag or get caught on anything, and leap through the doors just as they seal shut. A few odd glances point in my direction, but I ignore them, having been well-taught to maintain a stern demeanor, letting others think that I am always alert and diligent, ready to enforce the law at the tiniest of infractions. They turn away.

I feel my pants leg while trying to remain inconspicuous, but stop as the shuttle slants backward, leaving the central hub, and climbs high above the city, gliding through the highest levels of the tallest building, disappearing under their shadows before being re-born in the morning sun. My center of gravity shifts again as we head downward toward the eastern sector, my assignment. The lush buildings with their pristine windows and marbled plazas vanish, replaced by more rundown buildings with smaller yards, if they have any at all, crumbling walks, and sputtering lamps. For a mo-ment, the transport is level with the outer wall and I am able to look at the vast landscape beyond and some of the defensive structures that have been built around it, before we plummet below the barrier and the sun can no longer reach us.

The shuttle slows again, and I grip my duffel so tight that the strap cuts into my skin. I have never been one to give into fear or anxiety, but my nerves attack me without warning as I realize that this is it: this is the start of my life as an arbiter. The shuttle stops and the doors slide open with the same harsh ding that is more annoying than welcoming, but it does ensure that you do not miss your stop. I jump into the fray of people scrambling to get off while others try to get on. One woman snags my duffel in her attempts to board the shuttle and I yank it from her, forcing an apology from her when she notices my uniform and arbiter's badge. Being the keeper of the peace has its advantages. People respect you, but the look in her eyes seems to be fear. I am an arbiter, not someone to be afraid of. It is my duty to protect people like her and to protect Arel.

I hurry off the shuttle and onto the platform, forcing my mind away from my sudden curiosity. Now is not the time to wonder about one woman's reaction to my uniform. I have someplace to be.

I run across the platform and am amazed that some people

avoid me, possessing the same look in their eyes as the woman. It bothers me a little as I am not used to being feared. Back at the arbiter training center, no one is intimidated by me; instead, I was the one who tried to not anger certain superior officers; Molers springs to my mind. At least I will not be having to see him again.

Angry shouts catch my attention and I stop, turning in its direction where I see a man yelling at his wife. A passerby pauses to observe the scene and the man strikes him. I look around. No other arbiters seem to be nearby. The man strikes the stranger again, and I know I must do something. This is what I was trained to do. I drop my duffel bag and march over to them, knowing what I must do, even though I have not reported in yet, nor do I have the materials assigned to every arbiter, but I cannot allow this to continue. I have been trained for this. It is my duty.

"What seems to be the problem here?" I demand, my voice more authoritative than I thought it would be, though inside I am shaking. In training, recruits go through several mock scenarios to help them prepare for the real thing, except on the training grounds you know that it isn't real, and here, at this exact moment, the realization and knowledge that this is the real world hits me; but I am committed to it now.

The man backs away, his aggressive demeanor changing, and he seems more afraid of my uniform and badge, than me. "Nothing," he spits, but his face changes, betraying his regret at using such a tone with me.

"Nothing?" The anxiety welling up within me sneaks through in my voice so I arch an eyebrow, hoping it will have the added effect of making me appear bored with the situation.

"I said I wasn't doing anything," the man repeats himself and I know that he detected the nervousness in my voice.

Did he expect me to believe that he had done nothing? I saw him strike that man. Please, fella. I might be young and this might be my first time exercising my authority as an arbiter, but I am not stupid. Any fool could have seen that he was causing a disturbance, and he did strike another citizen—twice!

"You struck this citizen," I say, keeping my voice even, remembering what Molers had always said about fear being a sign of weakness, and a clear indicator that you are unfit for your job. I need to use this fear people seem to have of my uniform to my advantage, or risk failing to uphold the law and keep the peace on my first day as an official arbiter.

"Striking another citizen of Arel is against the law," I inform him, remembering the protocols I had studied since childhood; each offense was listed with the corresponding punishment and the actions an arbiter was to take. It had all been ingrained in my brain, so I know what I am supposed to do. I just need to put it into practice. "What is your name?"

The man refuses to answer.

"You can either tall me your name, or I can drag you to that information booth over there which will tell me." I keep my voice flat, hoping he doesn't force me to follow through on my threat, but the information booth is procedure when someone refuses to identify themselves.

"Hashan," grumbles the man.

"And your place of residence?"

Again, the man refuses to answer me, but his wife speaks for him. "Here, in the eastern sector."

The man strikes his wife, freeing the anger that he had kept in check while talking to me. I am on him in a second, my training dictating my movements, and pin him face first to the ground, stretching his right arm out behind him and ready to break his shoulder if necessary, while people scurry past the scene not wanting to get involved.

"Move and I break it," I warn him as he struggles a little before going limp. He is no match for a lifetime of training. I lift him to his feet, keeping his one arm behind his back, while I grab the other. "To the information booth."

The woman and other witness follow me to the nearby information booth; many, just like it, are spread throughout the city and each have a detainment box next to them. While holding onto the man with one hand, I place my other, with my arbiter's band, on the panel of the detainment box. It scans my palm, while another scanner reads my wristband, and my information appears on the screen.

"State the purpose for detainment," says a computerized voice.

I run through the list in my head, remembering what the law is and what is a punishable offense. "Five infractions: causing a disturbance in Arel, striking another citizen of Arel, attempting to strike an arbiter, resisting detainment, and for striking his wife, who is a citizen of Arel."

The computer logs my statement and I place the palm of the man on the screen. Within seconds, his information appears and is logged as well, with five red marks added next to his name. In the seconds that pass, I notice that he has been detained before and this is his second infraction. A person's first detainment results in a warning and four weeks of manual labor, spent repairing structures around the city. A person's second detainment is more severe. The punishment consists of time spent in the detention facility before being sent to reeducation. A third detainment... no one returns from a third offense; they just disappear, all records of their existence are erased, and the fires of the crematorium burn brighter. As I scan the information about his first detainment, I hope that the man learns from this incident and does not find himself arrested a third time.

A door appears and opens, revealing a dark space just large enough for a single person. I shove the man inside and the opening seals shut, followed by a hiss and a clang before falling silent. When a person is put inside a detainment box, the floor opens up and the individual falls straight down, landing in a sealed transport, which speeds through the underground rail system, taking the offender to the detention facility, where other arbiters process him and where he will await his hearing.

I turn to the other two, remembering that protocol dictates that they are to be logged as well, as witnesses, and must be present at the offender's inquiry.

"Scan yourselves."

They each place their right hand on the screen of the information booth and their names and residences scroll across the screen.

"You both are witnesses to the infractions stated earlier. You will report to the Ministry of Justice and will each receive a notice of the day and time you are to appear, where you will give your statements. Failure to show up will result in detainment. Do you understand what I have told you?"

Every time an arbiter exacts punishment and is forced to log witnesses of that punishment, they are to ask the witnesses if they understand what they have been told.

Both nod in silence.

"You are dismissed."

I watch as the woman and the stranger run off, disappearing in the bustling crowd, and let out the long, slow breath that I have been holding. I realize the time and curse under my breath. I am late. Very late and have already managed to make a terrible impression on Commander Vye before I have even reported for duty. I touch the screen of the information booth and get directions to her place of residence and frown. It is a bit of a walk. I stalk over to my abandoned duffel bag and heave it onto my shoulder, not surprised that it has been left untouched: it is an arbiter's bag with the seal on the side. Only fools would steal it.

I race to a stairwell that takes me from the platform to the main walkway that runs through the eastern sector. There are side streets and back alleys, and I will have to learn them at some point, but right now, I need to get to the arbiters' building. The sun is high in the sky now, though with all of the tall buildings and the towering wall that surrounds Arel, its light remains hidden, obscured by shadows that mirror the uncertainty that lies ahead of me and feeds my apprehensiveness.

People charge ahead of me, some rush right past me, while others dodge around me, all in an effort to get to where they need to be.

I join them, shifting my bag as its weight presses against the nerves in my shoulder, cutting off the circulation and causing my arm to become a bit tingly. It is a standard issue bag and not meant for comfort. A man walking ahead of a plebeian—the plebeian carries the man's bundles—strolls by me, heading in the opposite direction, while his servant keeps his head down, unwilling to chance looking anyone above his station in the eyes.

I stop. This is the first time I have been outside of the Martial Diplomatic Corps compound by myself and have never witnessed the regular activities of people. The compound had plebeians all over, and I have issued countless orders to them each day, but never have they carried my things, or any recruit's. We are expected to carry our own bags at all times to build physical strength, and an arbiter who cannot carry their own possessions is dismissed from their duties because, as Molers puts it, "They have no business being keepers of the peace." Seeing so many people with their servants walking the streets astonishes me because it is new.

A few times, while I was still a recruit, I was brought out of the compound with a group of other recruits and we walked the streets, receiving a tour of Arel. I do not remember seeing many people on the streets at the time, and as I think back, I believe that our commanding officers had the streets cleared so that we would not be bothered; or perhaps it was so we would not see the real Arel before we were ready.

A motorbike weaves around me, blowing black smoke out of the exhaust, while the cart behind it bounces along, almost hitting me in its effort to keep up. I watch as the driver pulls to the side of the narrow street and picks up two passengers. I get an idea. I need to get to the other end of the eastern sector and I have wasted enough time as it is. Each sector has it forms of taxis, much like the man on the motorbike with the cart, but there is also a trolley that runs through the city, in addition to the shuttle and moving walkways. I spot one a level above me, overloaded with people, much like the sidewalk is.

I jog to a low-hanging ladder and jump at it, grasping the lowest rung, and pull myself up, readjusting my duffel so that it sits across my back, and plop onto the grated causeway. I hurry across it, my boots striking the grate with deafening clomps, causing a few below me to look up, but they turn away the moment they spot my uniform. I hear the hum of the motor that moves the conveyor belt of the moving sidewalk. With a leap, I jump over the railing of the causeway and land on the belt, startling a group of women and children when I land.

"Sorry," I say to them.

They smile and step aside, letting me pass, and I have the feeling that I am not the first person to get on the moving walkway in such a fashion. I get on the left side of the belt—a red line runs down the center, splitting it in half; the right side is for slower moving people, while the left is for ones like me, ones in a hurry—and race down the moving sidewalk, its conveyor belt making it seem as though I am running twice as fast. I fill my lungs with air, loving the exhilarating feeling I have as I speed down the belt. A horn honks and I look down at the people meandering below me.

Another motorbike with a cart speeds through the street and swerves to miss the plebeian that had attempted to cross the road, but as the servant falls to the ground, I know that the bike has failed to miss him. I watch as the driver hurries away, not bothering to stop or slow down, while others ignore the injured servant as he rolls in agony in the puddle he has fallen in, and mud covers his snowy skin with each movement. The plebeian manages to get to his feet, pick up the bundle he had been carrying, and hobble away, while a man and his wife push past him without a second glance.

I refocus my attention on the people ahead of me as I charge down the moving walkway, using my left hand to hold my duffel bag close to me so that I do not hit anyone with it. "To your left!" I yell at two children (eight years?) in white suits, a sign that they are initiates in the medical corps, when they cross the red line into the fast lane. They both jump back into the slow lane and I rush by, giving them each a smile and receiving two grins in return.

An arm reaches out and grabs me, yanking me to a halt, and my heavy duffel slams into the lash marks on my back, causing me to wince from the pain it elicits. It is another arbiter, at least ten years my senior.

"What's your hurry?" he asks me in a gruff tone, but his expression softens when he notices my uniform and the crest on my bag. "Running a bit late aren't you?"

"Yes, sir," I gasp, trying to catch my breath.

"There's always one of you," he mumbles to himself, more than me.

I glance to the side, hoping he will let me go, but I cannot just leave without dismissal. He is my superior, as the four silver stripes on his sleeve indicate.

"You better get going. And take the next exit. There is a causeway that makes a nice short cut to the trolley."

"Yes, sir. Thank you, sir."

"And you better hurry. Commander Vye does not like tardiness."

I salute him and run off. Two people dash out of my way when they hear me coming and I charge past them. I spot the exit the arbiter who had stopped me had mentioned. Slowing down, I fall behind a couple and wait the five seconds before the belt positions me in front of the exit, and I jump to the right, taking the steps down to the causeway two at a time, my boots pounding the grate, creating rifts of thunder that echoes around me. A group of people approach me from the other direction and the causeway is not large enough for me to run by them without knocking one of them over. There is a walkway right below the one I am on and runs perpendicular to it, but still goes where I want to be. Gauging the distance, I know I can make it, and I climb on the railing, swing my feet over, and land on the walkway below, its solid surface making a different sound, compared to the metallic ring that its grated twins make.

I ignore the people who stare at me. Let them ponder my actions. I have someplace to be. My back stings from the constant thumping of my duffel onto the wounds I had received in the shower room, and judging by the extra amount of wetness I feel and how my shirt clings to my skin, I know that the wounds have started bleeding again. I hurry down the paved pathway and find a set of stairs leading to the street below. A set of chimes warns me that the trolley is almost there, and if I do not hurry, I'll miss it. I slide down the railing to the bottom of the stairs and run off the moment my feet touch the ground, not bothering to stop or slow my pace. I push my way past another group of people. Once again, they start to say something, but stop the moment they notice my uniform.

The chimes of the trolley sound again. It has already made its stop and collected its passengers and is off again. I quicken my pace, not bothering to control my breathing. I must catch it. The magnetic wheels of the trolley glide over the smooth, glossy rails, which still look like new, even though they have been there far longer than I have been alive, making a soft humming noise as it moves. I fall in beside it. It turns a little to the left, following the tracks and ignoring me, but I remain next to it, running so fast that my breathing sounds labored. There is a vertical bar I can grab onto if I jump for it. Two faces fill the window above me. I ignore them as I concentrate on the bar, playing in my mind what I must do, thinking of it as a test of my skills and commitment to my duty as an arbiter.

Keeping pace with the trolley, I speed up and lunge, gripping the bar with both hands and placing my feet on the side runner. I laugh to myself as I hang onto the side of the trolley, my body shifting with each jerk of the car. A few more faces from the top deck of the trolley lean over to catch a glimpse of me and, no doubt, my antics are the highlight of their day. The rocking motion of the car does not phase me, and I shift my hands for a better grip, while remaining aware of where I am and how far it is until my stop. A plebeian carrying a crate overflowing with onions stops, forgetting his station and his task, and stares at me with a dumbfounded expression, before remembering his place and trots off.

The chimes sound again, signaling that we are nearing another stop: my stop. I see the spires of the arbiters' quarters through a line of buildings and trees—their trunks as thick as my wrists—and know that I am close. I may make it in time after all. The chimes sound again and the trolley slows down. Once it is close to stopping, I let go of the bar and jump off, landing on the cracked pavement of the street and a little bit of mud splashes onto the edges of my boots. Not the impression I want to make, but I cannot worry about it now.

I race up the street and through the gates to the arbiters' quarters. The pavement transitions from concrete to brick, that looked like it had been a bright red at one time, but has faded to a moldy gray, and some of them are soft and mushy and crumble beneath my feet. I hurry to the main doorway. The glass is fogged and coated in crusted grime while the dirtied white paint of the building peels away around the window panes. My heart sinks. I had hoped that the building would at least look pristine like the training compound, but it appears that it is as rundown as the rest of the eastern sector, or what I have seen thus far.

I pull my mind away from my own disappointment. This is my assignment and I must see it through. I reach the path that leads to the door and stop, attempting to slow my breathing and make it look as though I have not been running across all of Arel, though my flushed and sweaty face says otherwise. Once I have controlled my breathing, I walk up to the door, my duffel hanging by my side, but before I can ring the bell and ask for entrance, the fogged glass door slides open and a woman stands in the opening with her arms crossed and a stern expression fills her face.

"You're late," she says.

Dammit.

Chapter 4

Commander Vye

I say nothing. What can I say to the woman—it has to be her—who is now my new commanding officer and mentor? I am late: the one thing I tried to avoid.

"Well?" demands the woman.

"What do you want me to say?" The words are out of my mouth before I realize that I have said them. This is not the time for a sarcastic response, but my pride, and mouth, gets me into trouble more often than not.

"Is that an attitude you are giving me?" The woman arches an eyebrow.

"No, commander," I reply. "I save my bad attitude for when I am in a foul mood." I bite my tongue. What is it with me today? This is the day, of all days, that I am supposed to make a good impression and demonstrate that I am the perfect recruit, willing to follow orders, and in control of my emotions, yet, here I am talking back to my commanding officer as though I am her equal.

I brace myself for her punishment. As my superior, she has the authority to punish me should I step out of line, and my rude remarks fall into the category of being way out of line. To my surprise, she steps aside and allows me through the door, which slides shut, releasing a soft thud as it seals.

The entranceway matches the dilapidated state of the exterior of the building with paint chips on the floor that a plebeian girl tries in vain to sweep up. Dulled paint, that must have been a bright white at one point, has yellowed, and in the fluorescent lights, it looks like urine—smells like it too. The faded green rug cushions my boots as I walk farther into the hallway, taking quick side glances into the two rooms it veers into.

"What makes you think that I am the commander?" asks the woman, her voice sharp and tight.

I turn back around and face her. Is this a test? "Who else would you be?"

"I could just as easily be one of the other arbiters that is stationed here."

"Unlikely," I reply.

The woman glares at me.

"Ma'am," I add as an afterthought. What is it with me today? I never would have spoken with such disrespect to Molers, but I also know that Molers would kill me if I did. The woman continues to stare at me and I realize that she wants me to explain how I came to my conclusions.

"You answered the door before I had a chance to ring the bell, so you were obviously waiting for me," I begin, "and the only reason you would have to await my arrival is if you are the one whom I am to report to. No other arbiter here would care if I was late or not because I am not their responsibility. You speak with authority, with the demeanor of one used to issuing orders and getting her way, and your demand to know why I am late without asking directly means that you expect me to offer an explanation for my tardiness and beg for forgiveness."

"Very astute."

The lighter tone in her voice tells me that I have pleased her, or passed some sort of test. I do not care which, just so long as she does not punish me for my rudeness earlier.

"I am Commander Vye. You were to be here thirty seconds ago." She taps the band on her wrist, which is similar to my own. Every citizen of Arel gets one. Not only is it an identification band, but it also serves as a timepiece, and by the way she is holding hers, I can tell that she was timing me, counting down the seconds until I was scheduled to arrive.

"You will address me as Commander or ma'am. Formality will be maintained here. There are seventy-five other arbiters in this house, and four other arbiter houses in the eastern sector with the same number, all which report to me."

We walk through the hall, stepping over the pile of paint chips that have just been swept up, scattering them across the floor again, and I notice that the plebeian's face scrunches up in irritation, but she refuses to say anything. I give her no more than a passing glance. Her kind are everywhere and it is their duty and privilege to serve us.

"The dining area is through this room and near the kitchen," continues Commander Vye. "In this area is what we call our recreational center. There are books to read if you wish."

I peruse the titles, silver words against fake, brown leather, and they are all ones approved by the council; nothing else is allowed. I pull one off the shelf—ripples form where my fingers touch the sides, waving across the holographic binding—and open it. Words appear on the page, and the screen changes its color, taking on the appearance of actual writing on paper. Books are not made from paper anymore, as it is considered wasteful. Instead, they are all digital, and each book is a computer that, once opened, will display the title which had been loaded onto it.

Rumor has it that some of the older citizens complained about the inhumanness of these digital books, so the council compromised, issuing that these readers be made to look like actual leather-bound volumes, designed to hold a single book, and when opened, the screen would change to look like paper. It satisfied the part of the populace who missed what they called paperbacks, and they do add a bit of hominess to the room, though I am surprised that Commander Vye allows it, considering the abrupt manner in which she greeted me. As arbiters, we are not encouraged to like comfort or luxury.

I put the book back in its place and turn my attention to an ornate chair, one I have never seen before, and touch the engraved spirals that run up the sides of the back until they meet, forming a curled peak. The silky smooth wood caresses my fingers, and the glossiness of the velvety material, which make up the cushions, look as though it can't be real. Losing my sense, and forgetting where I am and that I am being watched, I run my hand over it, back and forth, amazed that when I rub it in one direction, it feels rough, but when I go in the other direction, it is smoother than the wood. This chair does not belong in a room that has splotches of mold weaving their way along the molding that covers the edges of the wood floor.

"Aren't these items considered luxuries?" I ask.

"They are, but you will find that sometimes people perform better when they earn rewards."

That sounds reasonable. Sometimes, at the arbiter training compound, recruits were offered a reward for finishing first which, in most cases, consisted of being allowed an extra meal or an extra hour of sleep.

Commander Vye walks through another room, a short hallway, and through a third room before stopping. "This door goes outside to the main part of the grounds. Over there are a set of stairs that lead to the second and third floors. The main stairwell you saw when you entered the building. And that right there"— she points at another door, concealed in the shadows, it's gray color making it look as though it is nothing more than a smudge on the already dirty paint—"leads to the basement, which is the plebeians' quarters."

I hear rustling and look up into the blank face of another plebeian as he scrubs the walls.

Commander Vye stalks off again and I follow her through more doorways, until we enter the entranceway for a second time, where the servant I had seen when I first entered the building continues to sweep up paint chips.

"Sheila will take your bag."

I look at the plebeian girl—she avoids my eyes—and hug my duffel closer to me. "I can carry it."

"You've been lugging it around since you left the compound."

"An arbiter carries their own possessions. Failure to do so shows weakness and weakness…"

"Go prepare her room," Commander Vye tells the servant, cutting me off and stopping me from repeating the mantra I have been taught since the moment I could first speak.

The plebeian sweeps the final paint chips into the dustpan, dumps them in a trashcan, and puts the broom and dustpan away, before hurrying up the stairs without a word.

"This way," says Commander Vye.

She walks around the wide base of the carpeted wood steps—I cannot tell if the carpet has always been this brown or turned that way from years of grime—and to an oval doorway that leads to a small office nestled beneath the stairwell. Three square windows line the far wall, spilling sunlight onto a metal desk with its pens in a neat line on the left and a stack of forms on the right. A rag has been shoved under one of the legs, no doubt in an attempt to stop the desk from wobbling. Commander Vye walks behind the desk and sits in the chair, pressing a button that turns off the flickering screen, and in that split second, I notice that my face and recruitment record is on it.

"So, tell me why you are late."

I recognize the order for what it is and stand, feet shoulder width apart, arms behind my back, and my duffel still hanging from my shoulder, preparing to explain why I was tardy. "I witnessed a transgression after disembarking the shuttle."

"Transgression?"

"Yes, ma'am."

"Explain."

"A man struck two citizens of Arel."

"And your course of action?"

"In accordance with Arelian law, I cited the man for striking two citizens, and asked him to go to the information booth where he would be processed. He tried to strike me, so I put him down and placed him in a containment box, adding the charge of striking an arbiter to his citation. The two citizens involved have been cited as well and are aware of their duty to report to the Ministry of Justice and the punishment involved if they fail to do so."

Commander Vye punches another button on her desk and the monitor screen appears, showing her my first act as an arbiter. "Yes, it says here 'five infractions: causing a disturbance in Arel, striking another citizen of Arel, attempting to strike an arbiter, resisting detainment, and for striking his wife who is a citizen of Arel.' Does that sound about right?"

"Yes, ma'am."

"But that should not have prevented you from being on time."

Not prevented me? By the time I had finished detaining the man, I only had ten minutes, at most, to get here, and she has to know that it is not enough time. She is testing me, and if I answer wrong, I may be punished. Newly commissioned arbiters who failed to report to their first assignment on time have been known to disappear, never to be seen again. Some say they are sent beyond the wall, a fate worse than death, but another rumor is that they are sent to the crematoriums. Either prospect is dismal and I do not wish to be sent to either of those places. I will have to try harder if I am to serve Arel and prove my worth.

"Lieutenant Renal says that he detained you this morning," Commander Vye continues.

I am being baited. Of course, he has contacted her and told her of our altercation; failure to do so would result in him being punished, but the way Commander Vye informs me of her knowledge means that she is setting me up. This is another test—a measure of my commitment and quick wit. She wants to see me frightened, but I refuse to let her.

"An arbiter stopped me on the moving walkway. I was running and must have given him the impression that I was running from something."

"And why would he get that impression?"

"Because I caused a scene and he did not see my uniform. He released me when he realized that I am an arbiter."

"True."

This woman's snobbish attitude angers me and I do not understand the change in her behavior. One minute she is showing me around what is to be my new home for the next year, if not the rest of my life, and the next minute, she treats me like a plebeian. I clench my teeth to keep from opening my mouth like I did the time Molers played the same trick on me. He enjoys toying with others and catching them in traps. It is his way of testing your emotional responses and whether you have learned to control them, something I do not always succeed at. It was two years ago and he had lined all the recruits up in the courtyard to demand who had been stealing from the kitchens. We all knew that no one had been, such an action is foolish and results in severe punishment, but Molers was adamant that someone had.

He walked down the line, holding a green apple in his hand and asked us one by one if we had stolen it. When he reached me, unlike the others, I stared him in the eyes, refusing to avert my gaze or acknowledge his superiority. The entire incident was a hoax.

"Do you know who stole this?" Molers had asked me.

"Yes," I had replied in a strong voice, sounding more confident than I felt.

Molers had smiled, one of the few times I had ever seen him do such a thing, but his grin was not one of warmth or friendliness, but one of gloating as he reveled in his own sense of superiority. "Really?"

I could tell by the sound of his voice that he thought he had broken me; something he enjoyed most was breaking people's spirits.

"Tell me who."

This was when I made a fatal mistake, showing Molers up. "You did," I had replied. "Thirty minutes ago, I saw you enter into the kitchens and leave with that apple. You are the thief."

The next thing I remembered was a searing, burning pain engulfing my left cheek when Molers backhanded me, and warm blood oozing from a cut that formed in the center of the welt he had given me. Instead of hunkering to the ground, like I had seen so many in the past do, I straightened my back and glanced at Trevors, who shifted in his stance with a mixture of worry and pleasure on his face, but his concern came through the most. The only person Trevors hates more than me is Molers, and during that lineup in the courtyard, I had challenged the one man he fears most.

Molers had struck me four more times until a higher ranking officer stopped him, reminding him that it was his duty to train recruits, not murder them. I managed to walk away from there, though another recruit had to help me because of the dizziness I felt after taking five blows to the face. For a week after that, neither Trevors, nor Grelyn, harassed me, and I believe that it was because of my standing up to the man that had almost beaten Trevors to death. Though, after my face healed and I was cleared for duty by the senior doctor in the medical wing, they went back to their usual taunts.

A low cough rips me away from my memories and back into the room with Commander Vye glaring at me with her sharp brown eyes, waiting for a response, and I decide to chuck caution aside, as it is nothing more than a hindrance in this instance.

"If you wish me to say something, then I suggest you ask me a question," I tell her. "Otherwise, let's cut the game and you tell me why you have really brought me here."

"You have some balls on you," Commander Vye says.

Here it comes: my punishment.

"That's good."

What? Is she congratulating me? I was late in reporting for duty. I just challenged her authority. I have committed infractions, one that most high ranking officers punish, and she is praising me?

"As you know, the eastern sector is not the most affluent in Arel. We are the first to be attacked, and have suffered many over the years, which is why many of the buildings here seem to be in a state of constant disrepair. The people here are rougher and more prone to aggression, making our job as arbiters more difficult. I have seen too many get killed because they did not have the right temperament, or the pair of stones you seem to possess and, Molers has warned me about your brazenness. You will need that attitude of yours—"

I let out a small puff of air through my nose when she says that, but Molers' action does not surprise me.

"—if you wish to survive here. However, keep it in check. I am your superior and chosen to be your mentor for the next year. I will not tolerate disobedience or failure, and you will receive far worse than ten lashes—I will send you outside the wall myself if you cross me. Is that understood?"

The hawk-like gaze she gives me is my warning, my one and only warning to not fail her again. With everything that has happened since the shower room this morning, I had forgotten about the lashes on my back... until now, as the very mention of them brings the throbbing pain between my shoulders to the forefront of my mind.

"Yes, ma'am," I say, my tone even and unreadable.

"Good. Tomorrow, you will explore the wall. It is best to get the worst part of this assignment over with first. After that, you will be assigned your duties and will patrol the streets of the eastern sector, monitoring and keeping the peace as is expected of you. When I see fit, you will be introduced to other areas of this sector, such as the maternity ward, medical compounds, factories, and shopping centers, and there will be trips to the plebeian zone of this sector as well, as they must always be controlled.

"Your duties will be rotated and you will not have the same ones each day, and there will be times when you are asked to perform menial tasks, such as cleaning—we cannot allow you to become too accustomed to luxuries—and there will be times when you are assigned to patrol the outside perimeter of the wall or visit the outposts we have out there. If attacked, you will be among the first to respond.

"Breakfast is served at zero-six-hundred hours. If you are late, you will not eat. You are on your own for lunch, in which case, you can either eat here, or if you are on patrol, there are diners where you may grab a quick meal. I will have a list of them sent to your room. Here is your ration card."

Commander Vye picks up a disk, no bigger than the round tip of a ballpoint pen, and presses it into my wristband where it melts into the metal.

"On the first of each month, a stipend will be reloaded onto that. It is up to you to make your rations last until the next period. Any questions?"

"No, ma'am."

"You're dismissed. Take your bag to your room; it's number five on the second floor. You have fifteen minutes to eat your lunch and report back here, where another arbiter will be waiting to show you around."

I salute the commander and walk out of the room, hurrying to the stairwell, taking the steps three at a time, and jog down the hallway to room five. The room has no lock and the faded green door slides open the moment I step in front of it. I glance around. A single bed, just big enough for one person, with a pillow and folded sheets and blanket on top of it, rests against the wall to my right. A small closet is next to it where I will hang my extra uniforms, and on the wall opposite the closet is a desk with a single lamp framed by the window, which provides the only light in the room.

I place my bag on the bed, knocking the navy-blue blanket onto the floor, and stroll to the window, looking out onto the atrium below with its built-in gymnasium equipment. I watch as two men circle on a mat and wrestle with one another, no doubt continuing their training so as to remain in physical shape, and their toned, well-shaped muscles prove that they have succeeded. The wall looms ahead of me and I get a good look at it from the window: our only protection from what lies outside it. Sometimes, I wonder if the wall is meant more to keep people in instead of keeping invaders out.

A harsh cough jerks me from my reverie, and I realize that I have wasted precious time that I could have used to scrounge up some lunch, but it looks as though I will not be eating until dinner and what little nourishment the two eggs Faya had given me this morning has worn off.

I straighten my jacket and hurry out of the room, stomping down the hallway and down the stairs, shoving the plebeian girl, who still sweeps up paint chips, out of my way when I reach the bottom step. A low thud tells me that my actions have caused her to bang her head into the wall, but I ignore it, making no apology as I hurry to stand in front of Commander Vye, who waits for me in the entrance with another arbiter: the same one who had chastised me earlier while I was on the walkway.

"Noni, this is Lieutenant Renal. It is my understanding that you have already met."

I keep my face emotionless. Commander Vye knows we have already met and I find her false assumptions annoying, but I keep my mouth shut. I have been too forward as it is and must remain in control to prove to her that I am fit to be an arbiter of Arel, and perhaps I can get a transfer out of here to a more favorable post, such as the business or manor districts.

"He will be escorting you around the eastern sector today and show-ing you some of the patrol routes that you will be expected to keep under control. The two of you will report back by fifteen-hundred hours."

"Yes, ma'am," says Lieutenant Renal.

Before I pass through the door with him, Commander Vye hands me a belt.

"Put this on."

I strap it around my waist, noting that it has a holster with a semi-automatic hand gun fastened in it, a palm-sized flashlight, zip ties, and a baton that folded up into a stick the length of your index finger.

"These are your protection in this city," Commander Vye tells me as I fiddle with the baton. "You are to keep them with you at all times when you leave this facility, and they should remain within your possession at all times. Failure to do so will result in disciplinary action. Is that understood?"

"Yes, ma'am."

"Dismissed."

I follow Lieutenant Renal out the door and down the winding walkway to the gate which leads to the bustling street I had taken to get to the manor. A trolley jingles its bells as it speeds past, but I pay no attention to it. I must show that nothing intimidates me, and I am curious as to why Lieutenant Renal was kind to me earlier, but now acts as though that exchange between us this morning never happened. Ten minutes tick by as we walk down the street, heading to a more shrouded area of the eastern sector, where the streets are narrower, dirtier, and more crowded. I keep my eyes peeled for any suspicious activity, watching all the people that stroll past while keeping their distance from us, and the plebeians who keep their eyes focused on the ground.

Having tired of the silence, I worked up the courage to ask a question. "Where are we going?"

"Questioning a superior officer now, are you?"

I press my lips together, fearing that my luck has run out and I have overstepped my bounds, but when Lieutenant Renal faces me, his mouth is upturned into a sly grin and I relax my tense muscles.

"You needn't be so frightened of me."

"I am not frightened, Lieutenant," I quip. How dare he imply that I am letting my fear get the better of me. Fear is not allowed.

The bemused look on Lieutenant Renal's face betrays his thoughts and I know that he doesn't believe me. I just do not want to make another mistake.

"It's okay to be a little on edge," he says. "This is your first day outside the training compound and your first time being expected to perform your duties. I know it is intimidating. We all go through it."

He points at another arbiter who looks to be my age before continuing. "Bren over there came to us last year and he was off to a rockier start than you."

I watch as the man strolls down the sidewalk, whistling to himself, something I have never seen someone do before, while smiling at those who pass by him. His cheerful mood is off-putting when compared to the reactions I received this morning from any who saw my uniform.

"Are you sure that he is an arbiter?" I ask.

Lieutenant Renal chuckles. "I've wondered that myself a time or two. He is a different sort of character, but don't let his cheery demeanor fool you. Though he is pleasant to most whom he meets, when it comes time for it, he is all business. I watched him put three strong men in the same containment box once. Word got around, and ever since, people just mind their behavior around him."

A yellow ball rolls up to the man referred to as Bren and taps the tip of his steel-toed boot, followed by a girl and a boy. They stop when he scoops up the ball, glances at it, and hands it to them, patting the girl in the space between the two buns on her black head. Both children smile and run back to their teacher, who jogs up and escorts them back to the other children standing outside, tossing balls back and forth during the physical education period. Their yellow uniforms mark them as future teachers and, a part of me envies them, as teachers are not expected to follow such rigorous guidelines like arbiters. I shake such thoughts aside. It is not my place to question, but to serve. I must remember that.

"Where are you taking me, Lieutenant..."

"You can call me Renal when we are not at the manor or near the commander."

"Renal," I repeat, thinking it strange to address a commanding officer by his first name.

"I am taking you to a place where you can get something to eat while you are on duty. It isn't a fancy place, not that any here are, but it serves decent food."

I follow Renal as we walk down the dingy streets, past citizens hurrying along, some with their plebeian, making certain not to look us in the eyes, which is strange because we are all citizens. Their behavior reminds me of this morning and how the majority of those I had run into diverted their path so as to avoid me. After strolling down another block or two, we arrive at a building, tucked between two taller ones with the Arelian insignia on its sign, except instead of two spears and guns crossing one another, forming the shape of an x, this sign has two knives and forks doing the same. I stare at it a moment, perplexed as to why someone would do such a thing, remembering a rumor about someone else who had a similar sign, but his had two quills forming the x and it had been torn down by a squad of arbiters, and he was arrested. The more I think about it, the more I realize that the sign had been the least of his offenses, since he was accused of spreading ideals contrary to the Arelian system of government.

Renal glances at me, wondering why I have stopped, and I pick up my feet and hurry after him, straightening the bottom of my jacket for the umpteenth time. We enter the small establishment and the banging of cast iron frying pans, as well as the sizzle of frying bacon, chicken, and beef grilling over an open flame, serenade my ears with their enticing song, while my mouth waters from the tantalizing smells reaching far into my nose, beckoning me to sit down a spell and indulge. A mulatto woman places a loaf of bread, which has just come out of the oven, on the counter beside me, and its aroma reminds me that the two eggs I ate in a hurry are not enough to survive on. Something wet rolls down the side of my chin as my parted lips allow a small amount of spit to escape. I wipe it, hoping that no one notices, but a winking smile from Renal tells me that he has, and was expecting it.

Renal strolls to an empty table in the far corner and sits in a metal chair with his back to the wall, facing the entranceway. From his vantage point, he watches everything; every patron who enters passes under his observant gaze, which remains vigilant, despite his clear interest in the fresh-cooked food. I take the chair across from him and watch as his eyes roam the vicinity, but his face remains amiable, never portraying an ounce of ire.

The buoyant crowd ignores us as people continue their private conversations, unconcerned that two arbiters are in the room with them. My eyes roam over them, studying their jubilant faces as they talk and eat without a care, astonished that they do not care that Renal and I are here, considering the reactions I received from people this morning. As I wonder why no one in the building seems concerned that we are here, a man gallops up to us, carrying a tray brimming with two glasses of blueberry juice and a plate overflowing with scrambled eggs, buttered toast, and avocado halves wrapped in crisp bacon. I watch as he hurries up to us, dancing around the mishmash of tables and chairs with the occasional foot sticking out, not spilling a drop of the beverages he carries or losing his balance. He reaches us and bends down, holding the tray low as he moves the drinks and plate of food to the table, setting it in front of Renal.

"Haven't seen you in a while," he says, allowing the now empty tray to hang by his apron, and I note the grease and sauce stains that litter it.

"That might be because I haven't been here," says Renal, his tone light.

"You're not running out on me and eating somewhere else, are you?"

"Perhaps I am. There is a nice little place further in the district that serves an apple cobbler which makes yours seem… paltry in comparison."

I watch the two of them banter, my eyes flicking from one to the other, as their brows furrow and each struggles to maintain a serious face, before the man lets out a guffaw that shakes the entire establishment.

"Renal, my friend, you know how to hit me where it hurts."

"Not too hard, I hope," Renal replies.

The man claps Renal on the shoulder and gives it a tight squeeze in friendship before both of them turn to me, noticing the confused look that covers my face.

"And who is this?" asks the man.

"Sigal, I want you to meet Noni, our newest arbiter in the eastern region," Renal introduces me.

I smile and stretch out my right hand to shake his, only to have it swept up in two watermelon-sized monstrosities that squeeze it until it goes numb as he gives it a vigorous shake that bounces me out of my chair.

"A pleasure to meet you," he says, releasing my hand. I jiggle it a little, trying to get the feeling to return to my fingers, while also trying to not draw attention to it.

"Likewise," I mumble.

"You look like you need sustenance," Sigal says to me.

As though to add credence to his words, my stomach growls loud enough to be heard over the laughing crowd, and I glance over as the same mulatto woman places another steaming loaf of bread on the counter, unwrapping it from her towel, and its herbed aroma sets my stomach into another series of covetous growls.

Sigal chuckles and places one of the glasses of blueberry juice in front of me. "Drink up. It is our house special. You won't find a place that serves anything like it."

I sip the beverage as Sigal tromps off. It is semi-sweet with a hint of nutmeg, giving it a pleasant flavor. I take another drink and realize that Renal watches me and put the glass down.

"Oh, go ahead and help yourself," he says, "Sigal would be insulted if you didn't drain half your glass in one gulp."

"We do not have anything like this at the compound," I say, taking another sip of the juice.

"I'm not surprised. They keep everyone on a strict diet there to keep you from getting soft. You are expected to maintain that diet out here, but there is no reason why you can't indulge in a few things. Sigal's place here is a good one. He knows the arbiter's diet restrictions better than most, and keeps his menu in line with it, but has a way of making the food taste more palatable. I think you will find this to be a great place to catch a meal."

The door opens and two more arbiters walk in, settling down at the counter where the same woman serves them huge slices of bread, with steak and eggs, accompanied by a bowl of fruit. They thank her, and scoop egg into their mouths.

"We were never allowed bread, except at dinner," I say.

Renal snorts. "Just don't eat any at the manor. Not that it will be too difficult, as Commander Vye never allows it to be served."

His statement about Commander Vye does not surprise me, as I picture her and her disciplined manner doing pullups in the manor's outdoor gymnasium, living off a bowl of boiled beans, which was always the training compound's standby meal when they thought that the recruits were getting too used to savory food.

"There do not seem to be any plebeians around," I say, curious as to why they are absent here when I have seen them everywhere I go.

"Sigal does not use them."

"Why?" My question sounds harsher than I mean it to, but Renal takes no offense to it, as he must have been expecting it.

"He prefers to cook the food himself," replies Renal, "saying that it is the only way for him to know that it is prepared properly. His wife bakes the bread and some of the treats that are sold here."

"The mulatto woman."

A sharp glare from Renal tells me that I have pushed it too far, and I avert my eyes.

"Her parentage is something she had no control over. She was born of a plebeian woman who had entertained her master."

Entertained. He might as well just say that she was raped. It wasn't common, as most of us dark-skinned found thoughts of sexual relations with the fair-skinned abhorrent, but some people are unable to contain their desires and kept a few sex slaves to satisfy their needs and the needs of those like them. They are usually shunned by the rest of Arelian society, but are allowed to remain because of the services they provide.

"She would have been doomed to a life of drudgery if it hadn't been for Sigal," says Renal.

"How..."

"Papers can be forged, for the right price and if you know the right people," Renal leans over the table and whispers to me. "We do not speak of it here. She is dark enough and Sigal adores her. And there is no harm in them serving good food to the people here."

"And their children?" I ask, watching as Sigal bumps her elbow, on purpose, while she ices a cake, and she turns around, swiping a spoonful of frosting on his nose. All arbiters know that the water serving Arel has been fortified with certain compounds to prevent unwanted births, but sometimes the sterilization technique failed and unregistered children were born, which meant they were to be registered the moment the pregnancy was discovered and given an approved identity.

"They have none, except for Ian over there. He was assigned to them to work here as a server, much like we were sent to the Martial Corps, but they treat him more like a son than a servant. And Lilah over there. She was not wanted and Sigal's paperrs for adoption were accepted."

Somethings tells me that Renal had something to do with the acceptance of Sigal's papers, but I keep such suspicions to myself as I watch a young woman with frizzy hair joke with a few patrons.

"So they are not their biological children?"

"No. Do you remember when you turned thirteen?"

I nod. That was the day I was given my hysterectomy to prevent me from ever becoming pregnant, as arbiters are not allowed to have children.

"Sigal's wife was given the same treatment on her thirteenth birthday."

I lean back in my seat. The policy regarding children is complicated in Arel. Maternity wards are set up where women, through in vitro fertilization, where the embryo has been given certain traits to make them well-suited for the profession chosen for them, bear children on a regular basis, and those infants are taken from them and sent to their assignments. But not all children of Arel are born in such a manner. To keep the populace happy, some families are allowed to have their own children and keep them, but they are only allowed one child, and that child will work in the same profession and sector as its parents, the exception being the noble class: the council members, policy makers, and of course, our two presidents.

A plate is placed in front of me filled with Salisbury steak, coated in a sausage gravy, a thick slice of buttered bread, a fruit salad, and… beans. I pick up my fork as Renal winks at me with a smirk on his face, guessing what I thought of the last item on my plate, but Sigal stands next to me with his arms crossed, waiting for me to sample his entree. I could not let him down. I scoop up a forkful of beans—might as well get eating them over with—and place it in my mouth. My taste buds quiver from the overwhelming flavor that the beans hold. I shove another forkful of them in my mouth, savoring the texture and the smoky, sweet and sour flavor that they possess, followed by a huge bite of the bread, the herbed texture providing a nice accompaniment to the beans.

"Ha-ha! I knew she'd like it." Sigal claps Renal on the back and they both share a laugh, while a bit of icing remains on the bridge of his nose. "I can always tell the newly commissioned from those that have been here a while because you all have the same reaction. They don't feed you like that at the training facility."

He left us and Renal and I continue to eat our food until it is gone, relishing every bit of it. "We better be getting back," says Renal as he checks his wristband for the time, while I sop up the last bit of sausage gravy with the last bite of my bread and cram it into my mouth, glancing at the cake that Sigal's wife had placed on the counter moments before.

"Come on." Renal taps a corner of the table and a scanner appears. He holds his bracelet before it, allowing it to be scanned and a portion of his allowed rations to be deducted. I do the same and a number appears on my band, informing me of how many rations I have left for the month.

I follow Renal out of the building, but before we get out the door, Sigal runs up to us to say goodbye and shoves a small package into my hands.

"I noticed you eying it," he says to me with a wink, while Renal frowns. "You both come back anytime. My door is always open."

"Will do, Sigal," says Renal. "The food was excellent, as always."

We step outside and Renal leans close, whispering, "You better eat that quickly before someone sees you."

I open the small package and find a sliver of lemon cake in there. Glancing around to make sure no one sees me, except for Renal who already knows that I have it, I eat my cake in two bites as we head back to the manor.

Chapter 5

The Wall

I rise before dawn. Not even a sliver of sunlight covers the horizon. After having made a bad impression by arriving late yesterday, I am determined to report to breakfast early, eager to begin my duties as an arbiter in the eastern sector. I sit up, placing my feet on the cool floor, stretching my legs as I stand. I make certain to straighten the blanket on my bed and tuck it in on the sides, so tight that a coin will bounce if dropped on it.

As I step past the window, I pause to look out at the wall. It is a massive structure, built for our protection from barbarians and raiders. Kition is not the only threat we face in this world. It stands taller than the buildings, made of solid stone and concrete, blended together, forming a structure that is almost impenetrable, with barbed wire stretched across the top. At varying points are guard towers, placed between the inner and outer walls, and I have a feeling that I will be asked to be in one at some point. At other areas of the wall are flame throwers, which spew black fire, a concept based on Greek fire, but the word Greek was considered too white, so it was replaced, except that the fire that spills from the flame throwers is black, made that way by the chemical compound within them and impossible to extinguish. If touched by black fire, a person's skin melts from their bodies and they die a slow and agonizing death. No amount of medicine can cure a severe burn from it, leaving a victim of black fire with one remedy.

Movement catches my eye, and I look down into the yard where the outdoor gymnasium is. Is that Commander Vye? I lean closer to the glass, squinting as I try to make out the person in the semi-darkness. The woman stands beneath a bar and jumps at it, grabbing it with both her hands, her strong muscles visible despite the faint light, and pulls herself up until her chin is above the bar, repeating that motion 20 times before letting go. It is Commander Vye.

I watch as she moves to the two benches and places her hands on one and her feet on the other, doing pushups, never faltering or exhibiting tiredness. I hope I can be like her one day: strong, confident, the epitome of a true arbiter of Arel. She stops and stands up, pausing before she bothers to move on to her next exercise. Her head turns in my direction and I jump back, hiding in the shadows of my room, hoping that she didn't see me. When I work up the courage to glance out again, she is gone.

I tear myself away from the window, just as the sun peeks over the horizon, placing a faint red line of light on my face, and pull my pants up and put my shirt on. Breakfast will be soon and I do not wish to be late. I bolt out my door, making certain that the latch clicks when it closes, tugging on a sleeve of my jacket as I dash down the hallway and past a plebeian girl, the same one who had shown me my room yesterday. I stop at the top of the stairs and walk down them with dignity, not wanting to appear rushed.

"Nice to see that you are able to be on time," says Commander Vye when I reach the bottom step. One look at her, and you would never know that she had just been doing pullups as she stands there in her pressed uniform without a single bead of sweat on her face.

I keep my face impassive and say nothing, not wanting to bring her ire upon me or give her a reason to punish me. She motions for me to enter the dining room and I walk in there, eyeing the other arbiters around the table, each of whom stand at attention, waiting for the order from Commander Vye to begin eating. I spot the one unoccupied chair in the room and take my place behind it, mimicking the others, and stand at attention. Commander Vye stalks into the room and walks around its exterior, pausing by each arbiter and inspecting their uniform. Her steel gaze unnerves me, and I rub my sweaty hands on the seat of my pants while she is not looking at me in a vain attempt to dry them. Her boots clomp on the floor in steady beats, timed with the ticking of the only hand clock in the entire house.

Tick. Step. Tick. Step.

I continue to face forward, but move my eyes, following her as she circles the room, until she reaches me and stops. A lump forms in my throat. Her continued scrutinizing of me makes me believe that I have done something wrong. Sweat collects under the collar of my jacket and I feel the heat rise in my face. Why is she just standing there? I remember that Molers used to exhibit the same tactic while at the training compound, and that the only way to escape possible punishment was to not move or speak. I grip my hands tighter and stiffen my knees to prevent them from wobbling. Commander Vye steps closer and I feel her moist breath on my neck. With great effort, I control my breathing and keep my gaze focused on the man right across the table from me, refusing to shift position or make the slightest movement.

"You may eat," says Commander Vye, and she takes her place at the head of the table.

I breathe a short sigh of relief when she is not looking before sitting in my chair and helping myself to breakfast, determined to get a meal in so that I would not be operating on an empty stomach the entire day. The high protein is prevalent on the table and I realize that it was never just something done while in training. I heap some eggs, sausage, bacon, legumes, and strawberries onto my plate.

"Someone seems hungry," commented Commander Vye.

I stop piling food on my plate, thinking that I have done something wrong.

"Eat up," the commander says to me. "We have a long day ahead of us."

I place a spoonful of yogurt on my plate and start eating, taking extra care to chew my food.

"Everyone," Commander Vye announces to the room, "this is Noni, our latest addition and commissioned arbiter."

Soft claps sound around the room as everyone present gives the customary greeting and acknowledgement of my accomplishment and presence.

"I am certain that you all will treat her with the same respect that I have given you and expect."

No one speaks but just nod their heads.

The rest of our meal passes in silence and I struggle to not shove all my food into my mouth and swallow it in one gulp. Just as I finish my last bite of sausage, thus cleaning my plate, a group of plebeians walk into the room and take the dishes and leave.

"You all have your assignments," says Commander Vye. "Some of you, I will see here this evening, and some I will not. Good day to you all."

For the first time, I realize that there had been empty chairs in the room and this explains the reason for it. Some assignments must involve remaining overnight and missing a few meals.

"Noni."

Commander Vye's voice jolts me from my reverie and I jump from my chair, remembering that I am to be her shadow today, as she is taking me out to show me the wall, instead of delegating the assignment to someone else. I make certain that I have the items arbiters are required to carry with them at all times when on duty and follow after her.

Outside, the heat is sweltering, showering over us in an effort to overpower us and force us to succumb to its will. I wish it would cool off, but we are in early summer and this is how the weather is in summer. I do my best to ignore the humidity, as it causes me to sweat under my jacket. One look at Commander Vye tells me that I should not acknowledge, or even mention, the heat to her. She remains erect and proud as she strolls down the street, taking the shortest route to the wall. Not one drop of moisture dots her brow, nor does any fall down her face. Is she impervious to such heat? I shake the question from my mind. This is not the time for random musing or for my mind to wander. I must focus on this final part of my training.

The closer we get to the wall, the narrower and more crowded the streets become. The people who walk them do not smile or greet us, choosing to hurry away, their quick steps scattering the trash that idles on the ground, or ignore us instead. As I look around at the dull buildings with vines stretching up them, mixed in with the black filth that covers them, I realize that this is one of the unspeakable parts of Arel. Whenever our presidents gave speeches and spoke of Arel's greatness, they always had footage of the beautiful buildings and scenery that fills the city, giving the impression that areas like this do not exist. Sheltered within the compound of the training corps, I believed the footage, but this area tells a different story. I shake it off. No city is perfect, but Arel, my city, does offer beautiful, state of the art buildings with all the conveniences one could want, with plazas and nature walks for people to visit should they wish to relax and find some solemnity.

I match Commander Vye's long strides, doing my best to keep up with her quick pace. No word is spoken and she remains silent the entire time, and I conclude that she is not one for small talk, unlike the arbiter she had entrusted me to yesterday. As we move closer, a shadow appears, forming a rim around us. I glance up.

The wall looms before us, causing me to gasp at its massive

size and formidability. I had always viewed the wall from a distance or from its top, never from below like I am now. I pause and stare straight up it, marveling at the size of the structure. It looks impenetrable and it must be, considering how monstrous it is. As I continue to stare straight up, I experience a small bout of dizziness from craning my neck at such an angle and straighten myself, regaining my equilibrium and composure.

"Noni!"

Commander Vye stands near a seven-foot-high vertical rectangle in the wall that is just the right width for a man to go through, and her face betrays her displeasure at my dawdling. I scold myself and hurry over to her, not daring to look at her reprimanding glare, and pass through the entrance that leads to a stairwell. The narrow stairs wind their way upwards in a tight, square-shaped circle that seems to stretch upwards in a never-ending funnel. I place my foot on the first step and start the climb upwards.

The stairwell is an oven. No breeze is able to reach us, to soothe us and cool the sweat on my face and neck. The further I climb, the more burdensome the heat becomes, crushing me to the point where I struggle to continue my trek. Commander Vye is behind me, taking each step with ease, not bothered by the stifleness of the enclosure.

I cannot breathe.

I stop, leaning on the wall, trying to catch my breath, wondering why the summer's heat has affected me this way. I am not one to feel or be bothered by the temperature outside, but this stairwell, this dark hole of nothingness, causes my throat to clench and me to panic. Where is the light?

"Keep moving," orders Commander Vye.

I take a step, but stop once more.

"Keep moving." Her voice is less authoritative and softer, almost encouraging. "The wall frightens every new arbiter who climbs the stairs within it for the first time, but you must keep moving. The panic will pass."

I inhale, filling my lungs to the point where they refuse to accept more air before releasing it in a long, slow breath. Again, I take a step and continue climbing the stairs one at a time, refusing to think about where I am.

"You will find, Noni," Commander Vye continues, walking past me and taking the lead again, "that this sector is darker, grittier, and less forgiving than what you were accustomed to at the training compound, but always remember that the light always comes back."

She points her hand upward and I see a small speck of white light poking through at the top of the stairwell, outlining the last step: my current goal. Renewed with vigor, I charge up the stairs, taking them at a quick pace, refusing to look back or to pause, despite the attempts of the darkness to stop me. I place my foot on the final step, feeling the firmness of it beneath me, and allow the bit of light to form a stripe across the middle of my boot. I have made it. I have reached the top and can now escape this oppressive enclosure.

I charge out of the stairwell and onto the walkway of the wall. The relief on my face must have shown because the man at the top waiting for us smiles, before resetting his lips in a firm line when Commander Vye appears.

"Morning," she greets the man. "You may turn on the lights now."

What? There were lights in the stairwell the entire time, but she had them turned off to prove a point?

Commander Vye catches the sour expression on my face and I force it into an impassive look, but it is too late.

"This was a test?"

"Yes," replies Commander Vye. "You did better than some."

Better? It doesn't sound like I passed.

Irritated that she gave me yet another test, I follow Commander Vye as she walks along the walkway on the top of the wall, knowing that I have no other choice. She is my assigned mentor and I must do as she says, unless those above her deem otherwise. We move along and I take note of the people stationed along the wall at varying intervals in between the guard towers, standing at attention, prepared to act if we should be attacked.

While making certain that Commander Vye's attention is not focused on me, I run my hand along the edge of the wall that also serves as a rail to prevent one from falling. The sandpaper texture massages my palm, surprising me as I expected to be cut by it. A small nick stops my hand. I peer at it closer and realize that it is the place where a knife had once struck it, probably during an attack. There have been a few attacks on Arel that I remember, and there are stories of more that have happened in the past. I place my index finger in the small nick and it cradles it. Looking around, I spot bits of dried blood turned black from the passage of time, and more nicks in the stone, giving it a pockmarked look.

"This is the wall," says Commander Vye, not paying attention to my examination of the structure itself, or the fact that I have stopped following her.

"This is our first defense against any who wish us harm. Against outsiders," continues Commander Vye.

I spot a blackened mark on the outer edge of the wall. Glancing in the commander's direction, and seeing that she continues to walk and talk, ignoring my actions, I approach the black scorch mark, reaching out with my left hand to touch it. The tips of my fingers brush its silky texture, broken up by the feeling of small pins sticking out of it, waiting to strike.

My fingers burn.

"At some point, you will also be stationed here."

I wrench my hand back, ignoring Commander Vye's continued speech. The tips of my fingers feel as though I have placed them in an open flame and left them there. No amount of rubbing them on my clothes or on the stone of the wall itself eases the pain—it just makes it worse.

"The rotation is done in two shifts."

A memory floods my mind, drowning Commander Vye's words, a memory I wish to forget.

All recruits are taken to the wall at least once, to see it, to experience it, to know what to expect when they are commissioned as full arbiters, assuming they pass the gauntlet of course. I was brought here during one such time. We were shown the wall by Molers, who reveled in telling terrifying accounts of all the people who had died defending it and Arel. Each recruit was expected to handle some of the flamethrowers that line the outer edge and forced to watch as one of the guards threw a plebeian—one too sick to work—down into the space between the outer and inner wall to be torn apart by the ravaging, wild dogs kept there. I remember the screams of the boy, but watched with indifference, same as my comrades. He was just a plebeian.

That was when it happened.

A mortar round had slammed into the side of the outer wall, causing an earsplitting explosion that blew a massive hole into it and knocked us to the ground. I crashed into the side of one of the guard towers, covering myself as debris fell about me. My ears ringing, I looked around, dazed and confused as men rushed the hole that had formed, and other men, covered in rags and garments I had never seen, poured in. I watched as Arelian soldiers rushed to meet them, firing back with their weapons, while others ran to the flamethrowers and let the black fire loose upon our attackers, some of it striking the wall itself. I knew I should have moved, should have done something, but panic rose up inside of me, freezing my muscles, paralyzing me. I could not move.

Faya screaming my name forced my head to turn. She was trapped under a beam. Her cries, her frightened look, should have been enough to force me to act, but I did not. I gave into my fear.

Before I managed to do anything, searing pain gripped my right upper arm as burning embers settled on it, burning through my jacket and cooking my flesh. Still dazed, I had just registered the fact that my skin was on fire when hands seized me, ripping my jacket off, putting the flames out, and yanked me from what I had hoped would be my security. My savior dragged me to Faya, who remained trapped and said something to me, but my ears still rung and my mind refused to focus, so his words did not phase me.

A stinging slap had struck my cheek and my mind became alert.

"Grab one end," he had said to me.

I obeyed.

With me on one end of the beam, and him on the other, we lifted it together, heaving it off Faya, allowing her to scramble free of it. We dropped the beam. The man grabbed both of us by the shoulders and shoved us along the wall to where the other recruits huddled together and where ladders had been propped up, leading to the bottom of the wall and to a waiting transport.

"Stay here. Your instructors will take you back to the training compound," he had told us.

Faya and I just stared at him wide-eyed, nodding in response, unable to form the words to speak.

He ran off.

I watched as he hurried to join the fight. A harrowing roar jerked my head in another direction and I saw Molers, locked in a battle with two of the invaders, relishing every moment. He dispatched them with ease, but before I could see him do anything else, another set of hands seized me and shoved me to one of the ladders, forcing me to climb down it and to a waiting transport.

The memory fades, but my fingers still burn. I swallow hard, trying to forget my shame, my weakness, the one time I displayed fear and almost allowed my only friend to die because I was too afraid to act.

Just like in my memory, hands snatch my wrist and place a gel upon the tips of my fingers where I had touched the blackened mark. Within moments, the pain dissipates and my fingers feel better, as though they had never been burned. I look up at the guard who had noticed my plight, but his helmet obscures his face, much like with the man who had saved Faya and me all those years ago. I wish I could see his face. Do his eyes possess kindness, sympathy, or anger and disgust at my stupidity?

"Thank you," I say to him.

"Black fire, even after it has burned itself out, can still be dangerous. Best to steer clear of it," he whispers to me; his voice holds no anger toward me, and I realize that he is being nice for the sake of helping someone.

"I thought it always burned."

The man chuckles. "Everything burns itself out in time."

"I'll remember that."

"Here,"—he hands me the container of the gel he has covered my fingers with—"best keep this in case you need it again."

"Noni!"

Commander Vye has noticed my lagging behind. I jump to my feet and run after her, almost collapsing under her reprimanding glare, and a part of me swears that her gaze could freeze black fire itself.

"Keep up," she scolds me.

I hurry after her, tucking the container in my pocket and pulling my jacket over it so she will not notice it.

"Where is your head?" she snaps at me.

I do not answer.

"You need to pay attention, or you know what will happen to you. I have no time for idlers."

I continue to not respond.

"Now, from time to time, you will be asked to serve in the guard tower. It is small and cramped, but we all must take our turn in it. Some are assigned there more than others, but that is because they volunteer; but it will be good experience for you to serve some time there are well. That will be at a future time, once you've learned a bit more about the eastern sector."

She motions me toward the ladder, which had been carved into the stone of the tower, and I climb up it, pushing my way through the trapdoor that is above me. When I straighten up, I find myself in a small box, and that is being generous in describing its size. The room is just big enough for one person, let alone three. A communication device lies in the far corner, its video screen smudged from greasy fingerprints and dirt, tucked away on the side of the only desk in the room.

I turn in a circle, looking out the 360-degree window, with a sniper's rifle nestled in it, positioned in such a way so that it could turn as needed and face whichever direction it needed to. The window gives a tremendous view of Arel—a rail car glides over the city unaware of me watching—and of the outside world: the flat grassland surrounding us before morphing into dense foliage with trees whose broad, vibrant green leaves shield any who dwell among them. Stories are told of people who live there, barbarians who prey upon our convoys and steal anything they can get their hands on. As I continue to stare out the window, I notice what appears to be a small speck.

"One of our other compounds."

Commander Vye's voice interrupts my pondering. Arel has other compounds, spaced around the city, and some are a good 20 or 40 miles away, in an effort to keep the area free of any who wish the city harm and to warn of any attacks by Kition. I say nothing and just nod my head to let her know that I understand what she has shown me. As I do so, my eyes spot the arsenal hidden underneath the desk and along the wall, but fashioned in such a way so that it blends in with the dark stone.

"Everything good here, Lieutenant?" Commander Vye asks.

"Yes, ma'am," he replies.

"Any news to report?"

"I just sent my report to the central command, ma'am."

"That is not what I asked."

Commander Vye's harsh tone causes me to quake. I must not be the only one she becomes cross with or lashes with that steel tongue of hers.

"Sorry, ma'am," apologizes the Lieutenant, rethinking how to respond to her. "There is nothing to report. No sightings whatsoever."

Commander Vye's eyes turn to slits as though she reads his mind, making me glad to not be on the receiving end of her ire this time.

"Next time I ask you a question,"—she closes the distance between them—"you answer it."

"Yes, ma'am."

The commander strides over to the hatch and crawls down the ladder, with me following right behind her, not waiting to be told what to do. Once we reach the bottom rung, Commander Vye takes off, walking at a brisk pace to a crossway between the outer and inner wall. I hurry to catch up. I glance downward at the wild dogs below as I step onto the metal grate that the crossway is made of, wishing the rails were a little higher. Eight pairs of eyes glare back at me, each attached to a set of sharp teeth, dripping with saliva as they wait for their next meal.

I step off the metal grate with a resounding thud and gasp. I had thought that the view from the guard tower was mesmerizing, but as I gaze across the field of grass to the jungle, I realize just how small we are compared to what lies out there. I lean forward, being careful not to tear my uniform on the barbed wire, to look downward at the sharp drop below should I fall over the side. Burn marks and scars from recent storms and attacks cover the outside of the wall.

Something darts across the grass and to the wall. At first, I think that my eyes are playing tricks on me, or that it is an animal. Something else darts through the grass, leaving a thin trail, one that would go unnoticed if I had not witnessed it being formed, and the feeling that something is not right washes over me. I turn around.

"Commander!" I shout.

She whirls around with a displeased look on her face.

"There's some—"

I never get the chance to finish my statement. At that moment, a deafening explosion rocks the wall, knocking me backward and over the side that drops into the area where the dogs are kept. I grip the edge, clinging to it as I press my feet against the side of the wall to support my weight. The influx of gunfire, mired by another ripple of explosions, drown the incessant barking of the dogs as they swarm below me, hoping for me to fall so that they can have another meal. I heave myself up over the edge and roll onto my back, thankful that I did not perish in the first explosion. A fiery orb soars over me and I watch as it arcs in the sky before crashing into a cluster of buildings within the eastern sector of the city, swallowing the square of homes and businesses in its voracious flames.

A tar bomb. I have heard of barbarians using those to attack us before, but had never seen one until now. The screams from the people scrambling out of the burning buildings attack my ears, and that old fear swirls within me, giving rise to the panic that had stopped me from acting the last time I was on the wall during an attack on my city. I sit up and crawl to a corner where I cower, reliving the past, my shame. Gunfire shatters the air as people shout orders and arbiters rush to their posts, their boots attacking the ground in their haste. My breathing quickens and I am back to being the person I was five years ago and the feeling of failure consumes me.

Commander Vye's stringent voice yanks me from my stillness as she issues commands amidst the flying bullets and mortar shells that hurl themselves at Arel. A grappling hook appears over the edge of the wall and grips it, pulling taut as its owner climbs up its rope. I watch as a head appears. The man sees Commander Vye, who remains unaware of his presence as she commands those around her. He pulls out his weapon and aims it at her.

In that moment, I know who I must be. I am not the person of five years ago who cowered in fear, afraid of dying. I passed the gauntlet. I am an arbiter. I must protect my city.

I bolt from my corner, racing for Commander Vye, plowing into her and tackling her to the ground just as the invader fires his weapon. At first, she opens her mouth to criticize me, but when she notices the man who had almost killed her, she aims her own weapon at him and shoots him in the shoulder, but he does not let go of the rope. I seize a palm-sized piece of stone and hurl myself at the man, striking him in the head, ramming the brick into his temple over and over again until he drops to the ground below. I glance at Commander Vye.

"Get to that post over there! Kill any who try to get through," she orders me.

I hurry away to the little outlook area on the outer wall, snatching the weapon of a fallen arbiter along the way. After a quick check, I know that I have to be careful how many times I fire the armament, as the magazine is half-full and I do not have another one. I position myself on the wall and watch as more of the barbarians fling their grappling hooks on the structure and climb up by twos and threes. Leaning over the wall, I spray the people below me with gunfire and some let go of the line and plummet to the ground.

A roar fills my ears and I turn just as one of those with a flamethrower spews black fire across the land. It covers the people below it and they writhe in pain while their anguished screams fill the atmosphere, blending with a grenade that goes off right below me. I huddle to the ground, covering my face as dirt and debris pelt me, tearing holes in my jacket. Once it clears, I lean over the wall, letting loose another hailstorm of gunfire.

A grappling hook clinks on the stone next to me, chipping it as it embeds itself. The rope pulls tight and I wait for the person on the other end to appear. I point my weapon down to fire, but nothing happens. Ripping out the magazine, I realize that it is empty and that I must rely on my training. The hook shifts. I hunker low, waiting, hoping the person on the other side will not see me before it is too late. The hook scrapes the stone, leaving a white, jagged streak, and a head appears. I rise up, raising my weapon, and smash the butt of it into the head of the invader, forcing him to let go of the rope. More approach. I need to cut the line.

I search for something I can use and find a piece of glass from the shattered window of a guard tower. Seizing it, I ignore the sting as it cuts my skin and the warmth of the blood that follows, and saw at the rope with its edge. A hand reaches for mine. Wrenching myself free, I ram the piece of glass into the throat of the person the hand belongs to and return to cutting the rope. It frays. I saw faster, adrenaline fueling me. It snaps.

Another explosion shakes the wall as a series of grenades are detonated. I hug the ground, allowing my back to take the impact of the pebbles that strike me. Screams force me to sit up. An explosive device goes off near the flamethrower closest to me and it twirls around, covering the one in charge of it in black fire. He darts away from his station, crying in pain as he tries to put out the inextinguishable flames, and heads straight for me. I back away. He still runs in my direction, unaware of what he is doing, his desire to get the fire off him dictating his movements. A thud jerks my head around as an invader manages to clamber over the wall. Pinned between the two, I prepare myself for the only option I have. As the man from the flamethrower nears, I clench my weapon as though it is a bat and ram it into his stomach, while circling around him, kicking him from behind and shoving him into the invader that approaches from the other direction. They crash into each other. I hurry over to them and kick them both over the edge of the wall and to their deaths.

A low hum prickles my ears, growing stronger with each second; its sound vibrates my chest and I glance up. Our planes have launched, spilling from the depths of the mountain that my city is nestled into. The hangar doors stand wide open and small, one-man fighters swarm from it, flying overhead, their jets a welcomed joy, and release a barrage of fire on the invaders that dared to attack us. People crumble beneath them, ripped to shreds by the rounds that the jets release.

A deep horn sounds in the distance and a red flare shoots into the sky, giving a low pop, before dissipating. The ropes slacken and the grappling hooks release as the barbarians flee back into the jungle where they had come from, away from us, away from death. Low moans replace the grenades and gunfire as I take in the aftermath of this latest attack: wounded soldiers lay on the ground crying for help, while others stare straight ahead with lifeless eyes. I wander through it, taking it in, having never experienced what happens after we repel an attack, having never seen the streams of fresh, bright red blood, or dismembered bodies that must be disposed of. My stomach begs for release, but I clamp my mouth shut, swallowing several times to prevent myself from vomiting. I must not show weakness.

The toe of my boot strikes a metal shard, and it skitters across the ground. I pick it up. The insignia of Kition is on it. Strange. Why would a bunch of barbarians who swear allegiance to no one and nothing have a Kition weapon? How would they get it?

Something touches my shoulder and I whirl around, bringing my hand up to attack whomever it is, thinking that one of the invaders has not left. A strong grip seizes my wrist and wrenches it downward.

"It is only me," says Commander Vye and I relax my muscles.

"Who were they?" I ask.

"The barbarians that live in there," replies Commander Vye, pointing at the jungle beyond.

"Why?"

"Do they need a reason?"

No, they do not. They always attack us and are always envious of what we have, but something doesn't seem right. They have weaponry that they should not possess. I show Commander Vye the shard with the Kition symbol etched on it.

"This does not belong to them."

Commander Vye takes it, studies it a moment, turning it over in her hands, before tossing it aside, over the edge of the outer wall. "They most likely stole it from Kition, much like they steal from us."

I glance back at the grass below and the jungle that lies on its edge, and the bodies that now fill it.

"Come," says Commander Vye, urging me to leave, "it is time we return."

I follow her across the crosswalk to the inner wall and back to one of the stairwells that lead downward into my city, unable to shake this feeling that something is not right.

Chapter 6

Reliving Events

Morning dawns again, ignoring me as I sit on the edge of my bed, my hands clasping the bar that holds the mattress, disregarding the somber mood that plagues me. Yesterday's attack on the wall has spread throughout the city with images playing and replaying on the screens placed in every square. Kumi's voice spills from the speakers that dot the city, his troubled tone stirring sadness within me for those who have died, not that it would have taken much. They were good people, good arbiters who served Arel, and died defending my city.

I know that I must hurry. Taking a deep breath, I stand up, glancing in the mirror and at the cut on my cheek from where a pin-sized piece of rock had struck me. Rustling outside the door alerts me to the need to move. Snatching my jacket, and throwing my flowing hair into a tight bun, I hurry out my door and down the stairs, not bothering to apologize when I knock over the cleaning bucket that the plebeian girl had placed on the floor.

When I reach the bottom of the stairs, Commander Vye is waiting for me. "I suggest you eat something and do so quickly."

I do not question her. Before being dismissed yesterday and allowed to go to the privacy of my room, she had informed me that we were to report to the Command Division to give our testimony of the attack. I hurry into the dining room and snatch three slices of bacon, wrapped in kale leaves, and a chunk of cheese, gulping it down in just a few bites, before washing it all down with a mug of water. Once done, I run back to where Commander Vye waits for me with Lieutenant Renal standing with her. Before I have time to wonder about why he is there, she turns toward Renal, saying, "Lead the way, Lieutenant."

"Yes, ma'am." He salutes her and steps out the door, and I take my cue from the curt nod Commander Vye gives me and rush out after him, with her right behind me.

As I follow Renal, I move my eyes, taking in the people who gathered to watch us proceed down the drive of the manor and down the street, heading to the platform where an empty railcar, set aside for this occasion, awaits us. Most give us piercing stares, but some look frightened, while the plebeians stare at the ground like they are supposed to. They move once we pass them, going about their business, but still curious about where we are headed and what the outcome of yesterday's attack will be.

We arrive at the lone railcar—its sides and ceiling made of nothing but glass, giving one a 360-degree view of the city, with thin steel rods interspersed to add support—within 15 minutes and I step on it first, remarking that the doors are open as though they waited for us. I take a seat near the middle, maintaining an erect posture and staring straight ahead, keeping my face unreadable since arbiters are not supposed to show emotion. Renal sits in the row across from me and I watch as his neck muscles twitch from his efforts to not look in my direction, but his eyes flicker to me for a second before darting away. True to form, Commander Vye remains standing. With a ding, the doors to the railcar close and it moves, gliding along the rails in such a smooth fashion that I do not notice we are moving.

Despite the seriousness of the situation, I cannot stop myself from glancing up at the glass ceiling to look at the skyline and the thin, gold line of clouds that line the morning sky, obscured by the tall buildings. We tilt upward as the railcar glides over its rails, making itself level with the tallest buildings. Short memories of me traveling by railcar to get to my assignment fill my mind. They seem like they happened a long time ago, but only two days have passed. How much has my life changed? Why is it my time at the Martial Training Corps seems like it had been years ago?

We dip downward, going underneath another rail as its car passes over us before leveling out. I watch as the shadow of the other track covers us for a moment, blocking the sun, before allowing it to shine on us once more, a small act that describes my wrenching nerves. I have never been to the Command Division before, but remember learning that it is where you go to give reports, or explain your actions if what you had done was more than what your immediate superior could handle. I watch as we pass the central hub, and twist in my seat, wondering why we have not stopped. There is no car that goes straight from the eastern sector to the center of Arel, which is where the Command Division is. The transparent building passes by us, its cars and residents ignoring us as we turn and head north, weaving between skyscrapers and elevated walkways, with the ever-present smoke of the crematorium in the distance.

"We are not changing trains?" I ask, allowing my mouth to speak the questions on my mind, instead of controlling it.

Renal continues to stare straight ahead. If he has any thoughts about my outburst, he hides them well.

Commander Vye gives me a reprimanding look and I know that I have stepped too far. "We are not stopping at the central hub. This train was reserved for us to take us straight to the Command Division."

Judging by the tight tone in her voice, it seems that this ride is supposed to be one of silence and I have broken that sacred peace. I am going to break it again. "Have you ever been there?"

Commander Vye's jaw twitches as she struggles with reprimanding me, or answering my question.

"Once," she replies, choosing the latter. "I was like you: young and with much to learn."

"What happened?" I could not help myself. I wanted to know more about her. Why is she always so curt, so controlled? Will I become like her?

Commander Vye cocks her head to look me in the eyes, and for a moment, I wonder what she might have looked like in a different setting, one that allowed her to let her natural curls grow out instead of shaving her head.

"I learned to value silence."

Her sharp tone forces me to forget the other questions forming in my mind. I glance at Renal and he shifts, telling me that he had observed our exchange with interest, but did not wish to be noticed.

The railcar swoops downward, and I cling to the small bar on the side of my seat to keep from being thrown forward, though the ride is so smooth that I let go and watch as we sink below the towers as though we are delving underground. Just as the shadows start to overwhelm us, lights spring to life with screens displaying dancing images of products, newscasts, Kumi's speech, and images of the attack on the wall. The railcar decreases its speed and we slide into a small hub with copper archways crisscrossing one another, forming a web of shadows broken up by the people strolling past.

Both Commander Vye and Renal straighten themselves, rising to their full height, and I follow suit, remembering to keep my mouth clamped shut. We step onto the black aluminum platform; my boots blend in, matching its color, and hurry across it, ignoring the bustling crowd as they attempt to make their train. Once again, I am greeted by people who walk with pride, while their plebeians trail behind, heads bent low in a pathetic gesture. I spot the arbiters of this sector with ease, their uniforms standing out amongst the colorful clothing of the residents. A group of children dressed in red suits walk in front of us, carrying tablets, accompanied by their teachers who are dressed in the same red uniform. I pause to observe them as their instructors point at the high-rises surrounding us, explaining the structures and how they are supported and made to withstand the weather, and humid climate. They are from the engineering division.

A tight squeeze grips my shoulder. I glance to my right to find Renal's hand on mine as he shoves me forward, giving me a warning look to not dawdle. We are to be at the Command Division by 0900 hours and tardiness is never tolerated, nor do I wish to cast a poor reflection on Commander Vye. I allow Renal to guide me down the streets, wondering why he has taken the lead while Commander Vye and I trail behind. The walkways and streets glow as though they have been polished, while rays of sunlight refract off the buildings around us, sending small rainbows onto all who pass below them. Single seat transports hover past us, each with a passenger seated in them, while the walkways above us overflow with people walking in an ordered fashion, trying to get where they need to go.

Renal leads us to a glass elevator. When a few others try to board, he holds his hand up, stopping them. At first, I am confused as to why, before it hits me: Commander Vye and I are in his charge and he is responsible for making certain we report to the Command Division. The elevator floats upward, toward the topmost floor, and I watch as the people below transform into tiny, scurrying ants. The ride is over within seconds and the doors slide open, allowing us to exit.

"This way," says Renal in a tight voice and I find myself missing the warmth he had shown me when we were first introduced.

We follow him down a hallway—I glance out the windows, wishing I am out there and not in here—to a steel door with two armed arbiters standing on each side and one in between them.

"State your business," the one in the center demands.

"Lieutenant Renal reporting with Commander Vye and Arbiter Noni."

Arbiter Noni? I have never heard my name spoken like that before.

"Identify yourselves," says the man.

Renal goes first. "Lieutenant Renal. Serial number R26389."

Commander Vye steps forward. "Commander Vye. Serial number V21923."

The man stares at me. I take one step forward, wondering if the reason for the doors behind him being painted black, while others in this area are covered in a brighter shade, is to make us nervous. If that is the case, it is working. I feel as though I am going to an inquisition, but am unclear as to my crime. I stand at attention in front of the man, take a deep breath, and identify myself. "Arbiter Noni. Serial number N27461."

The man checks something on his tablet and scans our wristbands. "You may enter. Remember, speak only when spoken to and answer only what you are asked."

The solid black doors open before us and we step through, walking into a room with minimal lighting, except for a bright beam directed at a podium which I know is meant for us. A high table with three grim-faced people seated behind it lines the front of the room. Renal steps up to the podium.

"State your name, serial number, and business here," says the man in the middle.

Renal lifts his chin high. "Lieutenant Renal, serial number R26389, bringing Commander Vye and Arbiter Noni as requested by this council."

"Very well. You are dismissed."

Renal backs away from the podium, turns, and leaves the room.

"Commander Vye," says the man in the middle, "please step forward."

Commander Vye obeys and takes her place at the podium.

"You are the commander of the eastern sector, is that correct?"

"Yes, sir."

"And Arbiter Noni is in your charge, as you are her mentor for the next year, is that correct?"

"Yes, sir."

I watch in silence as the council questions Commander Vye and have a sinking feeling that I am the reason for us being here today.

"Tell us," continues the man, "are you in the habit of allowing our newest arbiters to fail in their commitment to us?"

"No, sir," replies Commander Vye. "Arbiter Noni had never been in combat before and this was her first introduction to it."

"Does that excuse this?"

A video pops up, filling the room, showcasing my shameful moment, where I cowered when the wall was attacked. I avert my eyes, wishing that I had reacted in a different manner. Wait. How did they get this footage? The drones. How could I have forgotten about them? They are used when recruits run the gauntlet, so it makes sense that they would be used whenever an attack, or anything important, happens in Arel. That also explains how the televisions across the city are able to broadcast the images within hours of the attack taking place. But why did I not notice them before? Is it because I was not looking for them?

"There is no excuse for such behavior," replies Commander Vye, "but if you have checked the footage that follows, as I'm certain you have, then you will see that Arbiter Noni protected Arel from two of the attackers and assisted another wounded arbiter. Fear is the first natural reaction when one is first thrown into combat. But Arbiter Noni overcame her fear and I have complete faith that she will prove a valuable asset to Arel as her passage of the gauntlet demonstrates."

The council members debate among themselves for a moment, turning off their microphones so that we cannot hear them, and I realize that they must have studied the footage of my time in the gauntlet and my reaction on the wall with such thoroughness that they already know my actions by heart.

"Arbiter Noni, please step forward," says one of the council members.

I walk up to the podium and Commander Vye steps back, placing my clammy hands on the cold metal, its smoothness forcing them to stick to it. "Ma'am," I say.

"Your actions within the gauntlet were exemplary, which is why you were placed in the eastern sector."

In the back of my mind, I wonder if the real reason was because of my tendency to question those in authority, especially when they irritate me, but now is not the time to be second guessing what the council says. What happens here will determine my future within Arel.

"As such, your actions on the wall call into question everything we thought about you," continues the council member. "What do you have to say in your defense?"

I say nothing.

"Arbiter Noni?"

What can I say? My guilt is on the screen, on replay, repeating over and over again how I cowered on the wall just when the barbarians who live outside attacked.

"Arbiter Noni!"

"What do you want me to say?" I ask.

The members of the council frown at me and I know that I have not given them the answer they wanted, but it is an honest one.

"If it pleases you all," I say, trying to sound humble and not pleading, "I would like a second chance to prove to you that I am able and worthy to protect Arel."

"We are not in the habit of granting second chances."

"A test," says one of the other council members.

The others stare at him in confusion.

"She should perform a test, as a measure of her loyalty." The man turns toward me. "You have proven that you are not the coward we see on this footage, but your recent actions do cause others in Arel concern over your willingness to protect our way of life."

"I shall do whatever you ask of me," I say, without thinking.

The man smiles and nods his head at one of the guards standing by a door in the shadows. I almost do not see him until he moves and opens the door, stepping through, only to return moments later with someone in chains. He drags the person to the middle of the room in front of me, the pale skin giving away the fact that this criminal is a plebeian. The guard forces the plebeian onto his knees and walks toward me, giving me his firearm.

"This plebeian," says one of the council members, "was caught stealing from his master. Steal from one and you steal from us all. We cannot tolerate thieves in Arel and the punishment is death. As an arbiter, you will be called upon to carry out such forms of justice. Are you able to do so?"

I look at the firearm and understand what it is they want me to do. Failure will mean my death. The plebeian looks up, his frightened blue eyes staring right into mine, pleading for me to have mercy on him, but mercy is a luxury that my city cannot afford.

"Arbiter Noni?"

I glance at Commander Vye and her unreadable eyes, which tells me what I need to know. She would do it; of that I have no doubt, and if I wish to be like her, if I wish to be strong and serve my city, I must feel nothing for this plebeian. And why would anyone care about a plebeian in the first place? I pick up the firearm, making sure that the magazine is full, turn off the safety, aim, and fire. The single shot rings through the tomblike atmosphere, echoing off the darkened walls of the room and ringing in my ears. The plebeian falls to the floor, unmoving, and judging by the way the guard checks the body, I know that my shot aimed true.

The members of the council look pleased and I place the weapon back on the podium, staring back at them with a stone face.

"Yes, well, punishing a plebeian is one thing," says one of the members, the one who had doubted my loyalty when I first entered the room. "How would she perform if it was a citizen who had broken the law?"

One of the council members nods at the same guard and he disappears behind the same door once again, reentering the room with a man in restraints.

"This man was caught helping a plebeian escape," says the council member. "As you are aware, we in Arel cannot afford to allow a plebeian to leave. It might lead to an uprising."

What he really means is that they cannot afford to allow anyone to leave: citizen or plebeian.

"Allowing a plebeian to escape," says another council member, "to the land outside these walls is the same as committing a theft and thievery is punishable by—"

"—by death," I finish.

The guard forces the man to his knees in front of me, next to the dead plebeian, but he shakes him off and drops to the ground on his own, remaining erect, staring me in the eyes with a determined look, and something else, something that I have seen elsewhere, in Mandi's eyes: pity. The firearm rests on the podium before me and I know what it is I am expected to do, and what it means if I do not do it. I pick up the weapon, aim it at him, and squeeze the trigger. Again, the single shot shatters the silent room and the man falls to the ground, dead. I have proven myself a true arbiter of Arel.

The guard retrieves his weapon, while others remove the bodies in front of me.

The council members look upon me with pleased expressions.

"In light of this testimony of yours, we have decided that you are to be granted a second chance to prove your loyalty and worth to Arel. Do not shame us again. You are dismissed."

I step away from the podium and join Commander Vye. She does not glance at me at all, but turns and heads toward the door with me right behind her, as is my place. Once outside, I spot Renal standing erect as he waits for us. He approaches Commander Vye and salutes her.

"We are pardoned, for now," she replies.

Her voice has a note of pessimism in it and I wonder if there is something she knows, but is not telling me. Neither of them acknowledge my presence as they hurry down the long hallway and back to the main floor where the exit is. As I follow them, I watch the people around me, feeling their eyes on me as though they are trying to tell me how lucky I am, as I had been very close to being sent to the crematorium. I follow Commander Vye and Renal outside and to the shuttle platform, where another car has been reserved for us. The glass doors hiss as they close and I turn to watch the building fade away, becoming smaller with each passing second, all the while shackled by hollowness and emptiness.

Chapter 7

Doctor Sahir

A month has passed since my embarrassment and punishment. After having trained to earn the trust of Arel as one of its protectors, I must now earn their trust again, and that of Commander Vye. I cannot fail again.

My feet fly over the grass as I run across the quad in the manor, heading for the hanging tires and bars, pushing myself to stay strong as I navigate the obstacle course that has been set up for the arbiters that live here. I leap into the air and dive through the lowest hanging tire, somersaulting on the damp grass before springing to my feet and jumping on the second tire. It shifts under my momentum, but I hang on, allowing it to propel me toward the third tire, which hangs high above the ground. I leap for it. My hands grasp the bottom of the tire and I pull myself upward to the rope that connects it to the bar above it as it swings back and forth, threatening to throw me off. It nears the first rung of the monkey bars.

I watch as the metal rung approaches, before being pulled away from it by the tire I am situated on. Since my arrival, I have watched as some of the other arbiters have tried to pass the course and failed. If I fall, I will break a leg, or worse. Yesterday, one of the arbiters tried to leap to the monkey bars, much like I am attempting to do, but he missed and fell to the ground, unable to move his arms or legs.

Commander Vye did the only merciful thing she could: she shot him in the head, saying, "If you are unable to move, you are unable to serve Arel. I would expect any of you to do the same to me."

I stare at the bar as it nears and drifts away, steeling my nerves and preparing myself for what I must do, glad that I had decided to wear my leather gloves. The tire swings me toward the metal rung. Just before it moves away, I jump off, stretching my hands out to the bar, and grab it, my feet swinging in the air as my breath catches in my chest. Focusing on the bars ahead of me, I reach for the second rung, and the third, hurrying across the monkey bars, grabbing the next one just as my hand threatens to let go of the previous rung. I reach the end and swing my feet forward, wrapping my legs around the pole that is there and slide down it to the ground, landing on my feet.

"Congratulations."

I spin around. Commander Vye stands behind me—I never heard or saw her on the quad—her arms crossed and her piercing gaze burning right through me.

"I am glad to see your commitment to staying physically fit."

"Commander," I say in a respectful tone.

"And I suppose I am glad that you did not break your neck like the last man who tried this course. It would have been such a waste if you had. Arbiters are not easy to train."

"Thank you, commander."

"Get dressed and meet me at the gate in ten minutes."

I salute her and run off to my room to grab my proper uniform, as it would be improper for me to enter the city in my undershirt, and against regulation.

When I reach the gate, Commander Vye waits for me, her hands clasped behind her back and her sharp gaze informs me that she had been counting every second as she waited. Afraid that I might have been tardy, I quicken my pace, stopping just as I reach her. She stalks through the gate and I trail behind her as we hurry down the walk and to one of the moving walkways. As usual, people keep their distance from us, taking extra care to avoid being in our path, and I notice that it is not only the plebeians who avert their eyes.

Curiosity burns within me as my mind wonders about our destination, hoping that it will not be unpleasant like the last time I had been escorted through Arel, but I keep my mouth shut, not wanting to anger my commanding officer. After 30 minutes of weaving through crowds and navigating the moving walkways, we arrive at a white building with pillars in the front and the insignia for the hospice: a staff with a snake wrapped around it.

"Today," says Commander Vye, "we are visiting the medical center of our region. I want you to pay close attention to all that goes on here, especially the maternity ward. Though it is rare for there to be any sort of unrest here, there are times when an arbiter is needed and it is our job to provide security and ensure lawful behavior at all times in all of Arel."

We stroll through the silver doors as they open before us and are inundated with doctors, nurses, and medical staff walking with purposeful strides through the pristine halls. The copper floor marvels me as I take a moment to glance downward at my reflection, while the stark white walls enable the lighting in the building to exhibit my better physical qualities. A woman hurries past with a tablet in her hands as she scrolls through medical charts, her white uniform contrasts against my own, forcing me to realize that I do not belong in this building.

A man and a woman walk past us, nodding in our direction. I turn my head to tract their movements, bewildered as to why they do not seem terrified like the people on the city streets. Though the doctors and nurses keep their distance from me and Commander

Vye, none of them act as though we are a force to be feared. Could it be because we are in their territory and so they feel some sort of confidence within these familiar walls?

Commander Vye's boots click as she moves down the hallway and I hurry to catch up, taking a moment to glance into one of the rooms at a patient lying in bed, talking to one of the medical staff. She stops in front of an elevator and the door opens with a soft ding. I do not need her sharp tongue to tell me to enter. We ride the elevator in silence until another soft ding tells us that we have reached our floor, and when the doors open, a man in an immaculate white uniform awaits us, while a line of young students walk behind him, following their instructor.

"Commander Vye," he greets us in a noncommittal tone.

"Doctor Sahir. Nice to see you again."

"And this must be your new arbiter." Doctor Sahir looks at me and gives a curt nod, allowing the sunlight spilling through the skylights to highlight the gray tips of his crew cut hair.

"This is Noni," Commander Vye introduces me.

Instead of shaking the doctor's hand, I decide to mimic the commander and maintain a rigid, yet alert, posture. He says nothing, but acknowledges my refusal to take his hand with a slight dip of his chin.

"If you will follow me."

Both Commander Vye and I follow Doctor Sahir down the hallway and to a room with nothing but windows for walls. If I thought that Commander Vye had quick strides, hers do not compare to the doctor's, as my rapid breathing attests to.

"We are hospice number eleven," Doctor Sahir says as he shows us around, "and for the moment, the only hospice for the eastern sector."

"I thought that each sector had three hospices," I interrupt him and bite my tongue the moment I do so. Commander Vye gives me a reprimanding glare as, once again, I have overstepped my bounds.

Unbothered by my interruption, Doctor Sahir faces me and

continues his tour of the facility. "That is true. Every sector is supposed to have three medical centers at the very least, but with the
recent attacks, I am afraid that we have lost one of ours, and the
likelihood of it being replaced is slim at best, while the second is
severely damaged and awaiting repair. Our presidents agree with
the Arelian council that it is not feasible to rebuild in a sector that
is constantly under attack."

A slight note of anger fills Doctor Sahir's voice. The other sectors are more protected than the eastern one, which is more exposed and bears the brunt of the attacks by the barbarians outside
the wall. With a flick of his wrist, Doctor Sahir commands us to follow him into a glass walled room. I stop the moment I step through,
unable to take it all in, and one glance at the doctor's face tells me
that I have given him the reaction he wants.

Glass encases me as I move forward, deeper into the gigantic
bay window, and look out at the compound below. More nurses and
doctors scurry about, performing their duties without a hitch, looking like glowing fireflies in the sunlight. From my vantage point, I
can see into every floor, some of which are one-room establishments
with beds in uniform lines, separated by curtains, while other floors
have more private rooms; where one is assigned when sent to the
hospice for treatment depends on their status and importance. Plebeians mop the floors, clean the glass, and cart the waste materials
away in silence, doing their best to remain out of the way of the
medical staff.

"You can see, no doubt, how efficiently we operate here," Doctor
Sahir says.

I glance to my right and almost gasp. A portion of the building is missing. Crumbled concrete fills the empty conclave and
sparkles in the bright sunlight as shards of glass still blanket it,
while metallic rods poke through as though they are claws reaching for something to grasp, wanting company in the dark depths
they reside in.

"Why has this not been repaired?" I ask, forgetting to control my mouth once again.

A harsh cough from Commander Vye silences me and I know that there will be punishment for my lack of respect.

Again, Doctor Sahir seems unconcerned about my outburst. "We are not deemed important enough at this time. You will learn, Noni, that here in the eastern sector, we make do with what we have, while the executive district receives whatever materials it needs. Of course, the fact that the presidents and council both reside there could have something to do with the fact that—"

"Doctor Sahir," Commander Vye's strong voice interrupts him, "as enchanting of a view as this is, perhaps we should finish showing our newest arbiter what the hospice does."

"Yes, of course."

Doctor Sahir charges down the corridor, away from the sea of windows and to a spiraling stairwell that allows one to see all the way to the bottom, if they lean over the railing for a look. His steps make no sound compared to the harsh clacks of Commander Vye's and my boots. After going down two flights, Doctor Sahir steps off the stairwell and heads down another pristine hallway.

"This floor is reserved for certain members of our society that would prefer to keep their identities a secret. Some of them suffer from illnesses that they do not wish others to know about, and so pay extra to have their privacy protected, while others are involved in more cosmetic practices."

I glance into a room where the door was left cracked open and watch as a doctor peels away some bandages from a patient's face, revealing a few stitches surrounding the nose and lips. I observe the delicate nature of the doctor's hand movements while she explain what surgery has been performed; but instead of being greeted by a worried face, the patient looks pleased, and when handed a mirror, she cries out with joy over how her appearance has been improved.

A tap on my shoulder forces me to look away and into Commander Vye's stern face. I hurry after the doctor, who has continued on, talking as though we have not dawdled at all.

"You will rarely be asked to serve on this floor," he continues, "as it is normally quiet. Though occasionally, we have had a few unsatisfied patients, but as a whole, the people here opt to be here."

He takes us to another stairwell and we follow him to the next lowest level.

"This is our trauma center," says Doctor Sahir.

I glance around at the fogged glass, the only room with such a thing, noting how they must have wanted to keep what happens here from being witnessed. Agonized screams fill my ears and I prepare myself for a fight, but Commander Vye's strong grip stops me as she points to a man on a gurney with a mangled leg. I do my best to remain on the sidelines as doctors and nurses hurry from one patient to the next in an attempt to save them, their white uniforms coated in blood and vomit, while the plebeians do their best to keep up with the sanitation of the area.

"I was unaware that there are this many citizens brutally harmed," I say.

"Most are," replies Doctor Sahir. "No one wants to know what darkness lies within their perfect world. We have an image to keep, which is why none, except medical personnel and arbiters, are allowed in the trauma center."

"Are there many instances of lawlessness here?" I ask, wondering how anyone so wounded could be capable of causing a disturbance.

"Rarely, but sometimes…"

As though to further prove the doctor's point, a man who had come in with a wounded plebeian screams, "What do you mean you cannot help her?"

"You know the rules," replies the attending physician. "All plebeians are to go to the sublevels for treatment."

"You mean to go there to die!"

"Sir, I am asking you to…"

"Are you going to do your job or not?" demands the man, fury filling his brown eyes.

The physician glances from the man to the unconscious female plebeian, and the children who stand behind him, making a connection between their muted dark skin and the man's reaction. "Is this plebeian important?"

"What kind of question is that?" demands the man, his dark face matching the color of a rose.

The youngest child starts to speak, but one of the older ones snatches her arm and forces her into silence.

"She is the only one who is able to calm my children when they are frightened," says the man.

The man's explanation does little to conceal what everyone in the room sees. Though relationships between citizens of Arel and plebeians are forbidden, they are not unheard of and most ignore them, as many of the children from such relationships can pass for dark-skinned. But how he managed to have three, despite the sterilization additives in the water supply, and without being caught perplexes me, until I notice the emblem on his shirt collar: he is a representative of the eastern sector to the Arelian Council. The physician does not bother to glance at the wounds on the female plebeian, but snatches a thumb-sized syringe and injects it into the plebeian's neck, stopping her heart.

"What did you do?"

"A favor," replies the physician.

"You heartless bi—"

The man charges the physician, wrapping his fingers around her throat, slamming her into the equipment behind her, knocking medical utensils and tools to the floor while all eyes focus on them. Within seconds, arbiters appear from the shadows and rush them, myself included. We seize the man, yanking him off the physician—she gasps and coughs while rubbing her throat—and pin him to the floor. I step back and allow the more experienced arbiters to stand him on his feet as Commander Vye approaches.

"For a disturbance within the hospice…" begins one of the arbiters, holding onto the man, but he stops when he notices Commander Vye. "Commander."

"Thank you, Sergeant," says Commander Vye. She looks the man in the eyes. "You seem a little too attached to a mere plebeian, a mere servant of your home."

The man remains silent, while the children huddle in a corner: the oldest tries to protect the younger ones, but fear is all over his face.

Commander Vye glances at the children. "Are they registered?"

The man still remains silent.

"It is a severe oversight of our regulatory board if they are not; and they must not be, since none of them are wearing badges or uniforms."

"It is allowed for a man to keep his children," says the man through gritted teeth, "until they have reached the age of majority, at which point, they are assigned to a sector."

"True," concedes Commander Vye, "and I am certain that you have the proper papers for such a thing."

The man says nothing.

"Just as I thought." Commander Vye looks at the oldest and the hate-filled glare he gives her as a smile creeps across her lips. "You have some fight to you." She glances at me for a moment and continues, "That can prove useful. I believe arbiter is best suited for you."

The arbiters snatch the boy, pulling him away from his crying siblings. Whatever rebellious nature he possess now will be eradicated when his arbiter training is completed, assuming he survives the gauntlet.

Commander Vye bends over the second oldest child, taking the electronic pad away from him, noting the book of mathematical equations he reads. "You understand all this?" she asks him.

He nods.

"Then it will be the engineering school for you."

An arbiter grabs him and hauls him away.

"Now what shall we do with this young thing?" Commander Vye cusps the girl's feeble chin.

"Please!" shouts the man, struggling to break free.

"In about ten years, she will have reached the age for bearing children."

"No! I beg you!"

"Breeder will be good for her," says Commander Vye.

"No!" shouts the man, but the arbiters hold firm to him.

My eyes dart to all within the room, but stop upon Doctor Sahir's and the fire within them.

"Commander," I say, knowing that I will be punished for this indiscretion, "according to the law, only a member of the Council of Registration, or those acting upon their orders, can decide if an unregistered child will be a part of the maternity ward. As arbiters, we have not been granted such authority to assign anyone anywhere."

If I have angered Commander Vye, she does not show it.

"And as this child has committed no infraction, it would be unjust to punish her for her father's misdeeds. Perhaps she has talents that are of better use elsewhere."

"You are correct, of course," replies Commander Vye, and I detect a hint of annoyance in her voice. "Where would you suggest she be sent?"

I look at the girl and realize for the first time that she holds a doll dressed as a cook. "Food Service."

Commander Vye concedes and arbiters grab the girl. As they carry her away, I steal a quick glance at the man, and for a moment, I believe that he has mouthed the words "Thank you." As part of the food service division, and if she does well and causes no trouble, the girl could find herself as a personal chef to a member of the council, a job that is both lucrative and prestigious, and the somewhat approving look within Doctor Sahir's eyes tell me that he would have done the same.

"And what would you do with him?" asks Commander Vye, putting me on the spot and testing me to see if I have the best interests of Arel in mind.

I do not respond right away, wondering what I should do with him. The standard punishment for his infraction would be the crematorium, but no one escapes that place and perhaps he would be of more use elsewhere. I stare into his eyes, seeing the same frightened look as what was within the eyes of the citizen I had executed to prove my loyalty, but his fear is not for himself; it's for his children.

"Disposal," I say, and while Commander Vye has a pleased look on her face, Doctor Sahir is disappointed, looking the way Mandi did when I slapped the plebeian at the banquet dinner.

"You have your orders," Commander Vye says to the other arbiters and they haul the man away. She stalks over to a wall monitor and brings up the detention facility, swiping her bracelet and indicating that I should do the same. Once she finishes processing the man and his children, as well as the proper reports, she turns to the director of the medical facility, saying, "Doctor Sahir, perhaps we should finish our tour."

Whatever disappointment resided within his eyes moments before has vanished as he hugs his tablet closer and leads us out of the trauma center and into another hallway. He takes us past more rooms filled with patients or students and to another set of black doors.

"Through here," says Commander Sahir, "is our maternity ward. Every sector has one."

He unlocks the doors and they open before us, allowing us to step through, closing the moment we have passed. I gawk at the sight before me, feeling as though I have stepped into another world. Instead of a tile floor, I stand on grass, broken only by the stone paths that weave through the indoor atrium, with each walkway leading to a separate room tended by medical staff. Fogged glass surrounds us, allowing sunlight in, but keeping prying eyes out.

I watch as women in various stages of pregnancy wander around the indoor courtyard and stop. Dark-skinned and fair-skinned women associate with one another, all of them expecting. Some talk among themselves, mixed together instead of separating themselves like they would outside these walls, while others remain alone, picking at the flowers (tulips, dandelions, and irises) that line the edges of the grass. A few glance in my direction, but just for a moment before averting their eyes. The same fear resides here.

Arbiters patrol the area, remaining hidden among the shadows, keeping vigilance on everyone. I observe while one arbiter watches Commander Vye and me as we are led around.

"This is our maternity ward," says Doctor Sahir, waving his hand around, showcasing the area.

"You do not separate the plebeians from the citizens?" I ask.

"Not here, we don't," replies the doctor. "We have found that they tend to have healthier pregnancies when allowed to associate with one another and share a common interest. None of them are allowed outside this area, so we have nothing to fear from their mingling. The plebeian women give birth to future plebeians, while the citizens give us future citizens of Arel. Each child is taken away from the woman that bears them, and when strong enough, sent to their assigned area."

We stroll past what could have passed for an outdoor shed, but was encased in glass with yellow zigzag lines across the panels.

"Here," Doctor Sahir points at the glass shed, "is our cryogenics. It is where we store all collected sperm that is used to impregnate the women."

Fruit trees and vegetable gardens loom before us as we continue our tour, tended by some of the pregnant women themselves, or other women who wear green uniforms, the color of our agriculturists.

"You grow your own food here?" I ask.

"We bring in some of what we need, but have found it best to grow what we can. Tending a garden provides good physical exercise and prevents any unnecessary attention."

"But those women are not breeders."

"No, they're not," replies Doctor Sahir. "They were sent here to help ensure that the gardens produce and to perform the labor-intensive tasks that our women here cannot do. We do not wish to harm any of the pregnancies here."

I look into the somber eyes of many of the women, including those in green, and wonder what they think of me, taking in every detail.

"There is where the routine medical exams are performed, and over there is where the infants are delivered."

I eye the rooms that Doctor Sahir points out.

"We have sleeping quarters on that end, and over there is where their meals are served."

"So, they remain here, separated from the rest of Arel," I say. I had always heard about the maternity wards, but have never seen one or know how they are run.

"It is best," says Commander Vye.

Though some within Arel were allowed to adopt children, or have managed to have their own, despite the measures taken by the government to prevent unnecessary births, the majority of infants were born in the maternity wards, in a controlled environment.

"Each female is chosen based on her physical attributes and capability of having children. The water supply for this place is kept separate from what feeds the rest of Arel." Doctor Sahir points at a water station where women brought their pitchers and filled them from the faucets there. "It wouldn't do to make our breeders sterile."

Commander Vye and I follow Doctor Sahir into one of the rooms and my ears hurt from the screams that meet them as I realize that he has brought us into the delivery room. I watch in horror as a woman cries in agony, with her legs propped up and spread apart while a doctor gives her instructions. Another scream escapes her lips just as the doctor pulls a baby out and cuts the umbilical cord, and the pain on the woman's face disappears.

She reaches out to hold her baby, but the doctor refuses to give it to her. Whispers of concern fill the atmosphere as the doctor consults with one of the nurses, before noticing Doctor Sahir standing there and holds the baby out for him to see it: it is an albino. With a somber expression, the doctor injects the infant with something, stopping its heart, before handing the child over to another member of the medical staff to dispose of it.

"What! No!" screams the mother as she watches in horror.

She pulls herself off the bed she is on and stumbles over to the dead infant, seizing it, her eyes widening in terror when she sees the unnatural white skin of the child. "No!"

The mother steps away, her legs faltering beneath her weight, but two arbiters appear behind her and grab her shoulders.

"It's not my fault!" screams the woman, but her pleas are met with silence.

As she is dragged away, her screams fade, but do not go unnoticed by those outside the room; their sympathetic eyes peeking through the doorway, knowing there is nothing they can do, except mourn.

"An unfortunate circumstance," mumbles Doctor Sahir, but his eyes seem more disturbed by the incident than his words suggest. He waves us outside.

Once more, we follow Doctor Sahir to another room where incubators have been set up, some with an infant and a tag indicating where the child was to be assigned, and some which are empty.

"This is where the newly born infants are kept until they can be delivered to their designated areas."

I stroll past the clear boxes, looking at the slumbering bundles, reading tag after tag, wondering if this is what happened when I was born. Was my mother never given a chance to hold me? Did she not choose my name? I notice it. None of the tags have names on them, just numbers and their chosen affiliation.

"They are not named?" I ask.

"No," replies Doctor Sahir. "Each child is given a number upon birth and assigned to a sector within Arel. Once delivered, they will be assigned a name, which is randomly generated by a computer program. We have learned that people function better if they have a name, something that identifies them as uniquely human."

Commander Vye gives him an odd glance. I sense it too: a note of despondency in his voice. "Doc—"

"Doctor Sahir," I cut off my commander, hoping to distract her from what she thought she had heard, "this is a remarkable facility. You must be proud that it runs so efficiently."

"Of course. Efficiency is paramount to an ordered society and we must all do our part for Arel. I do mine by making certain this medical facility runs competently, while delivering the quality care our people expect."

I glance at Commander Vye and her mouth is set in a firm line. She seems to have forgotten what it was she wanted to say, but I know that she has not forgotten my insolence.

"This way, please." Doctor Sahir leads us out of the maternity ward and spends the next hour showing the rest of the hospice to us, finishing our tour well before lunch.

Chapter 8

Patrol

My boots clomp on the moist, paved streets of the eastern sector as I wander to my assigned area. A slight shiver darts up my spine as an unusual chill in the air finds me, reminding me that the weather can be unpredictable, and reminding me of my punishment. Because I had challenged her, Commander Vye assigned me to night patrol. Though the days are warm and humid, the nights tend to be nippy.

A few droplets of water from the condescension that has formed on the edges of the buildings and street lamps fall to the ground, dampening my jacket as well. I swipe them off and continue my rounds, refusing to show weakness. I deserve my punishment; I know that, but a part of me wonders why I embarrassed Commander Vye in the first place. She is supposed to be my mentor, as well as my commanding officer. I should be following her every example, learning what I can from her.

The frightened girl's face fills my mind before morphing into the desperate one of her father. Though he deserved what punishment he received, punishing the child for his misdeeds did not seem right. This is where I have failed in my duties as an arbiter. I allowed my emotions to interfere and must not let them do that again.

"Emotions are burdens," Molers' voice echoes in my head as I remember one of his many training sessions.

"Anything to report," came Renal's voice over the intercom function on my wristband. He is on patrol as well, charged with monitoring me and ensuring that I do my job as this is my first night patrol.

"No, sir," I reply.

"Understood. Keep your eyes peeled. There have been unwarranted activities at night lately."

"Yes, sir."

I end my communication with him and wish this night would end soon. Patrolling the streets during the day is more interesting, as there are more people out and you are able to talk to them, or visit the various storeowners, and maybe pick up an extra meal or two; but guarding the streets in the dark means being plagued by boredom, a boredom that drags the hours and you with it.

A clinking sound draws my attention and I walk over to investigate, wondering why anyone would be out after nightfall as it is well past curfew. It happens again. I maneuver over to where the noise emanates from and ready my weapon. As I near the source of the sound, I realize that it has come from a craft store that Renal had taken me to on my fourth day within the eastern sector. Did he fail to put the trash in the incinerator?

All storeowners are to dispose of their garbage at the end of the day, placing it within the incinerators throughout the city, but sometimes they forget, or wait until it is too close to curfew, so they opt to do it in the morning. Sometimes, trash is left outside in the alley, an infraction that results in a warning, and stray animals find their way into it. A few years ago, an infestation of rats littered Arel because of the trash people failed to dispose of, blaming the lack of incinerators and the time it took to get to them. As a result, the council allocated resources to allow for more incinerators to be built throughout the city, but the eastern sector received the fewest funds. Always bearing the brunt of outside attacks meant labeling the spending of valuable resources to maintain its infrastructure as a useless endeavor.

I creep toward the noise, pulling out my small flashlight, turning it on and focusing the beam into a darkened alleyway, expecting to find some rats, a cat, or monkeys (yes, that happened one year, or so I'm told), but I am not greeted by any sort of animal. A mop of soiled hair with a few strands of pale yellow fills my light as a plebeian girl tries to lift a sack, while not allowing the items contained within it to tumble out of the hole that has formed in the bottom. She drops the sack the moment she notices my light, but holds something in her tiny hand, while using her other to smear mud over her face and keeping it covered with her grungy hair.

"Halt right there!" I yell at her, while I open a communication channel with Renal. "I have a four-twenty-six. A plebeian, female, possibly the age of eight, out past curfew, rummaging through garbage."

"On my way," Renal replies.

The girl quivers under my light as I keep it focused on her. "What is your name?"

She does not answer, but clutches the item in her hand, holding it closer to her body.

"What do you have there? Show it to me!" The harshness of my voice surprises even me, but she is only a plebeian.

The girl shakes her head and takes a step back.

"Now!"

"Behind you!" she screams, catching me off-guard.

I whirl around, expecting to see someone coming at me, but there is nothing there, just an empty and darkened street. Cursing at having allowed myself to be fooled, I whip back around and notice that the girl is gone, having darted down the alley, her bare, little feet making no sound. I chase after her, my boots pounding the cracked pavement of the alley, echoing off the sides of the building.

"Stop!" I yell at her and pull out my weapon, firing at her. The bullets miss her and bounce off the corner of a brick structure, causing her to release a shriek. "I said stop!"

She dives around a corner and into a street. I pursue her. Allowing my training to kick in, I control my breathing and focus on the girl. Who is she? Where would she go? She is small, so perhaps she will try to hide somewhere where I will not fit. Once I enter the street, I look around, lighting up the darkness with my flashlight. A wisp of hair catches my eye and I chase after it.

"Lieutenant Renal," I say into my communication device, "we are nearing the primary childcare center. What is your ETA?"

If he responds, I do not hear it. I push myself harder and watch as the tiny, dark shape up ahead veers to the left, heading to a set of stairs that leads to one of the upper walkways, and where the cameras are few. As I hurry after her, I realize that we are running in an area where the security cameras are not able to view us in any clear detail and a large number of them are broken, waiting to be replaced. A part of me admires her cleverness. As she climbs the stairs, moving with a speed I did not think she could possess, I change course and head for another set of stairs, going halfway up them before lunging to the railing of the walkway above it, and heave myself onto the platform. Turning, I run to where the girl is and cut her off. She stops with a start, in front of another stairwell, surprised that I have managed to get in front of her.

"Stop right there!" I yell at her, aiming my weapon.

She looks around for a chance to escape, but by her frightened actions, I know that she has found none.

"What is in your hands?" I demand.

The plebeian girl steps further into the shadows, making it difficult for me to get a clear view of her face. "Please," she pleads, "I need it for my mistress."

Needs what for her mistress? "Explain."

"She is very ill. This could help her," says the girl.

"Then your mistress should visit the hospice center."

"She has," wails the girl, "but they have deemed her incurable and refuse to help her."

If this is the case, why is her mistress not at the crematorium? Who is her owner? My piqued curiosity causes me to not pay attention to what is around me and not see the threat approaching from the side.

"Who is your mistress?"

"Ch—NO!" yells the girl.

A force slams into my left side, sending me over the top step of the stairwell, and I tumble down—my weapon flies from my hand—stopping at the bottom. Dazed, I look up and watch as two figures, the girl and the stranger who had helped her, flee down the walkway and disappear into the darkness.

"Noni!"

Renal's voice penetrates my confusion and I try to sit up, but end up falling over as his arms reach underneath my shoulders and heave me to my feet, leaning me against the railing. He retrieves my weapon and I place it back in its holster.

"Where is she?"

"Gone," I say, shaking my head as I try to clear it, but I must have banged it hard because the world still spins before me. "Someone helped her."

"Did you see who it was?"

I shake my head. "They both knew enough to stay out of the light."

"Be advised," Renal says into his radio. "We have two plebeians on the loose. One is a girl of about eight years, the other is unknown. They were last seen heading northwest." He clicks off his communication device and turns back to me. "Come on. Let's get you back and get your head looked at."

I allow Renal to lead me away and we head back to the manor. I have failed my city, again.

An hour later, I stand in Commander Vye's office next to Renal, listening to the drumming of her just clipped fingernails on the polished surface of her desk as her eyes glare at me, penetrating deep within to the depths of my most cherished secrets. An uneasy feeling that she can read my mind fills me, but I maintain an erect posture with my hands clasped behind my back and my feet spaced shoulder width apart, making certain to keep my eyes focused straight ahead, while avoiding her gaze. I wish she would speak. The tense silence unnerves me.

"Explain to me what happened tonight," Commander Vye speaks in a low voice, almost a growl, as she struggles to contain her anger.

"It is as I've reported…" Renal began to reply.

"I want to hear it from her," Commander Vye cuts him off.

"I assure you that my report is thorough," Renal begins.

I move my eyes to glance at him, wondering why he is trying to protect me. Is he afraid of the punishment I will have to endure? Does he know something and is keeping it from me?

"I've no doubt of the thoroughness of your report," says Commander Vye, "but you were not the one pursuing a suspect though the city, now were you?"

"No, ma'am." Renal salutes her and leaves the room, giving me a sympathetic glance as he closes the door behind him.

I maintain my stance as the tense silence fills the chamber again and I wait for Commander Vye to speak, while she continues drumming her fingers on the desk, a noise that irritates me to no end, but I know that I must keep my mouth shut.

"Well?"

"Well what, ma'am?" I ask, wanting to scream at myself for being so stupid right now. This is not the time for my usual brazenness.

Commander Vye rises from her chair, moseys around her desk, and leans against it, crossing her arms in front of her chest.

"I see tonight's events have not caused you to lose any of your flagrancy. Tell me exactly what happened tonight."

I suck in a deep lungful of air, trying to form the words and sentences that will explain what had happened, while presenting it in such a way so as to avoid too harsh of a punishment, but I know that I have failed my city again. Too many failures, and I know where I will be sent.

"I was on patrol in my assigned area when I heard a noise. Unsure of what it was, I decided to investigate."

"And what did you find?"

"A plebeian girl rummaging through some garbage that one of the storekeepers had neglected to take to the incinerators for disposal."

"Did you see her face?"

"No, ma'am. It was too dark for me to make it out."

"Then how do you know it was a female?"

"The plebeian had the height and build of a girl of about eight years and her hair reached past her shoulders with a few curls in it. No plebeian male wears their hair in such a way as it is forbidden. And her voice was too light to be a male's."

"And what happened next?"

"I ordered her to stop, but she ran, so I chased after her. I had managed to corner her on a walkway when I was sidelined by someone else. Whomever it was pushed me down the stairs, and I do not remember anything after that, until Renal found me."

"And you got no glimpse of the person who attacked you?"

"No, ma'am."

"Height? Build? Male or female? Weight? Nothing?"

"No, ma'am," I repeat, regretting that I had nothing more to give her.

"Did she say anything to you when you found her?"

"She pleaded with me to let her go, saying that she needed it for her mistress."

"Needed it?"

"Yes, that is what she said."

"And she said nothing else?"

"No, ma'am."

Commander Vye strolls back behind her desk, drumming her

fingers as she went, her mind mulling over what I have said to her. "It must be contraband," she says to herself.

I listen as she talks out loud about what the plebeian girl must have been after, wishing that I had managed to capture her.

"You will take me to where you found her. Meet me outside in ten minutes."

"Yes, ma'am." I salute her and head to the door, pausing when Commander Vye speaks again.

"You said she had curls in her hair."

I turn toward her, my hand resting on the edge of the doorway, feeling the Arelian crest carved into the wood.

"Interesting how you were able to notice that, but not see her face. Dismissed."

I left the room, heading to the kitchens, where I snatch an apple and wolf it down in six bites, wondering why I mentioned the plebeian girl's hair. How is it I noticed her hair, but not her face? Her hair covered her face, preventing me from seeing it, but I never paid attention to a plebeian's hair before. Why was she any different?

I need it for my mistress.

The words echo through my mind as I hear the girl's soft voice again. As I remain focused on the night's events, I swing my arm and knock over a stack of bowls by accident, having not seen them. A plebeian stands in the kitchen, keeping his distance from me as he waits for me to take my anger out on him.

"Clean it up!" I snap at him and hurry from the kitchen and outside the front door, not wanting to be late in meeting Commander Vye there, since I am in enough trouble.

When I step outside, a group of arbiters, all stationed at the same manor as me, stand there awaiting orders, but there is no sign of my commander. Relieved, I take my place next to then, waiting for Commander Vye to show up and the door slides open, revealing her imposing presence, allowing her to step out into the night air.

"One of our arbiters was attacked tonight," says Commander Vye to the others. "Though we have not located the two who attacked her, we can learn why they were out after curfew in the first place."

All of the arbiters salute her and move toward the gate, with Commander Vye in the lead and me by her side. She looks at me and I know what it is she wants and I obey. As we walk through the abandoned streets of the eastern sector, the snapping of shutters being closed fills the air as the local residents seal themselves inside, not wanting to be involved or witness what is about to happen.

I lead them to the alley where I first saw the plebeian girl and stopped, pointing at the bag that she had been holding when I had first found her. Commander Vye moves toward it and picks it up, holding it close to her nose, sniffing it before opening it and reaching inside, finding nothing. Her head pops up and she glares at the door in front of her. With a flick of her wrist, she commands one of the other arbiters, dressed in full gear, including a helmet, to knock on the door. He does, raising the butt of his weapon and slamming it into the door, creating an ominous thud that reverberates throughout the alley.

Another shutter closes; the creaking of its hinges slices the quiet around us.

No one answers and the man glances at Commander Vye, who nods her head, giving the order for him to knock once more before breaking the door down. Again, the pounding of his weapon against the wood door shatters the night around us. Seconds tick by and no answer. Just when two other arbiters approaches with a battering ram, the lock clicks and the door opens just wide enough to slip a few fingers through.

"May I help you?" the storekeeper asks in a shaky voice.

In answer to his question, the two arbiters push against the door, opening it all the way and shoving their way inside while the rest of us follow. Glass thrown to the floor mixes with the thudding of heavy objects being shoved from their place as we sweep through the room, knocking papers, books, vases, clay pots, and bags of soil over, creating a montage of broken ceramic pieces and dirt with footprints imprinted on it.

"Ma'am," an arbiter hands Commander Vye a small package.

She takes it and rips it open, revealing small vials of clear liquid. Her hardened eyes look straight at the storekeeper as he huddles in a corner with his wife; their frightened faces glitter with droplets of sweat.

"Take them outside."

Arbiters grab both of them, drag them through the front door, breaking it off its hinges in an effort to open it, and throw them to the moist ground.

"Please," begs the storekeeper, "spare my wife. She knew nothing!" His pleas fill the air, but are ignored as arbiters surround him and his wife, pointing their weapons at them.

Commander Vye stalks out of the store—her steps thump on the pavement in a slow, methodic rhythm—approaching the terrified couple as they hunker on the ground. "Where did you get these?" she asks, holding the vials out to the storekeeper.

He says nothing as he clutches his wife even tighter.

"Where?" The malice in Commander Vye's firm voice chills me as I watch the scene unfold in front of me.

The storekeeper glares at her, challenging her to force him to talk as he remains silent.

Commander Vye snatches the storekeeper's wife and yanks her away from him, pulling her weapon out of its holster and placing the barrel at the woman's temple. "Tell me what I want to know, or watch her die."

Tears spill from the woman's eyes, but she never screams, shaking her head at her husband instead. The two share a look, one that conveys that they have accepted their fate. "Do it, bitch," the woman spits at my superior.

Commander Vye rams her weapon into the woman's face, forcing her to her hands and knees. The woman coughs and spits out blood as she lifts her head and stares straight ahead at a figure approaching: Mandi.

I turn with the others and watch as Mandi advances toward

us, her uneven steps indicating that she had wanted to leave, but changed her mind when she realized that we are watching her. When she reaches us, I want to ask her what she is doing here, but change my mind. I am in enough trouble.

"What is going on here?" asks Mandi.

"What are you doing here?" Commander Vye replies with a question of her own, mirroring my own inquisitiveness.

"None of your concern," says Mandi, using a stern tone that I have never heard come from her before. "

"It is, when you are in my sector at this hour."

Mandi closes the distance between her and Commander Vye, speaking in a loud voice so that we all can hear her, "Commander, you may be in charge of this district, but you do not outrank me. My business here is above your classification level. I answer to the council, not you."

"I can bring this before the arbiter tribunal."

"You can,"—Mandi leans in and whispers in Commander Vye's ear—"but do you really want to go down this road with me, Vye? You will lose. I guarantee it."

Commander Vye backs away from Mandi. "Arbiter Noni caught a plebeian out past curfew going through this man's garbage. The plebeian got away, but upon further investigation, we found these." She holds out the vials. "Medicine, illegally obtained."

"And what is your suggested punishment?" asks Mandi.

Commander Vye looks at me. "Since it was Noni who led us here, she should decide." She faces me. "What do you propose we do with them?"

All eyes turn to me and sweat forms underneath the collar of my jacket. I glance from one to the other, trying to think of an appropriate punishment, one that would be deemed acceptable.

"But punishments are decided upon the offender's hearing, not by us."

"That is true," says Commander Vye, growing impatient with me, "but we can make a recommendation if we wish, which is what we did at the hospice. Sometimes our recommendations are heeded; other times, they are not. So, again, I ask you: what would be your recommended punishment?"

I step toward the man and look at him as he kneels on the ground, the defiance in his eyes evident. "Your crimes are as follows: failure to dispose of your garbage in the incinerator, illegal obtainment and hoarding of medicine, and refusal to answer an arbiter's inquiries." I study his muscular form and know just where he will best serve Arel. "A store is not much of a challenge for you. The fields are where you should go."

He spits on my boot and I kick him in the mouth before moving on to the woman. "Your crimes are as follows: failure to report your husband's offenses. As such, you are an accessary to his misdeeds." One look at her and I know that she would never survive the fields or anywhere else she is sent. "The crematorium for you."

"You bitch!" The storekeeper breaks away from the arbiters holding onto him and tackles me.

"Stay back," orders Commander Vye to the others when they move to help me.

The storekeeper and I roll across the ground, plowing through a puddle as we near the ledge of the sidewalk. He is on top of me when we stop and slams his fist into my face. Before he can strike a second time, I grab his arm, pulling it underneath his chest, and twist to my left, throwing him off-balance, and bring my knee up, striking him in the face and forcing him off me. I scramble to my feet and kick him in the stomach. He charges me. As he nears, I drop to the ground and sweep his feet out from under him, forcing him to crash into the ground on his back, but his head hits the ledge with a sickening crunch and blood pools around him. With caution, I shake him with the sole of my boot, but he never moves as his lifeless eyes bore into mine.

"Well done," Commander Vye commends me amidst the woman's

wails as she tries to cradle her deceased husband. "But do not think that you will escape admonishment," she whispers into my ear, her hot breath forming a misty coating on it.

I say nothing, nor do I smile as, once again, I see a look of pity in Mandi's eyes, but it disappears the moment I spot it.

"Dispose of him," Commander Vye tells the others, "and process her."

Two arbiters cart away the storekeeper's body, while two more drag the woman away, her screams drowning the night's sounds. I watch as they disappear. When I glance in Mandi's direction again, she is gone, and Commander Vye issues orders for me to follow her back to the arbiters' manor, but as we head back, my thoughts are consumed with the fresh blood that stains my hands: bright red against black.

Chapter 9

My Punishment

I stand in front of the window in my room dressed in my undershirt and uniform pants—my hands pressing into the sill—staring out the glass at the rising sun as it peeks over the edge of the wall that surrounds my city, while trying to avoid the line of black clouds that hover above it. Little specks of red-orange dance on the wall behind me, while the sun's rays change the color of my ebony face. I have not slept at all, knowing what waits for me the moment the sun rises: my punishment. I have had too many failures since my assignment here, and if I make one more mistake, I will be sent to the crematorium. Arel cannot afford people who are unable to protect it and uphold its laws, people who allow its citizens to suffer: people like me.

I release a slow, warm, vaporous breath onto the glass, admiring the way it fogs the window in a circular pattern that is neither perfect, nor ideal, but is unique, misshapen, and one of a kind. Reaching up, I run my finger through its center, dividing it in half as the shape fades from the glass altogether. I look out at the wall and the figures that line it, patrolling the top, doing their duty like I should have been.

Someone pounds on my door. I open it, knowing what to expect as Renal and two other arbiters in full gear stand just outside in the hallway.

"It is time," says Renal.

I glance at my boots, placed at the foot of my bed, and change my mind about putting them one. This is to be my humiliation, my castigation, my shame; the least I can do is not soil my boots. I step out into the corridor and the two arbiters fall in behind me, while Renal remains in the front. They escort me down the stairs, past a couple of plebeians who pause from their work to watch the proceedings, through the foyer, to the back where the doors that open onto the atrium are. My bare feet tingle from the cool, dampness of the grass as they press into it and bits of mud squish between my toes, making soft—*squishes!*—with each step I take.

Commander Vye waits in the center next to two poles, spaced an even length apart and which had been set up hours before just for this occasion, her hands clasped behind her back as she eyes me, while I approach my well-deserved chastisement. The other arbiters in the manor have gathered around to observe my reprimand, standard procedure, in the hopes that they will remember what happens when you fail, and not commit my mistakes.

I maintain an erect posture as I walk, refusing to show fear. If I am to be sentenced, then I will face it with the pride of an arbiter and accept it. I reach the posts and stop in front of Commander Vye, refusing to face her, showing her my side as I stare straight ahead, clenching my fists as I prepare for what is coming. Commander Vye gives her order without speaking and the two arbiters behind me and Renal fall in line with the rest, while two more hurry forward and each take a wrist. They place their hands on my back and force me between the posts, while raising my arms up and strapping the cold leather cufflets around my wrists, cinching them so tight that I cringe when the leather edges dig into my skin, certain that they will leave bruises in addition to a red impression. They tighten the chains attached to the cuffs, raising me until my toes brush the matted grass and I sway from the harshness of their motions.

"Arbiter Noni, N27461, you are hereby sentenced to twenty lashes," says Commander Vye as she strolls in front of me, facing the other arbiters, "for failure to apprehend a plebeian who was out after curfew, allowing her to escape with illegally obtained medicine, and for failing to adhere to Arelian law. As arbiters, we cannot allow anyone to disobey our laws, as it will lead to the disintegration of our way of life. Let this be a reminder of what is at stake, and of what happens if you forsake your duties. If one of us is weak, then we all are weak."

Once she stops addressing the other arbiters, a bit is placed in my mouth and hands tear off my undershirt, exposing my back and my breasts, making me glad that I did not put on my uniform jacket. The crack of the whip jolts my ears and I clench my fists harder, digging my short nails into my palms, preparing for what comes next. The whip cracks a second time and...

Burning, searing pain stretches across my back from the lower left to my right shoulder as the whip plows into my already scarred skin from previous penalties; the metal bits on the end tear my flesh off. I bite into the bit so hard that I can taste tiny splinters of wood that break off into my mouth, cutting my gums and the inside of my cheeks. Though I had been flogged before, whomever handles the whip this time uses a force that I have never experienced, and a part of me wishes that the training center had not been so kind to me, but had prepared me better. I moan as I realize that this beating will be nothing compared to the switches used at the training facility, preferring those over this torment.

Another lash stings my back, wrapping around my center and slicing my stomach just below the belly button. And a third curls around my diaphragm, causing me to gasp as I tried to breathe and I watch as bits of my skin are ripped away from me and tumble to the grass.

Four, five, six, seven...

My knees buckle and I sag as I hang from the chains and the leather cuffs burrow even deeper into my sore wrists. Again, the whip strikes me, leaving another stripe down the center of my back, mixing with the blood that coats me, sending a red spray across the pear-green grass. I have lost count of the number of lashes as I hang in the air, my head bent low, and my jaw relaxes, releasing the bit from my mouth, and it lands in the wet lawn with a small splash. Thunder rolls overhead, sending a low rumble across the sky as though it agreed with my predicament. The sun disappears behind the dark and heavy, bulbous clouds as though it wishes to hide from Commander Vye's wrath.

Another strike from the whip causes me to arc my back and rear my head up, but I bite my tongue, refusing to scream, refusing to give anyone there the pleasure of seeing me beg for release. I deserve this. I know I do, but in the back of my mind, 20 lashes seems excessive. I push the dissenting thought away from me just as the whip slices my skin once more. A speck of moisture touches my shoulder just as lightning flashes above us. As though it has been given permission, torrents of rain plummet through the sky and smother us, but Commander Vye and the other arbiters remain where they are. Though the rain washes the blood from my back, it appears to have strengthened the wrath of the whip as another stinging, burning sensation overtakes me.

"Enough!" yells Commander Vye. "I said twenty lashes, not twenty-one! Or can you not count?"

The man with the whip steps away from her and bows his head in apology, but Commander Vye's fury is visible despite the curtain the rain has placed between us.

"Do I need to refresh your memory?" Commander Vye says to him, a dark undertone to her voice.

Reading her thoughts, the man salutes her and coils his whip, saying, "No, ma'am."

I hang limp, unable to move, unable to lift my head as my back cries in agony from the torture it has suffered, made worse by the stinging pinpricks of the rain.

"Doctor Sahir!"

My head lifts just a bit at the sound of his name. I do not remember seeing him there when I first stepped outside. Was he hiding? He walks up to me with a case in his hand and two other medical personnel with him, placing his case on the soggy ground by my dangling feet, his white uniform remaining perfect, despite the storm's attempt to soil it. With a gentleness I never thought I would feel, his muscular hands touch both sides of my face and lift my head up as he examines my half-opened eyes.

"You've gone too far this time, commander," says Doctor Sahir.

Commander Vye opens her mouth, but is cut off before she can utter a single word.

"Do not threaten me. You have no authority over me and you know it." He examines my bloodied back and releases a puff of angered air from his lungs. "Take her down," he tells his two assistants, "and get her to her room."

His two assistants undo the leather straps and each wrap one of my arms around their shoulders, allowing me to place all my weight upon them as they carry me inside and to my room, which, to my surprise, has been turned into a hospital room with IV bags, monitoring equipment, and a bed. They lay me on my stomach and apply moist bandages to the wounds, mopping the blood as they attempt to clean them. I hear Doctor Sahir's strong voice issue orders, but it sounds far away and I have difficulty keeping my eyes open, until everything goes black.

Chapter 10

A Bit of Unrest

Isit on the edge of my bed as Doctor Sahir performs one last check up on me, monitoring my blood pressure, heart rate, and performing one last inspection of my back and the raised stripes that mark it.

"Your wounds seemed to have healed nicely," he says. "You may put your shirt back on."

I do as he says just as plebeians hurry in and cart out the medical equipment that had been set up in my room two weeks ago when I had received my 20 lashes, my repentance. As they empty my room, others bring the bed, desk, and chair that had been there the day I arrived. Once they have finished remaking my room, Doctor Sahir packs his utensils and leaves. I never asked him—and remain silent even now—about the confrontation he had with Commander Vye the day I was whipped, but the tension between the two remained the entire time he was in the manor overseeing my care.

"I wish you well, Noni," he says as he walks down the hallway and down the stairs.

I pull on my uniform jacket and zip it up, smoothing out the creases that always seem to form, despite my best efforts to prevent them. When the door to my room closes, Renal waits for me in the hall and I pause, wondering why he is there.

"Commander Vye wishes me to inform you that you are to accompany her to the school today. This is not some test, but more instruction on how Arel functions."

"Yes, sir," I reply, deciding to keep my responses simple and to the point so as to avoid any more reprimands.

Renal stops me. "You are not the only one to receive such a punishment." The empathy in his voice catches me off guard.

I stare at him. Why is he telling me this? The soft and compassionate tone of his voice is unusual, and I wonder if he has received the same and remember that most every arbiter does if they disobey, but not all. Some are good at following orders and manage to fulfill their duties without faltering.

"Have you…"

Before I can finish my question, another occupant of the house stomps up the stairs and into the hallway, marching past us without a single glance in our direction as he heads to his room. Anan: is that his name? Deciding that it is best to let the matter drop, and not wanting to be tardy, thus giving Commander Vye another reason to chastise me, I hurry down the stairs and to her office with Renal right behind me.

"Good," says Commander Vye as I open the door to the room, "you are here. Today, we will be going to one of the schools within the region. It is rare for them to be a place of disorder and misconduct, but it is a good idea for you to see how one is run." She steps around her desk and notices Renal standing in the doorway. "Renal, I believe you are assigned there today. Shouldn't you be there already?"

"Yes, ma'am. I was just bringing her down as instructed."

"Dismissed."

Renal leaves the two of us alone. I remain at attention, waiting for her to say something about my lashing, but she never does. Nothing needs to be said. What is done is done and I have had my warning. She puts on her own jacket and motions for me to leave. As I walk through the house and to the front entrance, I eye the other arbiters in the estate going about their duties. None of them look in my direction and no one speaks of what happened two weeks ago. It must be the rules of the manor.

The sun bears down on us as we walk down to the street and catch the trolley that will take us to the train station within the eastern sector. Hurdles of people bustle past us, each taking great care to give us room and to avoid running into us. I still find the entire ordeal interesting and confusing, but Commander Vye ignores it all, relishing the power her uniform gives her as she stalks up to an information booth, cutting to the front of the line, unconcerned about the others that had been there before her, and are too frightened to say anything. She checks the schedule for the train, noting when it will arrive, and strolls through the crowd back to me.

"Five minutes," she says to me.

A few give us nasty looks, but whirl around, facing away from me when they notice me watching them.

"Why don't we take the trolley?" I ask. "Will it not also take us to the school?"

"It will take longer. The particular education center we are going to is on the far side of the sector, well away from where we are. The train is fast and will get us within a block."

"How many education centers are there?" I ask, keeping my tone respectful.

Commander Vye gives me a peculiar look. "You seem—"

I give her a wide-eyed, curious expression, as though I am wondering why she is acting different around me.

"—different."

I shrug my shoulders, not wanting to say anything, still remembering the stinging slash of each strike the whip had made two weeks ago.

The shrill whine of the train fills the platform as it speeds toward us, slowing to an abrupt stop. The doors open and people struggle to push their way on or off the shuttle with us caught in the mix. I use my shoulders to shove passengers out of my way, receiving the beginnings of a tart response until they notice my uniform and take two steps away from me. A woman rushes past me with her plebeian in tow, but they get separated. As Commander Vye and I hurl our way onto the railcar, the plebeian tries in vain to board herself, struggling with the bulky package in her arms, but is tripped by another citizen and falls, dropping the package, which plunges between the train and the curb, landing on the tracks below.

"Well, grab it!" yells the woman, but the plebeian hesitates, knowing what will happen if she obeys. "Now!"

The woman backhands the plebeian, and she jumps onto the track with the train on one side and the ledge of the platform on the other.

I lean out the door to watch, my stomach becoming queasy as I realize what will happen next. The familiar ding echoes around us, and a few late-comers sprint across the platform, boarding the train just as the doors seal shut, sparing us from the screams of the plebeian as the train speeds away, slicing her in half.

The woman curses in frustration, unconcerned about the plebeian she had sent to her death. "That's the fifth one this week. Damn things are becoming too expensive to purchase or keep."

My eyes follow the woman as she forces her way to a seat within the car, heaving a brown-skinned out of his chair. Before I face straight ahead again, I glance around at the other passengers, noting the looks of indifference on some, while others attempt to mask their horror. Commander Vye grunts and I face ahead, staring out the glass windows that encase us, adoring mirrored images of the glass skyscrapers of my city as we ride upward on the rail, showered by rainbows as the sunlight spills through the translucent ceiling, before dipping lower again into the darkened depths of the eastern sector.

Within 12 minutes, we reach our stop and the train squeals to a halt. The harsh ding sounds again and the doors slide open, allowing the crammed passengers to begin the race of exiting the shuttle before the ones on the platform ram their way onward. I spring forward, pushing and shoving people aside, though many still jumped out of my way, allowing me to pass so as to avoid upsetting an arbiter and being put in a detention center. Commander Vye whistles at me, beckoning me to follow, and I hurry after her as she stomps up a set of stairs to a moving walkway. We stroll down it, passing those on our right until we reach our exit, and shove our way through to another set of stairs that take us up to the street.

Once at the top, I spot a tiered brick building, painted gold and shining bright in the sunlight, with towering panels of gold glass forming the exterior of the front and a sign with the word "Alpha" on it. Commander Vye strolls over to the entrance with me trailing behind. We pass through the doors that slide open for us and head to the front desk, where the staff, wearing pressed, daffodil-colored uniforms, prop their heads up to see who has just walked into their domain. Their chattering stops the moment they see our black uniforms.

"May we help you?" a man asks, his voice shaking.

"Commander Vye here to see your Headmistress."

"One moment, please."

As though to exemplify her annoyance at being asked to wait, Commander Vye places her fingers on the counter and drums them in a slow rhythm, while her eyes never leave the man who had talked to her, causing him to quake under her unforgiving gaze.

"She will be down shortly," says the man.

Commander Vye remains where she is, displaying her displeasure, and I copy her movements as we wait for the headmistress to meet with us.

"Commander Vye?" says a soft voice, belonging to a woman whose skin is a shade lighter than mine and whose hair is pulled into a low-hanging, loose bun.

"Headmistress Sminga, I presume." Commander Vye's voice provides a stark contrast to the director's.

"Yes. And this must be one of the new arbiters?"

"The new arbiter to the eastern sector," Commander Vye corrects her, placing emphasis on the word.

The new arbiter. This isn't the first time I have heard this. Am I the only one assigned to the eastern sector out of my graduating class?

"Yes, of course," replies Headmistress Sminga. "Follow me, please."

I follow the headmistress, with Commander Vye taking up the rear, as she leads us from the entrance to a hallway with skylights spaced four feet apart, decorated with drawings that the students had made of our two presidents. Doorways line the walls, each leading into a classroom filled with simple, wood desks, and each desk has a single child in it.

"Five and five is," says one teacher as she points at the equation on her electronic wallboard.

"Ten," reply the students in unison and the number ten pops up in bold, green letters.

I notice that some of the rooms have students wearing the same daffodil-colored uniform as Headmistress Sminga and others have students wearing uniforms in a darker color, a more mustard color. It is odd that they would be wearing different outfits. Are they not all going to be educators?

We stroll past another room where a group of four-year-olds repeat Arel's mantra. "Strength in our kind. Strength in numbers! Strength over weakness! Weakness is failure! Failure is death!"

"Headmistress,"—I snatch a glance at Commander Vye to make sure that I am not overstepping my boundaries, but her face betrays nothing—"I noticed that the students seem to wear two different uniforms. Why is that?"

"Oh, the answer is simple, my dear."

I give her a quizzical look when she addresses me as "my dear". Never have I ever been spoken to in such an affectionate manner.

"Those who wear the color of uniform that matches mine will be sent out to the other regions or to the education centers that accommodate the best of Arel's citizens. The ones in the darker color will either be kept here in the eastern region, or sent to the education centers that cater to those who are deemed fit for the other... more labor intensive parts of the city."

"So, they have already received their assignments," I say, thinking it odd that the future educators would get their assigned duties so early.

"Yes, dear. It is given to them upon their birth and they are trained accordingly."

We follow the headmistress through the hallway and to a foyer where on one end, a group of six-year-olds play a game, laughing and giggling as they went, while on the other end, a group of 13-year-olds participate in a series of roleplay scenarios where one is the teacher and the other is the student. The lack of discipline in this building astounds me. How can she run such a playhouse? If the Martial Diplomatic Corps were run like this, there would be no law and order. Judging by the expression on Commander Vye's face, she shares my sentiments, but keeps her mouth sealed, knowing her place and that this is Headmistress Sminga's domain.

"The first two levels are where our classrooms are and the top two are the dormitories. The boys are on one floor and the girls are on another. They are kept separate to avoid entanglements. Some have already been assigned partners, but some are designated to live at the education center they are assigned to once they reach the age of majority. Every weekend, they are allowed to visit their assigned parental units."

"Parental units?" The words are out of my mouth before I can stop them, but my surprise at them being allowed to have a semblance of a family is too difficult to conceal. Arbiters have no parental units. The corps is our family.

"Yes," replies Headmistress Sminga. "We have learned that for them to function as efficient educators, it is ideal for them to experience social settings outside these walls so that they will be able to form connections with the children they will be teaching. So, when they arrive here as infants, they are assigned parental units, usually a couple who lives close by to the center and are considered loyal citizens of Arel."

We head outside to a field of grass that has just been mowed, as the fresh scent of cut lawn prickling our nostrils attests to, and physical education instructors coach a group of children on the proper technique for running. One blows a whistle and two boys dart down a lane that is marked with white tape to the finish line, ending in a tie. Before they have a chance to bicker about who won and who did not, one of the instructors steps forward and says, "Now what have we learned here?"

"Nothing, sir," replies one of the boys.

The instructor raises an eyebrow, but maintains a calm demeanor. I think back to the one time I dared tell Molers that I did not learn anything from one of his exercises and the punishment I received in return, amazed at the gentler manner in which they treat the students here. "Nothing? Perhaps you should run the race again."

Both boys shake their heads and the distaste toward them for their objection to physical exercise fills my mouth.

"Sometimes," says the instructor, "it does not matter if you win in the immediate future. What matters is if you win in the long term."

Commander Vye grunts her disapproval.

"But," continues the instructor, unaware of her presence, "sometimes, no one wins. Sometimes, we all lose." The instructor sees us for the first time. "Line up!"

The students hustle in a mishmash fashion to form two lines, each standing with their hands by their sides, wondering why we are here.

"Hello, children," greets Headmistress Sminga. "Let us welcome two of our arbiters who are here to inspect us."

"Hello, arbiters," say the children in unison and my jaw almost drops at the way they greet Commander Vye and me.

In response, I salute them, snapping my heels together, an act that startles them.

"Would you like to inspect them?" asks Headmistress Sminga in that same soft voice, speaking to me as though I am a small child, which grates my nerves.

I do not answer her with words, but stroll over to the two lines of students, walking in the same manner I have seen Commander Vye use. I mosey past the first line and spot one child fidgeting and stop in front of him.

"Stand still!" I snap at him.

I continue to observe the daffodil-colored uniforms before me, reminded of the first flowers that bloom every spring, and pause in front of another student whose belly appears to be a little too soft. I pat his stomach with the back of my hand. "It seems that you need to lay off the sweets and exercise more. Do you all not run an obstacle course every morning?"

They shake their heads, an act that was never accepted at the training facility.

"Answer me!" I yell at them. Out of the corner of my eye, I notice that the headmistress jumped at my harsh command. Did she not discipline these students?

"No, ma'am," they say, and my ears pick up on a few that sound as though they are almost in tears.

I face the instructor. "You are their physical education teacher, are you not? Every morning you should have these students running an obstacle course to get them into physical shape so that they will bring honor to Arel."

"Yes, ma'am," says the instructor, stealing a quick glance at the headmistress.

I walk up to her. "I realize that this is your facility to run, but it is the Alpha Education Center. Should it not take pride in its students' physical well-being?"

"You are correct, of course," replies Headmistress Sminga, and I have the impression that she agrees with anyone who challenges her so as to avoid conflict, and a pang of disgust fills me as I turn away from her.

"Is there anything else, you wish to show us?" Commander Vye asks.

"Yes," replies the headmistress, and the remainder of the morning is spent with us touring the cafeteria, the classrooms, and dormitories.

"I have never seen a more ill-run school in all my years," Commander Vye grumbles as we leave, accompanied by the headmistress, but I remain silent, believing that I was never meant to hear that statement.

Our bracelets beep as a red dot flashes on them, warning us that there is trouble in the region. The headmistress gives us a quizzical look at first, but realizes that we are being summoned elsewhere, and as Commander Vye and I both rush out the entrance doors, she calls, "It was nice meeting you! Have a stupendous day!"

"What's wrong?" I ask, having never seen my wristband do this before.

"Trouble," replies Commander Vye in between breaths as we run.

I head for the platform to the railcar.

"No! This way!"

Changing direction, I hurry away from the platform and follow Commander Vye to a moving walkway. We hike down a set of stairs to a walkway that is just below the ground, allowing passerbys to only see the heads of those on it. Both of us shove people out of the way, not caring if they fall on the conveyer belt as we charge down the moving walkway, ignoring the shouts sent our way. We take the first exit off the loggia and jump on another one, ramming our way through a meandering crowd of people as they remain undecided about where they want to go. As we pick up our pace, the red spot flashing on our bracelets increases in rhythm, going so fast that it almost appears to be a constant decoration on it.

I notice Commander Vye veer to the left and do the same. She swerves to the right to avoid a man standing in what is supposed to be the passing lane and I follow suit, watching as she gets off the walkway and takes a set of stairs to the main road. The chaotic sounds of a mob hit my ears, telling me that we are close and it isn't long before I learn what has caused the problem. Other arbiters, with their batons and weapons drawn, join us as we reach the street and head for the source of the noise, while Commander Vye unholsters her firearm. We plow into the crowd, delving deeper into the mass of irate shouts, waving fists, and thrown Molotov cocktails that burst into a spray of flames.

Strong arms throw me to the ground and I land on all fours, receiving a kick to my stomach as I try to stand up. Gasping for air, I spot a blur of black and face it, seizing the boot that heads for me, giving it a hard twist, forcing the person it belongs to to plunge to the pavement, crashing onto the hard service. Another kick is aimed in my direction. I jump to my feet and dodge the blow, while bending low to evade a fist swinging for me. In the distance, I hear Commander Vye's voice as she issues orders to the other arbiters, while defending herself from a group of three people who have cornered her.

I pull out my baton, appreciating the snapping sound it makes as it unfolds into a forearm-length piece of harmful metal. A plebeian man charges me. I swerve to the side, spinning around, whipping him with my baton. Before he has a chance to react, I pounce on him, placing my baton around his throat, and fling him backwards until he slams into the ground with a grunt. His venomous eyes glare at me and I see the desire to murder within them. Lifting my foot high, I ram the heel of my boot into his face, rendering him unconscious, feeling his jawbone shift under my weight as it breaks and hangs at an odd angle from his mouth.

The violent crowd grows as I lose myself in it, swinging my baton, striking fair-skinned and dark-skinned in the face, shoulder, chest, and legs, all in an effort to avoid being harmed myself. A hard object strikes me between my shoulder blades, propelling me forward, knocking me off-balance as I stumble a couple feet. Two pairs of hands grab me, ripping my baton away from me, and drag me toward the center of the fray where more of the riotous mob wait, salivating over new prey. I struggle, kicking my feet. Managing to get an arm free, I ram my fist in the cheek of one and turn to the side, punching another, but before I can escape, more hands seize my free one and twist it around my back, threating to break it. I dread what will become of me, when a shadow appears and gloved hands seize one of my captors around the shoulders, ripping him away from me, while flipping him in the air and kicking another in the head. The same hands grab me, steadying me, while a familiar voice screams, "Go!"

I stare at Renal, amazed that he fights with such skill, wondering why he risked everything to rescue me.

"GO!" he yells at me again.

I find my baton on the ground, in the hand of a plebeian, and snatch it, while pulling out my weapon. Someone charges me when I try to run and I aim, squeezing the trigger, shooting him in the heart. A woman comes for me, screaming in a wild rage, and I shoot her in the neck, watching with a cold expression as she drops to the ground, clutching the wound as it sprays blood before her eyes rear up into her head, and she falls, face first, into a puddle of crimson water. Marching catches my attention and I look up, noticing the group of arbiters armed with flamethrowers for the first time. I sprint from my position, whipping my baton, striking any who get in my way, dodging, twisting, and swerving as I go to avoid being struck myself, bursting from the chaos just as the first spray of fire plows into the rioters.

Agonizing screams pierce my ears as dancing, humanoid-shaped fires dart and run in an effort to escape the pain that consumes them as their flesh cooks and falls from their bodies, until all that remains is exposed bone. One comes for me, waving her arms in a frantic motion, unaware of her actions, and I point my weapon at her, shooting her in the head before she reaches me. I spot another fiery rebel heading for Commander Vye and my weapon echoes around me, drowning the shrieks that plague the square as I fire at him, stopping him before he reaches her. Those with the flame-throwers step forward, moving past me and the other unprotected arbiters, pushing their way further into the dispersing crowd as they spray their lethal inferno on any who resist them.

People flee the scene. Not wanting them to escape, other arbiters chase after them, hunting them down, but I remain with Commander Vye, observing the manner in which she studies the scenario, her merciless gaze taking in every detail, and the most important one of all: hidden from us during the bulk of the chaos crouches a plebeian male with an Arelian female, clutching a pale-skinned child no more than four years of age. Wisps of smoke frame them as though attempting to capture this moment and seal it for eternity.

Commander Vye marches to the couple and I take my place beside her. She snatches the child by the hair, ignoring her screams.

"Please," begs the woman, her dark skin appearing luminous in the sunlight as bits of her permed hair stick to her tear-stained face.

Commander Vye says nothing, but she does not need explanations to know who the child is and why the couple are embracing one another; they are part of a forbidden relationship.

"Please, let her go," the woman pleads, her voice faltering with each word as the cries of her child tear at her heart. "We did not mean for this to happen. Just let us go, please!"

"Go?" says Commander Vye in a mocking tone. "Go where?"

"Outside the wall," the plebeian man replies, receiving a fist in the face for speaking without permission.

"Outside the wall?" Commander Vye's grip on the child tightens, causing her to squeal. "No one goes outside the wall."

The woman breaks down into a series of sobs, reading the unspoken message in Commander Vye's voice.

"Noni," Commander Vye faces me and I know that she is going to use this as a way of testing me, "you are the newly assigned arbiter to this region. I will let this be your decision. What are we to do with them? What does the law say?"

I eye the pair hunkered before me. "The law is clear. No Arelian citizen is to intermix with a plebeian, and any products of such a union are to be disposed of, unless they are of the proper complexion, or physically strong, in which case they can serve Arel and become productive members of our society. Those caught in a forbidden union such as this are to be sent straight to the crematorium with no hearing."

Commander Vye gives me an approving nod for reciting the law so well.

"This child is too pale and weak," I continue. "She should be disposed of accordingly."

An arbiter snatches the screaming child from Commander Vye and shoves her in the back of an armored truck, just as a small, fist-sized drone hovers nearby to capture every moment of my sentencing.

"No! Please!" the woman wails, reaching for her child.

"You," I approach the woman and the plebeian, "are found guilty of intermixing with a plebeian. There is no need to send you to the detention center for a hearing, as your infraction is obvious. You and the plebeian will be sent to the crematorium."

"No!" the woman screams as arbiters seize her and her plebeian lover, hauling them away to the armored vehicle, never to be seen again.

I look at Commander Vye and receive an approving nod, but when I glance at Renal, all I get in return is a somber expression. I have done my duty as an arbiter of Arel. I should feel pride and exhilaration, but I feel empty, hollow. I have become Molers.

Chapter 11

New Additions

The clinking of metal forks on ceramic plateware dances in my ears, transforming into white noise, as I eat a slice of ham, smothered in a semi-sweet sauce, surrounded by my fellow arbiters. We remain silent during our meal—pointless conversation is not encouraged. My eyes flicker to Commander Vye's chair as it sits alone and vacant among the monotony of our breakfast routine. Where is she? Most days, she is here, eating with us, making certain that we follow protocol and do not forget our place, but this particular morning, she has been difficult to locate, making her absence all the more mysterious and unsettling. Did something happen to her? Am I going to end up with a new mentor? I hope not. I have just memorized her eccentricities: what angers her and what pleases her, enough so that I should be able to navigate through the rest of this year without garnering her wrath too much.

I finish my last forkful of ham and drain my glass of water, wishing I could have some of that cranberry juice that was served at the banquet, but sugary drinks are not allowed for arbiters and our caloric intake is monitored. Though, judging by the beginnings of a round stomach on some, it does not stop them from sneaking in a few treats, and I know where I can go to get some juice if I wish. I just need to be careful not to overdo it, since I need to be certain that I can pass my biannual physical. Every arbiter is required to do a physical twice a year to ensure that we are maintaining our physical strength and well-being. I scoot away from the table, plopping my fork on my plate—a plebeian snatches it and wipes the area with a warm, moist, white towel—and leave the dining area, meandering into the corridor and to the lounge room, not knowing where I am to be assigned today: Commander Vye has neglected to inform me of it.

Where is she?

Changing my mind, I veer from the lounge area and creep over to her office. Most do not go near it, unless they have been summoned, or have something to report, as it is best to leave her alone when she has confined herself in there, but curiosity is difficult to ignore and shove aside sometimes. Muffled voices spill from the cracked door to her office, intensifying as I draw closer, remaining in the shadows, not wanting to be caught by another arbiter or accused of spying, even though I am snooping. I peek through the crack and see footage playing on the wall monitor of the riot that took place a few days ago. I watch as images of people brawling or maiming one another repeat themselves, remarking at how watching it on a screen is very different from being caught in it.

"You can see why our presidents and the council are concerned."

I freeze the moment I hear the man within her office speak. Molers. I thought I had left him behind at the training facility when I passed the gauntlet and received my assignment. What is he doing here?

"Yes, I can," Commander Vye replies in a cold voice of her own.

"This is the fifth riot in the last three months," says Molers.

"I'll handle it."

"Like how you are handling them now?"

"Are you questioning my methods?" demands Commander Vye. "I have been in charge of the security of the eastern sector for twenty-three years, and in all that time, we have had relative peace and stability."

"Relative being the operative word here," says Molers, "and in the last few years, that stability has been shaky at best."

"Perhaps if the council would let us rebuild our most important facilities: hospices, schools, factories—perhaps, then, we would see less unrest."

"Are you questioning the council?" The dangerous undertone in Molers' voice unnerves me.

"Stating a fact. We bear the brunt of these attacks, and our sector is always under a state of constant ruin because of it."

"It is up to the representative of this sector to… oh, that's right. You had him arrested and executed."

"He broke the law, and no one is above it?"

"I understand, of course. You were merely doing your duty."

"He was sent to the fields, not executed."

"Same result in the end."

"I'm sure that he has already been replaced."

"For now. If you are unable to control these riots…"

"They will be contained."

I imagine the scowl on Commander Vye's face as she mouths those words to Molers.

"I hope so," says Molers, "for your sake."

The false sympathy in his voice spills from his words and I know he has something planned. All my life I have known him, and not once in those 18 years did he ever exhibit affection for anything or anyone other than himself, and he always had a contingency plan to achieve what he wanted, I just wonder what it is he is after here in the eastern sector. Most people try to get to the northern or western sector as they are more luxurious, so what is his interest here?

"One other thing," Molers says. "Why was Mandi here in the eastern sector?"

"I wouldn't know," replies Commander Vye.

"You did not demand to know?"

"Of course I did, but I am a Commander and she is a Major. She outranks me and you know it. In fact, why are you asking me questions for which you already know the answer?"

"See to it that these riots are under control, or you might find yourself in a different position."

Molers heads for the door and I dart away from it, scurrying down the hall and hiding behind a corner, hoping that I was not seen or heard. I peek around the wall edge as Molers exits Commander Vye's office and stomps down the corridor in the opposite direction, passing through the entrance doors and to the outside world. A lump forms in my throat, and the thought of him being here, or worse, staying here, frightens me.

Commander Vye steps out of her office and screams, "Noni!"

Not wanting to be caught crouching behind this corner, as I know what will happen to me if I am, I creep down the hall, away from the corner and to a door that leads to another room, which I pass through, and reenter the same hallway on the other side of Commander Vye.

"NONI!"

I hurry up to my commanding officer and stop in front of her, saluting her.

"What took you so long?" she demands, her foul mood evident, and I know who gave it to her.

I say nothing, recognizing this to be a rhetorical question and apologies show weakness.

Before Commander Vye can say anything, an arbiter hurries up to us. "Excuse me, commander, but there is someone here to see you. It is urgent."

Her eyes flare in annoyance, but Commander Vye strides through the manor and into the foyer, with me trailing behind her, to see who has summoned her immediate attention. Standing in the middle of the grand room is Mandi, accompanied by two plebeians: a boy about my age and a girl who seems to be ten years younger than him. The girl hides behind Mandi, but the male stands to the side and defiance fills his face, while Mandi waits in that patient manor of hers.

"Major," says Commander Vye in a more respectful tone, compared to the one she used the day of the riot, "what might I do for you?"

"I am here to deliver to you two new plebeians," replies Mandi. "Their owner has died and they have been assigned here."

"I do not need more plebeians," says Commander Vye.

"Were you asked if you needed them?"

Commander Vye swallows back her retort, knowing what happens when one challenges assignments made by the regulatory boards of Arel.

"Sheila!"

The same plebeian girl who swept up a pile of paint chips on the day I first arrived here ran up to Commander Vye with bits of her hair spilling from the braid she keeps it in.

"Take these two to the plebeian quarters and assign them duties."

As they walk past, I realize that I have seen those two before. The girl was the one reprimanded by Molers on the night of the banquet for failing in her duties, and the male had wanted to do something, but Mandi had stopped him. Yet, something else seems familiar about the girl, but I cannot place it, and all plebeians look the same anyway.

"I thank you for bringing them here," Commander Vye says to Mandi, "but another arbiter, one of lesser rank, could have done the job."

"There was no point in pulling a man from his duties to do a task that I can do. I am being assigned to a post outside the wall. It was no trouble for me to bring them here on my way out."

"Is there anything else, Major?"

"No, that will be all." Mandi moves toward the door.

"Good luck with your assignment, Major."

Pausing, Mandi gives Commander Vye a sardonic smile before looking in my direction and leaving.

After Mandi has gone, Commander Vye turns toward me and says, "Grab your things. We're late."

Late? Late for what?

I check my belt and make certain that I have my firearm, baton, and the other items that arbiters are required to carry with them at all times when on duty.

"No need, ma'am," I say, standing at attention, showing Commander Vye that I already have everything and hoping to impress her, "I am ready to proceed when you are."

Her lips remain in a firm line and the scowl never leaves her face, a side effect from her morning encounter with Molers. "Come along. Lieutenant Renal."

As we march out the door, Renal drops the kale wrap he had been about to eat and runs out of the dining room, hurrying after us. None of us say a word as we follow Commander Vye to one of the stops for the trolley, hopping on it and taking it to the northern side of the eastern sector to a place where three cylindrical smokestacks form an ordered line with clouds of white smoke floating from their tops and vanishing in the sky. We have travelled to a factory.

Chapter 12

The Factory

Renal and I follow Commander Vye as we march down the road, it's pavement cracked and crumbling away in certain areas, to the gated entrance where five arbiters stand guard with their weapons raised and ready to shoot us, should we prove to be there for unsavory purposes.

"Stop!" yells one of the guards.

We all come to attention.

"State your name and purpose here," demands the guard and his confrontational demeanor toward Commander Vye surprises me. Shouldn't he be saluting her?

"Commander Vye. Serial number V21923. I am showing Arbiter Noni one of our factories so that she can better perform her duties. She is the newest arbiter to the eastern sector."

Renal steps forward. "Lieutenant Renal. Serial number R26389. I am here in accordance with regulations that two senior arbiters must be present when a newly commissioned arbiter visits a manufacturing plant for the first time."

The guard turns to me and I realize that I also need to give my name and serial number. "Arbiter Noni. Serial number N27461."

The guard looks at the holographic images floating above his arm, emanating from his own wristband, confirming our identities, before switching it off and motioning for us to proceed while the gate opens.

"Mind you. You will be under watch during your entire visit here. Any questionable actions on your part will result in you being shot. Understood?"

"Yes, sir," we all say in unison.

We pass through the barbed wire encased gate and I move my eyes, taking in the fence that spreads away from it, encircling the manufacturing plant, wondering what sort of factory this is that would require it to have such heightened security. Rungs of metal are latticed together, forming tight, impenetrable bonds that allow nothing through, except for the small holes, just large enough for the barrel of a rifle to fit through undetected. Interspersed at even intervals are more guards dressed in full gear and the visors of their helmets pulled down, patrolling their assigned area, each watching us, waiting to see if we intend to cause trouble.

"Keep your eyes forward," warns Commander Vye as we hurry down the curved road to the main building, our boots making soft thumps as we go, adding to the foreboding nature of this place.

"Permission to speak, ma'am?" I ask her.

Commander Vye nods, giving me her permission.

"Why did they not salute you at the gate? Are you not the head arbiter of this sector?"

"I am, but the factories are run differently. They do not answer to the head arbiter of the sector. Each factory answers to the Arelian Council or our presidents. They are independent from our authority."

This is news to me. Never in my training were the recruits ever informed that the manufacturing plants are beholden to the council alone.

"Each arbiter here is hand-picked," Renal says, "having undergone the strictest of security measures. They will kill us if we step out of line."

For the first time, I notice the red dot on his back. Slowing my pace, I spot a similar red dot on Commander Vye's back. Scolding myself for not realizing that snipers watch us, I match Renal's and Commander Vye's pace again, knowing that a third red dot is pasted to my back. I look up, without turning my head, and notice a small round shape along the roof of the building we head for, a shape that does not seem to belong, but can be missed by any with an untrained eye. More snipers line the wall that surrounds us, and the more guards I spot, the more curious I become about what is being produced. Not all factories are under such heavy protection.

A man stalks out of the steel door that melds into the factory building, stopping a few feet away, his eyes never leaving us, his simple uniform a stark contrast to the others who surround us dressed in full body armor. He stands at attention, his muscular arms by his side, his scowl growing by the second as we approach.

Commander Vye stops in front of him and salutes him. Renal and I do the same. "Commander Vye reporting as requested."

As requested? She did not set this up? It was set up for her?

The man's scowl could curdle milk, and for the first time, I see a trickle of sweat ooze down Commander Vye's temple.

"You are two seconds late." His sharp tone could slice through a beet with ease.

Commander Vye says nothing, maintaining a rigid posture and I mimic her stance.

"My name is Commandant Gazini. All within this facility answer to me. You are here by invitation only."

I know that last bit is a lie. We are here, because, as has been explained numerous times to me, every new arbiter must learn all the aspects of the sector they're assigned to, and that includes any that are considered off-limits most days. This means that he was instructed to have us here, but is saving face, which is no surprise, because I have caught Commander Vye doing the same, pretending that she is in control, when in reality, she isn't.

"You will do as you are instructed," Commandant Gazini continues in that punitive tone of his. "Touch nothing. Speak to no one. And do not wander off."

He walks around us, checking the tattoos at the base of our necks and the authenticity for each tattoo has a code written within it that cannot be duplicated or forged. Doing my best not to fidget under his sharp gaze, I keep my eyes peeled straight ahead, not daring to glance in any direction for fear that I will incur his wrath, and it occurs to me that his might be far worse than anything I have suffered under Molers or Commander Vye. He pulls out a scanner and runs it over our wristbands without a word and I control my desire to flinch when he snatches my wrist, his strong fingers digging into my skin and leaving a few bruises. Both Renal and Commander Vye maintain stoic expressions when he seizes their wrists to scan their bands.

"Enter," he barks.

We all march inside, passing through the smooth, steel doors as they crawl open before us and seal shut once we are on the other side, entombing us in a darkened interior where despair and hopelessness pours from the cold walls and hollow ceiling. Two guards await us, falling in next to us as we walk down the eerie hallway to another steel door that swings open upon our arrival, shutting on its own, like its predecessor, locking us in as we delve deeper into this sepulcher of fear, the unnerving silence broken only by the marching of our feet. I study our escorts, while pretending to not be interested in them at all, and notice something familiar about one of them. I would recognize that pompous gait anywhere.

"Trevors?" I whisper, forgetting to control my mouth. It travels throughout the corridor, bouncing off the walls and the ceiling, intensifying in its volume, despite the soft voice I had used to utter the name. In response to my unchecked outburst, the guard I have accused of being one of my fellow recruits rams the butt of his weapon into my stomach, causing me to double over as the world fades around me. A high-pitched squeal escapes my lips as I try to inhale, finding it difficult to breathe.

Within seconds, while I roll on the metal-plated floor, Commandant Gazini yanks the firearm from the guard I accused of being Trevors and strikes him in the head with it, knocking his helmet off, proving that I had been correct in my guess. I watch from my fetal position as Trevors falls to the floor, holding his head and trying to remain conscious, not daring to look into Commandant Gazini's callous eyes, while fresh blood dribbles from his mouth. He remains on all fours, and I almost do not recognize him as he seems to have lost his confident and cocky persona, one that I had come to know full well while at the training facility. I think it odd that he is here because I remember him being assigned to one of our wealthier sectors.

"I did not give you permission to assault my guests!" Commandant Gazini chastises him, while Renal and Commander Vye continue to stare straight ahead, not daring to move to assist me.

Trevors remains silent. Did he receive a more horrendous assignment than me? Despite how much I loathe him, watching him suffer this man's abuses tugs an ounce of sympathy from me.

"Get up!"

Trevors jumps to his feet, putting his helmet back on and hoisting his weapon to his side.

Commandant Gazini faces me while I remain on my side, steadying my breathing and doing my best to ignore the crippling pain in my stomach.

"I will excuse your inexperience for now, but one more unsanctioned act here and you will never leave. Understood?"

"Yes, sir," I say, trying to sound more confident that I feel. Realizing that I will receive no assistance, I roll onto my stomach, pushing myself to my hands and knees, before standing up, doing my best not to go too fast where I would become dizzy.

Commandant Gazini marches ahead of us and we all fall in line behind him, passing through a third steel door from a world of silence to a new universe drowning in noise—the harsh grinding of gears as they turn, begging for oil to relieve the tearing of their metal parts; the whomping of conveyor belts as they wind their way through the lines of workers whose swift hands snatch items, replacing them seconds later; and the sharp whistles of steam as it escapes from narrow pipes in a vain effort to relieve the pressure building up within the thundering furnaces—making my ears beg for a reprieve. As I watch the metal parts that snake their way through the sweat-soaked and grease-stained workers, I recognize them, realizing why this place has so much security.

"Welcome to the munitions factory," says Commandant Gazini. "This is just one of four within Arel." He stomps over to a rail and leans on it, spreading his hands wide as he looks down upon his domain. His gaze observes everything, taking in each sight, each movement of the workers' hands, each leap of the flames within the furnaces, while a satisfied smile stretches across his black lips.

I step toward the railing, my tentative movements not going unnoticed, wanting to see more, but afraid of angering this man who seems to frighten Trevors more than Molers ever did.

"Yes, come forward." Commandant Gazini wraps an arm around my shoulders, pulling me forward and into the grimy rail that sizzles when droplets of water land upon it. "Look upon this grand design." The pride in his voice is unmistakable, but it seems to be more than just egotism, but a firm belief that he serves Arel better than most.

I allow him to place me where he wants me so that I can glimpse this manufacturing plant in its full glory. Below us are 20 lines of conveyor belts, each littered with parts that will be fitted into weapons for arbiters like myself, so that we may protect Arel from threats. Workers surround each belt, their hands moving with a speed I never thought possible, as their attention stays focused on their task, never looking up to see who has come to visit them, not caring. They know their duty and perform it, never faltering, never wavering. At first, I do not see it because of the grime and soot that cover each of their faces, but as I study them, I notice that some of the laborers are dark-skinned, while others are fair-skinned, and they work side by side.

Commandant Gazini must have read my thoughts, because he knew what questions loomed in my mind before I had a chance to voice them.

"Here, there are no titles, no status, nothing, but the same goal for everyone: to manufacture arms and ammunition. The people you see here are plebeians deemed too volatile to operate outside these walls and former citizens of Arel who have been convicted of various crimes, but are able-bodied—sending them to the crematorium would be a waste—so they were sent here to work as a way of atonement. They have been stripped of their citizenship and have already had their trials, so any who break the rules here are dealt with swiftly and accordingly."

I watch the sea of deadened faces illuminated by the orange and yellow flames in the furnaces below them as they perform their tasks in mechanical fashion, appearing to be more machine than human. Narrow staircases lead to the factory floor, while another delves even further into the depths of hell, where the furnaces are, each the size of a two-story home, their wide bases thirsting for more fuel to feed roiling flames that stretch into the funnels above them, which allow the noxious fumes to escape. Tiny shadows move in front of the openings to each boiler, shoveling coal into them, never quenching the eternal hunger of the fires that yearn for more.

"Please," Commandant Gazini says, stretching out his arm over the factory floor, indicating that I should feel free to wander among those cursed to toil here.

I obey the commandant, not even glancing at Commander Vye for approval, as her authority does not exist here, a fact Commandant Gazini made quite evident. I mosey over to the top of a stairwell, unsure if I should wait for my superior officers to follow me or not, but soon realize that only I have been given permission to explore, as

Renal and Commander Vye remain rooted where they are. My left foot drops downward, settling on the first step, the metal grating creaking as it absorbs my weight. I descend further. The spiraling stairs shift under my movements and a bolt pops free of its hold, sending my heartrate racing at the lack of repair in this facility, and my hand reaches out, grasping the rail. Pursing my lips, I regain my balance and place my hands by my side, doing my best to maintain a regal posture, not wanting to display fear or weakness. A handprint sheds light on the rusted, copper exterior of the rail, standing out among the black soot and sludge that covers it. I crane my neck and look at Commandant Gazini. His phlegmatic expression betrays nothing as his unwavering eyes watch every move I make, waiting for me to make a mistake. This is another test: his test.

I place my foot on the next step, not bothering to grab any sort of support as the stairwell shifts, swaying to the side, reminding me of the ropes we were forced to climb at the training facility as they danced in the breeze when not in use. With determined steps, I descend downward, ignoring the rocking motion of the staircase, clamping my mouth shut and keeping my gaze focused on my goal, unwilling to show any sign of surprise. The soft clink of another bolt striking the floor stands out among the roar of the furnaces. Refusing to change my pace, I continue as though nothing is wrong and there is no reason for me to be concerned about my welfare. My foot touches solid ground. Relief washes over me, but I keep it to myself, maintaining my own stolid demeanor as I raise my head and stare into the apathic eyes of Commandant Gazini. He turns to his left, with Trevors, the other guard, Renal, and Commander Vye following after him, taking another staircase that had remained hidden from my sight.

"That staircase is used by our workers," he says, approaching me and I am incensed that he does not bother to congratulate me for passing his test. "I suppose that someday I shall have to have it fixed, but why deny others the entertainment of watching someone go up and down it, wondering if it will be their last act in this world?" His languid tone frightens me. Was I nothing more than entertainment during those few moments it took me to go down the stairs, all to fulfill his disgusting need for amusement?

He stalks off, and I take up my position by Commander Vye's side as we follow him through the factory floor, ignored by the laborers as they remain focused on their tasks.

"This is where the bulk of our manufacturing is done at this plant. There is another building just like it that handles smaller things. The residents here, live here. They do not leave. Beneath this building are their sleeping quarters and the mess hall where they are allowed one meal a day."

Beneath? That means that it is underground.

I study the people there, toiling over the conveyer belt, noticing—now that I am close enough to see their faces—their scrawny frames as their bones threaten to poke through their glistening skin, having no muscles to keep their skeletal structures constrained. Their hands move in automation, automatons whose sole purpose is to serve Arel. Not once did a pair of eyes glance at me or try to sneak a peek at me, not even to satisfy the smallest measure of curiosity, except one. A small flicker of movement attracts my attention. At first, I ignore it, thinking that it is just the way the light illuminates everything. It happens again. Pausing, I glue my eyes on the spectacle, watching as a woman pushes a cart, picking up the discards that have been flung into the aisles by those working the conveyer belt. I decide that there is nothing unusual happening and I am about to focus my attention back on the commandant, when I notice the woman glance in our direction in a manner indicative of someone who has something to hide—a secret.

Knowing that I am about to break protocol and incur the wrath of Commandant Gazini and Commander Vye, I sneak away from them, heading toward the woman. Commandant Gazini's continued talking means that he has not noticed my absence, but Trevors did. He stops me and I imagine the questioning look he gives me, shielded by his helmet. I point at the woman, her frayed hair sticking to her dark, sweaty face, as she meanders down the aisle toward a chute, picking up discards as she goes. Trevors nods his head and I wander over to her, trying not to garner her suspicion, placing my hand on the holster of my weapon. She notices me. Bending low and reaching into the bottom shelf of the cart, she pulls out a small bundle that had been concealed under scraps of rubber and runs.

I bolt after her, charging down the aisle as she heads for a disposal chute with her cherished bundle. Shots ring out as Trevors fires at her, striking the wall next to the chute, but missing her. She changes direction and heads for a set of stairs, leading to the upper floor, but Trevors fires another shot, causing her to detour. She charges to the center of the room, but I cut her off, ignoring the rage spilling from Commandant Gazini's mouth as he issues orders and other guards appear, while the people working the conveyor belts wake from their stupor to watch the chaos as it unfolds.

"Go that way!" I yell at Trevors as I pursue the woman down a staircase before he has a chance to follow behind me. To my surprise, he does not argue, but obeys my command. There is only one reason why he would do such a thing: to get back into Commandant Gazini's good graces.

The woman stomps down the stairs and veers to the right when she reaches the bottom. Not wanting to lose her, I jump over the railing and plummet the remaining five feet to the floor, scurrying to my feet and hurrying after her, while Trevors bursts from the other stairwell, cutting the woman off. She stops. Panicking, and unsure of where to go or what to do next, she reverses course and darts around me, heading for the furnaces where she stops, trapped.

She whirls around, clutching the bundle close to her, and the way her curls cover her brown face reminds me of the plebeian girl I had caught in an alley while on patrol. The angry cries spilling from it betrays the fact that it is an infant, another unregistered child. The woman's widened, brown eyes stare at us, realizing that she has nowhere to go and has sealed her fate as well as that of the child's.

The harsh clomps of Commandant's Gazini's boots march up behind Trevors and me, and a cold sweat pools at the base of my neck at the sound of his irate voice.

"What the hell is going on here?"

Commander Vye and Renal stand behind him, mingling with other guards, and for a moment, I believe I see worry on her cast iron features.

In answer to his demands, I grasp the bundle the woman clutches, wrenching it from her bony hands, and hold the child out to Commandant Gazini, and I am as shocked as the rest when they first see the infant. It's… it's a plebeian child. Why would this dark-skinned woman risk her life for a worthless plebeian? I glance at the woman, but she ignores my confused expression, delivering a steel one of her own, daring us to punish her and determined to meet her fate with dignity.

"Trevors, explain this."

Trevors salutes Commandant Gazini and stands before him, taking his helmet off so that his words will not be muffled. "I noticed this woman acting in a peculiar manner—"

That two-faced, lying—he noticed nothing! I grip the infant tighter, ignoring it as it wails in pain, allowing my anger to seethe through, and I open my mouth to speak, but Trevors talks over me.

"—and I instructed Arbiter Noni here to follow her, laying a trap for her."

"Whose child is this?" Commandant Gazini demands of the woman.

She refuses to answer.

Enraged at being challenged, the commandant slaps the woman, causing her to slam into the ground, her frayed hair covering her face.

"The mother is dead," she spits at him, never raising her eyes to look at him.

"Why did you not dispose of this child? Why risk your life for it?"

The woman turns her head, facing Commandant Gazini while remaining slumped on the floor. "It's just a child—innocent. But you—all of you—have smothered your hands in blood."

"Trevors!"

Trevors straightens his stance even more when Commandant Gazini calls his name.

"What is the punishment?"

For a moment, I am thrown back to the varying instances when I found myself being asked a similar question by Commander Vye.

"Death, sir," Trevors replies.

"Then what are you waiting for?" demands Commandant Gazini.

Knowing what he is supposed to do, Trevors walks up to the woman and lifts her to her feet, taking a step back before spiraling around and kicking her in the chest, sending her flying backwards and through the door to an open furnace. Her agonizing screams radiate around us as she is burned alive, and while a few grimace, hoping they are not seen doing so, a satisfied smile forms upon Commandant Gazini's lips.

He turns toward me. "I am certain that you know what is done with unregistered children."

I know. I glance at the crying infant, its deafening cries indicating that it has a strong set of lungs and could grow into an able-bodied worker, but this would be its life: despair and servitude. Unwavering eyes watch me, each belonging to an arbiter, each waiting to see what I will do—if I will uphold the law as is my sworn duty. The roars of the furnace pound my ears, drowning all other extraneous sounds and distractions and I think of the crematorium, my destination should I fail here. I turn the child over in my arms so that its back faces me and place my fingers at the base of its delicate neck. It is not difficult to do. It takes very little pressure. Its anguished cries cease the moment I feel the vertebrae in its neck snap and its arms and legs fall limp. My superiors' unforgiving gaze descend upon me, waiting for me to perform the next expected task. I toss the dead baby into the furnace.

Commandant Gazini steps closer to me, his icy gaze bearing down upon me, but I keep my focus straight ahead, not daring to look at him, unless ordered to. His sticky breath moistens my cheek as he whispers into my left ear, "An arbiter after my own heart."

I remain at attention and a brush of cool air slaps me when he moves away, snapping his fingers at his guards, who fall in line behind him, followed by Commander Vye and Renal, while I take my place at the rear, feeling dread as his words repeat themselves over and over in my mind.

Chapter 13

Guilt's Conscience

My face stings as raindrops stab my cold skin, despite how numb it feels from being out in the chill, moist air. Harsh breaths form before me, matching each step my flying feet take as I run the path in the outdoor courtyard of the manor, my heavy boots squishing into the soaked lawn that resembles a pond more than a mowed quadrangle of silky grass. The wind kicks up. My body screams at me to give in to the chill and go back inside, but I push myself to run faster, lifting my feet higher and smashing them into the ground, leaving jagged footprints in the soggy mess of the courtyard and ignoring the bits of mud that splatter on the sides of my boots, forming oval splotches. Rain pelts my bare shoulders, and for a fleeting moment, I remember that I should have worn my jacket, but shake my head because I do not want to get it dirty.

Thunder rolls through the clouds. The rainy season has arrived. I push harder. With each circle I make on the track, my steps splash harder in the water, sending droplets of brown water into the air, soaking the bottoms of my pants. I ignore the cold. I ignore the pain of the stabbing rain. My mind refuses to calm itself, to stop harboring the images of the infant. In vain, I tried to sleep last night, but sleep eluded me, flirting with me, allowing me a few blissful moments of dozing before jerking me awake and teasing me, reminding me of the way a cat toys with its prey before delivering the final stroke. If only I could have been allowed to close my eyes, but each time I did, I saw the infant's frightened face.

I run faster.

My arms swing at sharp angles by my side as I extend my legs, forming long strides to obey my demands. The rain pours, shielding me from prying eyes, preventing me from looking upon the city I am sworn to serve—to protect. But I failed to protect—it was a plebeian child. I upheld the law. I did as I was trained. So, why is there this gnawing sense of guilt pushing against the barriers of my mind, begging to be released?

I run even faster.

My lungs burn for air and scream at me to stop, to let them breathe and give them a rest. I cannot rest. I must keep running. Running keeps my mind occupied. It prevents me from dwelling on recent events. My foot slips on the slick grass and I lose my balance, tumbling forward, and I roll across the ground, getting covered in water and grass clippings, despite my feeble attempts to catch myself. Curtains of rain surround me, enveloping me as I lay on the ground in a puddle that stretches from my nose to my ankles, and mud oozes over my back while bits of it fall from my chin.

Soft plops echo in front of me. I look up and watch as the toes of a pair of black boots materialize in front of me, challenging the weather to do its worse. A hand appears before my eyes, opened in a welcoming gesture. I take it and a strong arm heaves me from my embarrassment on the ground and to my feet, while another hand wraps a jacket around my muddied shoulders.

"Not the best weather for a run, is it?"

The kindness in Renal's voice startles me. I have never heard him sound harsh, but nor has he ever sounded this benevolent, as though he cared about what became of me.

"I'm just trying to stay in shape," I say.

"Come."

I do not argue, not that I believe I am in any position to put up much of a fight, so I allow him to guide me over to an awning that is a few feet away from the nearest door into the manner, but protects us from the sky's furious tears.

"I have found myself out here on many occasions when I feel restless."

"I'm not restless," I snap.

In response, Renal gives me a doubtful look and raises an eyebrow, telling me that I am not fooling him.

"There comes a time in every arbiter's life when they start to be plagued by the faces they meet."

"You mean the people we detain."

He nods his head. "Some call it guilt. It troubles some sooner than others and it appears that it has latched itself onto you, for the moment."

I keep my mouth shut. Guilt? Why should I feel guilty for doing my duty to Arel?

"I think Commander Vye has been pushing you too hard, but yesterday, no one could have spared you from dealing with the unregistered child, except for Commandant Gazini, but he is a man... well, some believe that he is not human. You are a good arbiter, Noni, and you have more than proven your loyalty to Arel."

"Then why can't I sleep?"

Renal looks around and I notice a few stripes on his shoulder that stretch beneath his undershirt, stripes that match my own. "Listen to me very carefully. You did as you are supposed to. You must push these other thoughts away. Do not dwell on them."

"So, I am not the only one?"

Renal gives me a questioning look.

"You said that guilt plagues some sooner than others. That means that others have found it difficult to do their duty. What happened to them?"

"Some learned to separate themselves from it. Others could not escape it and the fires in the crematorium burned even brighter than in the past. I knew a man once. He was an arbiter like yourself and had to perform a similar task, dealing with an unregistered child."

"What happened to him?"

"He lost his mind. Tried to assassinate a member of the council, and the dogs that guard the wall had a feast that night."

The downpour continues, creating a melody that lulls one into a calm silence.

"Just remember your training. Remember who it is you serve."

"Is that what you do?" I ask Renal, trying not to stare at the marks on his shoulder.

"I have other reminders."

I give him his jacket back. He tries to refuse, but I shove it in his waving hands and thank him. The door is not far and I am already wet, so what does it matter if I get a little more rain on me? He takes it and gives me a reassuring smile, leaving me to wonder what other reminders he referred to, but I dare not ask. Some things are best left untouched.

Leaving Renal alone under the awning, I jog back to the manor and hurry inside, not caring that my boots track mud in, until I see the same plebeian girl I had seen my first day here. She tries her best not to show her ire at me leaving mud prints, but I read her facial expressions and know that she is thinking about the time she will now have to spend cleaning it up. Doing something I have never done in the past, I take my boots off, holding them so that no more mud will drip onto the carpet, and carry them up the stairs to my room, passing the new plebeian boy that Mandi had brought by as he cleans an adjoining room and tries to not watch me.

Once in my room, I change out of my wet clothes and into a

dry uniform, putting the rain gear on over it in preparation for my patrol duty. I stare at my boots, the last item I need to put on, and the mud that still adorns them, masking their polished exterior, a color that is a bit darker than my skin tone. I reach for them, but pause when I remember the girl cleaning the carpets. Sighing, I snatch a rag from the pile of dirty clothes that I need to send down for the wash and wipe the mud off my boots, performing another task that I have never done before. When done, I place my sore feet into my boots, the blisters on the balls of them burn as I put my weight on them, a constant reminder and side effect of my position, and I lace them up.

Ready to report for duty, I scoop up my dirty clothes, admonishing myself for not dealing with them earlier as untidiness is frowned upon, open my door, and stop when met by a startled squeak. In front of me stands the new plebeian girl that Mandi had dropped off. She jumps to her feet, the brush she had been using to scrub a stain out of the carpet dangles from the tips of her tiny fingers, and individual strands of her blonde hair frizzes, pulling away from her head because of the extra humidity in the air. I shove the pile of clothes into her slender arms, causing her to take two steps backwards.

"I want these washed and pressed by the end of the day," I tell her.

"Yes, ma'am," she replies in a quiet voice, keeping her eyes downward.

"What is your name?" I demand, knowing I needed to call her something other than "new girl".

"Gwen, ma'am."

I pause. Her voice sounds familiar. I remember it. The girl I had tried to stop during my night patrol had blonde hair, at least, it looked blonde in the pale light. I take bits of her hair, wrapping them in my fingers, but being careful not to cause her harm, and stretch it across her face so that only her gray eyes are visible. My mind works overtime, trying to piece together the fragments of that night, but something about her is familiar. Is she…

"I can take those and have them washed," says a voice. "It will allow her to finish cleaning the carpets."

Snatched from my attempt to remember why I thought I had seen her before, I look up and see the same plebeian boy—my age, I assume, so close to being considered a man—walking up to us with a duster in his grimy hands.

"Did I ask you for your assistance?" I snap at him.

"No, ma'am."

"Gwen, you will have these washed and pressed in addition to your other duties. If you cannot manage to accomplish your tasks, then we will find another place for you."

The girl, Gwen, bows her head and nods, indicating that she understands my threat.

I stomp down the corridor, but stop next to the boy that had interrupted me. "Name?"

"Chase," he replies.

Without warning, I raise my fist and backhand him across the mouth, drawing a few droplets of crimson blood. "You will not interrupt me again, and you will only speak when spoken too. Understand?"

The boy refuses to wipe the blood from the edges of his lower lip, keeping his eyes downcast, as he says, and the disdain in his voice is quite evident, "Yes, ma'am."

The rain beats against the pane of glass in the window, reminding me of what I will be spending my day in and a thought strikes me. If I have to spend the day soaked, there is no reason why he cannot also. "I want you to clean the equipment outside."

Satisfied that I have gotten my point across, I hurry down the stairs and out the door to my patrol duties.

Time passes at its normal pace as I make my rounds, following my own system of wandering the streets and checking each of my assigned areas, a system taught to me by both Commander Vye and Renal, which I modified to suit me. Anemic sun rays poke through the clouds at odd intervals before the sun disappears again behind the charcoal obstructions as rain continues to pour, making me glad that I have my raingear. The streets are quiet; even the walkways are sparse, as people must have decided to remain indoors on a day like this. I head to a moving walkway that is protected under a roof to get out of the rain for a while.

Something smacks into my back. Startled, I whirl around, wondering what has just struck me, and why. Mud slaps my face and I rear my head back, wiping its slimy essence off my skin as a boy's laughter fills my ears. He bolts. I chase after him, splashing in the puddles that fill the holes within the pavement, catching up to him, grabbing his coat and yanking him off his feet.

"What was the meaning of that?" I demand, my anger at having mud thrown at me rising.

"Arbiters are mindless drones that do the bidding of the council!" he spits.

Interesting. "Where did you get such a notion?"

No answer.

"Tell me!" I shake him in an effort to force him to tell me.

"No one!" wails the boy, not wanting to tell me the truth. It doesn't matter. There are ways of getting the truth from people.

"Do you realize that slinging mud at an arbiter constitutes assault and that assaulting an arbiter is a crime?"

Fear fills the boy's face.

"You'll have to answer for this," I say.

The boy struggles to get away, but my grip remains firm as I drag him through the streets to an information booth in the rain, which seems to have picked up. I place the boy's palm on the screen on the side of the booth and his information pops up, listing his name and guardians, telling me that he is one of those few children permitted to be adopted by a couple who had applied for such a privilege.

To give the illusion of familial relationships, Arel will allow some to adopt children. The parents do not get to choose the child, as all selections are random, and they will follow in the footsteps of their adoptive parents, meaning that if the guardians are bakers, then their adopted child will be a baker; though, sometimes exceptions are made.

I scan the screen. No prior infractions. "For the infraction of assaulting an arbiter. Recommend questioning the guardians as well," I say when prompted to give my reason for the arrest.

A panel slides open, revealing the detainment box, and I shove the boy into it, ignoring his protests and promises to never throw mud at me again. He clings to the side of the opening, forcing me to pry his fingers away from the doorframe. He is no match for me, and with one final push, he slams into the back of the box and the panel slides close, cutting off his pleas for forgiveness and cries of remorse.

My stomach growls. Checking the time, I realize that it is close enough to lunch and I know just where to go. Turning away from the booth, I head to the only place, according to Renal, to get a meal.

I open the door to the diner that Renal had taken me to my first day in the eastern sector and step through, entering a bustling world of cheerful banter, and I am inundated with the tantalizing aroma of sausage roasting on a spit. Listening to my stomach growl as my nose takes in the spiced vegetables, fresh-baked bread, and herbed chicken roasting on another spit, I take off my rain gear and wrap it around my arm, not wanting to drip water all over the wood floor.

"Come in! Come in!" greets Sigal, the proprietor, taking my rain coat from me and hanging it on a hook by one of the fireplaces so that it can dry. "I'll take that."

Again, I find myself amazed that he is not frightened of or even cautious around an arbiter, which seems to be the habit of many within Arel. I smile at him and stroll through the diner to a secluded table near the back where I can observe everything around me, but remain unnoticed. Within seconds of me sitting down, Sigal's wife places a tumbler full of a pink-colored juice drink in front of me.

"Whatever you have for your special today," I tell her when she looks at me for my order.

The woman smiles, the genuineness of it causes her face to glow with a natural charm that is not seen much in my city, and whisks away, the bracelets on her wrists clinking as she does, and weaves her way through the bustling crowds as though performing a waltz.

I sip my drink. Strawberry. I like it. Out of the corner of my eye, I spot a woman carrying a child, a jubilant smile on her face as she shows off her offspring to Sigal, who commends her on having such a beautiful baby. The green papers in her left hand indicate that she had been approved to adopt an infant, and it is only a few months old. Once all newborns reach three months, they are brought in to the hospices for a full physical examination, the second one of their life, and new papers are issued. I watch as Sigal's wife takes the baby and holds it in her arms. A maternal grin crosses her lips while memories of the woman in the factory fill my mind. Her ash-covered face, coated in streaks from the sweat that dripped down her skin, glares back at me with vehemence as she challenges the authority of Arel. She possessed a similar facial structure as Sigal's wife. Perhaps they were related. Cousins, maybe. I will never know.

A sharp wail strikes my eardrums, thrusting my wandering mind back to the furnaces in the factory as I recall the harsh screams of the plebeian infant while I held it in my arms, until I silenced it. It had no mother to wrap it in her loving embrace, much like the woman in the diner is doing to her child. It had no one to comfort it, to tell it everything will be all right, that the nightmare was just that—a dream. It only had me.

I place my hands over my ears to block out the harsh cries of the infant, but it passes through them, determined to taunt me, to remind me of what I should not be feeling. My hands slap the hard surface of the table in frustration, their sudden movements knocking my drink over and spilling pink liquid all over as it oozes over the edge and drips onto the floor, forming a sticky puddle. Before I have a chance to reach for a napkin, Sigal's wife is upon the mess and cleans it with a blue towel. She must have the eyes of an eagle.

"Sorry," I apologize, but she remains silent, giving me another of her genuine smiles, and places a fresh glass of strawberry juice on the table to replace the one I have spilt.

The chair across from me scoots away from the table as someone sits in it. "You should have told me that you were coming here," says Renal.

I scold myself for not seeing him, nor hearing him approach. Vigilance in a necessity if you wish to remain alive and I have failed, allowing myself to become wrapped up in my own thoughts, my own troubles, my conscience. Do not dwell on it, that was Renal's advice to me this morning, and I must adhere to it. Guilt is for the guilty and I am an arbiter performing my duty. So why do I feel otherwise?

"I did not know I was coming here until a few minutes ago," I reply. That is true enough. Some days, while on patrol, I do not have time for a meal, so I do not plan on stopping at any eatery, deciding that it is best to just wait and see, and take it on a day by day basis. "Been here long?"

"Long enough to enjoy Sigal's daily special."

"You recommend it?"

"Of course."

I lean closer, having a question burning on my mind that I've been wondering about for some time. "Might I ask you something?"

"Depends on what you want to ask."

"I have noticed that there are a lot of children in the eastern sector, and it's probably not just here."

"That is not unusual. We have a hospice here."

"Unregistered children." I lower my voice so as not to attract the attention of unwanted ears.

Renal gives me a pensive look, but remains silent.

"Back at the hospice, there was the councilman with three children, all unregistered. When the riot took place, another unregistered child was found, and at the factory was a third. That is a lot of children being born outside of the breeding centers."

"Where are you going with this?" asks Renal, but the cautious tone of his voice hints that he already knows what I am about to ask.

"The sterilization additives put in the city's water supply to control the population—is it not working?"

I do not intend to cause trouble, but I cannot help but wonder. Since I reported for duty in the eastern sector, I have seen an unusual amount of unregistered children. There have always been a small percentage of kids born because the sterilization additives do not work on everyone, but they work on the majority of the population, or so I was told at the training academy.

"You silence that questioning tongue of yours right now."

Renal's abrupt anger and unusual harshness catches me off-guard, and I back away from him. He softens his eyes and leans closer, glancing around to make certain that we are not overheard.

"Forget the question you just asked me."

"But..."

"Cast it far from your mind. What you have seen, what you have witnessed, forget it all."

"It is difficult."

"You must do it."

Disappointment grabs me by the shoulders, threatening to throw me off the chair as I stare at Renal, angered the he refused to answer my question. I cannot be the only one to have noticed this. The population must be controlled; otherwise, we will face famine and people will die, though, many have already died and some by my hand.

I cast aside the remnants of guilt that ebb at the base of my subconscious mind before it has a chance to take hold of me. I am an arbiter. An enforcer of the law. I have no time for remorse when all I've done is fulfill my duty.

"But, what if..."

"No ifs," Renal cuts me off. "The additives work. You must keep telling yourself that. And never, under any circumstance, speak of this again. If anyone were to hear you..."

Renal allows his voice to trail off, leaving his statement hanging open, but I understand his meaning. Asking unwarranted questions is not allowed. I knew a fellow recruit at the training facility who questioned everything around him. I never saw him again, nor was his name ever mentioned. It was as though he never existed.

"You are an arbiter. You will do your duty," Renal says to me. "You will find, Noni, that some things are not as they told you while in training. You will notice things. You may even start to wonder about these strange incidents, but do not speak of them, or ask about them. Promise me that you will never bring up this subject again."

A note of desperation fills Renal's voice and a part of me is curious about his past. Did he lose someone? Did he once ask the wrong question and was reprimanded for it?

"I promise," I whisper.

"And as for the plebeian infant," begins Renal, "remember what I said to you this morning: do not dwell on it. Emotions are luxuries that arbiters cannot afford to have."

Luxuries? I have never thought of them as such. Molers always described emotions as burdens best left behind. "I understand," I say.

A pleased smile crosses Renal's face and I look to see where my food is. On the far side of the room is Sigal whispering to another man. They split up and the man creeps over to a back room, looking around before disappearing behind a plain, rust-colored door, while Sigal chats and jokes with his customers, worming his way to the same door and ducking behind it. I sit up straighter, craning my neck for a better look, but before I am able to see anything more, a curved shape appears in front of me, blocking my view of the back room. Sigal's wife has arrived with my food. She places the platter in front of me, along with another glass of juice to replace the one I have emptied.

"Will there be anything else for you?" she asks, remaining between me and my line of sight of the back room.

"No, thank you," I reply.

"You enjoy your meal." She pauses next to Renal, before leaving, "And you, don't you go helping yourself to her lunch. You've already had yours."

"Wouldn't dream of it," jokes Renal.

When she leaves, Sigal is back in the main dining area, participating in a bout of banter with a group of customers as though he has been there the entire time, and I find myself doing the very thing Renal has just warned me about: wondering about something that is best forgotten. What was Sigal doing back there? And who was that man? I shake the inquiries from my mind as I glance at Renal and his warning about asking too many questions storms through my mind. My food grows cold and I have no desire to eat it that way.

I take a forkful of twice baked sweet potato and savor it, allowing the combined flavors of garlic, cinnamon, and parsley to waft over my tongue. As I savor every moment of my meal, my eyes dart in Sigal's direction and I notice him looking at me as he talks to his wife, but before I can wonder about their conversation, he looks away and continues bantering with the group he is with.

The television monitor in the room flashes red before blowing up and forming a wall-sized, three-dimensional image of Ulani—the premier news reporter of Arel—appears. All chatter ceases and people hold their utensils, filled with bites of food, in midair as they look up and wait for the announcement to follow.

"We interrupt your normal programming for breaking news," Ulani says in her usual businesslike manner, her rose-colored suit pairing well with the nature of the report. "Riots have broken out in the southern sector"—images of people running in the streets with homemade explosives, torches, and anything they could find to use as a weapon fill the screen, followed by footage of screaming children, a destroyed hospice, and a burned education center—"as people voice their discontent with the leadership of our presidents. Fires engulf the southern sector as our brave arbiters attempt to stop the rampage."

More images of arbiters in full riot gear tearing into the crowd, holding hoses that release powerful streams of water, while others resort to their weapon, fill the room, engulfing all within the diner.

"It is believed that a small group of terrorists are responsible for this riot, but we will not know for certain until an investigation can take place. For now, all citizens of Arel are encouraged to stay in their homes. Curfew will begin at three, for your safety, until the riots have ended. We will keep you informed of further updates."

The three-dimensional images disappear as the television screen returns to its normal size and goes blank. No one speaks. Sigal's wife hands boxes to patrons who wish to take their food with them, while their daughter takes the payments in a quick and steady fashion, scanning people's wristbands and deleting their rations from their accounts.

"Let's go," says Renal, standing tall and zipping up his jacket.

"Go?"

"Commander Vye will want us to report in before sending us where we will be needed, to make certain that the riot does not spill over into the eastern sector."

That makes sense. I take one longing look at my unfinished meal, cursing the rioters for interrupting my chance to eat—they could have waited another half-hour—as I zip up my own jacket and follow Renal outside, where we run to the nearest detainment kiosk, which also serves as a communication station in emergencies. He scans his wristband and a screen pops up, demanding to know his name.

"Lieutenant Renal. Serial number R26389."

The screen flashes green and a trap door opens, revealing a two-seater car. Before he is able to move, another screen opens, asking if he is alone.

"No," answers Renal.

In response, the screen angles toward me, demanding to know my name as well. I give it and scan my wristband. The trap door remains open, and before I have time to consider what I am supposed to do, Renal shoves me over the edge and to the track below.

"Get in!" he yells at me as he drops beside me and takes a seat in the underground car.

I situate myself in one of the seats, strapping the harness around me just as a glass casing closes around us, forming a protective barrier from what is to come next. It speeds forward. My body slams into the back of my seat, threatening to push through it and come out the other side as the gravitational force takes hold, making me glad that we at least had the protective glass shield to protect us from the rush of air. The track turns to the left and the shuttle follows it, causing me to lean sideways as I attempt to compensate for the sudden change in motion. The track takes a sharp swerve to the right. Again, the car follows it and I find myself jerked to the left and pressing into Renal, the straps of the harness digging deep into my skin and cutting through my jacket.

"Just follow my lead when we get there," Renal says.

I want to ask him questions. I want to demand what is going on. I thought we were to report to Commander Vye, but it appears that our orders have been changed without any forewarning.

Red flashing lights streak past us as we continue our trek underground. I try to look around at the tunnel I am in, its polished, steel walls reflecting the movement of the car, which looks more like a blur as we careen down the tracks, instead of an actual transport. Pipes run from the floor to the ceiling and stretch across it in an ordered fashion of parallel lines and sharp angles, all forming a sense of order with their symmetry.

We take another turn and my head slams into the side of the glass as I am thrust to the right. With each second, my heart beats faster, skipping every other beat as my breathing quickens from nerves and the uncertainty of where I am being sent. Before I have a chance to calm myself, the car jerks to a stop and I thrust forward; only the harness prevents me from flying through the glass shield, and I grip the edge of my seat for a bit of added security, though it does little to prevent the momentum from flinging me forward. Once stopped, my body slams into my seat and I remain there for a moment, regaining my senses, but that moment ends when Renal seizes my shoulders and yanks me from the car, pushing me toward a stairwell that leads upward and to another trap door. In front of the stairwell are other arbiters, some of whom hand out riot gear, while others take it and put it on.

Renal steers me to the people parceling out the gear. Before I have a chance to comprehend what is happening, an armored vest, helmet, and weapon are rammed into my arms. I do not need to be told what to do next. I place my armored vest on, having only worn one once before while as a recruit in the training facility, but this is different—now I will be wearing it to put down an actual riot, one that must be worse than previous incidents if they are handing out protective gear. Ripping velcro fills the tunnel around me, drowning the murmurs that spread among the other arbiters as they strap on their gear and ready their weapons with a series of clicks that rattle off the walls and to my ears.

Renal is dressed before I have secured the first strap of my vest. He takes one look at me, and without a word, his hands fly over the other straps, fastening them, and securing the vest, making certain that it fits tight against my skin. No smugness fills his eyes, just his methodical movements ensuring that I am prepared. I put on my helmet and hold my weapon, ready to meet whatever is on the other side of the door.

"Stay close to me," says Renal, his helmet muffling his words.

I nod.

Boots stomping on metal, grated stairs erupt into a chorus of rhythmic thumps as we run upward to the door and pass through it, spilling onto the street above. Sunlight blinds me for a second as my eyes adjust—which does not take too long thanks to the darkened visor of my helmet—and I follow the arbiters before me, allowing them to lead. A quick glance around tells me that I am no longer in the eastern sector, but the southern one.

A long, slender object flies overhead and plummets to the ground, landing in the middle of the crowd of arbiters that I am with, sending a metallic clink to my ears—a hollow sound that stands out among the shouts and screams that surround me. A hand seizes my right shoulder and shoves me to the ground, away from the mysterious object just before it detonates and sends a shockwave in a 360-degree radius that rips through anyone in its path. People writhe on the pavement, gripping their injuries as they wallow in pain, while a few try to stand, despite their wounds.

Stunned from the blast, I aim my weapon at a person running through the crowd and fire, not knowing if he is part of the riot and not caring.

Renal pulls me back to my feet. He points me toward the crowd and I nod, telling him that I understand and follow him. We charge toward the chaos, joining the other arbiters as they attempt to quell the riotous crowd. A man runs toward me. I fire at him and he drops to the ground, still clutching a Molotov cocktail. Before it has time to explode, I scoop it up and throw it into the melee where it bursts in midair, pelting those near it with shards of glass. Another charges Renal. I plow into him, shoving him out of the way, bringing my weapon up and blocking the knife that the rioter thrusts at me, kicking him in the stomach. He doubles over and I ram the butt of my weapon into the back of his neck, knocking him to the ground. In an instant, I scoop up the knife and throw it at another rioter as she runs for me, striking her just above her diaphragm.

The melodic dong of a bell fills the air. Looking around for the source, I spot a man with a sledgehammer, pounding the bell that sits in a plaza square as though he is sounding the charge. His antics fuel the rioters who shout with fervor and charge any arbiter they see, ignoring the streams of water that fall from the high-powered hoses that are being used on them. Some scream as a jet of water plows into them, knocking them off their feet.

This riot must end.

I do not know if the man ringing the bell is their leader, but he is urging them onward, which makes him a threat. Knowing what must be done, I race for him.

"Noni!" shouts a worried Renal.

I ignore him. I need to be closer to hit him, as the current distance is too great for my shot to be of any use. I swerve to my right to avoid an arbiter locked in hand-to-hand combat with a member of the rebellious crowd. Another breaks from the mob and charges me. Bending low, I dive to the ground, allowing him to trip and fly over me, smashing into the pavement. Without bothering to look back, I jump to my feet and head for the man ringing the bell once more. Just a few more steps.

The screams of the people mingle with the detonations of homemade explosive devices, filtering through my helmet, making me wonder if I wore it at all as it permeates the atmosphere and fills my ears, disorienting me. I focus on my target, dodging between people as I run and leap over bodies that litter the ground. I am in range. Stopping, I place one foot in front of the other, keeping my knees bent, and breathing slow, steady breaths as I raise my weapon and take aim. I have my target in my sights. Having not performed a feat like this since my training exercises, my nerves threaten to overwhelm me, smothering me with their agitation, but I release a slow breath, steadying my heartrate as I block out the chaotic sounds around me. I pull the trigger. The recoil knocks me to the side as I did not account for the power of the weapon handed to me, nor is my shot heard, drowned by the fray, but I watch as the man with the sledgehammer bangs the bell one last time, before dropping to the ground.

A blunt force slams into my back, knocking the wind from me, despite the vest absorbing most of the impact. I fall face first to the pavement, my elbows aching from the force of the impact as I land, and my helmet flies off my head, rolling a few feet away on the uneven ground. Rolling onto my back, I bring my leg up to kick my attacker, but he avoids it and is on my chest, straddling me. Pinned, panic rises within me. I jerk from side to side to throw him off, but his weight proves to be too much, and all I manage are a few twitches that are nothing more than mere annoyances to him. He goes for my throat and squeezes. I seize his wrists, but he is too strong for me. Choking, and fearing that I will pass out soon as my brain starves for oxygen, I release his wrists and flail my arms, searching for anything that will help. My fingers brush something jagged. I reach for it, desperate to grab it. Almost have it. Gasping, I snatch the piece of glass that had once belonged to a bottle, and plunge it into the side of the man's neck. He releases me. I throw him off me, crawling to my helmet, seizing it, and swing back around just in time to strike the man in the head with it, before he is able to attack for a second time.

A low whistle breaks the melee. I glance at my wristband and notice it flashing red, each flash happening faster than the previous, and I know that it is counting down. The attack drones are on their way. As the whistle grows, morphing into a thunderous roar, I seek shelter, joining the other arbiters who all know what is coming, but I do not have time to reach the buildings that the others have gone to, so I hunker by two bodies, pulling them over me. A spray of gunfire rains down upon the area, shattering the ground around me as I cling to the bodies I use to protect myself. I watch as feet race past me, unaware of my presence, belonging to panicked screams as people try to flee the onslaught, but many of them stop and bodies fall, unable to escape.

The ground rumbles. A smile crosses my lips. I know what is coming. The rumbling grows and the pebbles around me dance and bounce as armored vehicles appear, each armed with men ready to fire upon the crowd. I throw the dead bodies off me and crawl out from under them, jumping to my feet and hurrying to join the other arbiters as they fall in behind the tanks. Soon, the riot has been put down, leaving us with the aftermath: destroyed property, dead bodies, and wounded people who were executed on the spot as collaborators, a scene of death shrouded in the smoldering remains of what had been beautiful architecture serving as a testament to Arel's rise from the darkness.

Softball-sized drones appear, ready to capture the moment that another riot has been put down. I stand among the wisps of smoke as they trail across the pavement, reaching for the strands of hair that escape my ponytail, my helmet hanging from my limp grasp, studying the scene before me and the open eyes that look past me. What had started this? The southern sector is a good sector, protected from the attacks on the wall. What reason could they have to destroy their own home? I spot Renal and remember what he had told me earlier: do not ask, just do. He spots me and relief washes over him.

"Put your helmet back on," he says in a low voice when he reaches me.

I do, just as another group of arbiters arrive, the ones who will take our reports and submit them to the council.

"Remember," whispers Renal, "answer only the questions that are asked."

"What's going on?" I ask.

"They will want your account of what has happened."

"But they did not want one when the eastern sector fell prey to a riot."

Renal shushes me. "They want one now. Just give them direct answers."

An arbiter with red bands on both his sleeves, marking him as one of the council's investigators, marches up to us with a handheld tablet.

"State you names and serial numbers," he commands us in a stern voice, devoid of emotion.

Renal and I obey.

"Tell us what happened here," says the man.

The next ten minutes are spent with us each recounting our role in putting down the riot. I am careful to give short, concise answers, following Renal's lead. The investigator makes me uncomfortable and a line of sweat forms along my forehead, causing the inside of my visor to fog up, but his cold manner unsettles me, and I sense the same tension within Renal.

Once we are finished, Renal grabs my left arm and leads me away, back to the trap door we had come of, where we hand in our weapons, helmets, and armored vests before taking the two-person shuttle back to the eastern sector.

Chapter 14

Leave

I stand outside the door to the manor, allowing the sun to warm my skin as I study the wall that always looms over the eastern sector, watching the humanoid shapes walk across it as they stand guard, protecting us from the outside world. A gentle breeze brushes my cheeks, tickling them, teasing me, knowing that this is my one day of leave, my one day of freedom, before I embark on my little journey outside the wall. Commander Vye warned me last night that we would be visiting the outposts—another of my duties as an arbiter, and I have been here almost four months now—and allowed me to have a day off where I could go anywhere I liked in the city, so I chose to visit Faya, who agreed to meet me in the business district during her lunch hour, having decided to take it early.

A small squeak attracts my attention and I turn toward it, spotting the plebeian girl I had met when I first arrived—Sheila? Is that her name? —as she ducks away from the presence of one of the arbiters in an effort to avoid her. I study them, recognizing the arbiter—Trix?—but I had never met her beyond the simple introductions that

Commander Vye had made my first day here. I see her from time to time, patrolling the grounds or carrying out her duties within our sector, but we never talk. The most I have ever said to her was hello, or I just give her a simple nod of acknowledgement of her presence. Trix reaches out for the girl, but the plebeian shrinks away, uncomfortable with the entire exchange. I consider going over to them, but the door slides open and out steps an arbiter.

"Morning, Noni," she greets me. "Ready to enjoy your first day of leave?"

"Definitely," I reply.

"You better get a move on before Commander Vye changes her mind," she says as she zips up her jacket and walks off, heading for the center of our sector.

Following her advice, I hurry down to the street, taking one last glance where Trix and the plebeian girl had been, catching a final glimpse of them as Trix leads her away, passing it off as nothing more than a plebeian doing her duty, and if she was about to be punished, she must have done something to deserve her fate. The gates rush past me and I jog down the street, heading for an alley that I know I can take as a shortcut. I dart down it, jumping over discarded bins and trash, being careful not to slip on any of it, until I come to the end of the alleyway and burst out into a street bustling with activity.

Plebeians and their masters hurry about, while other citizens, dressed in their respective uniforms, rush to get to their assignments, all of us dwarfed by the shadow of Arel. Spotting a moving walkway, I run for it, darting across the street and hiking up the staircase to it, skipping the last step and jumping onto the walkway, startling a couple who already stand there. The woman jumps, but both turn away when they notice my uniform. I stare straight ahead, having gotten used to people's reactions toward me.

The walkway carries me to another that I know will take me to the rail station. Not bothering to excuse myself, I shove my way past people, getting off the current walkway, and hike up another set of stairs to the one I want, taking my place on it and ignoring any dirty looks thrown my way. Dulled and decaying tops of shanty houses pass underneath me, positioned on streets that match their depressed state.

I look ahead, not bothering to glance at the building we pass, as we leave a small housing area for a shopping center, the buildings growing larger as we approach the western edge of the eastern sector. A high-pitched whine races past us as a shuttle careens down its track, and a bit of its downdraft billows a few stray strands of my long hair that had somehow escaped my bun. I glace up, smiling as I watch the railcar pass, and stare at the towering buildings of Arel, remarking at how beautiful my city is.

I spot my exit. Not bothering to wait for the conveyor belt to take me to it, I push my way past those in front of me, my uniform forcing them into silence, and step off at my exit. A few shouts force me to turn around, and I spot two men involved in an argument, their voices growing with each passing second. Debating whether I should give up a few precious minutes of my leave, I start for them, but one of the men notices my presence and hushes the other. Both glance at me before turning away and walking off in two different directions, as though they do not want to be seen together. A moment of curiosity almost convinces me to go interrogate them, but the reason for my being here pops into my head, and I push all inquisitiveness aside, setting a fast pace down the walkway to the shuttle platform.

People huddle on the platform, pushing their way closer to where the shuttle will arrive, hoping to be the first on the car, and I join them, migrating my way to the front, glad that my uniform persuades others to step aside. The whine of the shuttle fills my ears as it approaches. Someone bumps into me and I glare at him, noticing the mark on his left forearm that marks him as a freed plebeian. He steps backward the moment he realizes that he had bumped into me, muttering his apologies. I watch as he disappears into the crowd, taking his place in the back like he is supposed to, ignored by those around him. A part of me considers arresting him for disrespect, but I decide to let it go. I am on leave. Work can wait until tomorrow.

The shuttle arrives, surrounding us with a tunnel of wind as it screeches to a halt and the doors open. The moment they do, people burst free of its confined space, each hurrying to their destinations, while those of us on the platform rush to board before the transparent doors close again. I choose a place in the middle of the car to stand, while others take a seat, clinging to the handholds that have been provided as excitement at riding the shuttle again bursts through me. The doors close. The railcar speeds off, floating just above the tracks and rushing past tall buildings that house offices and apartments, each one morphing away from their dilapidated state and into a more luxurious appearance the further away from the eastern sector we go.

Windows make up the entire shuttle, beckoning me to look out them at the magnitude of my city, the greatness of Arel, as the tallest, most pristine and magnanimous spires at its uppermost level, the core of our city, remind us all of its might. I marvel at the way the rays of the sun shine down upon them, bouncing off the tips of the towers being disbursed throughout the city as a sign of Arel's benevolence. The glow of day's light envelopes the presidents' manor, which can be seen from every angle of the city, proving their might, and pride swells inside me, reminding me of how honored I am to serve my city.

The shuttle rises upward and I shift my balance to accommodate for the ascent as it approaches the central hub, its transparent walls looming over us, concealing nothing and welcoming all who enter. I watch as people ride up escalators and stroll along the moving walkways in an effort to catch their connecting shuttle. As I pass underneath the marble archways, I find myself to be more in awe of them than I was during my first trip here. The shuttle levels out and slows to a stop. Mimicking the other passengers, I shift toward the doors, waiting for them to open so that I can jump out. A soft ding sounds and the doors slide open. People push and shove their way through and I get caught in the middle of it, allowing myself to be carted onto the platform, breaking free of the crowd the first chance I get and jogging to an escalator, remembering that when Faya and I had come through here, she had to head in this direction.

I pause by a monitor, scanning the various railcar schedules until I find the one I search for. Platform five will take me to the business district. I sprint away from the monitor and hike along a moving walkway to another escalator, taking the steps two at a time, arriving on platform five just as the shuttle pulls in. People dodge out of my way, no doubt wanting to avoid an entanglement with an arbiter, as I hurry onto the platform and join the crowd that boards the shuttle.

If I thought my original sight of the city had been spectacular when I had first been to the central hub, it does not compare to the effervescent view provided by this railcar. We soar high above the tallest buildings of the western region, and I press my face against the window to get a better look, watching as shuttles zip below me. My center of gravity shifts as the railcar banks north, heading for the uppermost levels of Arel, veering away just before it reaches the administrative district, descending as it heads for the business district.

A baritone voice pulls me away from my wonderment of Arel's infrastructure and I turn around. Two seats away from me is a plebeian girl wearing the emblem of the council, doing her best to ignore the two Arelian citizens harassing her. Most occasions, I would ignore it, but she wears the emblem of our council, meaning that she is stationed there. According to Arelian law, any plebeian who does the bidding of either of our presidents or the council are to be left alone and treated with the same respect as one would treat an Arelian citizen.

"Hey!" I shout at them, hoping that my stern tone will have the desired effect so that I do not have to find a detainment box. "Leave her alone!"

Others within the shuttle glance in my direction, moving away as best they can while pretending to ignore the entire ordeal, though their focused attention betrays their interest.

The two citizens glare at me, but take note of my uniform and the fact that my hand rests upon my weapon, something all arbiters are required to carry even when off duty. While they debate what to do, I calculate the distance between us, planning my attack should they disobey me. More people step away as the silence between us thickens. Just as I am about to take the first lunge toward them, the two citizens back off, worming their way through the crowd and to an adjoining car, and I let out a quiet sigh of relief, glad that I do not have to go through the trouble of arresting them. The plebeian keeps her gaze focused on the window, avoiding mine, while the people around us avoid getting too close to her.

Seconds later, the shuttle pulls onto a platform sheltered by a metallic building, constructed to look like an upside-down U, and screeches to a halt, causing me to pivot as I regain my balance from the sudden change in momentum. No one waits for the doors to open as they hurry out of the car to get away from me and the plebeian. I do not care. Let them go. I step off the train, leaving the plebeian on her own, and look up the name of the café that Faya had asked me to meet her at, stopping midstride.

Various structures made of copper, glass, and steel surround me, towering over me, reminding me just how small I am in this world as they stretch upward, reaching for the clouds above us. People dart about in crisp suits of every color—not a stain on them, nor a single wrinkle—going about their business while still making certain to give me a wide berth. A group of teenagers walk past me dressed in matching brown uniforms—our future economic planners—ignoring me as they keep up with their instructor, clutching their handheld tablets. The stomping of heeled shoes, followed by the constant whine of the railcars surrounding us, are a stark contrast to the organized chaos of the eastern sector.

"Excuse me," I say to a passerby and he stops, afraid that I might be detaining him for some unknown infraction. "Can you tell me how to get to the Belmont Café?"

Relief showers over him and he smiles, glad that I am just lost and in need of his assistance. "Go straight down that way and hang a left on the next street. Go straight for half a block and you can't miss it."

I thank him and run off. The white sidewalks reflect the sun, making them act as mirrors, and if I look close enough, I can see faint signs of my own reflection in them, all of which reminds me that I am no longer in the eastern sector with its grunge and dirt-ridden atmosphere. Glancing around to make sure no one watches me, I place my hand on the outer wall of a local store, rubbing it along the silky-smooth exterior, remarking at how, when I pull it away, not a smidgeon of grime coats it. A softball-sized drone floats by and I hurry away, not wanting to be late for my meeting with Faya, and turn down the street I had been instructed to follow, spotting the café with ease; it's outdoor tables and chairs are hard to miss.

Faya sees me before I even reach the café and calls my name. "Noni!" She waves me over and I join her at the table that she has reserved for us.

"Sorry I'm late," I say.

"Don't worry about it. I've only been here for a couple of minutes."

I take a long look at her. She seems changed, different from when we were at the training facility: more filled out, not obese, but muscular, and more confident. The business district seems to be doing her some good.

"Look at you," I say, noting how her face is a little less angular, though her brown curls still fall around her chin, accentuating her dark skin tone. "You seem different."

"I'm still the same me," replies Faya, "but this place is the best. My room has its own bathroom in it. Can you imagine? Not having to share a shower?"

I frown, unable to envision such a thing since I still shared a bathroom with other arbiters. I never thought about it until now. "The manor in the eastern sector is a little different."

"Oh. I didn't mean…"

"Don't worry about it," I tell her, not wanting her to feel sympathy for me. Needing sympathy is a sign of weakness and I refuse to exhibit either. "What have they got you doing?"

"All kinds of things. First, I was given a tour of this district and it is amazing. This is where everything is planned out and created to help the people of Arel succeed. Assets are doled out to each sector accordingly so they all get what they need. I've been to the school for economic planning. The children there are sharp, calculating numbers my head could never handle."

"The eastern sector is a little different," I say as I reflect on how it never seemed to have the necessary funds to make repairs, despite all the devastation it suffers. I had never thought about it before, but after seeing the luxury of this place and listening to Faya, I feel as though my sector is neglected. "Our buildings are not as pristine as the ones here and the constant attacks…"

"I heard about the attack on the wall. You weren't there when it happened, were you?"

"I was."

Faya covers her mouth and her eyes widen. Though we are all trained for such a thing, most never have to experience it.

"Noni, I'm so sorry. What happened?"

"Outsiders attacked the wall. They had more sophisticated weapons than I thought possible." I decide to leave out the part about them using weapons from Kition. "Many were injured, but I managed to survive. But, looking into their eyes… they're not human, Faya."

"I can't even imagine. The scariest event for me was last week when that riot happened in the southern sector."

I remember that incident, glad that it is over and not believing that only two weeks have passed.

"We were lined up at the edge of our district," Faya continues, "in case the riot spilled over into our area, but thankfully it didn't. I heard that they called arbiters from other sectors to put it down."

"I was there," I say.

"What?"

"Arbiters from the eastern sector were called in to help and I was among them."

"Geez, Noni. I can't believe that all this has happened to you. But enough of that. How is your commander?"

"Stern. Unflinching. She never laughs, nor smiles, and always expects me to do more than one hundred percent."

"Sounds like mine. Commander Frill—he would make Molers appear to have a sense of humor. He never laughs or jokes. I guess that is part of the requirement for training fresh meat like us."

We both laugh at her joke and the waiter comes out with a tray full of food, placing mashed yucca root, boiled beans, steamed broccoli, and candied carrots in front of us, along with a pitcher of water and two glasses. He scans our wristbands before he leaves. Every eatery in Arel is aware of the diet requirements for an arbiter and are not allowed to deviate from it, which makes me wonder how Sigal gets away with smuggling sweets to a few of us arbiters.

"I found where Trevors has been stationed," I say over a mouthful of broccoli.

"You have?" Faya leans closer to hear more.

"He's a guard at one of the factories in the eastern sector. I ran into him while my commander and I toured it."

"I never thought he would end up there."

Neither did I, but I didn't voice that thought.

"You know, perhaps being stationed in the eastern sector is a good thing."

"Why do you say that?" I ask her, since most arbiters would never say such a thing about another's assignment.

She puts her fork down and looks around, before leaning closer so that no one can eavesdrop.

"I've overheard others talking. The eastern sector is one of the more troublesome areas of Arel, mostly because of all the attacks by outsiders they suffer from. It is believed that if anyone can keep the peace there, they should be able to keep the peace in all of Arel. Most arbiters are sent there because they failed at their first assignment, but you were put there right after being commissioned, and you are not the first. I overheard my commander talking about how Arel needs strong arbiters. The unrest from the eastern sector seems to be spreading, but it is not stemming from there."

"What do you mean?"

"According to my commander," Faya whispers, "the riot in the southern sector was not the first one and its origins cannot be traced to the eastern sector. It's as though it sprung up on its own and there have been others."

"Others?"

"So, they are looking at training new arbiters to be able to handle these riots. Think about it, Noni. If you do well in the eastern sector, you can apply for a transfer to a place of your choice. They might even send you to the executive district!"

An assignment there is more than coveted; it would be an arbiter's dream. Those who have been stationed in the executive district have been able to attain seats within the council itself.

"You overheard all this?" I ask.

"Yes," answers Faya.

Three arbiters stroll past us and she stops speaking, straightening up and changes the conversation.

"But enough of that," says Faya. "Have you found someone?"

"Unfortunately, my time in the eastern sector has not allowed me to think about that."

"Which is why you need to apply for a transfer at the first available opportunity. Look." Faya points at two male arbiters on patrol.

"The one on the left is Joel. We met a month after I came here and have not been able to stay away from one another." She winks at me and I know what she refers to.

"Are there any other qualities you like about him?"

"He's funny," she replies, "but we don't spend a lot of time talking."

"Faya!"

She laughs at my reprimanding look. "You'll never change. You can't work all the time."

I chuck a piece of broccoli at her and she laughs even more. Though relationships between arbiters is forbidden, it happens anyway, and since we are all sterilized through mandatory vasectomies or hysterectomies, many believe that there is no harm in coupling, as long as you do not get caught. In my 10th year as a recruit, one couple had been caught in the act of sex and their punishment was used as a warning to the rest of us. One made the mistake of challenging the arresting arbiters and was executed that minute, while the other had been tossed to the dogs. A part of me wonders if, perhaps, the rigidity of the rules depends on where you are assigned and who your commanding officer is. Commander Vye denies herself every sort of pleasure and luxury and would never stand for my disobedience of the rules.

"Just be careful, Faya," I tell her.

"Don't worry about me," she says. "My commander sneaks people in all the time, and he's not particular about their proclivities. Secret relationships—it's common practice here."

I don't say anything.

"I'll be fine. Joel is applying for a transfer to the executive district. He may even get it."

"So, you like it here?" I ask.

"It's a lot better than the training facility."

I couldn't argue with her there.

Faya checks her wristband for the time and shoves one last bite of yucca root into her mouth. "I hate to leave you like this, but I have to get back. We're only allowed an hour for lunch."

'Hopefully, we'll be able to see each other again soon."

"I might be able to get some leave in a couple of weeks. Perhaps you can show me around the eastern sector."

"Can't," I reply. "In two days, I leave Arel to visit the outposts."

Faya's smile turns to concern as we both know that only danger lies outside the wall. "Noni, you be careful."

"I'll be fine," I tell her. "You better get back before they come looking for you."

Faya and I salute one another, and I watch as she runs off, disappearing around a corner, wondering how she had gotten lucky enough to be stationed here. Reminding myself that dwelling on her good fortune would do little to comfort me, I finish my lunch and leave, speculating about what my upcoming trip outside the wall will bring.

Chapter 15

Outside the Wall

I shove the last pair of uniform pants into my duffel and zip it close. Hoisting the bag, I slip the strap across my right shoulder, rubbing the slight sore spot where I had been given my inoculations yesterday, while allowing the bag to settle against my left hip. I glance out my window and at the wall. The sun has not risen yet, but I can still make out the figures patrolling the walkway that runs along it. My heart threatens to leap into my throat, while my mind plays scenarios of what lies beyond the protective structure, but I swallow twice and take a deep breath to calm myself. I have never been outside the wall. I have never been outside the city of Arel. Today is another test of my resolve, of my commitment to defending my city.

I hurry out of my room and downstairs to where Commander Vye waits for me. My stomach growls, wishing that I had time to eat breakfast, but the resolute look on my commander's face tells me that it will not happen. My gurgling stomach will have to wait. Next to Commander Vye is Chase, one of the plebeians that Mandi had escorted to the manor. A confused expression must have crossed my face, because at that moment, Commander Vye's voice interrupts my perplexity.

"He will be joining us."

I cannot think of a reason to bring some plebeian along, but Commander Vye always has a reason for what she does, and it is not my place to question her, but follow her and learn from her. "Yes, ma'am," I say to her.

"Our transport is outside."

I follow Commander Vye out the front door and it slides open, allowing us to pass through. As Chase steps outside, carrying three luggage bags, I notice him take a quick glance to the side, where behind a topiary hides Gwen with a worried look on her face. Before anyone else can notice them, they look away from each other, and Chase's eyes meet mine before darting downward, as is his place. I have no time to wonder about what secret message they had passed each other as Commander Vye's harsh grunt spurs me forward and I hurry into a waiting armored transport, settling in the back seat, keeping the strap of my bag around my shoulder. Another transport is in front of the car Commander Vye and I are in. I try to get a good look at the people within it, but cannot make out their faces.

"How long will we be gone, ma'am?" I ask.

"A week," replies Commander Vye. Her curt response forces me to clamp my mouth shut.

The engines grumble to life and the doors are closed, sealing me inside a moving cage. The transports pull out of the manor and onto the empty streets, and as we ride through the city, I watch as a few curtains are pulled back before falling back into place, as the curious onlooker pretends that he does not care about what we are up to. White lights spring to life, illuminating the two transports, and I see the wall from a different perspective; it towers over us, though intimidating when standing next to it, it is terrifying as we ride up to it and the steel gates that curve outward, ordering us to remain inside where it is safe. I press my face against the barred glass of my window to get a better look, but Commander Vye clears her throat as a warning, and I straighten up, pretending that I am not interested in the world outside my bubble.

The transports stop. Men walk up to the one in front, checking their orders before marching up to the one I am in. The driver hands the guard our orders and it is scanned and double-checked, and when it passes inspection, the guard hands the slim, translucent disc back to the driver and issues a command into a com unit.

The slow creak of turning gears, gears that have not moved in a long time and have rusted due to the rain and the dust, shoots up the wall and surrounds us, enveloping us in their own dreary song, as though they, too, are warning us not to go, but to stay where it is safe. The gates split open, showing us the world outside the wall and allowing us to pass through. The vehicle pivots and bounces as it starts up again and moves outside, following the one in front of it. Once we have passed, the gates seal shut, locking us outside, with an ominous boom, abandoning us to our doom. The muscles in my neck burn as I look behind, seeing my city for the first time the way an outsider would, and pride fills me as the first rays of the sun glint off the tiered arches of the presidents' home on the uppermost level.

Another harsh grunt forces me to turn around and look ahead before Commander Vye has a chance to chastise me for allowing myself to lose focus on what is to come. A pair of gray eyes watch me, but avert themselves the moment I glance in his direction. Not wanting to start something, I look out the window and watch as the world beyond passes by me, amazed at the tall grass that lines the edges of the road we are on, masked by the swirls of dust our vehicles kick up. I watch as the trees further away appear to not move at all, but study us as well, and wonder what lies beyond them. Is that where the barbarians live?

The left-rear wheel of the transport hits a bump in the road and it jostles me from my reverie, and out of the corner of my eyes, I see Commander Vye's sharp gaze boring into me, displeased that

I have relaxed my composure for a second time today. Straightening my shoulders, I look straight ahead, ignoring the green blades of waving grass, crowned in tips of gold as the sun rises above the horizon, imagining what it would be like to touch them, and allow the musings to fill my mind as time passes, while we carve our path through them, moving further away from home.

Another bump in the dilapidated road jerks me back to reality as the top of my head smacks into the ceiling of the vehicle and I see it for the first time: towers, spaced 50 yards apart, facing us, warning us to go no further. Upon closer inspection of the towers, I realize that there are no people in them and the weapons are unmanned. One glance at Commander Vye informs me that she has noticed the same, and the thin line on her lips portrays her displeasure at such slovenliness.

We pause at the gates and someone from the transport in front of us steps out, walks up to the gates, looks around, and knocks. The hollow echo of his knock filters through the steel door and reverberates around us, adding to the eerie silence that permeates every aspect of our situation. Where is everyone? The man places his gloved hand on the gate, giving it a slight push, and the door swings open just enough for a single person to squeeze through, releasing a low squeak from the rusted hinges as they whine about having to work. Worry creases Commander Vye's brow as the man steps through, his weapon raised and ready to defend himself if attacked, as the desolation of this place fills us all with concern. There should be guards along the wall, in the towers, and no one should have been able to just step through the gate unchallenged. Were they attacked?

The man steps back through the gate and waves us through, remaining in his wary and alert stance, as the two transports ease their way through the entranceway and into the compound. Bits of sand drift across the ground from where the grass has been cleared, adding to the portentous feeling that fills me as I wonder where all the arbiters are that are supposed to be here. If they had been attacked by outsiders, there should be bodies; or did the outsiders take them with them and...

A man bursts from the sliding doors of the building in front of us and sprints toward us, waving his hands. We all hunker and draw our weapons ready to fire.

"Stop right there!" yells the arbiter who had waved us through moments before.

"It's all right!" shouts the man running for us. "I'm unarmed!"

"Who are you?"

"Arbiter Gleeson. Serial number G26981." The man drops to his knees and holds his hands in the air in surrender, while two of us overlook him and check him for weapons.

"Arbiter Gleeson," says Commander Vye, approaching him, "where are your other arbiters?"

"Ma'am?"

"Where are the guards in the towers? Who is patrolling the wall surrounding this compound? Are you alone here?"

"No, ma'am," answers Gleeson. "Please." He wiggles his fingers as a way of asking permission to put his hands down.

Commander Vye nods her approval.

"Thank you," says Gleeson. "Well, welcome to Outpost 5."

His cheerful manner does not go well with the rest of us, and he soon realizes that we have concerns about the abandoned nature of this place.

"Perhaps you all would like to come inside and get some refreshments."

Commander Vye's sharp eyes roam the compound, noting the sand-snakes that drift across its surface, sprinting in an effort to escape the breeze that gives them life, and taking in the cracked siding of the buildings as they sag from disrepair. Even I recoil at the discolored paint splotching the bottom corners with rusty hue, mired by water damage and neglect.

"Lead the way," says Commander Vye in an amiable tone, but I detect a hint of sarcasm in it.

Gleeson smiles, but his nervous eyes betray the thoughts behind them, as he turns and motions for us to follow him, but only Commander Vye, myself, and two other arbiters comply. We step through the sliding doors that whish open for us, their rickety movements causing them to jerk and stick as they do so, and the green mildew that overcomes what had once been transparent steel, makes me appreciate the eastern sector, and its few luxuries, even more. Once through, the doors attempt to slide shut, but hiss and creak as they stick and vibrate from the pressure to move. Gleeson kicks the corner of one, freeing it, and the doors seal shut.

"Sometimes, they stick," he says with a shrug before turning and guiding us through a narrow corridor to an opening which leads to the main room.

I shift my bag to ease the pressure its weight puts on my shoulder as I walk, while a light above me flickers, turns off, and flickers back on, duller and not as bright. My eyes find Commander Vye, and I do not need to see her face to know that saying she is displeased would be underestimating her true feelings. Despite the flaws of the eastern sector, she maintains discipline and cleanliness and demands it from the arbiters under her command.

The main room resembles a gift box, but not the sort of gift you would give to anyone, not even your enemy. Urine-colored panels hang from the walls, and at first glance, I wonder how it is they are not on the floor as they dangle and sway from the slightest movement, while wires poke through small holes created by mice. Something hits my left shoulder. Curious, I pick up the object with my thumb and index finger and hold it in front of me, surprised that it is a bit of drywall. Looking up, I am amazed to find gaping holes in the ceiling with exposed pipes and wiring and discover the source of the drywall: a block of the ceiling hangs low, threatening to fall and drops bits of itself to the floor as a warning. I rub my fingers together, cleaning them of the particle dust and brush my shoulder.

Bare feet slapping the floor draw our attention. My eyes widen as a man walks up to us, wearing his arbiter shirt, but he has forgotten to put on his pants and undergarments, allowing his full glory to hang in front of him, exposed for all of us to see. Gleeson's face turns to fear, knowing how this looks and what sort of reprimand he will receive, but Commander Vye's stern expression never falters, nor do her eyes leave the half-dressed arbiter's face.

"Morning," he yawns.

"It's evening," says Commander Vye, testing him. It's really midafternoon.

"Oh, so it is." He stretches one arm above his head while scratching his balls with his other.

"You seem to be missing something, arbiter," says Commander Vye.

The man looks down and realizes for the first time that he has forgotten his pants. "Oh, so I am," he replies, walking up to Commander Vye and patting her on the shoulder. "I wouldn't worry about it."

Commander Vye seizes his hand and has him on the floor in an instant.

"It is commander," she hisses, "and never place you hand upon me again." She lets him up. "Put some pants on. Straighten your shirt. You should be fully clothed and your uniform pressed. Understood?"

"Yes, ma'am." He scurries away, hoping to escape Commander Vye's fury; his feet make clapping sounds as he runs.

"There seems to be a serious lack of discipline here." Commander Vye turns toward Gleeson, who swallows saliva in an effort to clear his mouth before he speaks.

"Would you like to see the rest of the compound?"

"By all means."

He leads us to another room with two long tables and benches on each side. One table is propped up where a leg has rotted through, unable to support the weight of the table itself, looking pathetic under the murky light that spills through yellowed shades rift with holes, adding a gloominess that this place seems unable to escape. I follow the dark grooves in the table, stopping when I spot a dead plant in a cracked ceramic pot with bits of dried, brown potting soil dropping from the clefts and littering the floor with its decayed, granular texture.

While Commander Vye takes in the dismal state of the building, I meander over to the window, pulling back the tattered curtain and taking great care to not damage it any more than it already is, and strain to look through the grease-stained glass, broken into sections by the crack that stretches from the top of the panel to the bottom. I scrape at the grime with the edge of my short thumbnail, etching away at the coating that neglect has placed on the glass, and peek through the small hole, looking out at a foreign scene of dust, mixed with trampled shoots of grass that never had the chance to grow, rusted nails and screws buried for a treasure hunter to find, and splintered wood that has fallen from its place on the sides or roofs of the surrounding buildings, all ignoring the lone arbiter who stumbles through it in her underclothes, while trying not to lose her untied boots as they shift on her feet.

"Have you no caretaker?" Commander Vye's voice breaks through my moment of inattention, and I drop the curtain, whirling around to face the room, hoping that her focus on Gleeson spared me from facing her wrath later on for allowing my mind to wander.

"I'm afraid," replies Gleeson, "that plebeians do not survive long out here."

"Are your arbiters incapable of caring for themselves?" The dark undertone in her voice reminds me of Molers and a shiver runs down my back as I think back to the time I overheard her talking to him in her office.

"No, ma'am…"

"Or, perhaps"—Commander Vye circles Gleeson with her hands clasped behind her back, scrutinizing him with that penetrating gaze of hers—"it is not them to blame."

Sweat forms under my collar as the heat and tension rises within the room, even though I am not the one she is disappointed in.

"I… I… do not know what you mean."

"Oh, I think you do."

"Commander," I say, doing my best to remain respectful, knowing how much she loathes being interrupted.

"Yes," she snaps.

"So far," I continue, "we have only seen the front courtyard and this building. I am sure there are more areas of this outpost that need inspection. Should we not continue?"

"You do have a point. Thank you, Noni."

I do my best not to smile, having never been thanked by Commander Vye before and find it odd that she is thanking me now, unless it is more for Gleeson's benefit.

"I wish to see your towers."

Gleeson nods and hurries to an exit, with the rest of us in tow, his pudgy feet shuffling as he goes. The tower he leads us to slants to its right side. One glance at the foundation and I see why: some of the bricks have crumbled away, and pieces of the gray mortar form a small pile near its base. I run the front edge of my boot against it and more grout drops to the ground, and a worried expression fills Gleeson's face as he tugs at his collar, before placing his hand by his side, as though he realized his panicky reaction for the first time.

"Are you going to take us up there?" asks Commander Vye in a sarcastic tone.

Gleeson opens a door that leads into a darkened interior with a metal ladder so coated in rust that the moment I place my hand upon the first rung, it ceases to be dark in color and copper red instead. One of us flips the switch, but the lights that scale the inside wall remain off.

"The power to this building went out over a mon—week ago and we have not been able—"

"Save it." Commander Vye climbs the ladder first, and the arbiter with us seizes Gleeson by the shoulder of his jacket and forces him to follow her, while I take my place in the rear, which seems to be my normal position in this world.

I once thought I had been in tight quarters before, but this makes the previous instances seem more luxurious and spacious as I inch my way up the ladder, my shoulders brushing the sides of the wall and becoming coated in dust. Soft clomps of each of our boots stepping on the metal rungs echo around us, and despite the sweat that drips from my chin and the clamminess of my hands as they reach for the rungs above me, the hair on my skin rises as though a sudden blast of chill air has engulfed us. I crawl through the opening at the top and stand up, allowing my eyes to adjust to the brighter—though not by much—room.

I do not need to see the room to know why displeased silence surrounds us. The 360-degree window allows a small amount of light through its soiled glass, and as though to prove how neglected they have been, a sheet of caked dirt falls away from it, allowing a rectangular stream of sunlight into the room, illuminating its disrepair. Layers of dust litter it, while fingerprints cover the computer consoles, desks, communication area, chairs, and even the floor, though our footprints have disturbed it all, overseen by a single cobweb dangling from the ceiling and resembling a limp piece of cloth more than the remains of a spider's home.

"Care to explain why there is no one here?"

I melt back into the shadows as the dangerous edge in Commander Vye's voice fills the tower room.

"We have no need for the towers," replies Gleeson.

Wrong answer.

"No need?"

"There have been no attacks here for the last two years or more. Even Arel does not communicate with us much. We are forgotten out here."

"No attacks?" The incredulity in Commander Vye's voice brings back memories of the attack on the wall when I had first been taken there under her supervision. "And are you implying that there are no attacks on the city as well?"

"No, ma'am. I wouldn't know anything about that. The last communication we had from Arel was four months ago. At least they remember to send us a supply convey once in a while; otherwise, we would be in worse shape."

"I'm curious," says Commander Vye, "if you are so forgotten out here, how is it you have managed to survive?"

Gleeson nibbles on the inner edges of his cracked lips.

"Well?" demands Commander Vye.

"Trade."

"Trade?"

Gleeson's feet shift a couple of inches as he debates whether or not to tell her the truth, and I hope he does because she will find it, one way or another.

"I barter with the people who live around here. They do not harm us! They are not all bad people!"

One flick of Commander Vye's hand and the arbiter with us rams the butt of his weapon into Gleeson's face, knocking him to the floor where he struggles to regain his senses. Before he can get to his knees, the same arbiter strikes him a second time and shoves him through the opening, allowing him to plummet to the ground. Two other arbiters, whom must have gotten out of their convoy when they saw us go up the tower, drag him away, unconcerned if has any broken bones.

"It seems things have gotten a little lax around here," Commander Vye says to herself. She turns to the guard accompanying us. "Summon everyone into the courtyard."

He salutes and climbs down the ladder.

"Noni!"

I jump from my corner and scurry down the ladder as well with her right behind me. We burst from the darkened tomb of the tower and into the sunlight, forcing me to blink several times as my eyes adjust to the glaring brightness. Scuffling noises draw my attention and I watch as the arbiters accompanying us drag Gleeson away, shoving a canvas hood over his balding head and throwing him in one of the vehicles. Commander Vye's steady footsteps command me to follow her, and I stand at attention by her side as she takes a megaphone, given to her by another arbiter, and turns it on, bringing it to her mouth.

"Listen up!" she yells into it. "All residents of this outpost are to report to the square now. Those who refuse will be executed on the spot."

Our guards storm the doors of the barracks, hauling half-dressed, half-asleep men and women from their beds and into the afternoon sun. Splintered wood and hinges popping from their holds jingle in the dirt as they fall, surrounded by terrified screams from the people within the buildings. I remain poised and erect as feet scrape the gravel, kicking up pebbles, and frightened yells and murmurs fill the courtyard around us, while the irate shouts of our guards bark at them.

"I want silence!"

The outpost arbiters fall silent as they form two lines in front of Commander Vye.

"Your commander has been detained and will be processed accordingly."

Whispers flow through the crowd. One of our guards strikes a man in the stomach, issuing a command for silence and the whispers cease.

"Because of his lack of discipline," continues Commander Vye, "you all have gotten soft, lax, complacent. That ends now. From this day forward, you will all be dressed in your full uniforms. Drills will be performed. The towers will be manned. And reports will be sent to Arel daily. A new commander will be assigned to you, but in the meantime, I will leave Arbiter Kurel in charge."

A man strolls up beside Commander Vye, pulling off his helmet, and scrutinizes the crowd before him with his brows scrunched together and his lips set in a grim line, causing his cheeks to draw inward, making the dark spots upon his ebony skin appear to multiply, mirroring the no-nonsense demeanor of those around him.

"This is your only warning," says Commander Vye. "This outpost will shape up, or you will all perish with it." She drops the megaphone and hands it to another arbiter before turning to me. "Noni, you will stay here."

I do not question her. Shuffling my bag on my shoulder, I turn in a circle, observing the frightened residents of the outpost as their eyes jump from guard to guard, unsure of what to do, and uncertain about their future. Their lax muscles, frightened demeanor, and jittery nature disgust me. How could they have allowed themselves to get like this? They are vital to the protection of Arel. If one outpost is overrun, all can be taken, which will leave Arel and its citizens defenseless. Yet, Gleeson had mentioned something about a deal he had worked out with the outsiders; what did he mean by that?

Wisps of sand brush over the tops of my boots while I wait for Commander Vye to return, and I am determined to maintain my proud posture as an example of how an arbiter is to behave, if only the strap from my pack would quit cutting into my shoulder, causing a sharp pain to build there. The crunching of gravel beneath resolute steps fill my ears and I turn toward it to be greeted by Commander Vye's return.

"Get in the transport," she orders.

I sprint to the transport I had ridden in earlier, wasting no time in obeying her, and slam the door shut just as she gets in the opposing side and sits next to me, accompanied by a guard. "What will become of them?" I ask her.

"Only they know," replies Commander Vye. "I have contacted the tribunal council of Arel, the same one you answered to earlier for your actions on the wall, and they will send someone to whip them back into shape. The man I placed there is just a temporary fix. It is up to them to decide if they wish to live or die. And I am certain that I needn't tell you about Mr. Gleeson's fate."

No, she does not. Images float through my mind about whom the tribunal would send, but I could only think of a few, none of whom I would wish to have in my life again. "We are not staying here?"

"No. We will head to the second outpost on our agenda and will rest there for the night, as we should be arriving before dusk. I hope it is in far better shape than this travesty."

Ignoring her reprimand of me earlier this morning, I crane my neck and stare out the rear window, watching as the outpost grows smaller in the distance, mired by clouds of dust, shadowed by knee-high, gold grass dancing in the breeze with just the road giving a clear view of the front gate. What will the other outpost hold?

Chapter 16

Commandant Paq

The sun hangs low in the sky, casting long, pale red shadows on the faces surrounding me, as our convoy speeds down the road toward our destination. The gate of the second outpost looms ahead of us, growing larger with each passing second, as the engines hum around us, drowning any extraneous sounds, not even allowing the soft roar of the wind or calls of the wild animals to reach us. I clutch my bag tighter, digging it into my lap, wary of what lies ahead and what I will find. The disastrous visit to the first outpost left a bad aftertaste in all our mouths and I hope that this one is better, considering the foul mood Commander Vye is in; we need something that will lift our spirits and let us know that Arel is well-protected. Both outposts are far away from Arel though; is it possible that each one regards itself according to its own set of rules?

Our convoy slows down, but jerks and speeds up again just as the front gate opens, allowing us passage. I stare out the window, taking in every detail, including the indentation in the gate, giving it a pockmarked look when the sun's light strikes it at a certain angle. One quick glance at the other passengers in the vehicle and I learn that I am not the only one interested in this new outpost: the plebeian is too. The moment we pass through the entrance, shouts ring out and sentries race toward us, their weapons raised and ready to fire if we prove to be a threat. Our transports ease to a halt, but no one makes any effort to exit the vehicles as the armed sentries surround us, aiming their weapons at us, and I squirm, wondering if I have committed some sort of infraction to warrant such a welcome.

"Hands up!" shouts one of the sentries.

We all raise our hands. This is a far different greeting compared to the blasé one we had received at the first outpost.

"Papers!"

Commander Vye maintains a calm demeanor as she unrolls the window and hands the man a rectangular disc, no thicker than a sliver of wood. He snatches it from her hand, receiving a glare in response, and sticks it in the tablet he keeps in his side pocket, scans through the files, grunts, and hands the disk back to her, after which, he scans her bracelet. A harsh rap on my window disrupts my observance of the proceedings and another sentry stands there, motioning for me to roll down my window. I obey. Before the glass has a chance to open all the way, he reaches in, seizes my wrist with my bracelet on it and scans it, having moved on to the next passenger while my mind still reels with what has just happened.

"Commander Vye," says a baritone voice, "I was not expecting you until tomorrow. I apologize for the harsh welcome, but your sudden arrival surprised us all."

"Yes, well, our time at the other outpost did not go as planned, so we continued on here," she answers, while stepping out of the transport and I do the same, rather than wait for orders. "I hope that we are not inconveniencing you."

"Not at all. The unexpected keeps one sharp."

"Commandant Paq,"—Commander Vye holds her hand out to

me and I close the distance between us—"this is Arbiter Noni, the newest arbiter in the eastern sector."

And her charge, not that she needs to say it. The expression on Commandant Paq's face conveys that he knows full well what she means.

"Welcome to Stryd, at least that is what we call the outpost around here."

The sentries back away from us, creating a path for us to walk through, as Commander Vye and I follow Commandant Paq. Some venture off and go back to their duties, while others remain, keeping watchful eyes on us, and the feeling that I am in a prison wafts over me, something I have never experienced before; but with each step, I sense that eyes watch me, waiting for me to make the wrong move, something the armed guards along the wall convey quite well as they watch us through the visors of their helmets, while also keeping vigilance on the land outside the wall.

Unified shouts catch my attention as we pass through an archway and into a brick courtyard. Arbiters practice drills (a combination of jumping jacks, running in place, push-ups, lunge squats, burpees, and balancing on one foot), standing out in their dark uniforms against the scarlet bricks behind them, as they count out their reps to the drill instructor in front of them. Commandant Paq strolls past them, not bothering to glance in their direction, until he spots one whom struggles to keep up. Her harsh breathing comes in ragged gasps and her face gleams from sweat, but her expression begs the instructor to stop as though each movement is a struggle for her, each rift with pain, and any casual observer can see that she is unwell.

Leaving us alone, Commandant Paq marches up to the woman, grabbing her by the bun on her head, and yanks her from formation, throwing her to the stone ground.

"You call that discipline?"

The woman looks up, her chest heaving as she attempts to slow her breathing. "Please, sir, I am not feeling well."

"I did not ask if you were ill!" shouts Commandant Paq, and for a moment, I see Molers standing in his place issuing the same statement. "Illness is weakness!"

The woman curls into a ball on the ground and vomits, its putrid smell attacking my nostrils, and I am forced to swallow three times in an effort to not expel the contents of my own stomach. Her involuntary actions anger Commandant Paq even more, and he kicks her with such brute force that her body lifts in the air and slams back into the pavement.

"How do we deal with weak links?" he addresses the other arbiters in formation.

"We cut them out, sir!" they all reply in unison.

A sinking feeling fills the pit of my stomach.

"What are you waiting for?"

The woman raises her head and watches with fearful eyes as her fellow arbiters approach her with murder and death overshadowing their own faces. They pounce upon her, kicking and punching her as she cries for mercy, but mercy is an unwelcomed guest in this world and an endangered commodity. She will find no mercy here. Steeling my face, my focus remains glued to the scene unfolding before me, until my gaze meets Commandant Paq's, and he motions for me to join in. I remain still. He waves me over again, more insistent, and I tremble at the thought of what will happen to me if I refuse. Commander Vye's arm across my chest spares me from having to make a decision as she holds me back, never needing to say anything as I understand her unspoken message: stay put. Commandant Paq's eyes narrow into thin lines, and now the fear for myself turns into trepidation for my commanding officer as her one act in defying him has angered him as well, and I have the distinct impression that Commandant Paq is not a man you want as your enemy.

A sharp whistle stops the beating and the arbiters saunter away, lining up in formation once again, participating in their exercises in an effort to remain in top physical condition. Alone on the pavement rests the crumpled remains of what had once been a woman, ignored by all—even the carrion birds that circle above have no interest in her.

"Perhaps you would like to see our facility," says Commandant Paq, and I note the hint of an order in his words masquerading as a suggestion.

A strained smile crosses Commander Vye's lips and she urges me to follow after the Commandant. Our short journey to the main building takes us past the woman smothered in a pool of her own blood, while more oozes from the various wounds on her body, mixing with the exposed brain from her cracked skull. I refuse to avert my eyes, not wanting to show weakness. Weakness is what put her in this situation.

A slow, ragged gasp escapes her lips, forcing me to pause. I look down. Warm, cherry-red blood molds over the toes of my boot, edging its way past, until I am surrounded by it, cut off from the uniform bricks that form the ground of the courtyard, all the while being watched by the one good eye of the woman. Remembering what Commander Vye had done for the one arbiter who had broken his neck, and what she had said, I lift my right foot and place it on the exposed neck of the woman, squeezing her airway closed, keeping my weight on it and not releasing the pressure, until her breathing stops and her eye closes, ending her suffering. Her fate had been sealed the moment she challenged Commandant Paq; I just granted her release. Keeping my face impassive, I pick up my foot and step over the corpse, continuing my trek to the main building, unaware of the trail of bloodied footprints that follow after me and the plebeian eyes that observe my one act of mercy.

I walk up the stairs and step through the sliding glass doors—their pristine nature marvels me after having seen the grime encrusted ones of the previous outpost—and into a world that knows no color. Coin-colored shade panels line the walls from the charcoal-colored floor to the pewter ceiling, where fluorescent lights amplify the achromatic nature of the room.

We stroll past graphite tables, made from a sturdy steel, with the slate-colored chairs pushed in, all placed in the four corners of the room, while white viewing screens—the only source of a different shade in this drab place—play messages from our two presidents. The messages repeat themselves, creating an incessant drumbeat for us all to march to, as we abide by their words of wisdom, and I find myself agreeing with what they say. The swish of water in a mop bucket causes me to jerk my head as an arbiter scrubs the floor while on his hands and knees, until it shines and he can see his face in the polished tile.

"There are no plebeians here?" The words are out of my mouth before I am aware that my mind thought them.

Commandant Paq faces me, amused by my question. "No. I find that the best way to maintain discipline is to instill a certain work ethic in our arbiters. The people assigned here do their own cleaning, laundry, cooking, and any other menial task that needs to be done."

Somehow, I get the impression that Commandant Paq has someone else do all his necessary chores, since he does not strike me as a man that lowers himself in performing degrading labor.

I remain silent as Commandant Paq leads us into the kitchen; the low hum of the wall refrigerators, fans, and the hiss of the grill as it cooks the raw slabs of meat placed upon it remind me of the training facility. Arbiters wearing white aprons, stained from the various cuisines they cook, dart about, ignoring us as they prepare the days' evening meal. Commandant Paq saunters up to a stainless-steel counter with a giant mixing bowl full of a red sauce and dips his pinky finger in, scooping up a glob of the syrupy liquid and licks it off his appendage, smacking his lips. Despite my disgust at him sinking his unwashed finger into what I assume is going to be our meal for the night, I clamp my mouth shut, not wanting to cause any trouble or give Commander Vye a reason to discipline me; though, judging by the odium expression on her face, she shares my sentiment.

For a moment, it seems as if Commandant Paq likes the condiment, but that moment turns into surprise when he slaps the arbiter standing next to it holding a whisk dripping with the red sauce. The poor man takes a step back, his eyes wide from the unexpectedness of the commandant's act, but lowers his head in response, refusing to challenge his superior officer.

"It's too bland!" yells the commandant.

"I'm sorry, sir," replies the cook in a low voice.

"Don't be sorry! Get it right the first time! It needs sweetness, some spice."

"Yes, sir."

Frustrated, Commandant Paq storms a pantry, yanking out bottle after bottle (cayenne pepper, turmeric, maple syrup, molasses, cinnamon, chervil, and dried saffron) and hauls his armload to the counter, dumping the spice bottles, allowing them to spill all over the immaculate surface, and I catch one just as it rolls over the edge. He opens container after container, dumping their contents into the bowl before snatching the whisk from the cook and stirring with such ferocity that the liquid splatters on the cabinets, floor, and countertop, leaving red splotches that resemble blood more than a dressing. He thrusts the bowl at me and I back away.

"Here!"

I give him a quizzical look, not wanting to consume his creation.

"Taste it!" Commandant Paq screams at me, garnering a piercing glare from Commander Vye.

Knowing I have no choice, I pick up a nearby spoon and ease it into the sauce, bringing it to my lips and taking a petite bite. I spit it out. I have no idea how the condiment tasted before Commandant Paq decided to play chef, but the sauce burns my tongue and lips, leaving a bitter aftertaste that reminds me of the time Molers forced me to eat mud. I had challenged him and that was my punishment.

"See what you have done," rages Commandant Paq at the cowering cook. "You have wasted what spices we have and ruined our supper!"

I can stand his abuse and absurdity no longer. "With respect,"

I say to him, the strong tone of my voice surprising even me, "you are the one who has destroyed our supper. You are the one who chose to empty all those spices into what was most likely a delectable treat, thus rendering it into something that is inedible. You have no one to blame but yourself!"

Commandant Paq raises his massive hand, its blackness warning me of what I am about to see in a second, and swings at me. I cringe and turn my head, waiting for the inevitable. Nothing happens. When I look up, I see his hand stopped in midair, with Commander Vye's fingers wrapped around his wrist in a grip so tight that his ebony fingers turn a shade of purple.

"Perhaps, you should show us to our quarters," she says, her stern voice informing everyone in the kitchen that her words are not a suggestion.

"Follow me," replies Commandant Paq, yanking himself free of her hold.

We trail after Commandant Paq, leaving the kitchen, but I turn back and watch the cook dump the sauce into a garbage can, while the others go back to their work.

The Commandant takes us from the main building to a smaller structure, which looks as though it houses the officers' quarters, and marches through the opening doors, stomping down the smoke-colored carpet, producing hollowed thumps as he goes. He presses his hand against two biometric reading pads and the doors to two rooms slide open.

"These are your quarters," he says to us in a curt tone. "I hope they will meet your expectations."

"They will do just fine," replies Commander Vye.

Commandant Paq grunts and stalks off, but before he can take two steps, Commander Vye stops him.

"You have neglected to tell us when supper shall be."

"Six sharp. Be on time, or go hungry." He glares at her for a moment before switching his venomous gaze to me and storms away, leaving us alone.

Commander Vye remains quiet and walks into her room, while I step into my own, breathing a sigh of relief as the door to my chamber closes, concealing me from unwanted eyes. I toss my bag onto the cot in the room, and it bounces off the spongy mattress and onto the concrete floor, its dull color adding to my dismal mood. Allowing my frustration to come through, I grab my bag's handle and throw it to the other side of the room.

Robust shouts echo through the window, snatching my attention. Curious, and having nothing better to do until supper, I stroll to the window—a small rectangular box high off the floor—and stretch up onto my tippy toes, grasping the edges with my slender fingers, and peek through the sheer glass. I watch the feet of the arbiters who are lined up in formation as they perform drill exercises, practicing their fighting skills: their protective stances, balance, kicks, and punches, while shouting "Arel" after each pause. I remember the moves, having performed them myself each day as a recruit at the training facility. As I look around, I realize that I am staring into the front courtyard, the same one where the woman had been beaten to the brink of death, the woman whom I spared agonizing pain. Her body is gone now, no doubt having been cleaned up by other arbiters, since Commandant Paq made it clear that he does not use plebeians.

A commotion rises near the entrance and the gates burst open, allowing armored vehicles through as they roar into the compound, kicking up plumes of dust that cover the area and block my view of the event taking place. I bounce on my toes, willing the dust clouds to dissipate, but it does little good; they care nothing for my desire to see what is happening. The armored cars roll to a stop, and with each passing second, the dust clouds become a bit more transparent. Commandant Paq rushes out to meet the arbiter who steps out of the first vehicle. She pulls off her helmet, saluting him, saying, "Commandant, we have found one."

Found one? One what?

"Good," he replies, unconcerned about what it is his arbiter must have discovered. "Bring it here."

The female arbiter waves at another in the vehicle behind her and two more arbiters jump out, dragging a man in restraints. A barbarian. The loose-fitting pants that hang from his hips, frayed and ripped at the hemline, the patched coat, and torn knit gloves on his boney and blistered hands give away the fact this this man is an outsider. At least, I think it is a man. The rags covering his face makes it difficult to tell, but as he struggles, yanking at his restraints in a crude attempt to break away, twisting and turning in their grasp, the rags fall away, revealing a face not much older than mine, possessing a thin, dark line on the upper lip, the beginnings of a mustache, I suppose. The arbiters haul him in front of Commandant Paq, who seizes his chin, lifting it up and turning his head to each side so he can inspect him. The man jerks away, disgusted with his treatment.

"A good specimen," says Commandant Paq. "Where did you find him?"

"He was wandering near one of our towers. Probably collecting intel for his barbarian allies," replies the female arbiter.

"That's a lie!" screams the barbarian, receiving a blow to the stomach in return for his outburst.

"Lock him up," orders Commandant Paq. "We'll have some sport in the morning."

Arbiters drag the barbarian away, and despite his attempts to slow them down, he is no match for them. As the courtyard clears, I notice our plebeian standing alone, near the transport that Commander Vye and I had ridden in, a speck of white in a sea of black. His nervous eyes roam around, taking in every detail, all the while keeping his head down so as not to attract unwanted attention. I never even thought about him until now, but there he is, still waiting by the transport as ordered.

A small beep sounds from my wristband, reminding me of the

time. I drop from the window, landing on my feet—my toes thank me for relieving them from the stress of supporting my weight—and hurry to the door, straightening my uniform jacket as I go. When the door slides open, I find Commander Vye exiting her room. She looks up at me, keeping her face unreadable, and steps into the hallway. "It's good to know that you are capable of being on time for some things," she says.

I step into the corridor next to her and the door to my quarters seals shut behind me. "Our plebeian is still waiting by our transport," I tell her.

"And?"

"He should be given something to do other than standing around waiting for us."

"A valid point. I'll see to it that he is given temporary duties here, until it is time for us to leave."

We set a brisk pace as we hurry down the hall, up the same set of stairs we had come down earlier, out the exit, and into the courtyard. Neither Commander Vye nor I say a word as we head to the mess hall, each of us wondering what supper with Commandant Paq will bring.

The ruckus stabs my ears before we reach the outer door to the mess hall, making me believe that Commander Vye and I must have entered the wrong room. From the strict discipline I have witnessed, I never thought that he would allow such frivolity. I glance at Commander Vye, but she stares straight ahead and strolls through the wide open, double doors into a slate-stained room with dust-colored, long tables stretched out, almost blending into the matching colored floor. I turn my head from side to side as I meander through the room, watching as arbiters seated at the long tables joke and converse in a light-hearted manner, oblivious to Commandant Paq's presence at the head of the table in the front of the chamber, while he busies himself with small talk with those sitting around him.

I head for a lone seat at the far end of the nearest bench, but a hand pats my right shoulder and directs me to Commandant Paq's table. Though reluctant, I go where I am told, following Commander Vye, who has received similar instructions, and walk to the front of the mess hall toward Commandant Paq's exuberant hands as he waves us over.

"Have a seat," he says, and his uncharacteristic jovial manner unnerves me, but judging by the alcoholic aroma exuding from his cup, I guess the reason for his changed behavior.

"Your arbiters seem to be in good spirits," comments Commander Vye, preventing me from speaking what is on my mind. "A stark contrast to earlier."

"Yes, well," replies Commandant Paq, sloshing his cup as he lifts it to his lips and droplets of amber liquid fall to the table, "I see no problem in letting them unwind once in a while."

"Prudent, considering the nature of the job out here."

Commandant Paq raises his cup in agreement and takes another long drink.

Our meals are brought out to us by other arbiters. They each carry two plates of food, setting one of the tin plates in front of us, before taking an empty seat, placing their own plate on the table before them. I stare at the bit of mashed, brown food sitting before me, covered in some sort of urine-colored gravy—well, I hope it is gravy—wondering what has happened to the red sauce I had seen earlier, which Commandant Paq had insisted on perfecting. I never expected any sort of high class cuisine, and the training facility never concerned itself with the palatability of the food it served, but at least we were able to decipher what had been served. This slop appears to have been put through a grinder before being plopped on a tin plate and thrust in front of its poor victim. Determined not to display weakness, I pick up my fork and scoop up a bit of the edible goat droppings and bring it to my mouth.

"Wait!" shouts Commandant Paq.

I put my fork down.

"What is this?" he demands, waving his hand at mine and Commander Vye's plates. "Is this what we serve here?"

Examining the faces around me, the answer is yes. I glance at Commandant Paq's platter and receive an answer into the mystery of the red sauce. Meat loaf, steamed carrots, and asparagus with the red sauce drizzled over each item fill his plate. It appears that he eats well, while those under his command eat dog food. Either way, it is clear that Commandant Paq lives by a separate standard.

"Clear this garbage away and give our guests some decent food," he orders.

Hands reach for my plate, but I grasp the sides and hold onto it, preventing our server from doing his job. Commander Vye takes note of my movements and places her own hand over hers as well, keeping it rooted to the table.

"If one does not eat what they are given," I say, quoting Molers, "it displays weakness and the weak shall perish."

A slight grin appears on Commander Vye's face before vanishing.

"What…" begins Commandant Paq.

"Our newest arbiter has been taught well at the training facility and still remembers her teachings," says Commander Vye. "She is right, of course. It is a pity that you do not seem to share the same sentiment."

Commandant Paq's face darkens and his eyes narrow, focusing on Commander Vye, not liking her unspoken challenge. "How dare you treat me differently and bring me this," he scolds one of the servers in a feeble attempt to save face.

The poor arbiter scurries away with his plate of delectable food and replaces it with the goat droppings and urine sauce. Commandant Paq glares at Commander Vye first before switching his noxious gaze to me. Following Commander Vye's example, I keep my expression unreadable and watch his every move, waiting for him to eat what he forces the arbiters beneath him to consume.

He snatches his fork with his thick, ebony fingers and shoves heaping amounts of the glop into his mouth, doing his best not to show his displeasure as he chews it and swallows, after which, he gives Commander Vye and me a challenging glare. Not wanting to be outdone, I place my original forkful on my tongue and gulp it down, refusing to taste the sludge, but my tongue insists on detecting a piece of carrot, which means that the preparers had placed everything in a blender and mixed it together, ensuring that the arbiters received their nutritional quota, but remained within Commandant Paq's requirement that they not enjoy their meal.

"Does it meet your standards?" growls Commandant Paq.

Deciding it best to quote another bit of Molers' teachings as a way of avoiding an answer, I reply, "Food is meant for sustenance, not pleasure."

The commandant chuckles, recognizing my reply for what it is: a regurgitation of what I had been taught since my birth. I do not care and ignore him as I finish my meal.

"Speaking of pleasure," he says, "one must do something for fun. Even your instructors at the training facility knew that."

"We did have moments of free time," I reply.

It is true. Not every minute of every day was dedicated to our training. Recruits became tired and needed a day of recovery, or their minds wandered and refused to focus. Though some were against the policy, Molers for example, the head of the facility decreed that a day of relaxation be allowed. In reality, we only received five hours devoted to ourselves, free to do as we please, so long as we did not leave the facility or break any of the rules, but recruits snuck out all the time, myself included. If the Martial Diplomatic Corps allowed its recruits a moment of rest, it makes sense that the arbiters in the field would be allowed the same, though I have a suspicion that Commandant Paq's day of relaxation benefits him and not those under his command.

"Out here, it is equally important to have periods where we let loose and rest."

I place my fork on my empty plate, listening to the Commandant's words, wondering where he is going with this conversation.

"There is not much we can do out here in the wilds, but we found a way to entertain ourselves."

"Entertain?" Commander Vye says.

"Yes," replies Commandant Paq. He leans closer to me. "Do you know what a hunt is?"

The notion is foreign to me. I have never heard of such a thing and do not recall anything being mentioned in any of my lessons at the training facility about a hunt, much less what it entails. "No, sir."

Commandant Paq smiles and my blood turns to ice. "It is most engaging and thrilling."

"And just what is the nature of this hunt?" asks Commander Vye.

"A very sporting kind."

My gaze darts between the two of them, wondering what Commandant Paq refers to, but I have a feeling that I am going to find out.

"Please tell."

The velvety nature of Commander Vye's voice unnerves me, and I know that she is just entertaining Commandant Paq.

"We go on a hunt."

"Hunt?" the word is out of my mouth before I have a chance to process what he is talking about.

"Yes, a hunt."

"And just what sort of hunt is this?" Commander Vye's voice darkens.

"The barbarians out here are numerous and need a bit of a reminder about whom is in charge. So, every once in a while, when my people are restless, we engage in a hunt."

I do not like the sound of this.

"Tell me more," Commander Vye encourages him.

"There is no good way to tell you, but you may join us."

Commandant Paq's offer unnerves me. It is one thing to uphold the laws of Arel, but hunting down another for entertainment does not seem right; but then, they are just barbarians, aren't they?

"We do not wish to impose," replies Commander Vye, but Commandant Paq refuses to listen.

"Nonsense. It is no imposition. I insist that you join us."

"We are on a tight schedule…"

"You must come. Your young arbiter here seems interested."

"No, I'm…" I begin.

"She is!" insists the commandant.

The hell I am.

"I'm sorry, Commandant…"

"It's decided," says Commandant Paq, interrupting Commander Vye.

"Well, then," Commander Vye raises her glass, "may the best hunter win."

Pleased, Commandant Paq claps me on the shoulder, almost knocking me over. "We will leave when the sun rises, and I thank you for agreeing to join me."

Do we even have a choice?

Chapter 17

The Hunt

Lines of burnt red peek through the rectangular windows of the room I stay in as I lay awake in bed, still on top of the sheets, having not bothered to cover myself; not that it matters since I had a fitful sleep. More red appears on the wall, transforming from slits to squares, to blocks. I get up and cringe when I notice how wrinkled my uniform is and scold myself for not taking it off before going to bed. At least I have another one. I pull it out of my duffel and put it on after straightening the wrinkled one, hoping that hanging it up will help it look less creased.

The soft swoop of the door across the hall as it closes alerts me that Commander Vye has already risen, dressed, and waits for me to report. Tucking my shirt in, I hurry out the door while still braiding my hair, so that it stays out of my face and is contained. She remains silent, but still manages to give me that scrutinizing look of hers, which always makes me feel as though I am being judged, before walking down the hall, up the steps, and out the door, while I follow without a word. Commandant Paq waits for us, pacing back and forth in an impatient manner, and I wonder how long he has been doing that, or if he even bothered to go to bed last night.

"You're both ready. Good. Good."

Neither Commander Vye, nor I respond, but Commandant Paq doesn't seem to care as he nods at a nearby arbiter who hurries off and returns with two more, dragging a man in chains: the same barbarian I had seen yesterday. The animal—he might as well be one with all the grunting noises that escape his mouth—yanks at the restraints, almost pulling the arbiters restraining him down with him, but they regain their balance and haul the barbarian toward us, throwing him to the ground. Hatred fill his eyes as he glowers at us.

"Let him go," Commandant Paq commands.

The arbiters nod and drag the barbarian to the open gate where they undo his restraints and jump back. The couth springs for them before darting away, as bullets riddle the ground next to his feet. A few seconds later, after he has assessed the situation, he runs off, disappearing into the brush.

"Choose your weapon," says Commandant Paq as another arbiter steps forth carrying an open case full of knives and holds it before me.

The entire situation unnerves me. My eyes dart to Commander Vye, who inclines her head, giving her approval. Knowing I have no choice, as Commandant Paq's presence bears down upon me, I pick a knife, weighing it in my hands and put it back, choosing another, handling one blade after another, until I settle upon one that feels natural within my palm. I say nothing as I take my chosen weapon and tie its sheath around my waist, next to my pistol, ignoring Commandant Paq's impatient sigh.

"You will not need that," he says to me, pointing at my pistol.

I glower at him. I go nowhere without it and do not wish to leave it behind while I am about to embark into unknown territory with a man whose temperament is less than ideal, or as Faya would put it: neurotic. He thrusts his beefy hand toward me and I unhook my pistol from its holster, placing it in his outstretched palm, cringing as he drops it in a box held by another arbiter.

"Everyone ready?" asks Commandant Paq.

People nod and mumble, "Yes, sir."

"On the count of three. One… Two…"

"What is the prize?" I ask, interrupting the commandant, and Commander Vye's startled expression informs me that she did not expect my inquiry.

"Pardon?" Commandant Paq replies.

"This is sport, is it not?" I say. "So, there must be a prize if one wins."

Commandant Paq's eyes darken.

An inward smirk gloats at how my question caught the commandant off-guard, but I keep my outward appearance impassive and unemotional. "There is a prize, isn't there?"

Commandant Paq's refusal to answer my question does not go unnoticed. "Go!" he yells and the arbiters allowed to join in the hunt rush out of the compound and into the brush, crashing as they go, making enough noise to frighten every critter in the wilderness. Did they not pass basic training? Or is all this noise their feeble attempt to strike fear into their prey? I watch as Commandant Paq leads the charge with Commander Vye joining in, though she seems to be going through the motions more than enjoying the activity itself, and after a minute passes, I am left alone, standing in the compound, while dust snakes slither through the wisps blown by the wind, winding their way to my toes.

Crunching footsteps attract my attention and I twist in their direction, spotting the plebeian Commander Vye and I had come with as he stops, holding an armful of garden tools—no doubt it is his job to clean them—and watches me. I cannot read his face as he masks his thoughts, but one thing is certain: the anger that had always been present is absent. I tear myself away. He is not important.

Touching the covered blade of my knife and reassuring myself that it is there, I pick up my feet and jog through the gate, after the others. I reach the edge of the grassy field and stop, looking around as the others charge forward and to the overgrown brush beyond. They will never catch the barbarian mottled in a group like that and thrashing around, mirroring a herd of buffalo as it flees a predator.

I change direction and head east, while they go south.

I hurry through the waist high grass, running for the overgrowth beyond, ignoring the stings of the blades as they strike my face in retaliation for disturbing their peaceful existence. There is no point in worrying about alerting the barbarian to my presence. He already knows that we hunt him, as Commandant Paq's arbiters had made certain of, but once I enter the trees, I should be able to disguise my presence. He will not head south for long, not with all the others rushing in that direction, leaving only three other possibilities, east being one of them.

I near the edge of the field and quicken my pace, bursting from the tall grass and into the dense vegetation, shadowed under the dwelling of the trees. I stop. Controlling my breathing, I creep through the jungle, past the trunk of a tree thicker around than the columns of the training facility, and those are a minimum of three yards in diameter, while its branches hang low from the thick foliage, weighed down by leaves the length of a cart. Being careful not to make any noise, I reach up and guide one of the jade leaves, which would serve better as a curtain, out of my path, ignoring the line of driver ants that crawl across the branch and up the tree, forming their own spiraling staircase. A trickle of wind sneaks inside this dark dwelling, brushing my flushed and moist cheeks, warning me of a change in the weather. Glancing up through the dense foliage above me, I manage to spot bulbous slate-colored clouds building in the sky. The wind changes, bringing with it an increase in humidity, which means that a storm brews on the horizon, leaving me no more than 30 minutes to find shelter. It will also make tracking the barbarian difficult. Good for him, not for me.

I hike the perimeter of the jungle, keeping the area where Commandant

Paq and his party had gone in sight, hoping to reach it before the rain starts and ruins any chance of tracking the barbarian. Climbing over logs and raised tree roots, I navigate my way through the wilderness, using my view of the compound as my marker, not wanting to become lost in this place. I have never been outside of Arel before, but remember the warnings about the outside world well. The fear of becoming lost and dying, something that the instructors at the training facility instilled in each of us, settles in the forefront of my mind, warning me to be vigilant. A flash of lightning rips my focus away from my hike. Jerking my head upward, I realize that the storm is almost upon me. Another flash of lightning lights up the darkening sky as the wind picks up, and I turn to seek safety underneath a tangled mesh of leaves, which might prevent the threatening rain from soaking me, when I pause. Rose moss carpets the moist ground before me, but a portion of it is broken off, jagged and smushed as though someone had stepped on it while in a hurry.

Kneeling, I lift the bit of damaged moss, inspecting it, trying to determine whether this had been done by an animal or a human. As I move some of the moss aside, I notice a footprint: human and made by a shoe with little tread on it. He did change direction once reaching the trees. Scraping more of the moss, sticks, and leaves away, I uncover more footprints. I glance in the direction they point to—deeper in the jungle. Intrigued, and not wishing to fail, I jump to my feet and follow the footprints, taking care not to make too much noise so as not to alert my prey to my presence. Silence is a skill taught to all recruits at the training facility, and I utilize mine to its fullest extent, avoiding sticks and rotted logs, doing my best to step on solid ground.

A bent orchid catches my eye, its white petals contrasting well against the dark green backdrop. I stop next to it and check it, noting that its petals are not wilted or dull in color, but still elastic and vibrant. A drop of rain dots my jacket. Undaunted, I continue, following his tracks and find more in the ground, unhidden, exposed for all to see. I jump onto my good fortune and follow them, charging through the trees, allowing the tracks to take me where they will. Some are close together from when he walked, while others are a little more spaced apart from when he ran. Underneath the lightning sky and the thunder that rumbles overhead, I chase after these tracks, expecting to find the barbarian any second when…

I stop.

A cliff drops away in front of me, having almost tricked me into charging over it and to my death. Panting, I stare down its precipice, considering myself lucky to have stopped in time and wondering where he could have gone, or if he had fallen to his death.

I'm such a fool!

Those tracks were too exposed and easy to spot. The barbarian had tricked me. He wanted us to think that he had gone over the edge and fallen to his demise, but, assuming he knows this area well, he would know better. More drops of rain pelt my shoulder as another roll of thunder warns me to seek safety. I ignore it. Angered over having been deceived, I want to find this barbarian and teach him that Arelians are not to be trifled with. I go back to one of the tracks that has led me here, dropping to my knees, skidding in the dirt as I do so, and reexamine the footprint. I notice that there seems to be two: one placed over the other. He had backtracked by walking backwards and restepping in his original tracks. To the unsuspecting person, it appears as though he had continued onward when, in fact, he did not.

I change direction and retrace the tracks, following back to where I had first discovered them, hoping to learn where my prey had gone. A burst of thunder strikes above me, releasing a downpour that soaks my clothes within minutes. The hounding rain fuels my rage and I charge ahead, forgetting to conceal my own presence within the wilderness, not caring if he knows that I am in pursuit as he appears to already be aware of it. My left foot stomps upon a cluster of moss and slides on the muddy ground, threatening to impede my efforts, but I regain my balance and continue. Dark lines of rain fill the void in front of me, making it impossible to see where I am going.

My foot smashes through a rotted log and I fall face first into the brown mud. Coughing and lifting myself onto my elbows, I wipe the muck from my eyes and blink several times in an effort to clear my vision, and stop. The mud looks to have been disturbed, as though someone has slid and fallen, much like myself. I crawl through the slick ooze and scrutinize my finding, spotting the broken branch of a nearby bush with a mud stain smeared on it. This new set of tracks is different. The uneven spacing and more indented nature of one footprint over the other means that the barbarian has injured himself and is limping.

I haul myself to my feet, allowing the rain to wash some of the mud from my uniform, and continue my pursuit. My boots squish in the mud as the slime oozes between their tread, while I trek through the jungle, taking great pains to remain silent, hoping to sneak up on my prey. My scalp stings from the rain that pounds it as it pours from the sky, punishing me for being outside when it appeared. My wet hands reach for the hilt of the knife Commandant Paq had me choose, but they keep slipping every time I try to grip it. Unable to dry them, I shake some of the water from them, knowing it won't do any good in all this rain, and grasp the knife again, freeing it from its sheath, and readying it for the unexpected.

I hear movement. Unable to determine if it is the barbarian or the wildlife that dwells in the trees, I keep my focus straight ahead, hoping that he will not suspect I know he is here. I creep across the muddy ground, doing my best to maintain my balance, lift a bit of foliage out of my view, being careful to not expose myself, and peek around the broad leaf. A dark shape hobbles 20 yards in front of me. Brushing past the frond, I dart behind the trunk of another tree, glad that the drumming of the pouring rain masks my movements. I peer around the tree's wide base and pull back just as the barbarian turns and glances in my direction. I hope he has not spotted me.

Taking two deep breaths, I ease around the tree and watch as the dark shape continues to stagger away from me, melding into the obscure shapes beyond us. I scurry from the tree and drop to my knees behind a thorn bush, cursing when one of its thorns pricks my exposed skin. Rain streams down my forehead, coating my eyes and causing me to blink with constant fervor in an effort to see. Certain that he is unaware of my presence, I dart out from behind the thorn bush and creep up behind him, walking on my tippy toes so as not to splash in the puddles, holding my knife behind me with the blade pointed downward.

His left leg drags behind him as he limps forward, and I notice the blood-soaked rag he has tied around his thigh in an effort to bandage a fresh wound. He pauses. The veins in my neck pulse from the adrenaline coursing through my body as I stop, mirroring him, willing him to not turn around. He stands still, his head up and alert, listening for anything out of the ordinary, making me thankful for the second time in mere minutes that the rain masks my presence. The hilt of the knife cuts into my palm as drops of water fall from the tip of the blade and to the ground, blending with the running streams that have formed in the mud, while I release the breath trapped in my lungs.

A whistle breaks the terse atmosphere.

I sprint the remaining feet between us just as the barbarian whips around and notices me for the first time. Despite the slick mud, I close the distance and spring for him, raising my knife. He ducks out of the way, but his injured leg impedes his agility, allowing me to catch him around the waist, dragging us both to the ground. We roll in the mud, its slime coating our bodies and making my grip on my knife falter. He knocks it from my hand. A sudden pain grips my face as he punches me with his free fist before ramming his elbow into my shoulder. Bracing my left foot on the slick ground, I push into it with all my strength and flip us over, penning him below me, a moment short-lived as he flings me to the side and we roll through the muck once more, stopping with me trapped between him and the earth and his right elbow pressing into my throat.

Choking, and unable to breathe, I flail my hand, scooping up a fistful of mud, and rub it into the barbarian's eyes. He jerks back, clawing at his face. Seizing my opportunity, I throw him off me, bringing both my feet up and ramming them into his stomach. He writhes on the ground, rubbing his fingers into his eyes to clear them of mud. I jump to my feet, searching for my knife. A small speck of metal glints in the torrent environment. I start for it, but notice that the barbarian has regained his senses. Changing direction, I tackle him, forcing him to the ground, but he throws me off. Staring at the sky, I see a blur of movement as his fist heads for me. I block it, seize his wrist, and wrench his arm, twisting in such a manner that I flip him over me and onto his back.

I scramble for my knife. Strong hands seize my left ankle, preventing me from reaching it and forcing me onto my stomach as mud splashes around me. Before he can pen me a third time, I ram my foot into his injured leg and he recoils, crying out in agony. I dart for the knife, scrambling through the mud, a predator desperate to kill its prey. I hear the barbarian's wrathful cries as he limps for me. My hand grasps the knife. The barbarian leaps for me, but I roll out of the way, spring to my knees, and stab him in his uninjured leg. He drops to the ground, clutching his wound.

Seizing my chance, I spring to my feet and kick him in the chest, knocking him to the ground, before straddling him, stretching my leg out to pen one of his arms and placing my left forearm across his neck, while raising my knife for the kill strike. His unintelligible grunts fuel his fury at having lost and he spits in my face, but I remain firm in my hold of him.

"Go ahead, you Arelian filth," he hisses.

I raise my knife higher.

"You attack my village and hunt me like a dog."

I stop.

Attack his village? It is the barbarians that keep attacking us.

A grin breaks across his face, exposing the missing teeth in his mouth as he realizes that I have no clue what he is talking about.

"Kill me!"

My knife hangs in midair.

"KILL ME!"

I lower my knife.

Looking into his vengeful eyes, I see a man who wants to die, while at the same time, wishes to destroy me, and I am reminded of the ones I killed in the name of Arelian justice; they still haunt me at night when I am alone, when I try to sleep. In that moment, I realize that he is correct about one thing: I have hunted him down the way any predator stalks their prey, participating in a sport that had disgusted me when Commandant Paq first mentioned it the night before. Am I no better than him?

Rising to my full height, I release the barbarian, refusing to commit murder for entertainment. I cannot give him what he wants. "Go," I say.

Keeping his eyes planted on me, the barbarian struggles to get on his knees, before forcing himself to his feet, standing at an odd angle to avoid injuring his leg any further. Realizing that he will not get far with his injuries, I search the ground for a stick that can be used as a staff and find one, picking it up and handing it to him.

"Go!" I wave the stick at him.

Still uncertain of my motives, he takes the stick and backs away. Before he can turn around and take his first step, a knife shoots out of the trees and strikes him in the heart. Stunned, I reach for him, and his hand stretches for mine as he falls to the ground, plummeting down a hill to be buried in the quick mud below, with only the robotic drumbeat of the rain mourning his demise.

Harsh footsteps stomp on the rotting vegetation on the ground as they charge from behind the brush and toward me as I stand poised in the rain, with water dripping from my nose and the ends of my braid, staring at the bottom of the hillside and the lifeless body below, still grappling with the harsh reality that a man who had once been alive is now dead. The footsteps cease once they reach me.

"Well?" Commandant Paq's harsh voice rips through the rain's drumbeat and drowns the voices of his hunting party. "Where is he?"

"Down there," I reply, my voice hollow, aware of all the eyes that watch me.

"Is he dead?"

I face Commandant Paq, my dislike for him intensifying beyond the point of loathing until it reaches a point where it boils over and transforms into utter hatred. "If you are so uncertain of your aim, then perhaps you should climb down there and find out for yourself. Or are you too lazy to do even that?"

"Why, you insolent"—he raises his fist to strike me, but just like before, his hand stops in midair held by the firm grip of Commander Vye.

"I believe I have warned you before about punishing my arbiter." Commander Vye's merciless tone causes a slight quiver in Commandant Paq's wrathful expression, but his anger at having been humiliated twice in one day by her outweighs any fear.

"I saved her life and this is how you thank me?" he hisses at her.

"Is this true?" Commander Vye asks me.

"No, ma'am," I reply.

"You lying…"

"Explain yourself," Commander Vye commands me, cutting off the commandant.

"He was no threat to Arel," I reply. Upon her questioning look, I continue. "We are charged with protecting Arel from threats both within and without. This barbarian had been captured by Commandant Paq, not because he meant Arel any harm, but because he was to be used for sport."

"And how did you come to this conclusion?" asks Commander Vye.

"Why else would the Commandant release someone he had captured hours before? Why else are we all out here?"

"And your insolence toward him?"

"No excuse, ma'am."

"There you have it," Commander Vye says to Commandant Paq while still holding his wrist in the air. "She is upholding the laws of Arel, and since you have failed to prove that the barbarian is an immediate threat to our city, she had no reason to kill him."

"And her insolence toward a commanding officer?" Commandant Paq demands.

"Will be dealt with, by me." Commander Vye releases his wrist and he jerks away, huffing in a manner to make his anger known.

Commandant Paq takes a step back, waiting for Commander Vye to turn her attention to me, before charging her with his fists raised. She ducks out of the way in an instant and counters his movements with a punch to his left shoulder. Furious, he leaps for her, but she sidesteps out of the way, forcing him to plow into the mud. Commander Vye stands over him, as though to ask if he plans to continue this nonsense, and in answer to her unspoken question, he grabs a fistful of mud and flings it at her. She turns and dives to the ground, having expected this maneuver, and lands in a push-up position before springing back to her feet and kicking him in the jaw, while the rest of us watch, and my amazement at her abilities causes me to forget, for a moment, about the reason we are here in the first place. Stunned, Commandant Paq lies in the mud, shaking his head and rubbing his jawline, debating whether he wishes to continue, but before he can decide, Commander Vye pounces on him, wrapping her arms around his neck and placing him in a headlock.

"Are you finished?" she asks him.

In answer to her question, he raises both hands in surrender.

She releases him and stalks away. I do not wait for her to tell me to follow and chase after her, knowing where I belong and what awaits me once we reach the compound.

Chapter 18

The Bell

The rain still beats down upon us when we reach the outpost. Shouts ring out, alerting those within to our presence, and the gates open, allowing us entrance as we wander inside with Commander Vye still in the lead and me right behind her, while Commandant Paq trails behind us both. The eerie silence warns me that the others within have taken notice of his demotion. Commandant Paq senses it as well, and he marches ahead, storming past us and to the center of the square where we all stop.

Strength in our kind! Strength in numbers! Strength over weakness!

The Arelian chant echoes in the background as arbiters performing drills repeat our most sacred beliefs. Without thinking, I chant along with them, repeating the words that have been drilled into my mind since birth under my breath.

"Listen up!" shouts Commandant Paq, and the arbiters inside cease their activities to hear what he has to say, except for the guards along the wall as they remain diligent in their duty to protect the compound from foreign invasion.

A circle forms around us. I suck in a deep breath, filling my lungs to their full capacity as I await what is coming to me for my unruliness. Speaking to the commandant in the manner that I did is unforgivable, and I should have been more respectful instead of allowing my emotions to control me. Dissent is not tolerated, least of all from a young arbiter such as myself.

"Arbiter Noni has committed an infraction: insubordination," continues Commandant Paq, "and because of that, she must now face justice. Her punishment will be—"

"The ringing of the bell," interrupts Commander Vye, undoing whatever plans the commandant had of demonstrating to me, and her, who is in charge.

"Pardon?"

"She is under my command," says Commander Vye, "and as such, it is up to me to decide her fate, not you. Or do you deny Arel's laws?"

The commandant's face turns purple as he struggles to control the rage roiling within him at having been put in his place by Commander Vye for a third time, but he rethinks his decision to lash out at her, no doubt concerned that there might be a marshal among us.

Marshals are elite arbiters, kept separate from the rest. They hide among us, pretending to be us, but their duty is to seek out arbiters who disobey the Arelian Council, and are therefore considered traitors, sworn to find these treacherous leeches and execute them, holding the power of life or death over us all. Commandant Paq has no way of knowing if we brought one with us—of course, neither do we—and judging by the way this visit to the outpost has gone, he must have concluded that one is here and rethought his reaction to my commander's interruptions.

"I deny nothing," he says.

The gathered crowd backs away, allowing a group of five arbiters through, while on the other end, past a cluster of outbuildings, a post is set up with a single bell atop it: my goal. I have only seen this punishment performed once, back at the training facility. The person being reprimanded is given a beating by five of their peers, after which, they must reach the bell and ring it, while avoiding certain obstacles, before the timer ends, which is set to five minutes. The person whom I watched perform this feat failed, and I remember his mangled corpse as they carted his body away, tossing it over the inner wall to be devoured by the wild dogs kept below.

Now it is my turn.

Taking off my uniform jacket, I stalk over to the center of the square, dropping it as I reach the start of my trial. The other five arbiters gather around me, each looking as though they relished the chance to take out their frustrations, their anger, and their disappointments on another, forcing me to suffer what they have endured under their commanding officer.

"You all know the rules," Commandant Paq's voice echoes off the walls of the buildings surrounding us. "You five are not to maim or kill the runner."

I am considered the runner since I must race for the bell after my thrashing. Sweat coats my palms as I ponder the obstacles I will be forced to face, not knowing what they will be as they are never the same, and depend upon the situation and who the runner is.

"You all know the punishment for failing to obey this simple command," continues Commandant Paq, "and I will not tolerate disobedience. When the gun fires, you will cease and get back in formation. The runner will have five minutes to ring the bell."

A timer is brought out to the edge of the square and bold, red numbers fill its transparent display.

Commandant Paq pulls out his weapon and readies it. A smirk crosses his lips as he glances at me, no doubt imagining my demise, confident that, in the end, he has won this power struggle between him and Commander Vye, thus proving his superiority.

"NOW!"

I gulp down a stringy glob of spittle that forms in my mouth as my heart races and glare at the irate faces surrounding me as they

close in. One charges me. I dodge, grabbing his leg and pulling him
to the ground before springing back to my feet. If I am to endure a
beating, there is no reason why I can't deal out a few blows of my
own. Another rushes me. I block. Before I can do anything else, a
fist rams into my back, between my shoulder blades, followed by a
kick to the back of my knee, forcing me to kneel. I try to stand back
up, but the sharp heel of another's boot cuts into the bottom of my
chin, forcing my head back. Air rushes out of my lungs, causing me
to gasp as someone kicks me in the stomach, before another strikes
me in the back, and I crumple to the ground in a fetal position,
holding my arms up by my face in a feeble attempt to protect it.

Blood spills from my mouth and mixes with the pool of water
on the pavement, turning it crimson. Every part of my body aches
and screams in agony as the blows keep coming, each more powerful than the last. I seize the ankle of one, causing him to lose his
balance and crash to the ground, but her retaliates by kicking me
in the face, and the world goes white for a second as I teeter on the
verge of unconsciousness before my vision clears, reminding me of
where I am. Pain engulfs my side and I feel the hard knuckles of a
fist burrow into it, bruising a rib. My rigid muscles slacken.

The gun goes off.

Though disappointed that their moment of dealing out torture
is over, the five people around me cease their onslaught and back
away, melting into the line of arbiters, not wanting to be on the receiving end of Commandant Paq's wrath for disobeying orders.

The slow, melodic ticking of the timer as the seconds vanish fill
the dismal atmosphere as I lie on the pavement, unwilling to move,
as each breath I take stabs me a thousand times in the chest. I plant
my hands in the puddles on the ground and struggle to push myself
up as my arms waver beneath my weight and give out, causing me
to drop and splash in the pooled rainwater. A drop of blood escapes
from the corner of my lips and plops in the water, forming a small,
red dot amongst the silver backdrop of the pavement. The timer

beats in my ears, reminding me of lost seconds, precious seconds that I will never regain.

I sit up, placing my right foot on the ground and haul myself to my feet, weaving from side to side as my head spins. One unsteady step forward and my legs buckle beneath me. I land on all fours, splashing in the water as the rain continues to beat against my back, delivering its own punishment for my insolence and failure as a protector of Arel. I glance at the stoic faces around me, waiting for me to fail, but one face catches my attention: Chase. The plebeian we had brought with us stands in the back, underneath an awning, in the shadows and away from the notice of others: a white face among a sea of black. Is that concern he has for me, or disgust? Whatever sentiment he holds toward me, his nonconformity is enough to propel me onward.

I stand up, rising to my full height, as water drips down the sides of my temples and my soaked ponytail sticks to my back, while the bits of black strands that have escaped their hold glue themselves to my bloodied cheeks.

Four minutes left.

Inhaling, I run for the bell.

Splashing accompanies my frantic movements, performing a chord as I rush to beat the timer. A swooshing noise prickles my ears. It takes me a moment to recognize it as a knife that has been thrown, and I jump backward just in time to avoid being struck, landing on my back. I roll onto my stomach just as a boot crashes into the pavement where I had been, snatch the knife, and jam it onto my opponent's shin. Ignoring his cries of pain, I dart away, heading for the bell once more, having defeated my first obstacle, assuming he does not follow me.

I stretch out my legs, timing my breathing with my feet, as I race for the bell, leaving the square and entering a walkway with buildings on each side, aware that time is against me and what my fate is should it win. Something long and solid slams into my back, knocking the air from my lungs and propelling me forward, and once again, I find myself on the ground. I roll onto my back and face the arbiter leering over me, holding her stock prod with triumph and noting the sparks that fizzle on the end. My second obstacle.

She jabs the ground with her prod, just missing me as I roll to the side, clinking when it strikes the concrete, while a buzzing sound is released from it as the electricity that charges through it curses its missed opportunity at harming its prey. I jump to my feet. Before I can swing around and face her, she stabs me with the prod and my muscles seize from the electricity coursing through my body, forcing me to my knees. She jabs me again with it. Unable to move, I scream from the pain that riddles my body, while my mind turns toward the timer and the ever-decreasing number of seconds. She lifts the prod. I crawl through the pooled rainwater toward the bell, focusing my attention on it, wiling myself to move forward, when she jabs me again, and I curl into a ball from the electric charge. A maniacal laughter fills the air. Is that her? Is she gloating over my failure?

Struggling to ignore the pain, I roll onto my back, seize the prod, and rip it away from her grasp. Stunned, she stares at me unsure of what to do, but I do not give her a chance to come up with a solution, as I strike her in the stomach, forcing her to double over. Though dazed, and still in pain, I haul myself to my feet. She charges me. Raising the stock prod, my knuckles turning white from my strong hold on it, I stab her in the throat with it, watching as it bursts through the back of her neck, skewering her. I let go of the prod. Her body collapses on the ground, convulsing from the electrical charge, as blood pools around her neck and head, her horror-filled eyes staring at the dark sky.

I rip the prod from her wound and run off, leaving her there to die. Something metallic skids across the ground, heading toward me, and I spot the small, cylinder that has appeared from the crowd watching me. Recognizing it as a flash bomb, I know I have seconds to escape its blast. A steel ladder runs up the side of the building next to my left. I jump at it, climbing upward to the top, keeping my focus away from the flash bomb. A pop sounds as it detonates, releasing a bright, burst of white light and smoke, just as I reach the top of the ladder and close my eyes, avoiding the worst of the effects. Unable to see what awaits me on the ground, I climb downward and jump off. My head still spins a bit from my beating, but I cling to the side of the ladder to regain my sense of balance as I envision the bell and refocus my attention, reassessing my bearings in an effort to not get confused or lost in the smoke.

The drone of the time still beats in my head, reminding me of its impending end. A clearing in the smoke appears and I spot the bell. Not caring what lies ahead, I run for it. Rain pours around me as I charge for my goal, desperate to win, to prove that I am worthy of being an arbiter. Almost there. The bell nears and for a moment, I believe that I have passed, that nothing will stop me when…

A burning sensation strikes my right arm, just below the shoulder, as a bullet grazes me, and the distinct sound of a gunshot echoes around me. I keep going. Bullets pummel the ground in front of my feet and I skid to a halt to avoid them, turning around, and my moment of triumph abandons me as the guard that had accompanied Commander Vye and I to the outpost steps from the crowd and into the middle of the walk, observing me. I should have expected this. I trusted him to ensure my safety while outside the wall of Arel. Of course, they would use that trust against me to cause me to falter and second-guess myself. Such tactics are the norm in Arel when chastising an ornery individual.

He raises his rifle. I duck behind the corner of a building just as he fires and the bullet strikes the corner edge, leaving a coin-sized nick in it. Still clutching the stock prod, I consider my options, always aware to the timer's countdown. Soppy footsteps approach, masked by the hiss of the rain, but I remain still, engulfed by the deluge and doing my best to control the involuntary shivers that threaten to take my body hostage. Knowing that I have reached an impasse, doomed if I do and doomed if I don't, I decide to end this like an arbiter.

Scooping up a handful of pebbles, I peek around the corner and take note of where my adversary is, before throwing the pebbles away from me and toward the other end of the walkway. I charge him, using his momentary distraction against him, and plow into him, tackling him, but he does not remain down for long. As I prepare for a second attack, he jumps to his feet and kicks me in the stomach, while raising his rifle to finish me off. I ignore the pain, grab his weapon with both my hands, and drop to the ground, flinging him over me, followed by a backward somersault, landing atop him, straddling him, pinning him to the ground as I press his weapon into his throat. He attempts to wrestle the weapon from me and knock me off-balance, but rage fuels me, and I jerk the rifle, striking him in the face with it. Before he has a chance to recover from being stunned, I rip his helmet off and rail into him, pounding my fists into his face, until blood squirts from his nose and covers my battered fists, only stopping when I notice the reflection of the timer in the glass of the building next to us.

My time is up.

I pick up the rifle and strike him once more with it, making certain that he will not move, and look around, staggering to my feet and wobbling in place, while my head feels as though someone has slammed a sledgehammer into it.

Ten seconds remain. If I run for it, I will never reach the bell in time. If I do nothing, I fail. I check the rifle, making sure that it still has a round in there, realizing that this is my best chance. Calming the storm within me, blocking out the harsh yelling of the pounding rain, I raise the rifle, aim, and fire, letting my last hope ride on that single shot.

It strikes the bell and the crystal, crisp ringing of it sings in my ears, drowning the harsh screech of the timer.

"Arbiter Noni," Commandant Paq approaches me, gloating, convinced that he has won, "you have failed."

"Failed?" Commander Vye's single word punctures through the

torrential rain, stopping the commandant in his tracks and his smirk turns into a scowl. "It is my understanding that she was to ring the bell. That is the rule you set forth."

"She never reached it."

"Did you say she had to? Did he?" Commander Vye stops in front a female arbiter, demanding an answer.

"No, ma'am," replies the arbiter, wishing that the commander had chosen another to answer her question.

The guard that I had beaten regains his senses and stands up, doing his best to pretend that I have not injured him at all, and watches the exchange between Commander Vye and Commandant Paq with interest.

"There, you have it," continues Commander Vye. "She did ring the bell, albeit in an unconventional way, but she did it nonetheless, and fulfilled the requirement you had set down. She followed the law of Arel. Are you choosing to do otherwise?"

Commandant Paq's scowl turns to concern as his gaze passes over the gathered crowd and considers the possibility that a marshal might be among us, knowing that if word gets back to the Arbiter Tribunal that he initiated the punishment of the bell, but failed to abide by its rules, he would be removed from command and not reassigned elsewhere.

"I am doing no such thing," he says, conceding his loss and allowing Commander Vye to achieve her fourth victory over him since our arrival.

I teeter a bit, exhausted, and on the verge of passing out.

"Arbiter Noni," Commandant Paq says so all can hear, "it appears that you have won the challenge of the bell and will remain as an arbiter of Arel, a true testament of our strength and commitment to order." He steps closer, closing the gap between us. "For now," he whispers to me and stalks away.

The guard snatches his weapon from me and walks off as well, while the other arbiters disperse.

"Come on," Commander Vye says to me, "let's get you cleaned up."

"Why?" I ask her, my voice almost undetectable in the thundering rain.

Commander Vye pauses, considering my question before looking me in the eyes, replying, "I chose the bell because I believed you could do it."

This sort of tenderness, if you can call it that, startles me, since the only side of Commander Vye I have ever witnessed was always the authoritative persona, doing what is necessary to ensure that I follow and enforce that law.

"How could you possibly..."

"I see a lot of me in you." Commander Vye notices my confused expression and continues. "I have only known three others who have ever passed the bell: two are now dead and the third was a lot like you in her youth."

Before I have a chance to say another word, she ushers me toward the medical wing, thus finishing the conversation.

Chapter 19

Attacked

The sun hides behind two long, boat-shaped clouds as I step out of the building that housed my sleeping quarters for the last two days, adjusting my bag on my right shoulder to ease the pressure of the weight I carry. Commandant Paq stands next to the transport vehicles, his hands clasped behind his back and a stern expression upon his face, no doubt still fuming over yesterday's events. Swallowing the warm salvia that has collected on my tongue, I walk to the closest transport vehicle, which also happens to be the one he is not standing next to, and start to open the door when he stops me.

"Allow me," he says, and opens the back door to the second transport.

"This one will do," I reply.

"I insist."

I know better than to try and argue with him. Closing the door to the vehicle I had wanted to get in, I step over to the other one, looking Commandant Paq straight in the eyes as I sit down, saying, "Thank you, sir."

"My pleasure."

His sudden niceness and smile unnerves me, and considering the way Commander Vye crushed his ego yesterday after the hunt, I wonder what his plans are, or if his ulterior motive is to placate us so that we deliver a favorable account of his behavior to the council back in Arel.

Commander Vye walks out of the barracks and straight to a transport vehicle—the one in front of me—and gets in, not bothering to speak to Commandant Paq or wait for him to say whatever prepared speech he had. Our next destination is another outpost, and I think she just wants to get there as fast as possible, having had enough of this place. A part of me wonders what she intends to report back in Arel, but I shake it off, knowing that it does not matter, nor will it affect me, not that I have much control over that anyway. I look around the transport I am in and notice that only me and one of the guards is in there, besides the driver. Is this on purpose? I think it odd that Commander Vye did not sit in the same vehicle as me, but remind myself that I cannot always depend on her to be there. I must learn to do things on my own, as one day, I might be running my own division within Arel.

The engine starts, and for a moment, I believe that I see the door to Commander Vye's transport open a little before shutting again as it moves. Had she been about to step out and find out where I am? I shake off the question. She must know that I am here, but we do have a schedule to keep and the drivers do not stop for anything because of it, knowing that arriving late at our next destination will not be tolerated.

We pass through the gates and Commandant Paq gives one final wave as we leave, causing me to ponder the reason for his sudden cheeriness, and deciding that it must be because we are leaving. I settle into my seat, clutching my bag tighter, as the right rear wheel sinks into a pothole, before popping out and jostling me and banging my head on the side on the vehicle. Grimacing, I rub the sore spot on my right temple, wishing that the road was smoother. The silence in the vehicle, aside from the roar of the engine, demonstrates just how isolated I am here, cut off from anyone I know. I would even welcome the plebeian boy's company just to have a familiar face.

I look at the guard in the front seat, his helmet concealing his face so that no one knows his identity. He could be a female for all I know. The guards of Arel always wear full body armor and keep the visor of their helmets down so that their identity remains anonymous, since they tend to be the ones that carry out the most brutal of punishments within the city.

As the trip drags on, I find myself desiring some form of conversation, anything to help pass the time. "How many times have you been outside the wall?"

No response.

I am not surprised by it and settle on staring out the window at the dusty road, grasses, and trees that dot the landscape and the ridgeline in the distance, as we drive along a road with a sharp drop off, reminding me of how far away from home I am. A muffled popping sound, drowned by the engine, pulls me from my musings. Craning my head and listening further, I recognize its familiarity and wonder why I am hearing it out here. Are we nearing the third outpost as they practice drills?

It happens again, and my mind jumps to action as I notice a flash from the ridgeline before the ground in front of the leading transport is struck, followed by a slew of gunfire. Another mortar shell strikes the space between my transport and the one ahead of me, creating an earsplitting explosion that causes my ears to ring as fire and smoke consume the ground, and I am unable to see the leading vehicle.

"Look out!" I scream.

The driver cranks the wheel and the transport swerves, skidding and stopping only when one of the rear wheels hangs over the

edge of the hill. I place my hands on the back of the seat in front
of me, catching my breath as I regain my senses from having been
tossed around in all the commotion, glad that the ringing in my
ears subsides enough for me to hear a familiar voice shout orders.
Shouts and gunfire shake me back into the present, and I look out
my grimy window as figures clad in black with their heads wrapped
in tattered rags race for us, weapons raised. I duck just as they fire
and the bullets riddle the side of the transport with holes, shattering the glass, its shards covering me and slicing the few bits of
uncovered skin I have, while what sounds like a hundred pebbles
pelting the metal sheeting pounds my ears. Knowing I need to get
out, I reach for the door handle, but stop the moment the transport
starts to tip over the ridge.

"Get us out of here!" I yell at the driver, but receive no response.

A part of me guesses the reason for his silence, and when I
glance at the driver's seat, a grim line seals my lips as my suspicions are confirmed: the driver is dead, but I cannot stay here, even
though the transport is my best protection from these raiders. More
gunfire echoes from behind me as the third transport arrives and
its occupants jump out, firing at the raiders, who turn their attention away from me and to their new opponent. Seizing my chance,
I ease out of my seat, balancing myself so as to keep the vehicle I
am in from toppling over the edge, and reach for the driver, shoving
him aside as I crawl into his bloodied seat. Chaos reigns around
me, outside of my protective barrier, as I settle into the driver's seat
and put the transport into gear, frowning as my hand slips from the
sanguinary gearshift, punching the gas, hoping that the other three
wheels would pull the fourth one onto solid ground. The whine of
spinning wheels fuels my already racing heart as my pulse thuds in
my ears, mixing with the gunfire outside.

A tremendous bang resounds on the hood of the transport as
the plebeian boy and another arbiter place their weight on it in an
effort to keep it from falling over the edge.

"Get out!" the arbiter screams at me.

I reach for the door handle and push it downward before pausing. A lone whistle breaks through the melee.

Instinct compels me to duck and cover my head, seconds before another mortar shell detonates five yards away from the transport, and the force of the explosion shifts the vehicle further over the ledge, and it drops over the ridge with me trapped inside. The transport turns end over end as it tumbles down the hill toward the bottom, and I am helpless against its momentum and the force that reduces me to the role of a bouncing ball, jostling me around without mercy, until crashing on the bottom. Through unfocused eyes, I glance out the opening where the windshield had once been, and at the crystal blue sky above, before everything goes black.

Chapter 20

Alone

My head begs for relief from the imaginary sledgehammers boring into it as my mind regains consciousness, and I open my eyes, blinking three times in an effort to focus them and clear the dust from them. Echoes from the attack above reach me, but I feel as though I am far away from it, as though a fog has enveloped me, shielding me from it. I wriggle my fingers and toes, satisfied that I can still move, despite the earthquake in my head. Twisting around, I realize that I have somehow gotten thrown back into the back and I am laying sprawled across it with my legs tangled up on the top of the seat near the rear window with my head near the footwell. Groaning from the pain in my skull, I maneuver myself, swinging my legs downward as I position myself right side up, taking a moment to pause as blood flows from my head to the rest of my body, and a tiny bit of dizziness wafts around me, dissipating in seconds, but the pain remains, making me wish the blood vessels would quit pulsating in my temple.

I place my arms on the seat in front of me and haul myself forward, crying out and falling backward as a crippling, stabbing pain seizes my left side. The fog surrounding my brain vanishes, allowing me to feel the full extent of my injuries. With shaking hands, I lift up my jacket and shirt, revealing a massive bruise, the size of two fists, and as I press my fingers against my ribs, I wince, taking in a sharp breath; my ribs are bruised at the very least, maybe even broken. Again, I place my hands on the top of the seat in front of me, forcing myself to ignore the pain like I have been conditioned to do, and haul myself over it and into the front next to the deceased driver. Taking a moment to steady my breathing, I spot the driver's sidearm and seize it, unstrapping its holster from around his waist and place it around mine, wincing as each movement reminds me of my unknown injuries. Though I know that I have the possibility of a cracked rib, there may still be other injuries as well: the silent, fatal kind.

Crunching brush alerts me to another's presence and I crouch behind the dashboard. A figure moves through the trees and underbrush, not bothering to practice any form of stealth, and as I peer closer, I spot the white skin and ragged clothing; the plebeian boy has been sent down to assist me. Before I have a chance to call out to him to be quiet, I sneeze, and the congestion in my sinuses clears for a moment, alerting me to another problem: gas. I glance in the side mirror and curse as I notice gasoline spurting from the tank, admonishing myself for not being aware of this earlier. One spark and we are both dead.

I turn the handle to the passenger door and push against it, but it refuses to budge and allow me to escape. The puddle of gasoline grows. I need to get out. I bring my feet up and kick at the passenger door, and continue kicking it, until it hangs open enough where I know I will fit, and crawl through it, clinging to it the moment I get out. The transport has landed a few feet away from another drop off. I lean forward to glance downward at the tops of the trees and their wide, emerald fronds and the faint mist that envelops them, obscuring the bottom of the gorge and the soft roar below. Is there a river nearby? I try to envision the landscape around me and my place within it, but the pervasive smell of gasoline jerks me back to my current predicament.

More crunching brush distracts me and I watch as the plebeian boy—Chase? Is that his name?—runs toward me. The fool! Does he not smell the gas? Easing my way around the door, while gripping it as tight as I can to avoid slipping on the loose, mushy soil, I inch my way to the front of the vehicle and onto more solid ground. I have no time to rest or be relieved that I have escaped what could have been my coffin, for the plebeian boy races for me unaware of the danger that awaits.

"Stop!" I shout at him, waving my arms, but he ignores me and continues, while the skirmish above us rages, unconcerned about our plight.

A single zap confirms my worst fear. Knowing I have no choice, I sprint away from the transport, catching the plebeian boy around the middle, doing my best to force him to turn around, but he stumbles, causing me to fall as well. Another spark lights up above the puddle of gas, igniting it. Before I have a chance to regain my balance, both the plebeian and I slide toward the drop off, propelled by the force of the explosion, and disappear over it, plunging to an unknown fate.

I gasp as I strike hard ground and continue to roll downward. I do my best to tuck and roll, but the force of gravity negates my efforts. Bits of dirt fly everywhere, surrounding me, clogging my ears and getting inside my mouth as my world spins, and I hear nothing but the sounds of my grunting and groaning as twigs snap beneath me. A searing pain grips my right leg, and despite me crying out, I never hear it as it is masked by my continued tumble down the steep hill.

The ground vanishes beneath me. I feel as though I am hanging in the air, until I drop, whipped by the wind, before smashing into something hard that gives way underneath me and covers me, drenching my clothes and my hair. I have fallen in a river. I manage to break through the surface of the water long enough to take a deep breath, before being sucked under again by the current as it whisks me away, twisting and turning me in so many directions that I have no idea which way is up or down, as the foamy water fills my ears with its roar, encasing me in a dark and soundless bubble. I kick my legs and I am struck by an intense pain. I open my mouth to cry out, only to find myself choking on frigid water instead, coughing, sputtering, and inhaling more water, despite my attempts to breathe air.

Someone tries to grab me, but I push him away, thinking that he is a threat. I thrust my arms downward, propelling myself upward and out of the water long enough for me to hear a voice shout at me.

"Grab my hand!"

A part of my mind realizes that the plebeian boy is still with me, and it is him yelling at me to take his hand. I fling my arm outward and he seizes it, gripping it in his muscled and callous hand as he hauls me toward him, while he uses his other arm to swim for the riverbank. I try to kick in an effort to help swim, but my right leg does not want to cooperate, and each movement sends a shooting pain up it, causing my injured side to ache even more—a momentary relief from the constant pain I am in. Water gushes over my nose and mouth, forcing me to gag and cough; my convulsions make swimming to shore more difficult. Despite the trouble my actions pose, the plebeian manages to reach the riverbank and drags me onto the moist sand. Bits of it get into the tops of my pants, grating my skin, but I do not care, thankful to be able to breathe without water finding its way down into my lungs. A few more rounds of coughing and I am able to breathe better, but all the relief from that brings is an acute awareness that my leg sits at an odd angle, and the massive bruise on my side beneath my ribs has turned a shade darker.

The plebeian boy lays next to me, gasping for air, no doubt exhausted from having saved both of us, but his presence so close to mine disgusts me. He should not be lying on the ground, but looking for survivors of the attack, or at the very least, getting me something to drink, since my parched throat has decided to make itself known.

"Fetch me some water," I command him.

"Are you kidding me?"

I smack him for his insolence, my reflexive action indicative of what I have always been taught.

He jumps back, but refuses to rub his cheek where my hand has left a mark, glaring at me instead. "If you please, ma'am," he says in a controlled voice, "how am I supposed to do that?"

I release an exasperated sigh. "Use one of those broad leaves from the trees. Cup your hands if you must."

He glances at the leaves on the nearby trees which hang over the river, either unaware of our plight, or unconcerned, and sets his mouth in a firm line, as though he hadn't thought of using one of them as a way to hold water. I watch, doing my best not to disturb my leg or side, as he climbs up the trunk of one of the trees, reaches for one of the larger leaves, and jumps to the ground, breaking the frond free of its hold. He twists it into a cone as he steps toward the water, kneeling down and allowing the river to fill it, remaining there as he drinks his fill.

Aghast at how he ignores my need to drink, I struggle to get up, but fall back onto the sand cringing in pain. "What are you doing?" I demand.

"Getting a drink," he replies as though it should be obvious.

"Bring me some water this instant."

His empty hand clenches into a fist, but I ignore his irritated demeanor, focusing more on the makeshift cup in his hand that has just been refilled with water. Doing his best not to spill it, he brings it over to me, and though he tries to lower it so that I can take a sip, most of the water tumbles from the cone, covering my face and chest.

"Look what you've done!" I yell at him.

"It was an accident."

Again, he speaks to me as though we are equals. I raise my fist and prepare to strike him, but he catches it in midair, striking me off-guard as no plebeian has ever done such a thing before. It is not allowed.

"Bring me some more water, now," I say.

He drops my fist and the leaf cone, saying, "No."

No? He is refusing my command? "I order you to fetch me some more water."

"Get it yourself." The plebeian boy walks off into the trees, leaving me alone on the riverbank with the few birds I hear singing, the trees, and the river for company, all of them mocking me. I listen as his footsteps fade and all my haughtiness and desire to prove my dominance disappears. Cut off from the people in the transport, and having no idea where I am, I am on my own for survival, but my injuries may kill me before morning. As my mind wanders into the realm of self-pity, I scold myself, reminding myself that I am an arbiter, trained to be strong and to survive, so as to protect Arel: my city. If I die out here, how will I serve my city? As I ask myself that question, my heart sinks, remembering the outposts Commander Vye and I have visited and the impression they gave, telling me that Arel ignores those outside her walls. I am on my own.

Determined to not go out without a fight, I seize the makeshift cup and force myself onto my stomach, steeling myself for the pain that follows, and grinding my teeth together in an effort to not cry out; though, a few guttural noises do break free from my mouth. Using my one good leg and arms, I crawl toward the river, while my damaged leg screams at me to stop, begging for some relief from the pain that grips it, and judging by the sluggishness it displays, I conclude that it has swollen a great deal; hence, why I am unable to bend it very well. The sounds of the river grow louder as I inch my way for it and lean over the bank, staring at the small waves as the water rushes past below me, unconcerned about my presence. Thankful that I have long arms, I reach down and fill the cone before bringing it to my cracked lips and drink the satisfying liquid in one gulp. I scoop up some more water, devouring that as well.

A shiver runs over my shoulders, and for the first time, I notice that the sky is darkening. Though it can be sweltering during the day, temperatures can drop at night, and to avoid hypothermia, I will need to find some means of staying warm, though I think most of my shivering means my body is going into shock. I wobble on my stomach as I turn myself around and crawl to the tree line where I spot some underbrush, leaving a mangled line in the sand, reminiscent of the trails left by worms in the dirt. When I reach the edge of the trees, I pause, sucking in air in an effort to soothe my burning lungs, while the pain in my leg and side continue to tear at my resolve to survive. A branch shifts, and I think I see a faint shadow dart away, but cannot be certain. Is someone out there?

"Hello?" I call. "Chase?"

I know that I spoke the plebeian's name on the off-chance that he is still nearby and would come back and help me, but when no one responds, I am not surprised, and somewhat relieved. What if a raider is out here, biding his time for the perfect moment to kill me, or make me his slave? Deciding that there is little I can do about it if someone is out there studying me, I inch my way further into the brush and pull it over myself, covering my entire body as best I can, even scooping some dirt over me, hoping that it will act as insulation and keep my body heat contained. My eyes grow heavy after I finish, and I lie on the ground, staring through the latticed canopy at the deep purple sky above me, wondering if I will wake up the next morning, but my desire to remain awake is weaker than my body's insistence that I sleep, so I give in.

A fitful sleep dominates my night as unwanted dreams of the attack, my time at the factory and maternity ward, the riots, and my uncertain future attack me, taunting me, beckoning me to follow them into some dark abyss of nonexistence. A hand touches my shoulder, jerking me awake, and I snatch the weapon I had taken from the dead transport driver and point it at the person who dared to touch me in my moment of weakness. My eyes meet the plebeian's. What color are they?

"It's me!" he says, falling on his bottom in an effort to get away from my crazed expression and weapon.

I relax, but remain uncertain of his motives, or why he came back. "I thought you had gone."

"I came back."

"Why?" I demand, not bothering to disguise the anger or arrogance in my voice.

The plebeian glances around and shifts his hand to readjust his balance as he remains on the ground, wondering what I intend to do with my pistol, but his fingers rattle something, and for the first time, I realize there is a flask in the dirt next to us.

"Well?" I prod him.

"Because I will not be allowed back into Arel if I allow a citizen to die out here, and an arbiter at that."

"So, you need me to get back home."

His eyes turn to slits. "We need each other."

I scoff at his statement, though I know he is correct; there is just one problem: no one is looking for me. I remember my lessons well as a recruit, and one of those lessons was about how those who get lost outside the wall are left to die. There are stories that arbiters whisper to one another when they think no one is listening, stories about how some among us were sent outside the wall, either on patrol or to one of the outposts, but never made it back home, having gotten separated from their unit, only to disappear in the wilderness beyond. No search parties were sent, nor was such a notion considered.

"If you are strong and worthy, then you will survive and find your way back. If not, then you will perish," Molers' voice echoes in my mind as I remember one of his many lessons, and this specific instance centered upon a single recruit asking about an arbiter, one whom had decided to initiate the Rite of Conquest—an act where an arbiter challenges a superior officer—and was said to have gone missing beyond the wall. Most arbiters initiate the challenge in the hope of gaining a higher rank or better assignment within Arel, but the challenge can be made for any reason and is one of the few rights that arbiters have. "The weak must be weeded out," Molers' voice finishes in my head.

Therein lies my dilemma. No one will come searching for me. If I tell this plebeian this, he will leave me here to perish, but if I keep this a secret, he will find out at some point when it becomes evident that no one in Arel cares if I am missing. This is to be another testament of my strength and will as an arbiter to prove that I am fit to protect Arel. The only problem is, I need this plebeian to survive out here because I will not get far on a broken leg.

"Plebeian..."

"Chase," he interrupts me.

"What?"

"You know my name, and you know that it is Chase."

Though I do not appreciate being spoken to in such a manner by him, I am in no position to argue. "Very well… Chase… there is something you should know."

A quizzical expression clouds his face at the change in the tone of my voice.

"No one is going to come looking for us."

"Of course they will."

"No, they won't."

He looks into my hardened eyes and the truth of what I have told him strikes him as his disbelief morphs into concern. "Then, how…"

"I'll have to"—his expression sours as I speak—"we'll have to find our way back to Arel."

"So, you know the way back."

That is another problem. I have never been outside the wall and relied on those who drove the transport vehicles to navigate the area and know where to go, and since I had been stuck in the back of the transport, I did not get to see enough of the surrounding area to get my bearings.

"You do know the way back?"

"No."

"Perfect. Don't they teach you people tracking and survival?"

"How dare you question the training of our arbiters! I may not know for certain the way back to Arel, but I can find my way to one of our outposts, and they will get us back home. You insolent…"

I try to stand up, allowing my anger at being questioned to force me to forget that I cannot walk, and the moment I put weight on my injured leg, I crash back into the dirt crying out in agony.

"Stay still, you idiot!"

Out of reflex, I raise my hand to strike him, but he catches my fist in midair and the vehement look in his eyes tells me not to do it again. I jerk my arm free, saying, "You'll have to set the bone."

His furious expression turns to worry. "How?"

"We'll need some sticks or anything that can be used as a splint to keep me from bending my leg. And we'll need rope of some kind. Those vines might work."

He gets up and wanders into the wooded area, searching for fallen limbs that are sturdy enough to be used as a splint. Minutes tick by as he picks up a few and tests them, before tossing them aside. One breaks the moment he touches it and I imagine my leg doing the same when we hit the water of the river yesterday. Soon, he finds two staff-sized branches, which must have come from the upper part of the trees, and sets them next to me, hurrying off to tackle the vines, ripping one from its hold and the strength of his muscles astonishes me. When he finishes, he coils the vine next to the wood and stares at me, waiting for the next set of instructions.

"Find something sharp. You'll have to tear the pants leg away," I tell him.

He does not question me, nor does he get insulted as I issue my command, knowing that setting my broken bone has to be done if we hope to get out of here. He searches the ground for something, leaving me to wonder what he is doing, picking up rock after rock before finding one that he likes and hurries back, using its sharpened edge to cut away my pants leg, exposing the swollen, black and blue skin on my calf and the small bump that indicates where the bone has broken.

"Feel where the bone has broken?"

The pleb—Chase gives me an inquisitive look.

"Feel my leg."

He runs his calloused hand over my lower leg and his expression changes when he feels the area where the bone has snapped. "I…"

"You'll have to push it back in place."

"I'm not a doctor."

I glance away from my leg and stare at him and the genuine concern in his eyes. Neither one of us is a doctor, and this is not an ideal situation, but I know that the bone must be set, or I risk losing my leg from the infection that will set in. Every recruit receives basic medical training—most of which consists of treating infections, tending cuts, sprains, and a broken bone—as part of their survival course. This is all I have to fall back on and my leg needs to be set, or I face amputation, and if I'm fortunate, I'll die out here instead. The crematorium awaits arbiters who are incapable of performing their duties and I have never seen one who was missing their leg.

"Look," I say to him, "we cannot stay out here, but I cannot move unless this bone is set. Otherwise, you might as well just kill me right now."

The plebeian's surprised eyes stare back at mine as though the thought of killing me had never occurred to him.

"You have to push it back into place and hope it sets. Afterward, you will place the splints on each side of my leg, tying the vine around it to hold it still."

Silence looms between us as his mouth forms a grim, but determined, line and he places both his hands where the protruding bump is, which is also the warmest part of my leg, and presses against it, putting all of his weight on it until a loud, crackling pop sounds. I have no time to register the bone-chilling sound, for at that precise moment, agony engulfs my lower leg and I scream from the torment, unable to keep it in, but he ignores my outcry as he sets the splints and wraps the vine around my calf, securing it in a firm bind, but not so tight that it cuts off the circulation. After he finishes, I stare at my leg, wishing for the agony to leave me alone when a knot forms in my throat from lack of water.

"Give me some water," I order him. "Please," I add when he crosses his arms in irritation.

He scoops up the flask and hands it to me. "It had water in it when I found it."

I snatch it from him, popping the top off, and take two big gulps of water before replacing the lid. "Thank you, plebe—" I cut myself off, remembering that I had agreed to refer to him by his name. "Thank you, Chase."

"You're welcome," he says in a dry tone, matching the same one I had just used when thanking him, an idea so foreign to me that I am surprised I managed it. "We need to get you out of here."

He wraps my arm around his shoulder and lifts me up on my remaining good leg, supporting me while I try to hop, as I am unable to put any weight on my injured leg.

"Does it hurt that bad?" he asks, concerned when I wince from the effort of standing.

"My leg isn't the only thing that I injured," I reply, as a sharp pain in my side reminds me of the bruise there and the possibility of a cracked rib. "Don't worry about it. We need to get going."

"Where to?"

"Where it all started. Where we were attacked."

Chapter 21

Unwilling Allies

The trek along the riverbank as we navigate our way back to where we fell into the river ebbs away at my patience as I envision snails moving faster than us. As though it is an attempt by the universe to tease me, I spot a slug creeping along a fallen leaf, leaving a trail of gooey slime in a parallel line to the path Chase and I walk along. Irritated, I kick at the disrespectful creature, forgetting about my injured leg for a moment, and lose my balance, falling to the ground and almost taking my only means of support down with me.

Chase sets me on a moss-covered log, which sinks under my weight, and sits on the ground himself.

"What are you doing?" I demand.

"Letting you rest."

"I do not need to rest."

"You really should…"

"The more time we spend here, the less time we'll have to find our way back." I know that I should stop for a moment, but my pride refuses to allow me that luxury, nor do I have any desire to stay out here longer than I need to, dependent upon a plebeian's generosity.

He slaps his hands on his bony knees and jumps up, walking over to me in a single stride and hauls me to my feet, ignoring my grimaces, and drags me along. A zigzagged trail follows behind us in the sand, as we make our way to the riverbank, with me hobbling beside him, doing my best to keep my weight off my injured leg, but despite my efforts, my body insists upon walking in my accustomed stride. The plebeian bears much of my weight, and I feel his muscles straining underneath the arm that he has placed over his shoulder as we move through some brush and take our place alongside the river, heading upriver, while its current insists we should follow its example.

If circumstances had been different, I might have thought the calm trickle of the water over the tops of the rocks poking out of its surface, timed with the sporadic calls of the native birds, pleasant, but such enjoyments are not encouraged at the training facility— too frivolous is what Molers referred to them as—and the constant pain shooting up my leg jerks me back to my current, and undesirable, predicament.

The recent rain we have had mocks me with the humidity it has deposited and left hanging in the air. I tug at the collar of my jacket, but refuse to remove it, as an arbiter is to be in uniform at all times, and removing a portion of it for one's own comfort is a sign of weakness. Or is it? My uniform is me; if I take off the jacket just for the immediate relief of feeling cooler, as the exposed sweat on my arms, back, and neck evaporates, am I not rejecting a part of myself?

Losing myself to the questions now roaming through my mind, I fail to notice the tree root protruding from the brown soil and trip over it, taking the plebeian with me, and rolling down the bank and to the river, screaming as both my leg and side explode in agony. The edge of the water nears and I claw at the sand, desperate to prevent myself from falling into it, but unable to stop. I hear Chase yell for me to grab something, but in all the confusion, I am unable to see what it is, until his hand strikes my shoulder in an attempt to grab me. I flail my arms toward him, knowing that he is the only thing that can keep me from drowning, and seize his wrist the moment I touch it, and he returns the favor with a strong grip of his own, heaving me away from the river's edge and back to solid, and dry, ground.

I lay in the dirt, staring at the sky, my chest rising and falling, as I breathe so hard that my lungs act as though they are unable to get adequate amounts of oxygen. My side, which had once felt numb, now burns and stabs me with a raging fire of its own, admonishing me for my ineptitude. Hands lift up my jacket and shirt, trying to examine my injuries, while a stern voice begs me to calm down, and for the first time, I realize that I am still screaming.

I clamp my mouth shut and force myself to not cry, while smacking the plebeian's hands away.

He jumps back, insulted, but not surprised. "It's not just your leg, is it?"

Knowing I will never get away with lying to him, nor am I in a position to do so, I lift up my shirt and jacket, revealing the gigantic bruise which has now swollen and turned an even deeper shade of purple. Once I get a good look at it, something I have not done since I first noticed it, I realize that my stomach has bloated a little, warning me of the possibility of internal injuries that I have yet to identify. My time is short, and depending on the severity of the wounds, and if I have internal bleeding or not, I may only have a day or two, or I could have an entire week.

"Don't touch it pleb—" I yell at him as he reaches for my wound, but stop myself.

He jerks his hand back and glares at me for not keeping with our bargain. He is just a plebeian. How can he expect me to respect him when he holds the upper hand? Splashing in the river causes me to turn my head, and I watch as a bird pulls a fish out of the water and flies away, reminded once again of my predicament and that my survival depends upon him helping me.

Swallowing my pride, and forcing my mouth to create some spit so that I can form the words, I calm myself and speak. "Chase," I say, my voice rigid and controlled, "I think I may have internal injuries. Touching it may make it worse, since you are not a doctor."

His face calms a bit, but the anger at my continued refusal to use his name still boils beneath the surface.

"Give me your jacket," he says.

I glare at him.

"Please," he adds, but sounds more like a command than a request.

Unsure of what he plans to do with it, and being in no position to refuse, I take my jacket off, relishing the momentary, cooling relief it brings, and put it in his outstretched hand. He twists it until it resembles a knotted rope and wraps it around my torso with a gentleness I did not think was possible, taking great pains to not agitate my injury, in much the same way he bandaged my leg. I watch as he fusses with it, until the jacket is secure and he is satisfied that it will not fall away. My side feels a bit better, but the constant throbbing and burning remains.

"What…" I begin.

"That should help prevent any broken ribs from shifting. It isn't perfect, but it's the best I can do for now."

"How…"

"Have you forgotten your treatment of us so soon? When was the last time you helped a plebeian who had suffered a beating?"

I do not answer, since he already knows it.

"We are left to treat our own wounds." He is half-correct. There are plebeian quarters in the hospitals, but if it is deemed a waste of resources, they are not treated; the same is true for anyone within Arel.

I squawk as he lifts me up, placing my arm around his well-muscled shoulders again, and we continue our monotonous trek back to where the transport had crashed.

"How long will it take us to get there?" he asks.

"I do not know," I reply. "It depends on how far down river the current carried us. We should move as fast as we can though." I do not need to say why because he knows the reason.

"Yes, mistress," he says in a robotic tone, no doubt his conditioning taking over in the same way mine has on many occasions.

"Noni." If we are going to be on a first-name basis, he might as well know mine.

"Huh?"

"My name is Noni," I say.

A rustling noise catches my attention and I jerk my head in its direction, staring at the bushes nearest us, trying to see beyond them and make out what could have caused that noise.

"What?" asks Chase, noticing my concern.

"Didn't you hear that?"

"It was probably just an animal." He takes a step and urges me to walk with him, ignoring the noise and what could have caused it, but my mind goes back to the water flask and who could have left it, and why.

My legs turn to rubber the more we trudge along the riverbank, easing our way over upturned tree roots and rotted logs that sit halfway in the lapping water. I desire to stop and rest, but push myself onward, while Chase holds onto my sagging body. Resting is for the weak—it is also a luxury I do not have. The heat bears down upon us, though I think I am more sensitive to it because of my physical condition, causing sweat to stream down the sides of my face as I breath harder and harder with each step. The more the day wears on, the more I feel as though something, or someone, watches us, following us to satisfy his own curiosity about our origin. Birds call to the sky, but my ears do not care, as my pounding heartbeat overwhelms the sounds of the wilderness.

When the sun dips behind the trees, I feel as though we have not walked far at all, despite Chase's assurances that we made good time. My one good leg is unable to support my weight any longer and I collapse into the moist sand, startling Chase. I try to stand back up, but he pushes me back down, being as gentle as he can.

"Sit," he says.

"We need to keep moving," I protest, trying to stand up again, but my leg gives out and I fall back to the ground.

"We should rest for the night."

I open my mouth to protest, but he cuts me off.

"The sun is almost down and I do not wish to wander around in the dark. We should wait until it rises again."

As much I hate to admit it, he is right. Traveling through the wildlands at night is never a good idea, as the possibility of getting lost is too high.

"We need a fire," I say, relenting.

Chase nods and walks off into the trees, but makes certain that I can still see his form through the spaces between the limbs, while I attempt to position myself so that I am more comfortable, but my broken leg twinges and admonishes me, making me wish I were back at the medical center in Arel's eastern sector. I snatch the flask that he had left with me and pop off the top, tipping it high into the air to get the last drops of its coveted and refreshing liquid. Nothing. Disappointed, I screw the top back on and plop the container in the dirt beside me.

Again, I hear something. I turn toward it, but all I find are trees and rocks. The hairs on the back of my neck stand up and the feeling of being watched washes over me for a second time today. Do the people who attacked us know that we are out here? Are they biding their time until they finish us off, having placed a bet among themselves over whether we make it back to the road or not? As I stare at the wide, jade leaves in front of me, I never hear Chase's footsteps as he walks up with an armload of wood. The branches clop together and thump in the sand when he drops them, causing me to jump.

"Didn't mean to startle you," he says.

"You didn't," I reply, trying to save face, but the look on his face betrays that he does not believe me.

"What were you staring at?" he asks.

"I heard something."

"It's the jungle. There's always something out here."

"Don't dismiss my concerns so lightly," I snap at him. "Pleb—"
Again, I cut myself off, reminding myself of our bargain, but a lifetime of conditioning is difficult to undo. "Chase," I say again in a
calmer tone, "I know I heard something and it did not sound like
an animal."

"Would you like me to go check it out?"

"Yes."

Sighing, he jumps to his feet and moseys over to where I poin,
his body language indicating that he thinks I have imagined the
whole thing, or have gone delusional due to my injuries. He pulls
back a few branches from some overgrown brush, but with each
passing moment, his shoulders sag and I know that he has found
nothing, making my insistence that he investigate my hunch seem
foolish. He stalks back to the pile of dead branches without a word
and builds a fire, using two stones to start the flame. Once the first
crackle sounds, relief showers over me, as I have no desire to spend
my night in total darkness like I had the previous one.

Remembering the empty flask, I toss it to him, saying, "It is empty."

His jaw tightens, but he picks up the flask and strolls over to
the river, refilling the small container and brings it back, setting it
upright in the dirt next to me.

"Anything else?" he asks.

"We need food," I reply, recalling the small bit of survival training I have had.

"We do not have any."

Aggravated by his response, I plunge my hand into the soft
ground and scoop dirt away, forming a hole, and keep digging until
I uncover what I am searching for: earthworms. Though not something I would chose to eat on a normal day, they are edible. I snap a
twig free of one of the pieces of wood Chase had brought, pick up a

wriggling worm between my thumb and index finger, and skewer it before dangling it in the fire. Once I believe it has cooked enough, I eat it, challenging my companion to do the same.

Unsure of this new menu item, Chase refuses to grab a worm, but his grumbling stomach forces his hand. He lifts a writhing worm into the air and holds it before him, studying it a moment until he places it on my roasting stick and hangs it in the flames. Once cooked, he holds the limp worm before him, his eyes darting from it and to me, before summoning the courage to eat it. His sour face almost makes the entire experience worth the trouble.

"Have you never eaten a worm before?" I ask him.

He shakes his head. "The texture I can live with, but I can't quite get past the taste."

"What does it taste like?" I hadn't registered any flavor with the worm I had eaten, having swallowed it whole instead of chewing it.

"Like dirt," he answers and we both laugh.

We finish consuming the worms, roasting each one before slurping it down. The wriggling earth dwellers fail to satisfy our palates, but for the moment, our stomachs have stopped insisting on being fed. Once I finish my final worm, I lean back as best I can, but my leg keeps sending twinges of pain, warning me to not move too much, not that I want to.

"Here," Chase hands me his last worm that he has just pulled away from the licking flames of our small fire.

"Keep it," I say.

"You don't have to prove how strong you are out here. This isn't the corps."

Shaking my head, I turn away from him, showing him my back as I take off my undershirt—a standard issue black tank top with the Arelian insignia on one of the straps—and wring out what moisture I can, as it has soaked up a lot of my sweat, and do what I can to brush off some of the dirt and grime that has collected on it. Even here, the insistence on keeping a clean uniform, something that has been instilled into me and drilled into my head since birth, dictates my actions. A light touch prickles my left shoulder and I seize it with my right hand, twisting the hand the fingers belong to and throwing it to the ground where it thuds in the dirt with a tremendous, but dulled, thump. Chase's surprised eyes stare back at me and I rip my hand back, feeling... feeling remorseful?

"I'm sorry," I say, but the words stumble out of my mouth as through my tongue has never spoken them before, and I realize that this is the first time in my life that I have ever apologized without being forced to by a superior officer—the first time I have expressed regret for my actions to a plebeian, and mean it.

Chase stares up at me in surprise, doing his best not to look at my exposed breasts.

Sensing his uncomfortableness, though I do not understand why it affects me, since this is not the first time my nakedness has been viewed by another, as privacy does not exist in the corps, and we are all forced to stand naked in front of the officers until we are no longer ashamed of doing so, I untangle my undershirt and put it back on.

"I didn't mean to startle you," he says.

"You didn't."

He gives me a doubtful look, but lets it go.

"Why did you touch me?" I demand.

Chase glances at the ground as it is now his turn to feel ashamed. "I'm sorry," he says, and for once, he does not use that robotic tone that so many plebeians practice, "I saw the marks and... and couldn't believe it at first."

I have never thought much about the scars on my back from previous floggings, as lashings are standard punishment when an arbiter steps out of line, but have not committed an infraction serious enough to warrant going to the crematoriums. They are just there, a part of me.

"It's nothing."

"It's not noth—"

"I said leave it alone," I snap, not meaning to be so harsh, but focusing on my admonishments would be focusing on me weaknesses, something that we do not do in Arel. Strength is unity.

Chase grimaces and walks away. "I guess plebeians are not the only ones who bear the scars of Arel."

Before I can respond, a bit of brush rustles again, and again I find myself believing that we are being watched. I touch the pistol I had taken from the dead driver of the transport I had been in, satisfied that it is still there, ready to be used if necessary.

"We should get some sleep," I say. "We have a long walk tomorrow."

Chase nods his head in agreement while also trying to stifle a yawn, evidence that he is exhausted from having carried me all day, and lays down in the dirt, near the fire. Within minutes, his soft snores fill the space between us.

Unable to shake the feeling of being followed, I remain awake, peering into the darkened jungle around us, hoping to find evidence that my suspicions are wrong, or that it is a harmless animal trailing us out of curiosity. I place my hand around the pistol, taking comfort from having it there, keeping my eyes on the ghoulish brush surrounding us with only the trickling of the river and Chase's heavy breathing for company, determined to stay up and protect us from any unwanted predators.

Sometime later, I feel a strange warmth on my cheek as I realize that my neck aches, feeling cramped from having been at an odd angle, while my numb fingers try to get the feeling back in them after having grasped the hilt of the pistol all night. My half-awake mind believes that I am standing guard and is unable to comprehend why I seem to be snoring. A hand nudges my back. When I do not move, it shakes my shoulder, more insistent that I move, and I jerk awake, realizing that I had fallen asleep, despite my best efforts, and I grab the hand, pulling its owner closer and pressing the nozzle of my weapon against the underside of his chin.

"It's me!"

The familiar voice forces my fogged mind to clear up and I drop the pistol as I look around, remembering where I am, who I am with, and what our situation is, and ashamed for having to be forced to wake up when I should not have been asleep to begin with.

"You fell asleep," he says.

"I didn't mean to."

"It's all right. I never expected you to try and stay up. I thought you had gone to sleep like me."

I holster my weapon and keep my eyes pasted on the sand.

"It's okay," he comforts me and I wonder why he is being so nice to me.

"No, it's not," I reply. "I should have been able to stand sentry all night. Failure to do so means…"

"Forty lashes?"

I give him an odd look and he points at my back.

"I saw the marks on them."

"Fifteen," I say, "or a night in the bunker."

"It seems that plebeians are not the only slaves."

Before I have a chance to retort, he stops me and points at a well-organized pile of items on the ground near us, and for the first time, I notice that someone has delivered us some gifts: clean bandages, a splint for my leg, herbs or plants of some sort, a staff, food, and another canteen of water.

"Your suspicion that we were not alone yesterday seems to have been correct," says Chase.

I hold one of the plants, inspecting them and wondering what they are.

"Medicinal herbs," Chase says, answering my unspoken question. "We use them sometimes for our own wounds."

A flood of questions stampede my mind as I grapple with who would have put these here, and why. The wildlands are supposed to be filled with bandits, wild men whose only goal is to destroy

Arel and the beacon of civilization it stands for. Me being injured would be the same as giving milk to an infant. They should have kidnapped or killed us already, not help us, or is it just one person, a loner who chooses to defy the rules of his people.

I reach for the new splint that our unknown helper has given us, but Chase jumps up and grabs it before I can, scooping up the bandages and medicinal plants as well.

"Let me," he says.

I do not argue and allow him to undo the vines holding the makeshift splint in place and relieve the pressure that the pieces of wood have put on my swollen leg. He tosses them aside, allowing them to fall where they will, while he places the new splint around the broken bone, taking great pains not to cause me anymore agony than what I already feel, and I bite my tongue to prevent myself from expressing my torment. Once in place, my leg feels better; though, I will still need a doctor once we reach Arel. After he finishes with my leg, I lift up my shirt and he removes my jacket from around my ribs, chucking it into the river, and places some of the herbs on the purplish, and somewhat black, spot on my side, securing them in place with the fresh wrappings.

The new bandages help me feel a bit better, but I am still exhausted and know that time is not on my side for returning to Arel and seeking medical attention, assuming the personnel at the medical facility decides that I am worth the necessary resources to treat my wounds. If they deem my injuries beyond repair, and cannot guarantee that I will be able to fulfill my duties as an arbiter, I will be decommissioned: a one-way trip to the crematorium. Everyone in Arel has their place and I must make certain that I can fulfill mine.

Once he puts the final touches on my final bandage, Chase picks up a pouch that we both assume is food, and opens it, revealing figs. He picks one out, studies it, and bites off the tip, chewing it for a minute before swallowing, satisfied that it is edible. He hands me one. I hold the fruit in my palm, uncertain about its origins or if

I should trust our mysterious guardian, but in the end, decide that it does not matter, since I do need to eat, and if I do not get any nourishment at all, I will die out here. Its semi-sweet taste bursts within my mouth, waking my taste buds as saliva trickles from the corner of my lips. I wipe it away, receiving a chuckle from Chase as he pops another fig in his mouth. We both finish what is in the pouch within minutes. The two remaining pouches offer more figs, legumes, and marula nuts, and we agree to save them for later since we have a long trip ahead of us and have no idea if this will be the only gift we receive.

As the sun rises higher in the sky, Chase helps me up, handing me the staff, and we make our way further upriver, with me hobbling behind him as I try to keep up, but still refuse to be carried. My staff stabs the soft ground, leaving a line of holes that weave from side to side, mirroring the meandering look of our footprints. We make better time than we did yesterday, but I still feel as though our pace is slow, and my leg keeps threatening to give out on me, despite my attempts to will it to support my weight.

An insect buzzes in my ear and I reach up to smack it away, causing it to hover next to my other ear. Annoyed, I bat at it again, but only seem to manage to make it fly back to the first ear that it had chosen to bother to begin with. Chase tries to hide his entertainment at my slight discomfort, but the slight smirk on his face and the few escaped snorts give his humor away. The branch from a nearby bush swishes and I jerk my head in its direction, trying to catch a glimpse of our mysterious follower.

"Probably just an animal," Chase says in response to my reaction. He knows I believe otherwise, and a part of him suspects it is something else as well, considering the two nights of gifts we have received.

Despite the hairs on the back of my neck standing on end, warning me of unwanted eyes watching us, I play along with Chase's suggestion that it was an animal I had heard and smile, shrugging my shoulders. I step forward, leaning on my staff, depending on it to support my weight, not wanting to rely on my only companion. I need to prove to myself that I am strong enough to do this, to find my own way home, that I did not pass the gauntlet by chance. An unwanted reminder of my profession stomps through my mind, drowned by Molers' unemotional and foreboding voice. Three weeks before we were to face the gauntlet, all recruits had been lined up for one last assembly where we were informed of the reality of our futures.

Molers parades in my memory as he strolled in front of us that day, his hands clasped behind his back, as he walked erect, showcasing his pride within himself and his contempt for us.

"As you know, your final test is in three weeks."

I must have seemed so small, so insignificant, as one within the crowd shivering from nerves about our final test, and wondering if I would survive, or be among the failures. I miss the simplicity of that time.

"If you pass," Molers continued, "then you will join an elite group, charged with protecting Arel, but know this, many who pass the gauntlet, fail within their first year as a commissioned arbiter."

"Brex," someone whispered beside me that day, and others did the same.

Brex had been five years ahead of my class. He had passed the gauntlet, and many among the training facility had believed that he would go far as an arbiter, being one of the strongest and most resourceful of all the recruits. Even Molers had been enamored by his skill, a feat that most believed to be impossible, since Molers praises no one. After he had been commissioned, something happened to Brex—he changed. No one knows for certain what happened, and the official story is that he had a mental breakdown, lost his mind, and thus had to be put down like a rabid animal. He never completed his first year as a commissioned arbiter. Rumors spread about how he had tried to take over the armory in his region and give weapons to the plebeians, while another rumor insisted that he had tried to assassinate one of the presidents of Arel. The official story said that he had contracted an illness, which allowed his mind to be poisoned against Arel, the very city that he had sworn to protect, causing him to incite a rebellion.

His licentious attempts to overthrow the leadership of Arel ended when arbiters, led by Molers himself—no doubt wanting to exact revenge on the one recruit he had once believed in—arrested him. Brex's trial had been publicized throughout Arel and his punishment carried out that same day. Back at the training facility, we watched as an airborne transport dumped Brex in the wilderness and left him there with a few drones to monitor him and transmit his punishment to the television screens throughout the city. We watched for a week as he struggled to survive in the wildlands outside of Arel, a grim reminder of what lies outside our walls, until a group of barbarian raiders found him and murdered him. Brex's promise as an arbiter turned into a nightmarish ending, and serves as a reminder for what happens to those who fail to protect Arel. The crematorium is preferable to his fate.

"Do not," Molers had said, three weeks before my gauntlet, when the whispering finished, "follow his example."

A slender branch poking out of a nearby trees snaps, startling me from my musing, and I jump as a squirrel leaps from the branch, landing on the ground and scurrying away with a nut in its mouth.

"See?" Chase says to me. "Just an animal."

My side throbs and I grimace instead of smiling at his comment, not sure why he is attempting to comfort me, or draw my mind away from my worries about being followed, unless this is his attempt to force his own mind to not focus on our dilemma. I stab the ground with my staff and take another step, forcing myself to keep going, hoping that we find the place where we had fallen into the river soon, though I am unclear about its exact location. Everything had happened so fast that all I can do is guess, and the further we go, the more I question my memory of where the vehicle is. Neither of us talk much as we walk, which I am thankful for because it takes every ounce of effort I have to control my breathing and appear to not be in pain, despite Chase's constant eye on me; but he keeps a respectable distance, only lending me a helping hand when I ask for it. His gray eyes, the same shade as his sister's, harbor concern about my continual struggle to walk.

I stop.

In our path, rests a lone tire, leaning against the protruding roots of a tree as though it had been placed there. The trickling of the river fills the foreboding atmosphere around us as I glance around, searching for signs that we were not alone, wondering who placed the tire there, and why. I hobble over to it, but Chase stops me.

"Let me go," he suggests.

I glower at him, not liking the idea that he thinks I am incapable of looking at it myself, and I want to know if it had been on the nearby ground before it was moved, or if it had been carried there. Reading my mind, he points to my leg and my side and I know that he is right; my injuries prevent me from being able to move with ease, meaning that he should be the one to go. I nod my approval, still not liking the idea, and watch as he stalks over to the tire, taking great care to not make so much noise, marveling at his adept ability to remain silent, since he displayed none of it yesterday, and wonder how often he used that in the past to sneak around Arel past curfew. Thoughts about his sister fill my mind, and as I study his movements, I ponder over where I had seen her before, a question that has plagued me since I first met her, and it hits me—she is the girl from that night!

"It's you!" I blurt out.

He turns around, a quizzical expression on his face.

"You're the one who almost got me killed that night!"

Judging by the confused look on his face, he still does not understand what incident I am referring to. "The bag of medicine in the alley. The girl. You are the one who knocked me down those stairs. You are the reason she got away!"

"Look, I…"

"A man was arrested because of you!"

"I…"

"You stole valuable medicine from Arelian citizens, and for what?"

"Do you know what it's like to have nothing? Do you know what it is like to starve—to work until you can no longer stand? To be beaten for not doing your tasks quick enough?" An anger that he must have kept buried just below the surface lashes out, exposing itself, knowing that I am in a weakened state, alone, and unable to defend myself. "Each day I am treated as though I am nothing. An insect has more value than me in your perfect world. My sister and I are forced to watch as those we love are murdered one by one, and you sit there and judge me for stealing a few vials of medicine that would have been disposed of anyway because they had passed their expiration date?"

"How dare you."

"You are the filth, not me!"

"I received twenty lashes because of you two!"

"You received them because of your own failures."

His cold tone inflames my already building anger to the point where it matches his own resentment, and I reach down for a rock, scooping it up and chuck it at him, missing his face, but I do clip his left ear.

He touches his earlobe, allowing some drops of blood to settle on his fingers before examining them and the damage I have done.

"You bitch."

He charges me. I poke the bottom of my staff out, catching his feet just before he reaches me, causing him to stumble, but my damaged leg prevents me from darting out of the way, and he grabs my good ankle—his strong grip surprises me—and pulls me down. I use my staff to prevent myself from falling over and kick him with my other leg, releasing a muffled cry from the pain that shoots up it. Before he can recover, I yank myself free of his grasp and jab him with my staff again, hobbling away and putting some distance between us. Enraged, he stands up and glowers at me, desiring blood, and I return his glare with my own murderous scowl, unsurprised that he betrayed me: it's in a plebeian's nature to do so, which is why they need a firm hand.

"I am tired of your kind always treating me like filth!" yells Chase.

"Then don't act like it, plebeian!" The words are out of my mouth before I even realize that I thought them.

He charges again. I raise my staff, jabbing him in the stomach with it. He doubles over, and while he catches his breath, I twist the staff and strike him between the shoulder blades, forcing him to the ground. He lunges. Unable to dodge, he catches me around my legs, knocking me to the ground. I struggle to get back up, but his strong hands seize me around the waist, turning me over on my back. I seize one of his thumbs and twist it, breaking it. He loosens his grip for a second, but it is not long enough for me to get him off me. As I try to sit up, he throws me back into the dirt, straddling me, and presses my staff into my throat.

"Go ahead and kill your sister," I spit at him.

He relaxes and sanity returns to his eyes, but it does not matter, because at that moment, a low growl captures both of our attention. Our eyes move toward the direction of the snarl. More growls fill the air and my stomach turns into knots, as I realize that our scuffle has distracted us from the unfortunate fact that we have been followed by a pack of wild dogs. Their ribs poke out of their skin and their sunken features indicate that they have been starving for some time now, and I recall that some time ago, the council of Arel had decided to shorten the food supply for outsiders by spreading poison that made it where, no matter how much an animal ate, it still starved. It would take years for the wildlife to rebuild their populations, making it so that those who depended upon them for survival would perish. Now it seems that their moment of brilliance will be my downfall.

The growling intensifies, followed by wrathful barks. Chase's eyes look into mine, but there is nothing we can do. The dogs outnumber us, and despite their state of starvation, will overpower us the moment we attempt to flee, not that I would get very far to begin with.

An object strikes the wild dog nearest us, bursting into a powder that hovers in the air with the scent of citrus and peppermint. The animal backs away, not liking the smell. More fist-sized balls arc through the air, striking the dogs on their muzzles or sides, each one exploding into a powder that hangs in the air, creating a thick, powdery fog that overwhelms one's nose with the combination of peppermint and citrus. A blur of movement streaks through the dry mist, carrying a cudgel, and strikes the lead dog with it, knocking it to the ground. Startled and afraid, it scrambles to its feet and hurries away. Howling, the pack of wild dogs run off, after their alpha, disappearing into the brush, while Chase and I are reduced to a series of coughs. Once the dust settles and we can breathe again, we are alone.

Chase climbs off me and gives me his hand to help me up, but I refuse it, snatching my staff instead, using it to haul myself to my feet. I hobble over to the tire, not caring how much noise I make, since it is evident that we are not alone in this wilderness, and inspect the rubber sphere, noting an impression in the dirt where it had landed. Someone had picked it up and leaned it against the tree just so we would find it. Craning my neck, I scan the precipice above us and spot a bit of metal. It might be the transport vehicle that had carried me down here. I scour the side of the steep hill, searching for a place where we can climb. To my right towers a tree, growing out of the ledge, but its roots dig deep into the earth, poking out of the hill in such a way that it mirrors a ladder of sorts, though more haphazard and precarious, but it could work as a way of climbing upward. Either way, if we stay here, we are dead.

"Look," Chase says in a soft and apologetic tone, "I'm..."

"There," I cut him off. "We'll climb up there." Though I detest the idea, I still need his help to get up this hill, assuming he does not allow me to fall on the way up there.

He looks at where my finger points and nods his approval.

I start for it, but he grabs my arm, stopping me, but jerks away the moment I face him.

"We should wait for tomorrow," he says.

"We should go now."

"Look around you. The light is fading. It will be dark soon."

"And the wild dogs?"

"I'll make a fire and we'll keep our backs to the cliff. That should provide us some protection."

I glance at the steep hill again, my legs threatening to give out on me from the day's hike. I need to rest, but do not wish to show my defeat. "Fine. We'll climb it at dawn."

I stumble over to a mound of rocky dirt as sweat drips down the sides of my temples, falling from my jawline, and ease myself into a sitting position, groaning from the pain in my side and leg, but relieved to be able to relax for a bit. I feel nauseated and realize that our scuffle has taken more of a toll on me than I wish to admit.

Chase hands me the water flask. "I'm sorry. I should not have lost my temper."

Still incensed over our fight, and my discovery of who he and his sister are, I refuse to look at him when I respond. "No, you were right. My lashings are a sign of my failure as an arbiter. Let's not pretend to be allies. You only need me so you can get back to your sister and I need you to get back to Arel."

The angry mood between us permeates the air, settling upon us with a weight that is heavier than all the buildings in Arel combined. Chase stalks away, but before he leaves me, he says in a soft voice, which I almost do not hear, and perhaps he hopes I won't, "Your punishment is my fault."

I stare after him as he walks toward a bush and breaks branches away from it, observing his ragged clothing, more haphazard after our ordeal in this place, having never noticed it, nor cared, before. A plebeian's attire depends on what their master decrees. Some prefer their servants to be well-dressed and frown upon those who force their plebeians to wear tattered clothing. At the manor, plebeians are given simple attire that is devoid of defects, but Commander Vye has stressed that she can ill afford to purchase more than a certain number, so they are expected to take care of their allowed possessions.

While he busies himself with gathering fuel for a fire, I lift up my shirt to inspect the bruising on my side, grimacing from the jabs of pain I feel as I ease the material over it and peek under the makeshift bandage. The coloring has turned darker and spread. Frowning, I know that this does not bode well for me. Being as gentle as I can, I place two fingers upon the wound and bite my tongue to prevent myself from screaming, as my side is gripped in agony. Knowing there is little else I can do, I place the bandage back over the bruise and slide my shirt back down, just as scuffling feet disturb the dirt next to me, and I look up to find Chase standing there, holding an armload of wood and leaves. I tuck my shirt into the top of my pants, ignoring his sudden look of concern.

He places the wood in a pile near me and proceeds to gather some rocks, building a boundary with them to try and prevent any flames from leaping out and igniting a nearby tree or some of the dead vegetation rotting on the soft earth. I watch as he puts two blocks of wood in the center and tries to light them from rubbing two rocks together, but even though a few sparks are created, the humidity in the air and the damp wood prevents a fire from starting.

"You need an accelerant," I tell him.

He ignores me and continues to struggle against the will of the elements.

Irritated at his refusal to listen to me, I snatch one of the rocks from his hands, take the ends of my hair, its once long silk strands, now frizzed and tangled, and cut off a chunk, holding it out to him. He takes it and the stone I had snatched from him and places it on the wood. One of the sparks from the striking rocks ignites the hair, and we both shove some dried leaves on it until the broken branches catch fire and burn with a strong blaze, for which I am thankful, but refuse to show my relief to Chase. My eyelids grow heavy as I watch the bouncing flames until I am no longer awake.

Crackles drowned by a buzzing sound fill my ears as my fogged mind struggles to wake from its dreamlike state, but my body desires sleep, and I find myself dropping off before a sudden snapping sounds jerks me awake. Still groggy, and exhausted, I struggle to open my eyes and focus on the smoky scene before me, discovering that someone had put green brush on the fire.

"Nice to see you're awake," says a familiar voice, and to learn that Chase is still there surprises me.

I try to sit up, but a hand pushes me down.

"You should stay put."

"How long was I out?" I ask, my voice cracked and hoarse from having not spoken in a while.

"A day," says Chase.

A day? I was asleep for that long?

"But it is dark," I say.

"Okay, then. Maybe a little longer than a day. The sun hasn't been down for long though."

His quiet and subdued tone provides a stark contrast to the anger that had filled his voice earlier, before I had fallen unconscious.

"Why didn't you just leave me?" I ask.

"You said it yourself. I need you to get back into Arel."

I swallow a load of spit that has filled my mouth, not surprised by his answer, as I had expected it, though he could have just taken some of my clothing and shown it to the authorities in Arel, claiming that he had tried to save me, but couldn't. It wouldn't be that far from the truth, and every breath I take reminds me of this fact. The idea that he had already thought of it, but had decided it wouldn't work, enters my mind and I push the whole notion away.

"Thank you," I whisper.

Chase stares at me with a bewildered expression, wondering if I have lost my mind, and a part of me wonders it as well, as this is the first time I have ever thanked a plebeian—and my gratitude is sincere.

"For what?" he asks me.

"For not leaving me."

Shame fills me as I realize that a part of me had been afraid that I would be alone out here, wounded, unable to move, and forced to die in the wildlands, carnage for the scavengers to feast upon. Fear is not accepted in Arel, and the training facility does all it can to stomp any phobias out of its recruits—memories of being six years old and left alone in a blackened room with only a copper rod to use to find my way out fill my mind—yet the fear of being alone still resides within me, even in the smallest measure. I have failed. I am not fit to be an arbiter.

Chase cocks his head to one side and his brows scrunch together, forming a dark shadow across his face in the firelight. "Are you crying?"

"No," I snap, reaching up and brushing away a single tear that has escaped my eye without my permission.

"No, of course not. Arbiters have no feelings," he says.

"Neither do plebeians."

He grins at my response. "You're probably right. I guess there isn't much difference between us in how we are treated."

Puzzled, I observe him for a moment, wondering why he would say such a thing.

"What do you mean?"

"I noticed the marks on your back."

"And?"

"I always thought that only plebeians were beaten as punishment."

"My punishments were deserved," I say.

"Were they?"

"They remind me of my negligence in my duties, so that I will not fail again."

"'Those are an awful lot of reminders,' he mutters to himself, but not low enough where I am unable to hear him. "How long have you been an arbiter?" he asks me.

I think back to when I had passed the gauntlet and received my commission. It hadn't even been a full year, but perhaps just six or seven months, though it does not seem like it had even been that long, as so much has happened that I never noticed the passage of the weeks.

"Almost half a year," I reply.

"That's an awful lot of punishment for such a short time," he says aloud, voicing what he had first meant to say only to himself.

"Arbiters are made," I say with pride, "not born."

"Tell me about it."

The probity in his voice disquiets me, and his genuine desire to learn about the training an arbiter goes through frightens me a little, since none of the citizens within Arel ever want anything to do with arbiters, but are afraid of us instead. Despite my qualms about trusting him, my pride at being an arbiter compels me to brag about my experiences and the training I had gone through.

"An arbiter is chosen at birth, and as an infant, is brought to the Martial Diplomatic Corps' training facility. From that moment on, we are taught to be strong. Disobediences is met with swift punishment. When we are able to walk and until the age of five, we are forced to stand in the cold rain without any clothes on, until we learn not to shiver or show weakness and embarrassment or be humiliated because our naked bodies are exposed. Those who perish are considered the weakest and are not mourned. Their bodies are thrown to the dogs. Those who survive, move on to the next stage of our training: learning to read a map, use our navigation systems, to study the law, learning battle strategy, but besides the mind, we are subject to physical training as well, because without strength and endurance, what use is a mind?

"By the time I was eight, I could climb a fifty-foot rope without tiring. When I was nine, I climbed a one-hundred-foot rock wall. At ten years of age, I defeated my first opponent in hand-to-hand combat. At eleven, I faced my first live training exercises, and only the strongest survive those. At twelve, I completed my first success-ful mission."

"What was that?"

"Each recruit is supposed to sneak into a designated area and steal something. I was assigned to pilfer something from one of the com-manding officers. I took the magazine right out of Molers' sidearm while it was still strapped around his waist. Of course, I had bribed an older recruit to distract him, allowing me to complete my mission."

I know that Chase has no idea who Molers is, but the way I speak about my former training officer must have told him all he needed to know about the man, or at the very least, my sense of accomplishment at what I had managed to do.

"By the time I was thirteen," I continue with my story, "I com-pleted a survival training course. Each recruit is dropped off in an undisclosed location, after receiving two weeks of classroom in-struction, and expected to survive for five days. By the age of fifteen, I had completed several mock battles and witnessed my first execu-tion of a criminal. In the end, those who survive their training must pass the gauntlet.

"Emotions are not allowed, except anger. We are the pillars that Arel stands upon and are expected to uphold its laws at all cost. Failure means death."

When I finish speaking, I study Chase's face as he listens, and my curiosity about his interest in my past overrules my mouth. "Why do you care?"

"My sister and I were born plebeians, always forced to serve the citizens of Arel and always reminded of our place and where we be-longed. Our lives were chosen for us because we are fair-skinned and I hated everyone in Arel for it, thinking that people like you have it easy. But it appears that I am wrong. We are both slaves in the end."

"I am no slave," I scoff at his notion.

"Did you choose the life of an arbiter?"

"Of course not, but that is how our society has survived. Everyone has their... has their place." My voice trails off and I dislike the direction this conversation has gone in.

"Your sister," I say, the one question plaguing my mind now pushes its way out of my mouth, and I wish to change the subject, "why was she there that night?"

A somber expression covers Chase's pale face. "We needed medicine for our mistress."

I remember that his sister had made a similar statement when I had questioned her, before she ran off and escaped.

"Could your mistress not go to a medical center? As a citizen, she would have been treated."

"No, she wouldn't have been. Her illness had been deemed untreatable, and the medicine had been denied to her because it would be a waste of resources to treat someone who was already dying. That is why Gwen was there. Not everyone within Arel agrees with its laws, and some will do anything for a little extra comfort. I stole my mistress' favorite piece of jewelry and sold it for the money necessary to purchase the medicine. In the end, it did not matter. She had passed that night while Gwen and I had been trying to escape from you."

"Why did you care so much about her? Aren't all Arelians the same to you?"

"Gwen's and my first master treated us with an iron hand. I took most of the beatings, but it wasn't enough to prevent him from splitting us up. Our mistress had seen Gwen at auction, and when she learned that we were siblings, she promised to pay our first master triple for the both of us. He took it, believing that he got the better part of the deal.

"She was kind, our mistress. A widow. I think she just wanted company and she treated Gwen and I well."

"So, you thought of her as a mother."

"As family."

I guess a kind mistress would be the closest thing to family a plebeian could have. Like the rest of us, they are taken from their mothers after birth and given to a surrogate who trains them to be proper servants until they are old enough to be sold. Siblings are rare, which is why it is odd for Chase and his sister to exist, much less still be together, not that it can't happen; it's just rare.

"You said that you sold some of your mistress' jewelry," I say, my arbiter training kicking in. "To whom?"

Chase clamps his mouth shut, knowing just where I intend to go with this line of questioning, and regrets having revealed so much about his past.

There are rumors of an underground movement, a place where people go to trade for items that they need, and where fair and dark-skinned mingle as equals. The problem with rumors is that they are just that, unsubstantiated bits of information, but he knew where to go.

I drop that trail of thought. This is not the time to ponder over what might be or how I could use it to help myself. Visions of the woman holding a plebeian infant fill my mind again, and the sense of remorse that I had hoped had left me, comes crashing back, seizing my conscience and admonishing me with its own lash. It is her eyes—the determined look within them still haunts me—and her willingness to die just so a wailing bundle, whom Arel considered less than human, could have the chance to live unravels me.

"Did you get dust in your eyes?" Chase asks me, and the concern in his voice throws me off. Why would he care?

"No," I reply, brushing the few tears that have welled up and escaped. Tears? I have never cried before, not since the first time I had been forced to stand naked in the pouring rain amongst others like myself and the hardened officers who patrolled around us with their switches. On that day, I learned what tears bring forth: they create misery.

"Are you sure? I can get you some water."

"I'm fine," I snap, and my voice indicates that I have no desire to pursue this matter any further.

Chase's disbelieving expression informs me that he does not buy my story, but he allows the matter to drop, much to my relief.

"Emotions are frivolous and useless," Molers' voice echoes in my mind, "and will only serve to get you killed."

Perhaps he is right. Acting out of emotion can lead one to make stupid decisions, which can lead to one's demise, but if that is the case, then why do people seem to act upon them anyway? Could it be that it depends on the emotion and the situation? The woman with the infant acted out of emotion, but she also harbored a certain amount of self-control. I shake it off. Such thinking is dangerous, but dangerous to whom?

"How did you end up at the manor?" I ask, hoping to distract myself from my own thoughts.

Chase squirms a little, his discomfort at my question obvious.

"If I recall, Mandi brought you two."

I think back to the banquet and how Mandi had not recited the oath of Arel with the kind of enthusiasm that the rest of the room had. The more I dwell on it, the more I realize that she had always been a bit different from the other commanding officers, more subdued and less likely to discipline someone for a minor infraction. I shake my suspicions away. Mandi had always been kind to me and even helped me evade a few of Molers' disciplinary measures.

"Are you hungry?" Chase asks me.

The mention of food makes my forgotten stomach growl and ache, forcing me to remember that I have not had a decent meal for a few days now. He tosses me a pouch that still has a few figs and nuts in it. I open it and take out a fig, biting the tip of it off and chewing on it with some amount of dignity, not wanting to put my eagerness to eat on display, as I have shown enough of my invulnerabilities in front of him. The sweet juices from the dried fruit engulfs my tongue and mouth, causing saliva to burst from its crevice, and a few bits of drool escape from the corner of my lips. I wipe it away before he can spot it. The dried fruit and nuts are not much, but enough to quiet my stomach's insistence at being fed, for now.

"I never thanked you," says Chase.

I stop chewing on my meager meal and look at him with a puzzled expression as his statement has caught me off-guard. "For what?"

"For what you did at the last outpost with Commandant Paq."

With everything that had happened in the last few days, I had forgotten about Commandant Paq, a man I hope to never see again, but the ominous feeling that I will not be so fortunate envelops me as I remember that glacial look in his eyes when we departed the outpost.

"I did nothing," I reply.

"Not according to your Commander Vye."

My eyebrows fuse together as I give him a pointed look.

"After you had gone to your sleeping quarters, she and the commandant had a discussion outside, regarding me, and I remember overhearing her say that you insisted I be given some sort of temporary duties."

"Why would you thank me for that?" It seems odd for a plebeian to be so grateful for being given extra work, since they are expected to perform certain tasks anyway.

"If you hadn't made your request, the commandant would have disposed of me in much the same way as when he disposed of that one arbiter."

Images of the female arbiter lying on the ground, pulverized and beaten by her fellow arbiters because of her failure to perform the physical exercises, flood my mind.

"How do you know..."

"I overheard his subordinates talking about his plans."

"So, you were eavesdropping?"

"People talk in front of plebeians, unafraid of us revealing their secrets, not that anyone would take what we have to say seriously anyway."

That much is true. Plebeians are servants, meant to serve us more deserving people. Citizens speak in front of them all the time without the fear of them talking, because they are to be seen, but not heard.

"And you believed her?" I say, not wanting to be thought of as having even the slightest bit of caring for what happens to him.

"Is there a reason for her to lie?"

No. If Commander Vye wants something, she demands it. And her actions in front of Commandant Paq demonstrated that she is no pusillanimous individual.

A yawn creeps up on me and I do my best to stifle it, but Chase notices it regardless of my efforts. "We need rope," I say, looking up the hill, pondering over how we are to climb up it.

"Huh?"

"To get up there." I point at the hill. "We'll need a rope of some sort to help us climb up."

Chase reaches behind him and pulls out two sets of braided vines. "Ahead of you on that one," he says. "You were asleep and I didn't have much else to do."

I feel the makeshift ropes, marveling at how he had the knowledge to do such a thing, or the foresight to create two.

"I thought that one we would tie around ourselves and the other I will use to hoist you up with."

"How did you…"

"Like I said, you all talk and I listen."

I hand the braided vines back to Chase, doing my best not to show how pleased I am with his ingenuity and the fact that it might help me get home.

Leaves rustle nearby and I jerk my head in their direction, as the sense that someone watches us overwhelms me again, but another yawn forces me to recognize how exhausted I am, and I ignore the movement of the brush. If something is out there, I am in no position to defend myself. I lay my head back, knowing that I am about to fall asleep again at any moment, as the increasing difficulty of keeping my eyes open takes root until it almost controls my actions.

"Sleep," Chase mumbles. "I'll keep watch."

For a moment, my eyes pop open, but exhaustion takes over and they close as my mind drifts off to sleep and his words blur together, making me think that his statement is just a part of my imagination.

Sunlight drapes over my face as my mind returns to the conscious world and I blink a few times before my eyes open and focus on my surroundings. Though the fire has dwindled and burnt itself out, leaving a pile of smoldering charcoal that glows when the moist breeze graces it, the pouches and the wilderness are right where I remember, never changing, never moving, with Chase seated next to me with his head resting against a protruding rock from the hillside. I scoop up a pebble and fling it at him. He jerks awake and turns around to face me.

"What?" he says.

"You fell asleep," I chide him, but keep the judgement in my voice minimal.

I reach down for the pistol strapped around my waist, checking to see if it still remains there and notice that something is different. "Did you take my weapon?" I ask him.

Chase gives me a perplexed expression, as though he does not know what I am talking about.

"Did you touch my weapon?" I ask again.

"No," he replies.

"The holster strap is not fastened," I say, and his face falls, admitting his guilt.

"I thought I had heard something while you slept, so I took your weapon as a precaution when I went to investigate. I hoped you wouldn't notice."

"Never take my weapon again."

"I could take it from you right now if I wanted."

His bold statement angers me, and it seems that being out here alone, and forcing me to use his name, has emboldened him. He may not have a busted leg, but he lacks training, and even if he did manage to unarm me, he would still be out here on his own, and would die from starvation.

"Try it," I command him.

Chase arches an eyebrow, trying to discern if I am serious or joking, but I have never jested with him before and he knows it.

"Try it," I say again.

He stands up, dusting his grimy hands on his soiled pants leg as he inches his way closer to me, playing out in his mind how he would disarm me. Once he is within range, but before he can touch me, I raise my staff and jab him in the stomach with it, causing him to double over. Incensed, he approaches again. I raise my rod again, but he snatches it and tears it from my hands, flinging it aside with a victorious look on his face. I will hand that one to him, but keep my face impassive as I await his next move. He lunges downward and reaches for the pistol, but I seize his wrist with both my hands and twist, flinging him onto his back. Before he can move, I position his arm to that I can break it if he tries anything.

"All right! All right! I concede."

I release him.

"And what have you learned?" I ask him, following Mandi's example; she always abhorred punishing recruits for minor mistakes and, unlike the other instructors, insisted that we learn from them. I'm not sure why I have never thought about it much, until now, until this very moment.

"That brute strength isn't everything."

"And?" My tone matches the one I had heard Mandi use so many times when she advised me to learn from my mishaps.

"That even an injured person can be dangerous, especially when cornered and with nothing to lose."

"Whereas you have everything to lose. Congratulations. You just passed your first lesson."

Chase scowls.

"Do you even know how to use it?" I ask, referring to the pistol.

"You know I don't. Teaching plebeians how to use weapons is illegal."

It is, but as I sit here thinking about our situation, and our mysterious benefactor, I realize that it is in my best interest to demonstrate how to use the pistol in case I am unable to, even if it means taking the risk of him turning it against me. I take the weapon from its holster, take out the magazine, and hold it out to him. "Here."

He remains where he is, unsure of my motives.

I wave it at him, beckoning him to take it.

With caution, he takes the pistol from me, holding it out to the side in an awkward fashion like one who has never handled a weapon before would.

"Never point it at anything you do not intend to shoot," I tell him, "and use both hands to hold it. You have more control that way."

He wraps both his hands around the handle, placing both index fingers on the trigger.

"Fingers off the trigger. Never put your finger on the trigger, unless you are ready to fire. And you will only use one finger, so decide right now which one will be your trigger finger."

I watch as he obeys my instructions.

"Now aim for the tree over there. Pick a spot on the trunk and line it up in your sights. Your feet should be shoulder width apart and stand up straight. And remember to breathe, slow, steady breaths. Don't lock your elbows. Keep both your eyes open. That's it. When you are ready, fire."

The gun clicks and Chase lowers it, giving me an exasperated look. "It's not loaded."

"Of course, it isn't, and not for the reason you are assuming. Before you can use a loaded handgun, you must first be accustomed to its weight and how it feels to hold it."

Memories of my first moments of holding a pistol flash into my mind. When recruits are taught the use of weaponry for the first time, they are given guns that are not loaded and forced to carry them around until they become used to the weight, how it feels to hold it, and how your arms can tire after holding it in the air for several minutes. We spend weeks carrying the weapons until we are allowed to use live ammunition.

Something snaps in the distance, distracting both of us and reminding us that the morning is disappearing, and if we hope to scale that hill, we need to go now. Chase hands me the pistol, handle first, and I take it, putting the magazine back in, before placing it back in its holster. Fearful that the wild dogs might have returned, or that bandits may have found us, I snatch my staff and press it into the ground, gauging out a hole in the brown earth, and haul myself to my unsteady feet, doing my best to not put too much weight on my broken leg. Chase reaches out to help me at first, but changes his mind and picks up his makeshift ropes. He ties one end of the first one around my waist and the other end around himself.

Chase places his foot on the steep slope of the hill and digs his hands into the rainy dirt to haul himself upward.

"What are you doing?" I ask him as he starts to leave me behind.

"Going first," he replies as though it should be obvious. Before I have a chance to question his motives for going first, he drops back to the ground and says, "I'm going to the tree right there. I'll tie this"—he lifts up the second makeshift rope—"around it and then pull you up."

His words make sense, and a part of me regrets assuming the worst of his character, thinking that he planned on leaving me here. If he had wanted to do that, he would have already; he's had several opportunities to do so.

"Sorry," I mumble and step back, giving him the room he needs to restart his ascent.

He digs his hands into the dirt again, placing each foot in a strategic foothold so that he can push his way upward. Black pebbles clack as they tumble to the bottom, having been disturbed from their resting place by his efforts. I watch from the bottom as he inches his way upward, pushing with his legs while pulling with his arms. He slips. My breath catches in my throat, but I fail to notice it, as my entire focus remains on him, knowing that my survival rests on his success. He reaches the tree he had pointed out to me earlier and pauses, catching his breath. He uncoils the braided vine from around his well-toned shoulder and ties one end around the trunk of the tree, giving it a good yank to make certain that it does not budge, before dropping the other end to me.

I snatch it and knot the end underneath my shoulders. Before I signal that I am ready, I slide my staff through both ropes, binding it to my back in an effort to keep it with me, but soon learn that it will not work and I am forced to ditch it. Disappointed, I toss it to the ground and give the line two tugs. It pulls taut and my feet leave the ground, bringing with it the unsettling sensation of floating in the air, unable to control my own actions. My body scrapes the side of the hill as it is dragged upward, and each bump sends a wave of pain through my leg and my side, causing me to grimace, but I endure it, not wanting to show weakness. Bits of dirt sneak down my shirt, much to my ire, but there is little I can do about it as I look upward and keep my eyes fixed upon Chase and the tree.

Once I reach him, I grab the base of the trunk, wrapping my arms around it, and heave myself upward, while Chase's hands seize my waist and pull me the rest of the way. He situates me between the slope of the hill and the base of the tree trunk, both of us gasping for air as we rest, and I study the streams of soiled sweat trickling down the sides of his temples. Without a word, Chase unties the rope from around the tree and starts the trek upward again, heading for a small ledge encompassed by a green climbing plant bursting with flaming orange, tubular flowers, each with four petals forming a perfect square, just big enough for a single person, and visible only from below, that lies just below the crashed transport vehicle.

I watch with bated breath as he presses his knees into the soft dirt as he scales the side of the hill, reminding me of a spider as it climbs a wall, but with less skill and ease. He grips a rock protruding from the slope, and the sweat coating his toned muscles shines in the sunlight, making me realize that not an ounce of fat exists on his body. He reaches for what appears to be an exposed root, but it breaks free of the ground the moment he grasps it, causing him to hang in the air for a moment as he braces his feet against the slope and reaches for another protruding stone. I release the lungful of air I did not even know I had been holding.

Small rocks tumble down the hill not far from me, creating a musical series of clicks and clacks and I jerk my head in their direction. Peering into the brush that grows on the hill, I squint as I try to see through it and the bushes that somehow grow above me, but see nothing. I glance at Chase before turning back to the falling pebbles, convinced that he could not have done it. My desire to know the cause of this disturbance overwhelms me that I do not hear Chase calling my name at first and only realize his desire for my attention when he yanks the rope around me. I look up and we lock eyes for a moment, allowing me to glimpse the perturbed expression on his face.

Again, the makeshift rope pulls taut and the sensation of dangling in the air grips me as I'm lifted up and my feet scrape the sides of the hill. I do my best to use my one good leg to help push my way upward, while pulling with my arms, grinding my teeth each time a jolt of pain grips my damaged limb. Almost there. I reach for the same rock that Chase had used moments before and ignore the sharp edges that poke my palm as I squeeze it tight, using all my strength to lift myself up so as to ease the burden on Chase. Whether he appreciates my miniscule efforts or not, I do not know.

Pebbles rain down upon me, surrounding me, cutting my exposed skin with their fury from being disturbed from their resting place— their form of revenge, I assume. Another tug and I reach the ledge. I grab it and pull myself up, but before I can get in a seated position for a chance to rest, Chase shoves me toward the edge, urging me to keep climbing, since the plateau where the transport vehicle stopped rolling is just an arm's reach away.

Though disappointed at not having a change to rest my tired muscles, I do as he says, knowing that if I stop now, I will never continue. I stretch my right arm upward, reaching for the ledge above me. At first, I believe that I have caught it and start to pull myself up when I slip. The sharp rock slices my fingers, and I would have tumbled downward if Chase hadn't caught me and balanced me on the narrow crevice he sits on. Taking three deep breaths, I reach upward a second time and grasp the ledge above me, my bloodied fingers wanting to slip once more, but before they do, I reach with my left hand and seize the edge, heaving myself up while Chase lifts me with his arms. I role onto semi-flat ground, the fine dust coating my grungy uniform, turning it a light brown, and stare at the blue sky with its few bulbous clouds that drift across, unconcerned about our plight.

I take the second line we have and crawl over to the front end of the transport vehicle, being careful not to roll off the slope, and tie the free end around the front bumper before inching my way back to the edge. Once more, I lay on my back, exhausted and look at the migrating clouds above me. Scratching on the ground next to me reminds me that Chase still needs to make this last leap. I roll over onto my side to reach for him, but just as my hand grips his wrist, his foot slips and he plummets to the bottom. I gasp as the rope around my waist pulls tight and squeezes my insides to the point where I am afraid that it will cut me in half.

"Chase!" I scream, and my frantic cry echoes around me, bouncing off the steep slope of the hill and the rocks above me, mocking me.

He reaches the end of his line and it jerks him to a halt while yanking me over the edge I lay upon in one simultaneous motion, and I grip the line tethered to the transport, screaming as it burns my hands, branding them. We both dangle in the air the way noodles swing from a fork as they are brought to their demise. Straining, and my arms burning, yearning for relief, I haul myself upward, climbing the rope back to the precipice that the transport vehicle, our shared goal, rests. I scramble onto the ledge, my side chastising me for my negligence of its injury, while my leg also begs for my attention. Positioning myself in a seated position, I do my best to use my legs to support me as I attempt to pull Chase up, but my injured limb refuses to bear any weight, while my one good leg wobbles, unable to bear it all. The rope slips and I squeeze tighter, clenching my fists around it to the point where I think that there will be nothing left of my stinging palms. I heave him upward, struggling against my failing body and gravity as my strength threatens to give out.

My mind wrestles with what to do, presenting two solutions: die or cut Chase loose. I shove the latter solution away, unable to bring myself to do it, to cut him loose as though he is nothing more than a piece of refuse to be discarded when its use is spent. My brain yells at me to let him go and cut the line, but I just sit there, unable to do it, wondering why I cannot. My butt slides an inch across the ground toward the ledge. As I come to the realization that this could be my last moments, I decide that I would rather die than live with the guilt of killing the one person who tried to help me escape this place.

Another jerk threatens to pull me over the edge. I take a long, slow breath and stare straight ahead, unsure of what has changed within me, or why it has come about.

Brown hands, with specks of coarse black hair on the fingers, seize the rope I cling to and pull it upward, saving Chase from the fate of smashing into the ground below us. The top of his head appears, followed by his face, neck, and shoulders. Relieved, I reach for his arm and grip him just below the shoulder, while the mysterious hands grab his other one, and together, we pull him onto the crevice away from the edge and to more solid ground. Once the adrenaline of almost dying, or losing Chase, my only companion in this wilderness, wears off, I remember the strange hands and whirl around to see the face they are connected to. Brown eyes stare back at me. Ragged strips of dark cloth cover the stranger's face, attached to a vest that has more tears and holes in it than solid cloth as stray threads sprawl away from it, swaying in the humid breeze.

I snatch my pistol, freeing it from its holster, and aim it at him.

"Who are you?" I demand.

The stranger holds his hands up in a defensive posture, begging me not to shoot him.

"Who are you?" I scream at him.

"Please," he pleads, his voice hoarse as though it is unused to speaking.

It hits me: the water flask, the pouches of food, the staff, the medicinal plants and bandages, the constant feeling of being followed—it had to be this stranger, this barbarian standing before me.

"You're the one who has been helping us."

He nods.

"Why?" I ask.

"Please," he says again, "not all of us are savages."

My face hardens. How can I trust him? He must have a motive for helping us; I just need to learn what it is.

"Answer me!"

The stranger stares back at me with wide eyes as though the answer should be obvious, and confusion fills his face as he wonders why I do not understand, but Chase seems to. I never hear him move, nor notice that he has crawled away from the edge of the crevice. A white hand on the barrel of my weapon startles me as a soft voice speaks.

"Because, sometimes you help someone when you are able to and when they need it."

My eyes shift to his, marveling at the tenderness within them, corresponding with the gentleness of his voice, as his words go against everything I have been taught.

I remember a time I had tried to help someone. The recruits had been summoned for a live fire training exercise, the goal of which was to make it to the other side of the field without being injured. Those who failed were left to die from their wounds as the carrion birds feasted upon them, regardless of if they still breathed or not.

Faya had gotten pinned down by two machine gunmen. I watched as she hid underneath an overhang in an effort to avoid being hit while gunfire rained down upon her, pelting the surface above her and coating her in bits of rock and dirt, despite her effort to cover her head and face. Her screams as the bullets drew closer—and one clipped her right shoulder—pierced my ears and haunt me to this day: a constant reminder of our reality. I had just made it to the end of the field and had crossed the white line that had been painted on the ground when I had noticed her plight.

Memories of the instructors' irate shouts, melding with Faya's frightened screams, fill my mind as I recall what had happened next: I turned back, racing through the field, ignoring the holes that appeared in the dirt near my feet, as the gunmen attempted to strike their target and bring me down. I swerved and dodged, hoping that my random movements made me a difficult target, but kept my focus on my only friend in the training facility who knew my deepest secrets and fears.

She had always helped me with my academic studies. I could not stand by and watch her be killed in a training exercise.

Another recruit headed straight for me, desperate to reach the end of the field and was angered that I stood in his way. The moment he lowered his head and shoulder, I knew that he planned on plowing into me and shoving me out of his way. To avoid him, I darted to the left before veering back to the right, heading straight for Faya, where I dropped to the ground and slid underneath the overhang beside her, as she hunkered low to the ground with her hands covering the back of her head.

"Come on!" I had yelled at her.

She remained in a fetal position, too afraid to move, but I knew that if she remained where she was and avoided being hit, the instructors would still have her sent to the crematorium for cowardice. I snatched her arm and yanked her from the ground, pushing her to her feet, and shoved her away from her place of security.

"What are—"

"Run!" I screamed at her and pushed her forward.

She refused to move at first, but a mortar shell detonating near us jerked her out of her zombie-like state and propelled her forward with me right beside her, urging her along. We raced across the field, amidst the chaos of gunfire and explosions, our gaze fixed upon the white line as we crossed it together.

The moment I stopped running, a fist struck my face, knocking me to the ground.

"What did you think you were doing?" Molers had demanded, his demeanor more enraged than usual.

I had kept my mouth shut.

"One dead arbiter is better than two. Do not waste your time helping one amongst yourselves who is too much of a coward to complete a simple task! You either make it on your own, or you do not make it at all."

I glared at him, and the venom in my glare was all that he needed to strike me again, except I blocked him and broke his nose to an overwhelming series of gasps from the other recruits as they watched our battle of wills.

Enraged, Molers seized me by the throat, lifting me up, and whispered—his mouth so close that the stench of the salmon he had eaten for lunch that day attacked my nose—so that no one else could hear, "If you were a full-fledged arbiter, I would accept your challenge in the Rite of Conquest. As it is, I have a better punishment for you."

He snatched my hair and dragged me to the white line on the ground, facing the field as the last recruit ran across. "You will watch as your friend here runs back to the starting line before returning here. If she lives, then I will forget our little altercation here."

From the corner of my eye, I saw Faya shake her head in fear, knowing, as I did, that her chances of making it back were slim. One of the other instructors grabbed her and threw her back across the white line. She rolled across the ground before coming to a stop, looked at me, jumped to her feet, and sped off, sprinting for the start line. I watched, transfixed, as she raced across the field, touched the start line, turned, and headed back for the rest of us. The ground erupted beside her and I thought for moment that Molers had won, but a darting figure shrouded by smoke ran across the field, coming closer and closer until Faya popped out of the murky veil and stepped across the white line.

Molers dropped me to the ground fuming at having lost.

As the vivid scene fades and I am brought back to the present, I think back to the gauntlet and how I had helped some of the recruits there, unsure as to why I always ran to the assistance of my fellow arbiters, despite the directives of our instructors. An image of the barbarian I had refused to kill during Commandant Paq's hunt fills my mind, as though my subconscious is trying to tell me something about myself.

"Why have you been helping us?" I asked the stranger again.

"My grandfather and my father before me have always helped those who escape the tyranny of the wall, and so do I."

"The wall… you mean Arel."

He nods.

"We have not escaped," I say. "We got separated from our transport after we were attacked and got lost."

"I know you are."

His response reminds me of riddles and I despise riddles. "It was people who looked like you that…"

"They are not my people. My clan do not attack your kind."

"Clan?" I ask, having always been taught that those outside the wall were one and the same.

"There are many of us, but we all serve different leaders. My clan do not care about your people, but others out here, the other wild men are different. They are the ones who attack you, and with weapons they have not made themselves."

"They come from Kition," I say.

"No, not Kition."

"What do you mean?"

The stranger looks around, wanting to leave. "Please, it will be dark soon. I can help you get to the road above us, but let me go after that."

My muscles strain under the weight of the gun as my mind wrestles with allowing him to assist us, or doing what I have been trained to do. He is an outsider, an enemy of Arel, and it is my sworn duty to protect my city; but as I stare at him, I see someone who is no threat at all, just like the barbarian from the hunt. I lower my weapon.

Chase takes one arm and the stranger takes my other. Together, they lift me up, my side screaming at me for relief from the agony it has suffered the last several days, while I seem to not feel anything in my broken leg. Chase starts for the slope, but the stranger stops him, pointing out a path with less of an incline. I wince as they carry me there, trekking up the hill at a faster pace than my mangled body agrees with, but I keep my mouth shut, wanting, more than ever, to get back to Arel. The shadows of the trees lengthen and the temperature decreases by a degree or two as they struggle to climb the hill, bearing my weight, panting as they go, but neither of them complain, and I notice that Chase's desire to help me seems to have changed from a purpose that would serve him and his sister to something else. The more I ponder it, the more my mind tells me to stop worrying and to just give in to my tired body's desire to sleep. I shake my head. I need to remain awake.

A cool breeze brushes my chin and I look up, thrilled that we have reached the road and that the worst part of this experience must be over. Relishing the breeze as it dries away the sweat that streams down my chin, neck, and chest, I forget for a moment that one of the people with me is an outsider, but the moment is short-lived and reality strikes me upon the head, reminding me of my dire situation. Chase and the stranger set me down and the stranger backs away, having fulfilled his end of the bargain, but instinct and a lifetime of training is hard to ignore. I pull out my pistol and aim it at him.

"Noni!" Chase says with surprise.

"I meant what I said," the stranger says. "I mean neither of you any harm and will leave you both alone now."

"If we are attacked, or if my city is ever attacked by your people," I tell him, my voice cold and void of emotion, "I will kill you."

"I believe you," the stranger replies.

I lower my weapon. "Get out."

The stranger turns and runs, disappearing into the trees and blending in with the landscape as though he is a part of it.

"We should rest here tonight," I tell Chase.

"What if he returns with more people?"

"It doesn't matter. He already knows where we are, and has been following us for the past two days at least. If he has set a trap for us, what does it matter if we spring it today or tomorrow?"

"You trust him?"

"About as much as anyone," says Chase.

"He is not telling the whole truth about his reasons for helping us. You had to have sensed that something was missing from his story."

Chase says nothing, but the look on his face conveys that he thinks the same as me regarding the stranger. He hands me one of the last pouches with food and I open it, offering him some of the dried fruit inside, but he refuses. Giving into the demands of my growling stomach, I finish the contents of the pouch before falling asleep.

Drops of water splash on my soiled and chapped cheek as my enervated body refuses to allow my eyes to open or my mind to join the conscious world, desiring rejuvenating sleep above all else. Another droplet of water dabs my cheek, followed by a soft humming that morphed into a melodic pattering, as more water falls from the sky, splatting my body and the world around me. Forcing myself to wake up, I struggle against the weights on my eyelids, forcing them to open, to show me what life has brought to me this time. A drizzling rain encompasses us, soaking us, as once again, the sky decides that we need another obstacle to overcome before achieving our goal: reaching Arel.

Wiping the pool of water from my cheek, I crane my neck to look at Chase, who remains asleep, despite the puddles forming around him as he sinks in the forming mud on the once dry and sandy road.

"Chase," I hiss.

I receive a groan in response.

"Chase."

He stirs.

Frustrated by his refusal to get up, I prepare myself to repeat his name once more, making certain I am not too loud where I attract unwanted company.

"Chase!"

He raises his head, shaking, before rubbing the sand out of his sleep-encrusted eyes, and looks at me. "What?" he asks, still focusing his own mind as he drags it away from the bliss of unconsciousness and what dreams he might have been having before I woke him.

"It's morning." Even though I cannot see the sun, since it hides behind the gray clouds above us, I know it has risen, judging by the amount of light we do have. "We need to get going."

I attempt to get in a sitting position, but stop as a bed of sharp nails seizes my injured side. Concern crosses Chase's face and he jumps to his feet, reaching me in a single step, lifting my shirt and checking the bandage—now brown with black splotches on it and soaked in my sweat—he had applied days before. He does not need to form the words to express the thoughts rolling through his mind as I know what they are. I need help and I need it now.

"It needs changing, but we do not have any more bandages. I think it will hold."

He examines my leg. "Do you feel that?" he asks, poking me, but I shake my head.

I have not felt much in it for a day now, and I am concerned that the circulation may have been cut off because of all the swelling, which has remained the same and neither increased, nor decreased.

"Can you wiggle your toes?"

I manage to move the chubby stubs on the end of my bloated foot.

"Well, that's something at least," he says, more to himself than to me. "We really need to elevate your foot, but…"

"There isn't time."

I struggle to get up, but it proves useless as my body refuses to obey my commands, a sign that it is shutting down. Chase places his strong arms underneath my shoulders and lifts me up, wrapping one arm around his shoulder so as to support me as we walk. I take a step in the direction the convoy had been headed before the attack, but Chase stops me.

"Shouldn't we go back that way? We know that there is an outpost there."

I pause and glance in that direction, but a deep-seated feeling that had sat silent for the last few days bursts to the surface, warning me of the foolishness of venturing there. Something tells me that if I go back there, seeking Commandant Paq's assistance, I will seal my fate instead.

"Somehow," I say to Chase, "I don't think Commandant Paq will help us."

"You don't think…"

"No one will question him if he says that all he found were our bodies, or that I died of my injuries soon after reaching his outpost. It's not like I impressed him."

None of us spoke about the fact the he cares nothing for plebeians, and one less plebeian in Arelian society would not be questioned or mourned since they are expendable and replaceable, or the fact that Commander Vye had challenged him and succeeded in making him appear weak; killing me would be his way of achieving revenge against us both.

"I would rather take my chances searching for the other outpost," I say.

Chase offers no protest, but holds onto my arm, which he has wrapped around his shoulder, while placing his other around my waist, taking slow strides so as to not to aggravate my crippled state any further, thus making it worse. We navigate our way down the muddy road, me hobbling more than walking, sloshing in fresh puddles as the rain floats around us, falling in a delicate motion to the ground, coating everything with its life-giving shroud. The refreshing rain brings a sense of renewal, having calmed the raging heat from the last few days, but I know it will not last as the weather comes and goes in cycles. A miniscule breeze, not enough to motivate the leaves of the trees to move from their static state, but enough to revivify us, cools our water-soaked skin and I relish it, enjoying the sensation while I can, as such pleasures are unusual.

Without the sun to guide us, I have no idea what time of day it is or how long we have walked as we continue our trek, never stopping, not even for a moment's rest, refusing to show weakness by allowing our tiredness to expose itself. I stumble, but Chase catches me and puts me back on my feet, never letting go. I study him from the corner of my eyes, being careful not to make him aware of my interest in how he conducts himself. He left me alone in this wilderness when we first became stranded here, but he came back. Why? Despite my harsh words flung his way, words I have been taught to think and say, he bestowed upon me a kindness by continuing to help me get back to Arel; though, he has his own reasons, his sister being one. That must be his entire reason for existing, and it hinges upon the hope that I will defend him once we get back, though my mind refuses to let go of the notion that he seems more human than the citizens I am sworn to protect, and that frightens me.

My foot splashes in an ankle-deep puddle and bits of water grip my leg, oozing down my calf between me and the top of my boot, past my ankle, settling beside my heel, causing my foot to squish inside my footwear. The clammy sensation tickles my foot and I frown, having never liked water in my shoes, as it wrinkles the skin on the soles of my feet, making them smell terrible with an odor that would even cause Molers to faint.

A low rumble caresses my ears. I pause, straining to listen to it, wondering what it is, as it never changes in pitch, tone, or rhythm, but remains constant, like that of an engine. That's it! It is an engine, and as the rumbling intensifies, a mixture of fear and joy grips me as I have no way of knowing if this means we are about to be attacked once more or if it means that we are to be rescued.

"To the trees," I say, erring on the side of caution, as the distrust that has been beaten into me over the years takes over and dictates my reaction to this new development.

Hearing the rumble for the first time, Chase shares my reluctance to expose ourselves until we know whether we are dealing with a friend or an enemy. He guides me to a more level area within the trees and we stop just beyond the veil of the brush, watching the road with intense interest, waiting, and hoping. The ground vibrates beneath our feet as nail-sized pebbles bounce along it, doing a little jig of their own in anticipation of who approaches and what it might mean.

A sliver of hope starts to well inside me, but I shove it aside, reminding my internal self that hope makes one careless, which leads to death, as I have been told over and over by my instructors at the training facility. The reverberations grow louder, snaking up my legs, through my stomach, and into my chest, rattling my ribcage as the tank-sized vehicles appear around a bend in the road, heading straight for us. Being careful not to get too excited, I observe them as they inch their way closer. As they amble past us, I recognize the Arelian insignia on them and release a sigh of relief.

I have no way of knowing who is in those vehicles, but know

that I must take a chance on flagging them down, since my chances
of making it on foot to the nearest outpost is slim. I nudge Chase,
urging him to help me out of the tree line and to the side of the
road. We scramble up the slight slope, slipping in the gelatinous
material that had once been solid ground, as we crawl up it and
to the road, and I plop in the mire, face first, its slick, grease-like
substance burying me. Chase's hold on me falters and he reaches for
me three times, his hands sliding off my mud-covered body before
he regains his grip around my waist and heaves me back to my feet,
dragging me up the small embankment to the thundering vehicles
as they trudge past us. Once we reach the road, we both yell, waving
our arms in an effort to get their attention, but as they continue
on by us, that one speck of hope that I had allowed myself to feel,
despite my better judgement, fizzles out and the realization that I
would die out here stabs my heart.

"They didn't see us," I mumble as the last transport rolls past, my
voice hollow.

"I'm sorry, Noni," Chase replies.

I stare into his gray eyes and I see genuine sympathy and sadness,
when before, there had only been contempt. In the short time that I
have been an arbiter, Chase is the first plebeian I have met that has
demonstrated kindness and spoke sincere words of apology, not the
fear and loathing I have become accustomed to and expect.

The rumbling slows and dissipates as the two vehicles stop.

"Look!" Chase points at them and I turn toward them, wondering who will step out.

A door opens on the front vehicle and out steps an armed arbiter,
followed by a female arbiter wearing a uniform similar to Commandant
Paq's. She glances at us, and we must have made quite a pair, one dark-
skinned and one fair-skinned coated in slime, clinging to one another
for support, as both fear and hope consume our thoughts. The woman
waves her hand at the second vehicle and the passenger door opens,
revealing a form I have become very familiar with: Commander Vye.

"Commander," I squeak, unable to contain my joy at seeing a familiar face, and I try to hobble over to her, but stumble and drop to my knees instead, forcing Chase to help me up again and half-carry, half-drag me over to her.

"Noni," she whispers, but low enough so that the others near her do not hear it, and I detect a note of relief in her voice, something I have never heard come from her before, as it goes against her hardened nature.

She realizes that Chase still has his arm around my waist and marches up to him, slapping his right cheek, leaving a red mark, a perfect mirror image of her hand, on his face.

"Let go of her, you filth!"

"Mistress," says Chase, reverting to his ingrained manner of speaking to an Arelian citizen, "she—"

"Did I give you permission to speak?" demands Commander Vye.

"Commander," I interrupt her, my breathing labored as I force my thoughts to turn into words, "he is the reason we are here now. He has helped me, tending my wounds. According to the law, he should be rewarded for assisting an arbiter of Arel."

Commander Vye gives me her usual icy stare, but remains silent.

"She knows the law well," says a new voice, as the arbiter who had stepped out of the first vehicle approaches us. "She is correct."

"Yes, Commandant Jensen," replies Commander Vye.

My weight proves to be too much for Chase to handle—he is just as weak as I am—and before I can hit the ground, Commander Vye swoops in and takes me from his arms.

"Get a stretcher over here now!" yells Commandant Jensen, and two other arbiters burst from the vehicles, carrying a stretcher and first aid bag.

I allow myself to be put on it, not caring if I give in to my exhaustion and close my eyes as I am carried away, while another arbiter shoves Chase into the back of a transport, not bothering to tend his bruises or cuts. The last conscious thought I have is that I am going home, home to Arel.

Chapter 22

The Final Outpost

I stare out the window of the room that has been assigned to me before my arrival at the third and final outpost that Commander Vye and I were scheduled to visit. At least five weeks have passed since Chase and I were found on the side of the road. Instead of taking me back to Arel, Commandant Jensen thought it best to bring me straight here, since the compound has a medical wing with all of the most up to date equipment. My memory of what happened soon afterwards is spotty at best and jumbled, and according to Commander Vye, I had gone in and out of consciousness for at least two days. Being bedridden for so long frustrated me, not to mention the boredom that follows, and I was thrilled when they took the cast off my leg, though I still have to wear a brace for the next week. I will be grateful when I can start exercising again and get back into shape so that I can continue to perform my duties as an arbiter, besides the fact that I detest being cooped up in a room, unable to go anywhere or do anything.

Jealously builds in the back of my mind, nestling in as it weaves its web of deceit and desire, while I watch a group of arbiters strolling outside, and I wonder when I will be able to do that again, instead of hobbling with a cane by my side for support. To my right is a stone square, similar to the one in the outpost run by Commandant Paq, where arbiters perform drill exercises, but instead of fear filling their faces, they are confident and resolute, ready and willing to defend their station if called upon to do so. One man stumbles a little as he runs in place, and I watch as the commanding officer leads him to a shaded area, believing that he has been in the hot sun for far too long. The memory of Commandant Paq's swift punishment for any who did not meet his impossible standards hovers in the back of my mind—an image of the woman whose pain I helped relieve flashes before me—warning me of just how different some places are.

Tired of being confined to my quarters, I shamble over to where my cane is, one assigned to me by the senior physician stationed here, put on the fresh uniform jacket that has been given to me, and approach the door, scanning my wristband.

Passage Denied.

The words scroll across the door in bold red lettering, reminding me, once again, that I am supposed to be in bed resting, but I if I stay within these suffocating walls for much longer, I will lose my mind. Irked, but not deterred, I grab the knife that had been brought in with my breakfast and use it to pop the paneling off the tiny square box near the doorway. Using a trick that Faya had taught me once when we both wanted to sneak out of our room at night to meet up with some other recruits for a nighttime excursion, I strip the two copper wires in the control box and intertwine them together. A hiss sounds and the door slides open, allowing me to stumble through, and I smile to myself when they close behind me.

The sunlight hurts my eyes for a minute when I step outside, having gotten used to being indoors due to my injuries and at the insistence of the head physician. I amble down the asphalt path, my cane tapping one beat at a time in tune with my slow steps, as I head toward their gymnasium, which is outside and similar to the one at the manor back in Arel. Other arbiters stroll past me, saluting me, something that I am unfamiliar with, since it is I who is supposed to salute them; my rank is lower than theirs. I return the gesture, still intrigued by their show of respect for someone of my rank.

"One!"

I turn in the direction of the unified shouts and find another group of arbiters participating in their exercise routine where a single rep consists of a pushup, jumping to their feet and doing a jumping jack, before finishing with another pushup.

"Two!" they shout in unison.

I pause my slow stroll and observe their movements, remembering the times I have had to participate in such exercises, and if I were not still recovering, I would be joining them.

"Three!"

One of the arbiters glances up and notices me. His faces morphs from concentration to excitement and he jumps to his feet at attention. "Arbiters," he shouts, "attention!"

The others spring to their feet and face me.

"Arbiters, salute!"

They all salute me.

Taken aback, I stand still for several moments before I remember that I need to return the salute out of recognition and respect, so I reign in my initial shock and bring my right arm up in a salute. Pleased, the arbiters return to their exercises, while I remain in my statuesque state, grappling with their response to my presence, wondering what has warranted it.

"They respect you," says a voice.

Startled, I turn and face the commanding officer of this unit. "But I have done nothing, sir."

"You survived outside the wall."

Not without help, I think to myself, and as a tidal wave of memories and self-reprimands slam into me, I remember how I managed to survive in the wildlands and who had helped me: Chase. Since our return, I have not seen him, nor do I know what has become of him. I scold myself for dismissing him and allowing myself to be deluded into thinking that I had rescued myself.

Before the commanding arbiter can wonder about my standing there in a pensive state, oblivious to the world around me, I nod at him, salute, and walk away with my cane, continuing its single drumbeat on the coal-colored asphalt. I head to the plebeian quarters, which are on the other end of the compound. The closer I get to it, the more sparse the arbiters are, and I find myself in a pond of white faces, feeling outnumbered and as though I do not belong. A few hollow eyes glance in my direction before diverting themselves back to their tasks, doing their best to ignore my presence, hoping that I do not desire theirs. The further I go, the more I wonder if I have stepped onto forbidden ground, as the clean, polished buildings are replaced by shanty shacks, with warped wood constructing the walls and holes for windows, as no glass fills the hollow spaces.

I pass by a tent-like structure with a v-shaped roof, its cracked tiles have fallen to the dusty ground, and four metal posts supporting the structure. No walls fill the spaces, but have been left open, allowing the warm, moist breeze to blow through, while plebeians work the industry-sized washing machines, wring out the clothes, and iron the uniforms. At first, I wonder why there are no walls for this laundry facility; but as I step closer, I feel the heat radiating from the machines and the irons, presenting me with an answer to my unspoken question, not surprised that they are not allowed a building that has the ability of climate control: luxuries are not to be wasted on the servant class.

I spot one plebeian pulling a load of uniform jackets out of a dryer, separating them and laying them flat in preparation for ironing. Not knowing where else to look, I approach her, startling her, causing her to drop one of the jackets on the unswept floor, and her surprise turns to a frown as the fresh-washed jacket collects every particle of dirt scattered across the wooden floor. I bend down and pick it up, brushing it off as best I can, but my feeble efforts seem to make matters worse, and hand it to her. Unsure of my motives, the woman hesitates before taking it from my hand, while never taking her hazel eyes off me.

"I'm looking for Chase," I tell her.

A quizzical expression crosses her face.

"The plebeian that was found with me."

She jerks her head to her left, motioning for me to go in that direction, and when I follow her movements, I see Chase standing next to an incinerator with his shirt off; my eyes, without my permission, take in his well-formed muscular physique from having spent a lifetime performing manual labor, and I find myself admiring his physical attributes. I shake such thoughts away and thank the woman before hobbling over to speak with Chase. He lifts his head when he hears me approach and we lock eyes for a moment.

"Non—mistress," he greets me, tossing another armful of waste into the incinerator. "What can I do for you?"

"Nothing," I say.

"Then, why are you here?"

I stare past him, asking myself the same question, having not thought through my desire to see him, and not sure why I wanted to in the first place.

"Mistress?" he prods me.

"To thank you," I reply. "You helped me out there, and if it wasn't for that, I would be dead."

"We used each other," he says to me.

Used? That is not how I described it. "Pardon?"

"You used me to get back here just like I used you for the same reason. It was a fair trade and it worked."

"Chase, I..." My voice trails off as I ask myself why I am here, thanking him for something he was supposed to do anyway, while also curious about his new cold and dismissive attitude. Why am I fumbling to find words to speak with? Why am I insulted that he refuses to accept my sincere gratitude? Instead of me thanking him, he should be thanking me, but something deep within me tells me that my actions were the right thing to do.

"You should go," he tells me.

I turn and stroll away, never aware of the sorrowful look upon his face, but the other plebeians see it; their expressions mirror his.

Confused, but unwilling to go back to my room, I meander back to the outdoor gymnasium, returning the salutes of arbiters who run past me, but my automatic movements fail to conceal that my mind rests elsewhere, grappling with thoughts and emotions that I have never experienced—rejection, dismissal, and indifference—struggling to understand why this depressed mood has overtaken me. I tell myself not to dwell on it, that he is just an arbiter and is correct: I did use him to get home. Despite my self-lecturing, my subconscious remains aware of my true feelings, but respects my wishes to lock them away for the moment.

I reach the gymnasium and head over to the free weights that they have, picking up two 15-pounders and settling on a bench, resting my cane on the ground. The least I can do is maintain my upper body strength, and this will cure my boredom for a while. For the next hour, I perform a series of arm exercises, consisting of chest presses, biceps curls, triceps extensions, and lateral raises; and I lose myself to the motions, allowing the tension within my muscles to work its way out, while forcing my mind to focus on the exercises and not the thoughts rattling around in my head.

When my arms tire, I decide to try strengthening my legs. I walk over to the leg press and sit in the seat, adjusting the weight. First, I work my good leg and confidence builds up in me as it pushes the bar upward with ease, so I switch legs. My recovering leg crumples under the weight. Frustrated, I adjust the machine to a lighter setting; and, though my left leg manages to push it up-ward, it shakes and wobbles under the pressure, and I am forced to give up, allowing the weights to slam back into to place with a resounding—*clap*!

"If I remember correctly, the doctor forbade you from physical exercise for another two weeks."

Startled, I turn, staring straight into Commander Vye's eyes, but instead of their usual sternness, they are softer and more maternal.

"I detest being stuck inside, locked away for later use," I reply.

"I figured that you had just gotten bored."

That, too, I think to myself.

"If you are going to rebuild the strength in your leg, you need to start small."

Commander Vye motions me over to a bench and I follow her instructions, sitting down, waiting for her next set of orders.

"Lift your leg," she tells me.

I extend my mending leg, the muscles strain and pull from the effort, not wanting to cooperate, but I force them too, doing my best to not show how much it tires me.

"Good. Now, do it again."

I bend my leg and extend it, doing two more repetitions.

"Lie on your back and lift your leg five times, holding it in the air as your lower it."

I do as she says, positioning myself on the bench so that I am on my back and lift my leg, lowering it, allowing it to hover instead of settling on the bench, before lifting it again. My thigh muscles tire after the second leg raise, but I ignore it, pushing myself to complete the task given me, desperate to regain my strength and agility.

"You're doing well," Commander Vye encourages me, and this new, gentle attitude of hers makes me wonder what challenge she has in store for me. "I want you to walk two laps around this gym, without your cane."

I stand up and hobble over to the dirt track that circumferences the outdoor gymnasium; my right foot crunches in the gravel as it presses downward, while my left shuffles, leaving a streak.

"Pick up your feet!"

There is the Commander Vye I am accustomed to. I concentrate on walking in a normal stride, lifting both my feet, but my recovering leg resists my efforts, preferring the laziness it has become accustomed to. Struggling against my body's desire to be indolent and my personal wish to regain my physical strength, I lift my foot higher with each step, forcing it to walk the way it should and not drag in the dirt, picking up my speed as I go.

"Lift those knees in the air. Higher. Higher!"

Commander Vye's commanding voice echoes in my mind, fueling my efforts, adding strength to my own will and stubbornness, reinforcing the mental commands I give my body. My knees rise high in the air as I walk, performing high kicks with each stance, forcing myself to balance on my left leg, reminding it of how it should function and that its time for languor is over. I complete my first lap.

My leg screams at me to stop as the muscles burn from the exertion I put them through, but a lap around the track is child's play, something I have done since I took my first step as an infant. This should be the easiest exercise I will ever perform. I charge into the second lap, lifting my knees high, only taking a normal step when needed, so as to avoid stumbling or falling down. The more my leg admonishes me for being so harsh, the more I push it, taking deep breaths to stop myself from gasping, welcoming the stream of sweat that pours down the back of my neck and between my shoulder blades. Only three more yards to go. I quicken my pace. Again, my mending leg begs for mercy, but I refuse it. Mercy will not help it regain its strength.

Weakness is death!

The chant taught to me so long ago, repeats in my mind as I push myself onward. With one final stretch of the leg, I cross the finish line, completing my second lap and stagger over to the bench, plopping down on it, allowing myself a moment of rest, while my leg continues to chastise me for being so cruel to it.

Commander Vye stands over me. "You've done well."

I look up at her, surprised by her praise as she does not give it often, or at all.

"You are not the first arbiter to suffer a broken limb, Noni, nor will you be the last. If you wish to regain your strength, you will need to reteach your leg the motion of walking and lifting, adding weights as you need to, until you have worked your way up to what it was able to do before the injury. Recovery takes time, but sitting idle is the worst thing you can do now that you know you are capable of more."

A trio of arbiters stroll past and salute me. I return it, though I am still unused to this newfound respect. I take a side glance at Commander Vye, who beams from the reactions of the other arbiters in the outpost.

"You should welcome their respect," she tells me, having noticed my reluctance to accept the honor they are intent upon giving me.

"But I have done nothing."

"You achieved two feats that most arbiters never do and you did it in the same week: you survived the wildlands—"

"I had help," I whisper, but she does not hear me.

"—and you outwitted The Bell."

I had almost forgotten about that and memories of The Bell fill my mind with Commandant Paq's irate face in the center.

"You are proving yourself to be an interesting arbiter," Commander Vye says, "and don't think that the arbiter council has not noticed."

My heart sinks at her last statement. The last time they took notice of me, I had not acted the way an arbiter should, and they feared that my cowardice would return. I hope that their second opinion of me is more favorable, but would prefer to never stand before them again.

"I thought I had told you to rest." The head physician marches up to us, with two other arbiters by her side, placing her hands on her hips, gesturing how upset she is at my refusal to stay in bed, making me wonder if she had ever been in my position before.

Commander Vye opens her mouth to speak, but one of the other arbiters, who I assume is Commandant Jensen, beats her to it, saying, "I don't think it is such a terrible thing for her to be testing her limits in an effort to become strong again so as to return to her duties."

I try to get a look at the arbiter standing behind the commandant, but the individual remains hidden from my view, shifting her stance every time I get close to sneaking a peak, while something in the back of my mind warns me that I have seen this person before.

"Commandant, if you please..." begins the physician, but the commandant cuts her off.

"You can't blame her for having grown tired of staring at the same four walls she has been in for the last five weeks. Allow her to get some fresh air. Besides, I think it is time for you to see this place, since that is why you were scheduled to come here in the first place.

"Grelyn, pick up Arbiter Noni's cane for her."

Grelyn.

Now the suspicion for the other arbiter seeming familiar hits me. She steps out from behind Commandant Jensen, her unnatural blue eyes unnerving me like they always did, holsters her weapon, picks up my cane from where I had left it on the ground, not bothering to shake some of the dust off its stem, and shoves it in my hands in a manner that conveys just how displeased she is at having to do something kind for me. When we received our assignments, I never thought about where she, Trevors, or anyone else would be sent. I only cared about Faya's assignment and that is because she is my only friend. The more I think about it, the more it makes sense to have her out here. With her ability to see in the dark, thanks to the procedure that she had opted for, she is an invaluable resource out here beyond the wall. After she takes her place by Commandant

Jensen's side again, the head physician opens her mouth to badger me once more about the importance of not overusing my leg so soon after having the cast taken off, but the commandant cuts her off.

"She will be fine. I will see to it personally that she does not reinjure herself. You are dismissed."

A final huff escapes the physician's mouth, but she remains silent and stalks off, perturbed at having been ignored and her professional opinion rejected without a second thought.

"This way," says the commandant.

Commander Vye and I drop in behind her, walking next to Grelyn, who remains erect, keeping her eyes pasted on the commandant's back, refusing to give me or my commander a moment's notice. We follow a concrete path, leading from the gymnasium, to the nearest building, and I find myself looking all around, instead of maintaining the proper military posture, allowing my curiosity to dictate my movements again. Unlike Commandant Paq's outpost, the slate-colored buildings are less dull and dreary, but shimmer in the sunlight, mirroring the way glitter reflects it. I do not know if it is because he is such an unlikeable person, or if it's because, out of the three commandants I have met on this trip, Commandant Jensen seems to be the most normal.

"This is the brig," she says to us.

I study the windowless building, knowing that locking someone up in a room, allowing them no chance of seeing the sun, is a good way to ensure that they are thankful to be allowed out, and will do almost anything to avoid being shut away again, as my most recent experience with being put on bedrest will attest to. We stroll around the square structure to a small enclave where the door is, the only way in or out of the building.

"How long is one sentenced here?" I ask, forgetting my place and receive a reprimanding glare from Commander Vye as a warning.

"Three weeks," the commandant replies. "If an arbiter is sentenced here for a third time, they are sent back to Arel to be dealt with. Grelyn, tell our guests one offense that will have an arbiter sent here."

"Disobeying orders," Grelyn replies, but the malice in her eyes does not match the even tone of her voice.

While observing the exchange between Commandant Jensen and Grelyn, I sense the tension between them as though there is a power struggle going on here; Grelyn's hatred for the commandant is evident, as well as the commandant's insistence on demonstrating to her just who is in charge. Only one thought goes through my mind: this will not end well.

"Explain to her what that disobedience consisted of."

Grelyn glares at the commandant, incensed at being put in such an embarrassing position. After having been used to getting what she wants at the training facility, I am not surprised that she loathes her new position. "I was on night patrol," she begins, "and…"

"And…" Commandant Jensen's stern voice prods her when she trails off.

"And I disobeyed a direct order to return to the outpost immediately."

Grelyn should have known better. Disobedience is not tolerated. Even she had been punished for it while we were still recruits, despite her being some of the instructors' favorite pupil.

As silence fills the void between us, Grelyn continues, knowing just what Commandant Jensen wants her to say. "I was on night patrol when I thought I had seen something of interest. I pursued it, ignoring a direct order to return back to the outpost, garnering three weeks in the brig. This was my second offense."

Second offense? What was her first?

"But if I had been allowed to pursue my suspicions, I could have—"

"You almost got your entire unit killed," Commandant Jensen interrupts Grelyn, preventing her from telling her side of the story.

"I might have been able to find their base of operations," Grelyn challenges her.

"At the expense of everyone else."

"But…"

"Sometimes, it is not worth risking the lives of your fellow arbiters, and your reckless actions put them in danger so that you could achieve some sort of self-glory."

"We are all expendable," Grelyn protests.

"Not out here. Out here, our numbers are limited, and you cannot recklessly risk your fellow arbiters' lives for you own use. We are finished here."

Commander Vye and I watch the exchange between Grelyn and Commandant Jensen with interest, and a little apprehension on my part.

Once she has finished scolding Grelyn, Commandant Jensen walks off to another part of the compound, motioning for us all to follow. She leads us down another path that passes by the plaza, where another group of arbiters participate in some drills, and to a gray building with a pair of red stripes painted in a horizontal fashion, wrapping around the entire perimeter of the structure. Next to it is another building, but with yellow stripes mirroring the red ones. I look at them with interest, wondering what they signify, having not seen them on the previous two outposts I had visited. As we walk further, I spot a similar building, but with blue stripes. Commandant Jensen veers toward it and the fogged glass doors slide open, allowing us through.

Ivory tiles with an ebony diamond pattern on it stretch out before us, illuminated by soft lights emanating from five chandeliers hanging from the pale gray ceiling. One corner of the room is vacant, with a ring around it, indicating that it is a sort of boxing ring, though the two men within it fighting one another gives its purpose away as well. I marvel at the pool table in the center and the chairs spread throughout, each with plush cushions.

"This is our recreational area," says Commandant Jensen. She laughs at the perplexed look on my face. "If you perform your duties well, you are allowed a few luxuries. Life out here is harsh and this helps to mitigate it and make it somewhat bearable."

I glance around the spacious room and the two plush sofas in a far corner with people stretched out on them asleep; the holographic chess game taking place in another secluded area; and the two arbiters sitting at a table, locked in an arm wrestling contest, wondering what thoughts go through their minds, or if they are content to be here. Shouts of praise mixed with groans of disappointment fill my ears as the arm wrestling contest comes to an abrupt end with one participant as the victor, while the other rubs his arm, refusing to conceal his sour expression.

Commandant Jensen waves us along and I trail after her in silence with Commander Vye by my side, unsure of where she intends to take us next. She leads us through the room to a corridor, lit by three egg-shaped lights that provide a white glow upon the ashen walls and floor, before hiking up a set of stairs the same color as a dove's feathers.

"The outposts serve as a buffer between the wilderness and Arel," Commandant Jensen says as she guides us through the building. "It is our job to keep watch for any movement or suspicious activity that goes on and report back."

I step upon the solid steps. The short fibers of the plain carpet stick to the bottom of my boots for a second before letting go, cushioning any sounds that my steps would have made. Once at the top, we dart around a corner, stalking down another corridor—its walls match the color of the clouds outside—and through a solid steel door, which slides open the moment Commandant Jensen swipes her pencil-thin wristband; its anchor color matches my glum mood.

"Do you have any questions," the commandant asks us as she moves behind her glass desk, which housed nothing more than a transparent computer pad, a stylus, and a tin cup of unfinished tea. The giant window behind her, which also serves as the inner and outer wall, illuminates her muscular silhouette as she squares her shoulders, maintaining an erect posture that commands respect from all within the room.

"The attacks on the wall," I say, averting my eyes from Commander Vye's stern face, "you say that you are to serve as a buffer, but Arel still suffers attacks on the eastern wall."

"Unfortunately, we cannot stop all of them," replies Commandant

Jensen. "We do our best, but there is only us and a few other out-posts out here. Sometimes, the barbarians sneak through unno-ticed. Though…"

Commandant Jensen's strong voice trails off as she allows her thoughts to dissipate, refusing to voice them in front of us.

"Yet?" prods Commander Vye, her interest in the commandant's unspoken words evident.

"Nothing," the commandant dismisses her. "You will learn, Noni, much like Grelyn has, that though these outposts are to provide a sense of security for those of you back in Arel, they do not always succeed. The uncivilized people who live out here are smart, and they have learned how to avoid our methods of detection. That is why she is here"—Commandant Jensen points at Grelyn, who stands at at-tention with her hands behind her back and her feet spread shoulder width apart—"her ability to see in the dark is most useful out here."

Commandant Jensen motions for me to stand next to her. I obey, doing my best to use a normal stride, instead of limping and showing weakness, as I move toward her, past a set of shelves with our digital books, masquerading as old-fashioned printed volumes, and I notice a small corner of one cover propped open just enough to allow a paper map to peek through. Allowing my curiosity to take root, I pause and stare at the paper, wondering why someone would print a map when they could just put it on a monitor for viewing. The familiarity of the lines on it draw me in, but before I can think too much about it, Commandant Jensen pulls me closer and places me in front of the tinted window, turning me so that I face it.

"Out there is the world we are charged with protecting Arel from."

I focus beyond the field of grass and sand, beyond the wilder-ness of gnarled and entangled trees, twisted and knotted together in an effort to form a forbidden maze to discourage any who might dare to think of entering their domain. A murky line across the landscape, marking the far horizon, fills my vision, and a moment of musing that I have not thought about since the day I received my commission bursts into my mind, demanding to be heeded and not ignored: the mysterious and mythical place where everyone lives in harmony, does it exist?

"Our lives out here and at other outposts may seem rough and a bit uncouth to some, but this is our reality," Commandant Jensen explains. "Arel is the only place where civilization thrives."

"And Kition," I say.

Commandant Jensen gives me a startled look, before hiding it away, placing her stern façade back in its place, the mask that she shows the people around her. "Yes, but Kition is not Arel and is always trying to undermine our efforts to bring stability to this world."

As I listen to her, I recall that her statement matches what my instructors at the Martial Diplomatic Corps and presidents Tapiwa and Kumi have said. Before, I never wondered about it, but at this moment, at this time, the words make me pause.

"This is the reality you have seen for yourself when your convoy was attacked and you found yourself alone out there."

"But I wasn't alone," I say, forgetting to keep my mouth shut.

"You might as well have been," muttered Commander Vye.

"But Cha—" I stop myself from finishing his name, remembering where I am and how it would look if I appeared to be on a first-name basis with a plebeian. "The plebeian proved to be an invaluable resource."

"Some do have their merits," Commandant Jensen adds, "and he told us about how you fought off a barbarian outsider, even though you had a broken leg and bruised ribs, how your refusal to quit led to both of your survival."

Chase lied? I open my mouth to contest the story she tells me, but snap it shut upon reconsideration as confusing thoughts enter my mind; and I struggle to grapple with Chase's actions and why he said what he did, but Grelyn's hawk-like gaze pierces through me, as though she knows my thoughts and knows what happened. I ignore it.

"If the outposts fail, Noni," Commandant Jensen starts again, "then it falls on those of you within Arel to protect our way of life and everything we hold dear. I tell you this because your actions out there, on your own, prove that you are the epitome of what we strive for, a testament to the sacrifices of those who came before us and the struggles they endured. You, Noni, give those of us out here hope for the future. But, I digress. You are probably tired and hungry. Grelyn, take Noni to the kitchens so that she can eat."

Whatever Grelyn's thoughts are on being Commandant Jensen's errand girl, her face conceals it well. She salutes her commanding officer and marches out the door, motioning me to follow her. We walk down the corridor and down the stairs, my cane making a single stomp on each step, in terse silence. A part of me is hopeful that I will be able to escape her wrath, but I should have known that I would not be so lucky, because once we reach the last step, Grelyn peeks around the corner, making certain that we are alone, before grabbing me by the shoulders and pinning me against the wall.

I slam the palms of both my hands against her ears, causing her to stumble backwards for a couple of steps. Using this chance, I tackle her, smashing her against the other wall. She coughs and I know that I have knocked the air out of her, and I relax my grip—my mistake.

Grelyn is a formidable opponent, something I should have remembered. She uses my reluctance to finish her against me, using her powerful legs to push herself away from the wall, and slam me back into the previous one. I try to kick her, but my healing leg proves to be my undoing as it refuses to hold all my weight, and I fall down with her on top of me. I reach for my cane. Grelyn shoves it out of the way and sits on my chest, placing her forearm against my throat, choking me as she leans close, speaking in a whisper.

"Don't get too comfortable with your new position," she says, her moist breath leaving a film of saliva on my cheek.

"What do you want?" I manage to say, my voice harsh and raspy because of her arm against my throat.

"I heard about how you embarrassed Commandant Paq," she replies. "Everyone here has."

I stare at her in confusion, unsure of why she is telling me this or what her motives are.

"Commandant Jensen still believes in Arel, in the law, but I've been out there every night since my arrival and have seen things. Things are changing, and you are going to wish that you had made a friend of Paq, instead of an enemy. And when that day comes, I'll be there."

As I lay pinned to the cold floor, I realize that Grelyn would have preferred being under Commandant Paq's tutelage; not that it surprises me. The two are a lot alike, and I know she would have excelled under his command, maybe even have become one of his favorite arbiters.

"I'm glad you're enjoying yourself out here," I hiss at her, hoping that my next statement will strike a nerve, "while Trevors wastes away in a munitions factory."

The irate look on her face tells me that I have accomplished my goal of angering her and she raises her fist to punch me; but the sounds of marching footsteps stop her, and she realizes that she cannot mark me up too much, or Commandant Jensen might ask questions, and she is still in charge here. Grelyn gets off me, removing her arm from my throat, allowing me to breathe. She grabs my shirt and hauls me to my feet before snatching my cane and thrusting it into my left hand.

"You have to be wondering, Noni," she says to me, "the attacks on the wall, the constant unrests. The people of Arel need a firm hand, firmer than what they have right now."

Two arbiters appear from around the corner and stop, staring at us in confusion, as though to ask why we are there. Grelyn and I both salute them and she stalks off, taking me to the kitchens, while I trail behind her, wondering what her words mean or what the purpose of her actions were. We have always had attacks on the wall of Arel. I think back to my first engagement there, remembering the weapons used from Kition. Does Grelyn know something I do not? What did she find on one of her patrols in the wildlands?

Chapter 23

An Enemy Formed

The transport bounces along the pothole-ridden road—its right rear wheel hits one square on, causing the back to jump up and me to strike my head on the roof of the vehicle—toward the giant gates that allow entrance through the wall and into Arel. My... my city. Elation at seeing my home eludes me, running away and hiding as though ashamed of being associated with such a place. Where is the pride I had once felt? Why do I feel so... empty?

I glance at Chase, who sits in the back seat with me, but his gaze remains straight ahead, focused on anything, or anyone, but me. We had spent an additional three weeks at the outpost; and in all that time, he never spoke to me. My mind still wonders why he lied about what had happened in the wildlands. He had the opportunity to embellish his role in saving my life, to advance his status and prove his worth, but he chose not to. I realize that I have been staring at him for the last several moments and jerk my gaze away, passing over Commander Vye, who had turned in her seat in the front and watched me. We lock eyes for a moment before I turn back to the window, watching as the scant amount of brush disappears and the road widens the closer we get to the gate.

I move my leg a little, glad to have the brace off. After the extended stay at the outpost, and the excellent care provided by their doctor, my broken leg healed quite well and faster than anyone thought possible. My station as an arbiter, and the fact that my age meant I had an excellent chance of healing quicker than most, and with little to no lasting side effects, made me the doctor's number one priority, though a part of me wonders if Commander Vye had a little something to do with all the extra medical attention as well. Her behavior toward me seemed changed, different outside the wall than before we left.

Grinding and creaking fill the air, drowning the roar of the transport as it plods along and I look ahead. The black gates, dulled from the constant sand, wind, and rain, creep open, allowing one to see inside the city. Guards in their towers turn their attention on us, aiming their weapons, poised and ready to strike should we prove to be a deception, should we prove to be the enemy. As the transports pull in and nothing happens, their rigid stance relaxes, but behind their helmets, I know that they watch us, waiting, and ready.

I prepare to get out, thinking that the vehicles will stop, but they do not. Hoping that no one noticed my mistake, I nestle back in my seat and watch as the leaning buildings of the eastern sector pass by us. People scurry out of our way. Plebeians walk behind their masters, but even their masters do not dare look at us, choosing to avert their eyes instead. I am taken back to my first day within this region as I hurried to report for duty, remembering all the people who refused to look at me, hastening away instead, hoping that I did not notice them. Again, the same question I had thought about that day enters my mind: why are arbiters feared? We guard the citizens of Arel. We defend them from outside invasion. We protect them from uprisings. Yet, all I ever see in their faces is fear or anger.

Long shadows pass over us as we make our way through the

bouncing streets that feel as though they have not been repaired in over five years. One of the rear wheels finds another pothole, and I clutch my stomach as it is jarred from its peace. The silence within the vehicle ebbs at my nerves, broken only by the roar of the transport's engine as it climbs the small hill to the manor, and I look up, staring through the windshield at the building that grows as we approach. Elation at seeing my home eludes me for the second time today, and I am left with a hollow pit in my stomach.

We pull onto the driveway that leads up to the front door and the vehicles stop. Not waiting to be told to get out, I open my door, grab my duffel bag, and place my boots on the pavement, relishing the warmth of the sun as it covers my face. Commander Vye strolls to the front of the vehicle, while Chase hurries inside, no doubt to get a head start on his chores for the day and to make up for the ones he missed while gone. He never glances in my direction and a part of me is hurt by it, a puzzle that plagues me as I try to understand why.

"Noni," Commander Vye says to me and I turn toward her, remaining at attention, "there will have to be a report written, but that can wait until tomorrow. Take the rest of the day to rest."

"What about my patrol duties?" I ask, wanting to get back into a routine so that it would occupy my mind, freeing me of the events from the past nine weeks.

"Let me worry about that."

"Yes, ma'am." I secure my duffel over my right shoulder and head for the front door. As I place my hand around the knob, it jerks from my grasp and opens wide, forcing me to come face to face with Molers. My breath catches in my throat, forming a hard lump that refuses to dislodge and allow me to breathe. I swallow, forcing the lump downward, as I keep my gaze fixed on Molers, wondering why he is here. I know that he has applied for a transfer out of the training center, asking to be assigned elsewhere in the city for a position similar to Commander Vye's; he does it every year. When I was still a recruit, we always knew when his request had been denied, as his already temperamental mood turned more foul and the least little thing set him off.

"Arbiter Noni. Commander Vye," he greets us, but I do not buy his façade of pleasantries, having witnessed it before. "Please, come in." He opens the door wider.

"Master Arbiter," says Commander Vye in a controlled tone, keeping her own curiosity at his sudden presence muted as she strolls through the door and I follow after her.

"Shall we go to your office?" asks Molers, but his request is more of a command than a suggestion.

I do my best to keep my face impassive, but some of my curiosity and hatred toward him must have shown through since he turns and gives me a warning glare. Swallowing the lump in my throat, I wooden my expression, and he once again focuses on Commander Vye. She inclines her head and leads the way to her office, and he trails after her while I reposition my duffel on my shoulder and head for the staircase.

"Arbiter Noni," says Molers, and I stop, unsure of why he insists on calling me by my formal title, while at the training facility, I was referred to as recruit, little shit, or maggot, "you will join us."

I will? Why? Whatever business he has with Commander Vye could not include me; at least, it never has in the past. Knowing that I would not be allowed to escape whatever he had planned for me, and not wanting to be on the receiving end of his wrath like I had been countless times as a recruit, I follow after him and Commander Vye, tightening my grip on my bag, making up the caboose to a train as it creeps through a darkened tunnel to its impending doom. We enter the office and Commander Vye takes her place behind her desk, refusing to sit, preferring to stand when dealing with Molers, who positions himself right in front of her, his expression unreadable, while I sink into a corner, wishing I am somewhere else.

"Please," says Commander Vye, motioning to a chair.

"I prefer to stand," Molers replies.

For a moment, I am thrust back to when I had stumbled upon them while they were in here, arguing. The door had been ajar and I had allowed my curiosity to get the better of me. He wanted something then, something that angered Commander Vye. What does he want now?

"As you wish," Commander Vye says, remaining on her feet so that she can look into Molers' eyes and face him as an equal.

The tension in the room strangles me and I hope that neither of them notice the beads of sweat dripping down the sides of my face.

"It has come to the council's attention that you had a little bit of trouble during your trip," says Molers.

"That is not surprising since I sent word to the Command Division about it eight weeks ago," replies Commander Vye.

"They wanted to clarify a few things."

"I left nothing out."

"Maybe so, but some things are a bit confusing for them."

"For them, or for you?"

Molers' brows furrow, not liking how Commander Vye goes straight to his real reason for being here. "I've warned you before to not make an enemy of me," he growls.

"Perhaps, you should clarify what questions you had about my report."

"Commandant Paq had interesting things to say about your visit."

"Indeed." Commander Vye's tone darkens.

"Most of it, concerning, you." Molers faces me, and a wave of heat fills the space between the collar of my jacket and my skin. "Defeating the bell. That is quite a feat. Of course, the reason for you engaging in it is even more interesting."

I stare at him, trying to keep the fear off my face as I know where he is headed with this line of questioning.

"Why is it you failed to kill the outsider when you had a chance?"

My mind goes back to that moment. I feel the rain on my skin and it envelops me, drowning me, causing the stray strands of my hair to plaster themselves to my face as I prepared to kill him. For a moment, the room and people before me fade away as I travel back, reliving that exact moment when I had decided to release him, only for him to die at the hands of Commandant Paq. I jerk myself back to the present, realizing that two pairs of eyes are on me, waiting for me to answer Molers' question.

"He was not a threat to Arel, sir."

"And how is it you came to that conclusion?"

"Commandant Paq had decided to release this outsider so that he could have a bit of fun and hunt him down. If the man was a threat, shouldn't the Commandant have executed him the moment he was captured?"

"A fair question," says Commander Vye.

"And yet, it is not yours to answer," Molers reminds her. He turns back toward me. "It has also come to our attention that you went missing for a few days."

"Yes, sir." I reply.

"Care to elaborate?"

"It will all be in my report, sir."

"Master Arbiter," Commander Vye interrupts me, "I must protest. This interrogation of yours is out of line."

Molers slams his fist on her desk; its resounding thud echoes around the room, silencing her and causing me to jump. Again, I am reminded of the previous time he had come to this manor and talked with Commander Vye. I never thought too much of it, but now, I wonder what was said before I had stumbled upon them and eavesdropped on the last few minutes of their conversation. Commander Vye had not been happy with what he had said and remained in a terrible mood the rest of the day, but this current situation makes me wonder why he is here as Grelyn's warning to me resurfaces, forcing its way to the forefront of my mind.

"Answer me!" Molers bears down on me, and I realize that I had been so consumed with my own thoughts that I never heard him speak.

"It will be in my report, sir," I repeat, hoping my response answers the question he had asked me.

"In your report. You and that plebeian boy were alone for some time," continues Molers, and I begin to understand what this is about, "and his statement was interesting. In the preliminary report that your commander sent back to Arel, she states that the plebeian boy helped you while you were lost and wounded in the wildlands, but she also stated that he mentioned how you saved both your lives at least three times, all while you had a broken leg and a possible broken rib."

"Bruised," Commander Vye corrects him, Molers ignores her.

I wish I knew what Chase had said to Commander Vye while I was unconscious in the medical wing of the third outpost. All I know is that he credited me with our survival, refusing to take any for himself or to embellish his own role.

"He helped me as much as I helped him," I say.

Molers' doubtful expression conveys his disbelief toward the entire incident, and my mind races to think of what I can say that will match Chase's story; otherwise, we will both be punished.

"Did you run into any of the locals?"

"Locals, sir?" I ask.

"Any of the people who live outside the wall."

I harden my face, willing myself to not show fear to this man, as I try to moisten my cottonmouth with what saliva I have left so that my words will be crisp and clear and not have a hint of anxiety in them.

"We found one, sir."

"And?"

"He ran off," I answer.

"How do you know it was a he?" demands Molers.

"I do not," I reply. "It was an assumption, but the individual could have easily been female. The rags it wore made determining its sex difficult."

"Did you speak to it?"

"No, sir. The outsider ran off. I believe we surprised it as much as it surprised us."

Molers weighs my words, mulling over them, trying to determine if I lied or told the truth. I maintain my rigid posture. He seems too interested in what happened to me out there and I know it has nothing to do with him being concerned about my welfare. He hides something. But what?

"Are you finished?" Commander Vye demands.

"Anxious to be rid of me?" says Molers in a sly voice.

"Master Arbiter," replies Commander Vye, "I have a sector to manage, and you keeping us here, demanding to know answers to questions that will be in both our reports, and which you will have access to in the next two days, prevents me from doing my job."

Molers' brow twitches, a sign I know well, one that indicates his anger is close to bursting through the calm façade of his. He never liked being challenged.

"So it does. Very well, commander, I look forward to reading both of your reports."

He will be reading our reports? An instructor from the training facility never reads the reports of other arbiters, unless they are under his command or are a recruit. What happened while we were away?

Molers salutes both Commander Vye and me before leaving her office.

"Commander," I ask, "what was that about?"

"I don't know," she replies.

"What does it mean?"

"Nothing good." She waves me out of her office and I clench my duffel, hugging it close to me as I leave, spotting Molers as he finishes talking with Chase, who squirms underneath his towering physique and unrelenting gaze. Molers stalks away from Chase, walking past me and the same plebeian girl whom I saw when I first entered this manor as she sweeps the front entrance. Without warning, he raises his hand and backhands her, knocking her to the floor, relishing the scream she releases when he strikes her.

I drop my duffel.

"Molers!" I shout at him, not using his formal rank, as my mouth speaks the words flowing through my mind before I can stop them. I don't know what compels me, or why I react this way, but his cruelty toward the plebeian sparks something inside of me, causing me to seethe with anger. "Striking a plebeian who has done no wrong and who has not failed in performing their duty," I say to him, loud enough for all to hear, as I approach him and stand inches away from him, "is a violation of the law. According to Arelian law…"

Strong hands seize me around the throat, shoving me into the wall, while the edge of a table scratches my side as I slam into it, choking me as I struggle to breathe. My first instinct is to panic and grab the hand around my throat, but I stop, remembering my training and reach for the side table, feeling for anything I can use as a weapon.

"Are you threatening me?" Molers growls into my ear. "Because if you are, there is a better way to settle this."

My fingers brush something long and slender. I snatch it, but before I am able to act, another hand grasps Molers' wrist in a firm grip and the knuckles turn white from the pressure.

"Master Arbiter," Renal's voice echoes around us, and I glance in his direction, having never noticed his presence or heard him approach, and judging by Molers' startled expression, neither did he, "that is enough."

Molers releases me.

I lean against the wall, coughing and gasping for air, doing my best to not show just how close I was to losing consciousness. I glance at Renal, who looks at the slender object in my hand, a broken handle that had belonged to the single drawer in the table, which someone must have placed there earlier and forgotten about it, and I drop it, allowing it to thump on the rug on the floor.

Molers heads for the door, but Renal stops him.

"Master Arbiter," his calm, yet commanding voice demands obedience, and no one questions him, not even Commander Vye, as she stands in the doorway of her office, "Arbiter Noni has not issued your punishment."

"My punishment?" The fury in Molers' eyes could melt stone, but he contains himself, an act that unsettles me, since he is not known for taking orders from anyone deemed to be below his station and rank, but something about Renal's stance conveys that disobedience of his command will not be tolerated, and Molers senses it.

"You did disobey the law and no arbiter is above it," Renal says.

Molers faces me, standing at attention. "Very well. Arbiter Noni, what is my punishment?"

I survey the others in the room, each of them watching me, awaiting my decision. The prohibition of striking a plebeian as they perform their duties is a law in Arel, but it is one that is ignored by most; even I paid little attention to it, until now, until something within me changed. As my eyes pass over the other arbiters I read their expressions: most believe that this is just a simple power play between me and my old instructor, a way for me to demonstrate that I am capable of being firm in my duties, even when it is someone I know, while others probably believe that I have overstepped my bounds. My gaze meets Chase's. He shakes his head at me, pleading with me to let it go, but I cannot. If I do, I will forever be marked as weak and given an assignment that will result in my death. No, I started this and now I must finish it.

"Master Arbiter Molers," I say, doing my best to keep my voice from shaking and to not cough, "for your failure to follow the law, a law set down by our ancestors in their wisdom, you will…" My mind races to think of a proper punishment. As everyone stares at me waiting for me to finish my sentencing, I think of the factory I had visited with Commander Vye and how plebeians and Arelian citizens had been sent there because of unforgiveable infractions. Though I know that he will not be there for long, perhaps I can make his life a living hell for a while, giving him a little taste of what he delivered to us recruits. "You will be assigned to the munitions factory here in the eastern sector for a period of three months."

Molers' face darkens.

"Master Arbiter Molers," Renal says, "you have been given your punishment. You will report to the Command Division within the hour, where a marshal will be assigned to you to ensure that you are not afforded any special treatment."

Molers salutes Renal and stalks out of the manor. His demeanor tells me that I have made a dangerous enemy, one that I will have to face in the future.

"Don't you all have somewhere to be?" demands Commander Vye, and those who had gathered to watch our exchange make themselves scarce. "Noni, you can file your report in my office."

I do not argue with her, knowing that after my exchange with Molers, I must file a report, and the sooner the better. She steps away from her office and I reach for my bag, but before I can grab it, the plebeian girl snatches it away from me and runs upstairs, taking it to my room. Composing myself, I go into the commander's office and swipe my bracelet against the wall monitor, watching as it flashes to life, confirming my identity. Before it allows me to access it, it asks for confirmation from Commander Vye that I have permission to use her computer. She gives it and leaves, closing the door behind her.

I take a deep breath, preparing what I am to say. "Arbiter Noni filing a report of formal reprimand for Master Arbiter Molers. Molers struck a plebeian performing their duties, violating law 2265-A. For such a violation, Arbiter Noni recommends a sentence of three months in the munitions factory of the eastern sector. End report."

Though the Ministry of Justice determines a violator's final punishment, when it comes to arbiters, the law is a little different. When an arbiter commits an infraction, the arresting arbiter can determine the punishment, anything except the crematorium, and the Ministry okays it in the majority of cases. I know that my recommended punishment will be upheld, but I have a sinking feeling that my actions have made my situation worse. Molers will never forget what I have done.

I turn off the wall monitor and it morphs back into the wall, giving no indication that it had ever been on, much less that it exists. When I open the door, Commander Vye fills the doorway and I force myself to meet her gaze.

"You should not have done that," she says to me.

A quick glance down the hallway tells me that we are alone. I step past her and head for the stairs.

"A plebeian can be replaced, but a good arbiter cannot."

I remain silent.

"When you won the bell, you asked me how I knew you could do it and I told you that you remind me of me. Don't be like me."

I look into her eyes, seeing compassion for the first time. Before, whenever I stared into her gaze, only a cold stern look greeted me, but right now, something has changed, something is different. Pity fills the dark depths of her pupils, but not the sort of pity I had witnessed Mandi display. This is different. It is directed at me.

"Take the rest of the day off."

"Yes, ma'am," I reply and make my way to the staircase, but she stops me the moment I place my foot on the bottom step.

"Noni, this job will either harden you, or kill you. Remember that."

I hike up the stairs after she goes into her office and closes the door behind her, unsure of what has just happened. Not wanting to think about it—Chase, my time outside the wall, or the barbarian that Commandant Paq murdered for no reason other than the thrill of it—I run up the stairs, not caring that my boots pound each step, mimicking the way a masonry worker hammers stone. I reach the top step within seconds and hurry to my door, not waiting for it to slide open all the way as I shove my way through and stop short. The plebeian girl stands in the center of my room, her head hanging low as she stares at the floor, allowing the tangled mass of her hair to fall around her, covering her face. I spot my duffel. She has placed it at the foot of my bed, still zipped closed and with no sign of having been rifled through, as though the thought of stealing something valuable had never occurred to her.

"What are you doing here?" I ask, more surprised than upset.

"Waiting, ma'am," she replies in an inaudible voice that I have to strain my ears to hear her.

"Waiting for what?"

The girl reaches up and tugs at her dingy shirt, soiled and grayed from use, pulling it down, bearing her pale skin while keeping her shoulders hunched and her head bowed low, not daring to look at me. My eyes widen as I grapple with her actions and rush toward her, seizing her shirt and pulling it back up over her shoulders. I cannot believe that she thought... I would never... the thought disgusts me! She is a child. I drop to the floor as I realize that, for the first time, I do not think of her as a plebeian, a slave meant to do the menial chores that my job prevents me from doing, but as a young girl, too small and weak to protect herself in a world intent on forcing her to fulfill the tasks of a grown woman.

"What made you think that I..." I allow my voice to trail off, unable to finish the question as the thought continues to make me want to retch. I prefer men, ones closer to my age, and I would never force myself upon someone.

"You saved me from the other arbiter. Did me a favor," she whispers, afraid to speak up for fear that I may decide to punish her myself. "I owe you now."

"Not like that, you don't." I grab the only chair in the room and encourage her to sit down. "Do the other arbiters here force you to..."

"Only two," she replies.

It is forbidden for an Arelian citizen to force themselves on a plebeian. Such unions are outlawed altogether to prevent an inferior population from being produced, but most of what is prohibited happens anyway.

"Tell me their names," I say to her.

"Anan," she says to me, "and..."

"Continue," I encourage her, keeping my voice gentle.

"Trix."

I know Anan. Well, in passing. I run into him from time to time, but we have never been on patrol together, nor have we ever talked. Most days, he can be found harassing the plebeians, and as I think about it, I remember that the women and girls always tried to keep their distance from him, and now I know the reason why. As for Trix, I only see her when we are all expected to report to the dining area; she keeps a low profile, though she was on the receiving end of Commander Vye's temper before we left for the outposts, for failing to remain at her post.

I look at the girl, thinking back to when I first arrived at the manor, trying to remember her name. As I force myself to remember something that I had once thought trivial, the girl sneezes and I notice her shivering. There does seem to be a bit of a chill in the air, but I never noticed it until now. I reach into my closet and pull out one of my spare arbiter jackets, wrapping it around her shoulders the way I think a mother does when tending to her child, the way I had witnessed Chase tend to his sister when she was scared, but I never knew the love of a parent.

"Sheila, right?" I ask her.

She nods her head and starts to cry. I am confused as to what I should do. I have never witnessed anyone cry like this before, nor have I ever been sought out for comfort. A part of me fears that her sobbing will attract attention, and considering how well today has gone, that is the last thing I want. I turn toward the door, expecting to see someone standing there, demanding to know what is going on, but it is empty. As tears stream down her freckled cheeks, I wrap my arms around her, feeling clumsy and awkward, but she nestles into them, allowing me to embrace her in a comforting hug, surrounded by the pale sunlight that creeps through the window. I lose track of time as she weeps, waiting for her to regain her composure, but she stops, falling silent, and yawning from the exertion.

"Feel better?" I ask.

She nods, wiping the last tear from her eyes.

"Why don't you rest," I suggest to her, laying her down on the bed and tucking the blanket around her.

"I can see why Gwen thinks you are nice," Sheila yawns again.

Nice? I had tried to arrest her when we first met. "She said that to you?" I ask. She had to have been close to Gwen's age, maybe a year or two older.

Sheila nods, but her face turns somber again.

"What's wrong?"

"She's sick."

"What?"

"While you and her brother were away, she was forced to beat the rugs in the rain as punishment for burning a pot in the kitchen. She hasn't been out of bed since. Some of us try to get her chores done in addition to our own so that she won't be missed, but she isn't getting better."

"Where is she?" I ask, knowing just how well Chase would take her illness, and I find myself worrying about him.

"In the plebeian quarters." Sheila yawns once more and closes her eyes, falling asleep within seconds.

I step away from the bed, determined to find Chase and his sister. The door to my room makes a small—*soomf!*—sound as it closes behind me and I sneak down the dim and gray hallway, heading toward the back stairwell used by the plebeians, leaving Sheila in my room, asleep on my bed. No sounds escape from the main floor or the stairwell. Taking it as a good omen, I slip down the stairs, hugging the wall and being careful to step over the fourth step from the top so as not to cause it to creak, like it always does when someone steps on it. Muted silence swirls around me, encouraging me to continue my descent down the servants' staircase.

When I reach the bottom step, I crane my neck to peek around the corner, looking into the kitchen and the corridor that leads to the main entrance and the main stairwell. No one. Unnerved by the lack of activity, I force myself not to dwell on it, but to take advantage of it. Perhaps Commander Vye had decided to send everyone out on patrol, or because of my entanglement with Molers, they might have been confined to quarters. Regardless, the lack of their presence is my chance to see Chase and Gwen.

I dart from the back staircase to the main hallway, tiptoeing as I creep along it, making my way toward the plebeians' quarters. A cough echoes from up ahead. Startled by it, I bump into a narrow table, causing it to shift. The cough stops. I duck into a doorway just as a head pokes out from the main living area, using the shadow to conceal my presence. The man looks up and down the hallway, pausing to listen for any more sounds that might indicate that he is not alone, and judging by the way he reacts to my clumsiness, I realize that he isn't supposed to be down here either, meaning that Commander Vye had put everyone in lockdown. I watch him creep to the main stairwell and climb them, doing his best to not make a sound.

Several seconds pass as I wait, making certain that no one else is down here with me. Before another can interrupt my skulking around, I hurry to the door that leads to the plebeian quarters and open it, cringing when it releases a slight creak, which to my ears, sounds as though a raging storm has just opened its fury upon us. Glancing around, I see no one, nor do I hear any footsteps racing to investigate, so I slip through the door and close it with a soft clink. I lean against the door, shrouded in darkness with only a single light hanging from the ceiling, coated in cobwebs, to provide any escape. My hand stretches out and finds a rail. Clinging to it, I take each step one at a time, doing my best to remain silent as they sink under my weight, threatening to give way and allow me to tumble downward.

Water pools at the bottom, and I almost slip when I step into it, but manage to catch myself. My antics attract the attention of a plebeian woman. She rushes to the doorway of her room and gasps when she sees me, placing her hand over her mouth to keep from screaming, in case her actions bring punishment down upon her. I place my index finger over my lips, motioning for her to remain silent, as I remember Sheila's reaction toward my sparing her from Molers' wrath and realize that arbiters do not come down here, unless they intend to inflict some sort of punishment, or are looking for something else. Once again, the thought of someone using her in such a manner causes a small swell of vomit to enter my mouth, and I force myself to swallow it, maintaining my rigid composure, not wanting to show disgust or fear in front of this plebeian. If she suspects that I am disobeying orders, she might use that to her advantage.

"I am looking for Chase," I tell her in an authoritative tone.

The woman points further down the dismal corridor, her pale skin reflecting the murky light emanating from the few lanterns allowed down here.

I stalk toward the area she points to, stopping when I reach a corner that takes one down another hallway and follow it after receiving an approving nod from her. Manual doors line the walls, each hanging from rusty hinges, swaying from the slightest movement, as no latches remained to lock them in place. Stale dust fills the air, enveloping me, causing me to choke as I breathe, unused to such a toxic atmosphere. I poke my head through the nearest door, but the room is empty. Continuing my search, I scour room after room, discovering a plebeian or two in them, each surprised to see me, but too frightened to do anything, finding no sign of Chase or Gwen; and, as the minutes pass, the soft plops of my boots on the grungy, dirt ridden concrete floor remind me that I do not belong down here.

I reach the end of the hallway and stop. Two doors remain for me to choose from. I pick the one on my right and open it, freezing in the archway at what greets me. On the only cot in the room—if you can call a moldy mattress riddled with tears from which its stuffing pokes out, supported by crooked and bent metal rods a cot—lies Gwen, her eyes closed with beads of sweat dotting her face as she shivers underneath a thin and tattered blanket. Chase sits by her bedside; his worried eyes focus on her, and he never notices my presence. I open my mouth to speak, but the words stick in my throat, refusing to come out, to allow me to speak.

Swallowing, I force the lump in my throat downward, moistening my mouth and whisper, "Chase."

He jumps up and stares at me, unsure of why I now stand in his room.

"Noni! You shouldn't be down here!"

Ignoring his statement of the obvious, I enter the room and close the door behind me as best I can, though it just swings on its crooked hinges, mocking my efforts. "I came when I heard about your sister."

"Why would you care?"

His words stab my heart, slicing through me as though I am little more than softened butter being spread on a piece of bread. He notices my wounded demeanor and softens his tone.

"I'm sorry," he says.

"Sheila told me about Gwen," I say, stepping closer, gasping when I see her ashen face.

"Where is she?"

"My room. Sleeping," I add when he gives me a questioning look. "How is she?" I ask, pointing at Gwen.

Chase bows his head and turns away in an effort to hide his tears from me. "Not well. She needs antibiotics, but no medical center will waste such resources on her—on a plebeian."

He says the last word with disdain, and for the first time, I agree with such sentiment, remembering the man at the medical center Commander Vye and I had visited, insisting that the plebeian woman he carried be cured. A pang of guilt struck me as I recall his fate and that of his children, a remorse I have never experienced before, but as I watch Gwen's small chest rise and fall from her shallow breaths, I pity her.

"They say she has been like this for a few days now," Chase talks more to himself than to me. "Some of the others here have tried to cover for her by doing her chores, but they cannot keep it up for long. I should have been here."

I place a hand on his shoulder in an effort to comfort him, something I have witnessed others do, but it feels awkward and unlike me, so I release my grip.

"She doesn't deserve this," Chase whispers to himself.

"What happened?" She had been well when we left for the outposts and her sudden illness made little sense, unless...

"Vaccinations," spits Chase, "or that's what they call them."

Every five years, all residents of Arel are required to receive vaccinations against various diseases, including the plebeians. During that period, we line up for our routine inoculations, or personnel from the medical centers will visit areas within Arel, distributing them. Our wristbands are scanned and we are given the appropriate shot. I received one before leaving Arel and never thought much of it, and I am certain that Chase received his as well. Though, there are rumors... rumors that not all of the immunizations are legitimate.

I remember a few years ago we all had our routine vaccinations, but despite the efforts of the medical centers, a small outbreak took place, preying upon the old and the already infirmed, as well as spreading among the plebeian population. The only areas not affected were the maternity wards and the training facility. They do not receive any injections to avoid harming any children they might be carrying, but they are also segregated from the rest of Arel. The only visits they are allowed are from medical personal and arbiters, all of whom are given complete health scans to ensure that they will not infect anyone within the ward itself. And though I have received my immunizations every five years since I was three, we are also kept separate from the rest of Arel to ensure that our training is not infringed upon.

During the small outbreak, one of the instructors at the training facility voiced his concern that perhaps some of the vaccinations were not immunizations at all, but the disease itself, used as a way to control the population. I never saw him again. Gwen's current condition brings these memories back to my mind, ones I had forgotten about, until now.

"What do you mean?" I ask him.

"You know we received our vaccinations before leaving Arel."

"Yes."

"After we left, the rest of the city underwent its five-year health inspection where everyone is given a health screening and vaccinations against what are considered the deadliest diseases."

That sounds about right.

"Haven't you ever wondered what is in those shots?"

I stare past him, not wanting to look upon Chase's tortured face. The truth is, I never thought about it. I just did as I was told.

"She was like this when we returned. According to the others, she fell ill soon after receiving her vaccination, the same day she was forced to clean the rugs in the rain, and she isn't the only one. Emma died a week ago."

The name is not familiar to me, but I keep my mouth shut, allowing Chase to speak.

"They say that the southern sector got hit the hardest from this small outbreak, and according to the presidents of Arel, it is now on the decline. Most who were affected have died, but she is strong. She won't succumb." Chase brushes away a strand of hair that has plastered itself to her cheek, swallowing back a tear and doing his best to control his breaking voice.

"Are the plebeians the only ones affected?" I ask.

"No," says a small voice, and both Chase and I whirl around. Sheila stands in the doorway, having snuck in without making a single sound, and I chastise myself for allowing someone to sneak up on me, but push it aside since Gwen's current state is more important.

"Sheila," I say, yanking her inside, "what are you doing here?"

"You were gone when I woke up and I…"

"It's okay," I say, hugging her, unsure where this sudden protectiveness of her comes from, or why I feel the need to keep her safe.

She pulls away and takes a quick glance at Gwen's still form. "You all talk when you think I'm not listening. Some of you even brag about what happens to us."

I listen to her speak, knowing that her use of the word "you" refers to people like me.

"Some of the old died within a few days," continues Sheila. "A friend of mine mentioned that her master's wife—she had been wheelchair bound for a few years now—died from this outbreak. He died a week later after kissing her good-bye. Those too weak to keep going are dead: citizen or plebeian."

A lifetime of conditioning rebels against accepting her words, but Sheila's demeanor harbors no deceit, and I find myself believing her as my thoughts turn toward Gwen and what she means to Chase.

"Haven't you noticed the fires burning brighter since you returned?" asks Sheila.

No, I have not.

Gwen coughs and mumbles something, but her inaudible words are impossible for any of us to discern, and my heart aches for the loss Chase will suffer if she dies. I blink my eyes several times in rapid succession to prevent myself from crying. What is wrong with me? I have never felt sympathy for a plebeian before, but ever since Chase saved my life, ever since he lied for me, I am compelled to help him, to return the favor and… and I have been referring to him by his name, not his station. Conflict reels within me as my mind and heart struggle to overpower the other, wrestling with what I have always been taught to believe against what now stares back at me: one sorrowful face worried that someone he loves will die and another just grateful to be spared a beating, or worse.

I watch as a bit of dribble spills from Gwen's open mouth as she struggles to breathe. I do not know how much longer she has, but know what will happen if no one helps her. As I ponder the last few minutes and what Sheila has told me, it occurs to me that disease can be spread from one individual to another by saliva, and before my mind can stop me, before my heart is controlled by years of training, I ram a finger into her mouth, coating it in her spittle, and shove it into mine.

"What are you doing!" Chase jumps to his feet and yanks my finger out of my mouth, but it is too late.

"Returning the favor," I say.

He stares at me, his eyes wide and mouth open in disbelief. Is that worry on his face? Does he no longer just consider me another arbiter?

"You saved my life twice," I tell him. "I owe you."

Chase opens his mouth to speak, but I cut him off, knowing I have wasted too much time down here.

"If I get sick, they will take me to the medical center for treatment. I will try to steal some of the antibiotics they use to treat me and get them back here. But I will need your help—both of you—to get it to Gwen."

"Noni…" Chase begins.

"It's the only way to save your sister."

"You are gambling your life that they will want to save you," says Chase. "What if they decide that you are not worth the resources?"

My eyes pass from him to Sheila before locking onto his again, and for the first time, I do not fear the consequences of what I have done. "Then the crematorium will have two new fuel sources."

Chapter 24

A Plan in Action

Whispering fills my room and I open my eyes, but they refuse to do as I command and close themselves, only opening enough for me to get a small glimpse of huddled shapes surrounding me. I try to lift my head, and it flops back onto my pillow, weighed down by anvils, or it might as well have been since my neck muscles are too weak to support it. Again, I try to lift my head, but a firm hand pushes me back down onto the mattress. Why am I so exhausted? Sweat drips down the sides of my temple, soaking the sheet beneath me, while more covers my neck, mocking my curiosity as though the answer to my question should have been obvious.

"How long has she been like this?" asks a familiar voice, and it takes my fogged mind a few seconds to attribute it to Commander Vye.

"I do not know," says another familiar voice: Sheila's. A small yelp escapes from her when Commander Vye slaps her. "She was like this when I came in to see why she had not reported for breakfast, as ordered."

I open my eyes just in time to watch as Commander Vye raises her hand again, before rethinking her decision and lowers it, noticing that I have awakened.

"Noni," she says, her voice gentler than I am accustomed to. "Noni, can you hear me?"

My mouth opens to speak, but the only words my ears hear are jumbled and softer than the slightest murmur in a crowded room, making me wonder if I have spoken, as my voice does not sound like it belongs to me.

"Call for a medical transport," orders Commander Vye and Sheila runs out of the room.

Time creates its own pace as I lay in my bed semi-aware of the activity around me, slipping in and out of consciousness. Seconds—or was it minutes?—later, heavy boots race up the stairs, drawing closer as they pound the hallway, heading for my room. My mind remains locked in its fogged state as gentle hands lift me and place me on a stretcher; their white uniforms pierce through the small slit in my eyes as I struggle to open them again, and they carry me to the main floor. Chase's head appears at the banister, but vanishes just as fast, and I wonder if I had seen it at all, or if it had been my imagination. As warm sunlight touches my skin, I turn my head and I am met by Renal's worried gaze, burning his concerned posture into my mind, troubling me.

My eyes close again as the medical personnel lift me into the transport and the doors slam shut. My breathing quickens and more sweat forms on my face, dripping down the sides of my temple onto the stretcher, forming a pool of salty liquid beneath me. Opening my eyes again, my head spins from a sudden jolt that jerks me from side to side, and I turn my head in an effort to keep from vomiting. We stop. The doors open, allowing the sunlight inside the dark interior, causing me to squint from its intensity. Before I have time to adjust to not moving, hands seize my stretcher and haul me into the daylight, darting to a doorway that slides open as they approach, granting us entrance and thrusting us back into the cold glow of fluorescent lights.

"What's her condition?"

Is that Doctor Sahir? Again, I attempt to sit up, but I am shoved back down and told to take it easy.

"She has a fever. Is in and out of consciousness. Not lucid at all," replies one of the medics.

I open my mouth to refute the medic's claim, but my tongue remains glued to the roof of my mouth, reminding of a time when Faya and I dared each other to place as many cotton balls as we could in our mouths to see who could fit the most in. A thermometer is shoved under my tongue.

"One hundred and three," says the doctor.

A bright light fills my eyes as he shines one in them, testing my pupils, before feeling the lymph nodes of my neck and listening to my heartbeat and breathing. My arm swings at him to force him to quit manhandling me, but a pair of strong hands snatches it and holds it by my side, keeping me still.

"She has the symptoms—"

My head burns and I cannot stop shivering as chills run through me, attacking every part of my body, tormenting me.

"—but I need some bloodwork done."

A pinch, followed by a small prick, pierces my forearm as a nurse follows Doctor Sahir's orders, and my blood gushes from my vein into a tube, filling it with a red, viscous substance. I try to watch, to remain aware, but my will falters and I am unable to fight my weakened body's demands for rest. Relentless spinning attacks my mind, despite my eyes being close, and the sensation of the gurney moving underneath me jerks me back into consciousness, but my eyes refuse to tolerate the bright, white lights bearing down upon me with merciless fervor.

"Arbiter Noni?"

The distant voice fills my tumultuous mind as it wavers between the conscious and subconscious, unable to determine which reality I belong in. Only the jerking of my head and the twitching of my muscles provide any indication that the blurred people, the fading whispers, and the icy gurney beneath me are real.

More murmurs. More whispers. My unfocused mind struggles to hear them, to understand their words, but my body desires sleep. Sights and sounds meld together, fusing into one confusing world, until the distinct clinking of glass vials bumping into one another pierces the air, stabbing through the jumbled mess that fills my mind and catapults me back into my present situation, and the reason for me being here. I open my eyes. Concentrating, I force them to focus, and walking toward me is a nurse, carrying a tray with five vials of clear liquid—the medication I need for Chase's sister. She sets the tray on a table next to me and turns away, heading toward Doctor Sahir as he sits by a monitor, awaiting the test results. Desperate, I reach for the tray, forcing my weakened body to move. It refuses. I flop back down on the bed. Glancing in their direction, I see them huddled by the translucent monitor, still awaiting the results. The nurse peeks at me, taking in my condition, and turns away. This is my last chance. Swinging my arm out, I lift myself up enough to snatch a vial of what I hope is the medication that Gwen needs, and shove it in my pocket.

"It's positive," says Doctor Sahir, rushing from the monitor and toward me. He scoops up a package with an unused needle in it and tears it open, placing the paper-thin tip into one of the vials, filling the tube with the clear liquid.

My hand remains glued to my pocket with the coveted prize as he inserts the needle into my vein, injecting me with the cure. A warm sensation fills my arm, starting at where he has pricked me and spreading outward in waves up my bicep and down my forearm to the tips of my fingers, followed by drowsiness. Unable to stay awake any longer, I turn my head toward the doctor, taking one last look at him before the world goes black and all the voices around me cease.

Sometime later, my mind pulls itself form a deep slumber. I

have no idea how much time has passed or how long I have been asleep. I turn my head, wanting to go back into the blissful abyss of unconsciousness, where pain does not exist, but my mind rebels, jerking me awake. Murmurs spill in from the hallway. The voices sound familiar and I struggle with my memories to place them.

"How did she get this sickness?" comes a demanding and curt voice: Commander Vye's. "She had the vaccine."

"Vaccines are not foolproof," says Doctor Sahir.

I imagine Commander Vye's disapproving glare as she stares at the doctor, demanding answers in that silent way of hers.

"I'm sorry, commander," continues the doctor, "but you did say that she had been lost for a few days in the wildlands. Perhaps she picked it up there, maybe a more virulent form of the disease. Her charts indicate that she had a broken leg, bruised ribs, and was suffering from dehydration and lack of food. In such a weakened state, vaccinated or not, she would have contracted anything."

I open my eyes just in time to watch Commander Vye unfold her arms, placing them by her sides.

"The important thing is that we caught it in time."

A nurse bustles into the room with a tray, her white uniform making the immaculate walls appear dingy and soiled. "Oh, good, you're awake," she says, her burgundy lips curling into a smile, as though she is happy to see me alert and aware of my surroundings. "You gave us a bit of a scare for a moment."

"How long was I out?" I ask her.

"Two days."

Two days? Gwen! What if she did not survive this long? She was already ill when I found her and if she doesn't...

"Something wrong?" asks the nurse.

I shake my head, scolding myself for allowing my internal emotions to show through. Arbiters are supposed to be stronger than that. We are supposed to compartmentalize, but as I try to remember my training, thoughts of Gwen lying dead on her cot with a lugubrious Chase looking down on her, holding her hand as though trying to hang onto what was left of his world ravage my mind. I need to get back.

"When may I leave?" I ask, doing my best to sound casual about it.

"Eager to get back to work?" replies the nurse, her rose-colored cheeks complimenting her black skin and reminding me that I must look terrible in comparison. "You were pretty sick. It is preferable if we keep you here for another day or two just to make certain that you are well enough to return to duty."

Another day or two?

"I'd much prefer to return home," I say, spotting my uniform folded into a neat pile atop the only dresser in the room. For the first time, I realize that I am wearing a hospital gown, and a wave of panic washes over me, fearing that they found the vial of medicine that I had stolen earlier.

The nurse grins at me again, giving me one of those knowing smiles as she places the tray in front of me and reveals the plate of food on it. I stare at the eggs, bowl of fruit, and buttered roll.

"How do you feel this morning?" asks Doctor Sahir as he steps into the room with Commander Vye, who shoots a disapproving glare at the buttered roll on my tray.

"Better, sir," I say.

He takes my wrist into his smooth hands, checking my pulse. "Pulse is good." He shines a light into my eyes, testing my pupils before smiling to himself, pleased that I seem to be doing so well.

"Is there any way I can return back to the manor today?" I ask.

Doctor Sahir gives me a quizzical look and I try to keep my face unreadable. "You do need to rest and I would prefer if it were here where we can monitor you."

"What if," I begin, controlling my voice and hoping it does not sound too desperate, or there will be questions, "a nurse were to come with me and keep an eye on me. I've never been fond of medical centers and would prefer more familiar surroundings."

Appearing to be afraid of something is a sign of weakness and frowned upon, but I gamble that they will forgive such a childish fear on my part, considering my brush with death. Their softening expression tells me that my moment of apparent meekness has worked.

"I am off duty in an hour," says the nurse. "I could go with her and monitor her for the next few days."

"On one condition,"—Doctor Sahir looks right into my eyes—"that you eat everything on that plate. And don't scarf it."

"Yes, sir," I reply, reaching for the buttered roll. Commander Vye clears her throat when I do, displeased that I have such a food item on my plate, since it violates the strict dietary restrictions of arbiters.

"Certainly, commander," Doctor Sahir says to her, "one roll will not harm her. She needs to regain her strength, and for the next three days, I have rescinded the restrictions to her diet."

Commander Vye backs away, knowing that his orders concerning my wellbeing supersede hers, for now, and the doctor winks at me before leaving.

"Shall we?" he says to Commander Vye, and she follows him out of the room.

"I'll be back in an hour," the nurse says to me.

Alone once again, I push the tray away and crawl out of bed, pausing for a moment, when my rubbery legs threaten to buckle beneath me. One unsteady step at a time, I make my way to the dresser and grab my uniform pants and reach into the side pocket, relieved when my fingers touch the smooth glass of the slim vial, but stop when I feel something else. I ease the mysterious object out of my pocket and almost gasp when I discover that it is a needle, still wrapped in its sterile package. In my sickened state, I never remembered to grab a needle at the same time that I snatched the medication, so what is a fresh one doing in my pocket? And who put it there? A note is stuck to the plastic encasing the needle.

Administer 4ml every two hours until the medicine is gone, it reads.

I shove the vial, needle, and note back into my pocket, wondering who wrote that note, and how they knew what I intended to do with it, but the biggest question plaguing my mind is: why did this mysterious person not inform the medical board of my infraction? Not wanting to risk being caught with these items by having someone else handle my clothes, I take off the gown I am in and put on my uniform, smoothing the wrinkles out before hurrying back to my breakfast.

I pick up the buttered roll and take a bite, chewing it with care, not wanting to upset my empty stomach by eating too fast. Drops of melted butter roll down the sides of my chin, and I wipe them away with a napkin, relishing its salty taste. Once I finish with the roll, I munch on the eggs and fruit, taking small bites. The nurse walks back into the room the moment I swallow the last bite of fruit.

"Good," she says, "you cleared your plate." She pulls a wheelchair into the room.

"I don't..."

"Doctor's orders."

Knowing I will not be allowed to walk out, I sit in the wheelchair and allow myself to be pushed through the medical center until we reach the entrance, where Commander Vye waits with a transport.

"Nurse Natalie," says the commander.

"Commander Vye."

One does not need a knife to slice the tension between them. It is so taut that a simple tug will snap it.

Not knowing why the two acted curt with one another, I rise from the wheelchair and sit in the back of the transport, reassuring myself that the medicine for Gwen still remains snug in my pocket. Once Commander Vye and Nurse Natalie are in the transport, the driver puts the vehicle in gear and we drive off, down the meandering streets of the eastern region, and receive a few glares from people who were forced to jump out of the way, but unwilling to do more than glower. I stare out the window. Plebeians follow their masters, looking at the ground as usual. I have never paid much attention to them before now. One Arelian citizen smacks their plebeian so hard that he falls to the crumbling pavement and receives an approving nod from a nearby arbiter. My fist clenches at the sight, but I release it before anyone notices.

A shadow spreads across the transport, covering it, and I look up at the towering wall as it makes its presence known, the one barrier between us and the outside world. I study it (the missing pieces of mortar and the plebeians rushing to repair it, the guards on its uppermost level, patrolling its walkways) and the feeling of protection that I once had whenever I looked at it withers away, replaced by dread and the sense of imprisonment. I push the negative thoughts away. Arel is civilization. It is the one beacon of light in this dark world. It is... the mantra of what Arel is, words that had been programed into me since my childhood, slip away as I watch a scaffolding give way, dumping the plebeian upon it to the hard, unforgiving ground and crushing those unfortunate enough to be below it. Their agonizing screams cut through the barrier of the transport. I turn away. No one will help them. They will be disposed of, like anyone who is deemed useless, and the fires of the crematorium will burn brighter.

They are just plebeians, I remind myself. Not even people. The hollow words bring a pang of guilt, and I grip the side of my pants once more, feeling the slim vial and needle, a reminder that they were for a plebeian, but not just any plebeian—one I care for.

Relief fills me when we pull up to the manor and I know that I can go to my room and lock myself away from the world for the next few days. Nurse Natalie helps me out of the vehicle. I wish she would not fuss over me so much, but clamp my mouth shut, remembering that it is her job to ensure that I get my health back. We walk past Commander Vye and the nurse hands her a small disk.

"This is the list of what she should eat for the next three days. Doctor Sahir's orders."

Commander Vye takes it with a quick swipe of her hand, not

thrilled at being forced to obey the orders of someone who is not part of the Martial Diplomatic Corps.

Once inside, I spot Shelia. Knowing that I will not be allowed to leave my room, much less sneak down into the plebeian quarters, I turn toward her and say in a commanding voice, "I'm thirsty. Bring me some water."

Shelia nods and scurries away.

As Nurse Natalie leads me to my room, the other arbiters of the manor gather around. Some give me approving smiles and nods, no doubt remembering my encounter with Molers two days before, while others glare at me as though I am still diseased. Renal stands by the stairs and pats me on the back as we go up them. Once in my room, the nurse sits me in the chair. I need a way to get the medicine to Shelia so that she can deliver it to Chase. My mind races to think of a plan.

"Nurse Natalie," I say.

"Just call me Natalie."

"Yes, ma'am. May I have another blanket? It's a little chilly in here and we are only issued one."

"I'll see to it." She hurries out of the room.

When she's out of sight, I jump up and move to the door, looking up and down the hallway for Shelia, but there is no sign of her. Thinking of a contingency plan, I look at my bed and rush to it, pulling the medicine, the needle, and note out of my pocket and shove it under the pillow. I reach my chair just as Natalie returns, followed by Shelia.

"Here you go," Natalie says to me.

I smile at her, hoping she takes it as an act of appreciation, before turning to Shelia. "Put the water on the table. After that, you can take the blanket and make up my bed and be sure to fluff the pillow."

Shelia obeys and I watch as she unfolds the blanket, stretching it over the bed and tucking in the corners. When she moves to the pillow, I realize that Natalie is watching her. Needing a distraction,

I take off my jacket, pretending to struggle with it, and she turns her attention away from Shelia and toward me, helping me get my arms out of the sleeves, and taking a minute to check my pulse. I glance at Shelia and watch as she finds the vial of medicine and the needle with the note attached to it. He small fingers scoop them up, and she hides them under her shirt, using the waistband of her pants to hold it.

"You may go," I tell her and Shelia runs out of the room, taking our only hope at saving Gwen with her. I just hope that we are in time.

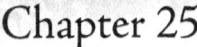

Chapter 25

Back on Duty

The cold steel of the metal bar looms over me, taunting me, daring me to reach up and grab it, to bend it to my will. I stare at it. Eleven days have passed since my brush with death—since my own rashness almost caused my demise, but that does not concern me right now. All I can think about is Chase. Did his sister survive? I have not heard from him or Shelia since I managed to smuggle the medicine into the manor and sneak it to her, not that it surprises me, since Commander Vye has kept a close eye on me, concerned that I may fall ill again.

A breeze stirs around me, caressing my bare neck and shoulders, carrying with it a hint of a chill, warning me that the season will change soon. Looking at the steel bar above me, I push all thoughts of Chase, Shelia, and the events outside the wall out of my mind, determined to gain back the only value I have to offer as an arbiter: my physical strength. Bending my knees, I leap upward and grasp the cold metal, wrapping my fingers around it, until I feel blisters form on my palms.

One.

I pull myself upward, ignoring the strain on my biceps, before lowering myself down.

Two.

Again, I pull myself upwards until my chin is above the bar. Sweat drips down my temples as I hold myself there, refusing to give in to the shaking of my arms, until I release the tightness of my muscles in a controlled action.

Three. Four.

On the fifth pull-up, my biceps give out, forcing me to lose my hold on the bar and drop to the dull green grass, landing on my side. As I lift myself up and lean on my elbow, I spot a familiar face staring at me from the hedges on the other side of the quad, and I lower my head in shame. Once again, Chase witnesses one of my failures.

"You shouldn't push yourself so hard." Natalie walks up behind me, carrying a towel.

I watch as Chase turns away, going back to his chore of trimming the hedges, before I stand up, rubbing the sore spot on my right hip, which I know will form a bruise later.

"The sickness has weakened me," I say.

"Illness does that," Natalie replies in a soothing voice. "You must allow yourself time to rest and recuperate. You will get your strength back."

She means well, but for the last 11 days, I have been secluded in my room on bedrest and have grown antsy. I need to do something, to get back into a routine. Natalie notices my downtrodden expression and places a reassuring hand on my shoulder before handing me the towel. I take it and wipe the sweat off my face, appreciating her efforts at cheering me up.

"Take it slow," Natalie warns me. "If you try to do too much too soon, you will just make yourself sick again."

"I can't just sit in my room all day."

"Which is why I asked Doctor Sahir to clear you for duty, but if you start feeling fatigued, weak, or exhausted, you let me know immediately."

"Yes, ma'am."

Natalie smiles, not a fake or forced smile that so many within Arel give, but a genuine one, as though she cares about my well-being and happiness. Whomever had decided that she should go into the medical field upon her birth had made not only the right choice, but an accurate prediction of where she belonged. I thank her for her comforting words and stroll back to the manor, taking one last quick glance for Chase, but he is gone.

"Noni!"

Commander Vye's sharp voice catches me by surprise and I whirl around to face her.

"You will be on day patrol today with Renal. Keep your emotions in check."

"Yes, ma'am," I reply, knowing just what she referred to. When I had allowed my emotions to dictate my actions, I ended up picking a fight with Molers, and though I won it, for the moment, I know that he sits in the munitions factory plotting his revenge. Dread fills me at the prospect of having to meet him again once he is reinstated.

"And someone has requested to speak with you," continues Commander Vye. "I transferred it to your quarters. Make it brief."

I salute the commander and charge up the stairs, taking two at a time, knowing just who had called me. Friendships are not encouraged among arbiters, but they form anyway, despite what our superior officers say, and Commander Vye's delicate manner of telling me about the call means that she knows that I have at least one friend in the corps. I burst into my room and tap the smooth button on the wall across from my bed after the door closes and Faya's face appears on the wall monitor.

"Noni, are you all right?" she asks with concern.

I frown. Somehow, news of my sudden illness had gotten to her and I never wished to cause her to worry. "I'm much better, thanks. How did you know?"

A mischievous grin creeps across her lips, the same mischievous grin she always got when she did something she wasn't supposed to, or was about to do something that went against the rules. "Well, I was worried about you going outside the wall, so I asked Joel to volunteer to accompany one of the economists that was assigned to inspect the eastern sector, and while he was there, I asked him to find out if you were okay. He's the one who told me about your illness. I can't believe it! We were all vaccinated."

"It doesn't matter anymore," I say, trying to console her. "I'm fine now. I just need to get back into physical shape."

"I'm sure you will. So, what's it like outside the wall." The eagerness in her voice tells me that she has been dying to ask that question ever since she learned that I had been assigned to tour the outposts.

I take a deep breath, wondering how I can tell her about it without divulging everything. I consider what would have been reported to the citizens of Arel, and what she would have been told by the few arbiters who like to tell stories, and choose my words with care. "It's very different from here. The wilderness is barren, cruel, and filled with wild people. Life at the outposts is harsh and rugged."

"I heard there was a skirmish."

"Our convoy was attacked by outsiders. I managed to get away, but suffered a broken leg." I left my other injuries out.

"How did you survive?"

"We had a plebeian with us and he happened to be in the same transport as me when we were attacked. He…" I pause for a moment, remembering that Chase had told Commander Vye that it was me who had saved us both, and in case anyone is listening, I do not want to jeopardize that, for both our sakes, "helped me, as is his duty, but the skills we learned at the training facility helped us survive such an unforgiving place." I leave out the part about the barbarian who helped us both in the end, knowing what would happen if anyone learned that I did not kill him, but let him go.

"That sounds terrifying. Even some of the most seasoned arbiters would have failed if they were in your position. You continue to do well there and you could easily apply for a transfer."

My wristband beeps, warning me that I am in danger of being late for my shift. "Faya, I hate to cut this short, but…"

"I understand. You have to get back to duty. Take care of yourself, Noni."

"As long as you promise to do the same."

Faya grins and switches off her monitor, causing mine to go blank. I press the button and turn it off before snatching my jacket and putting it on, making certain that it is wrinkle free, as I brush off any lint that might have gotten on it. This is my first day back on duty, since leaving for the outposts, and I want to make a good impression.

Renal waits for me at the bottom of the stairs when I rush down them, but instead of giving me a stern look like Commander Vye often does, he brandishes a sly smirk, pleased to see me up and eager to perform my duties. Neither of us say anything as we walk out the front door. It slides shut behind us, allowing its foggy exterior to block our view of the interior. Wisps of clouds float in front of the sun, dimming it a bit, as we stroll down the driveway to the manor and exit through the gate, stepping onto the main street and head for the interior of the eastern district. The hum of a passing railcar draws my attention, and I glance up at the railway as it whizzes by, blowing a loose strand of my hair into my face, remembering my first day as an official arbiter—the day I first arrived in the eastern sector. I catch Renal watching me and I increase my pace in an effort to prove that I had not been dawdling. A slight chuckle escapes his lips.

We hike deeper into the eastern sector, taking a moving walkway to minimize the time it takes us to get there. Everything looks to be the same as when I had left for the outposts. Citizens hurry down the streets and walkways with their plebeians in tow, carrying packages or bags. A railcar passes overheard every few minutes. It all seems unchanged, yet it is all so different.

A plebeian girl, about the same age as both Shelia and Gwen, rushes past us after her master as he steps onto a moving walkway, carrying a bundle half her size. It falls from her grasp. Fretting, the girl tries to pick it up as the conveyor belt carts it away, but each time she manages to reach it, someone kicks it, pushing it further away from her. An impatient huff escapes her master's lips as he watches her vain efforts, his face contorting into anger with each passing second. No one bothers to help her. No one notices her plight.

As I watch her, I remember Gwen's frightened face the night I had seen her, the night I had chased her for the crime of trying to help her former mistress. As the plebeian girl reaches the package and is about to pick it up, a pointed shoe rams into it, sending it skittering further down the walkway, and I recall Shelia's frightened face when Molers struck her. I leave Renal's side. With quick, purposeful strides, I hurry down the moving walkway, toward the package, encouraging people to move out of my way, not that I have to give them that much incentive to do so, since one glance at my arbiter's uniform forces them to jump out of the way on their own. I reach the package and pick it up, handing it to the girl. She gives me an apprehensive look, the distrust evident in her opal eyes, and we stare at one another in awkward silence as the conveyor belt carries us away. I hold the bundle out to her, urging her to take it. Her nimble fingers snatch it from my hand and she runs away, back to her master who eyes me with suspicion, but refuses to say anything.

Straightening up, I stroll down the moving walkway, against the direction of the crowd, my head held high, daring any one of them to challenge me, but none of them do, settling for sending me a few odd glances. One woman glares at me. I face her in response, boring my gaze deep within her brown eyes and she turns away. When I reach Renal, he motions for me to follow him.

"That was an odd thing to do," he says to me, once we are away from the crowd.

I try to think of a good excuse, but do not have one. "Not really," I reply, and it sounds weak, even to me.

"Oh?"

"What purpose was served by taunting her?" I ask.

"I suppose there was none, but you shouldn't have helped her like that."

"She is not their property. Toying with her like that was not necessary. They should have ignored her and tended to their own plebeians." I hope he accepts my reasoning.

Renal stops. I look at him, curious as to why he has stopped, but he points at a lower level, where a group of three boys dressed in green uniforms draw on a poster that has the images of our presidents on it.

"Go that way," he whispers to me.

I race to another stairwell, following Renal's instructions, and charge down the staircase, my heavy-soled boots clanging on the grated steps, as I barrel my way through a group of citizens as they climb upward to the moving walkway. They start to speak, but stop when they see my uniform and the determined expression on my face, realizing that I have spotted a crime and am on my way to rectify it. I leap from the third to last step, landing on the platform with a bang. Not missing a beat, I jog toward the boys, hurrying down the causeway, while Renal charges from the opposite direction.

The boys notice us. They split up. Renal chases two of them, while I charge after the third. He tries to dart around a corner, but I cut him off, snatching his arm and twisting it behind him, allowing my training to control my movements. My grip remains firm, while the boy struggles, and I drag him back to the poster where Renal waits for me with the other two.

"What's the meaning of this?" he demands of them.

They lower their heads and shuffle their feet.

"Why aren't you in class?" Renal asks, his tone stern.

No answer.

I glance at the poster and gasp when I notice what they have done. The poster depicts both Kumi and Tapiwa standing side by side staring at a distant horizon, as though they looked into the future, with a halo of sunshine enveloping then, bestowing heaven's approval upon them. This is what the poster is supposed to look like. The boys had colored in the presidents' faces to make them look fair-skinned and colored in the sun so that the scene appeared to be nighttime. On the bottom, in handwritten scrawl, reads:

THE INCESTUOUS DUO.
HYPOCRITES AND MURDERERS.

What were they thinking?

"Do you boys understand the penalty for this?" I ask them.

"For what?" replies one, challenging me. The venom in his eyes unnerves me, but he rethinks his decision and waves his black hand at the poster. "We were just having some fun."

"Mr. As—"

"SHH!" The one who had challenged me silenced the other before he could finish his statement.

Fun or not, they have all committed a grave offense, one where the only road leads to the crematoriums.

"Noni," Renal says to me, "I believe Commander Vye would prefer you decide their punishment."

I take the boy in my grasp down another flight of stairs, dragging him through the bustling crowd, as people swarm out of our way not wanting to get involved. Renal follows behind me with the other two. The boy makes one last attempt to break free of my hold, but I jerk him back, slamming him into the side of the booth. His frightened eyes stare into mine, and I regret my rough treatment of him. Placing my palm on the panel on the side of the booth, I prepare my statement and the recommended punishment in my mind and watch as a light scans both my hand and wristband, followed by my information appearing on the monitor screen.

"State the purpose for detainment," says a computerized voice.

"Two infractions," I say "three detainees. Speaking misinformation about Presidents Kumi and Tapiwa and vandalizing a presidential poster."

I place the boy's palm on the panel and it scans it. Once done, Renal hauls the other two to me, and I put their palms on the same panel, allowing the computer to scan them. On the screen next to it appears their information. The oldest is 16, while the others are 12 and 14.

"Though the standard punishment is assignment to the crematorium, due to the young age of the perpetrators, this arbiter recommends reeducation."

"It will be taken into consideration," the computerized voice says, and a door on the side appears before opening, revealing a dark hole.

One by one, Renal and I shove the boys in there and it closes, dropping them to the prison transport waiting in the tunnel beneath us, which will take them to the Ministry of Justice.

"Reeducation?" Renal asks me.

"They are young enough," I reply with authority, "and the law allows them that chance."

Renal gives me an approving nod.

I am not wrong. The law does say that any person under the age of 18 is allowed a chance for reeducation for their first infraction, as it is believed that they are young enough to learn from their mistake and be reassimilated into Arelian society. Any transgressions afterward result in an immediate transport to the crematorium.

"I believe that it is lunchtime," says Renal and he walks off, leaving me with no choice but to trail after him without a word.

Chapter 26

Strange Curiosities

My stomach grumbles as we approach the door to Sigal's café, reminding me that not only has it been a while since breakfast, but that I had not eaten much of it either. Reminding me of the first time he had brought me here, Renal opens the door and beckons me to go through first. Once again, the overwhelming aroma of baked pasta, roasted beef, steamed carrots, and fresh-baked pies and cakes blend together, tantalizing my nostrils and palate, urging me to indulge in their forbidden flavors. I reach for a piece of sliced carrot cake, sitting alone on its serving plate, daring someone to snatch it. Renal stops my hand.

"Remember the diet restrictions," he says with a smile.

I glare at him, knowing full well that he came here often and helped himself to a few sweet treats, but this time, I have a secret weapon. "You forget, sir, that for the next twelve hours, I am allowed certain liberties with my diet."

Renal laughs, and I realize that he has been toying with me the entire time. He picks up the cake, folding it in a nearby napkin, and hands it to me with a grin so large that I think his face will freeze in that position.

"And so you are, my little arbiter."

I take the slice of cake, unable to contain the smile that breaks through my feeble attempts at maintaining an irked demeanor, and we both chuckle.

Renal leads me to a table nestled in the back, much like he did the first time he brought me here, where we can watch and observe without anyone sneaking up on us. Eyes glance in our direction as we pass jovial patrons indulging in rich foods that are banned to arbiters, but no one says a word, nor do they make a move to challenge us, as Sigal's affinity for serving arbiters, and keeping us happy, is well-known. A few other arbiters who have also stopped by for a bite to eat wave at us and we both return the gesture.

"You better eat that before it disappears," Renal says to me when we sit down, and I realize that I am still holding my piece of carrot cake.

I take a bite. My mouth waters as saliva spills over the piece of cake that my teeth chew, surrounding my tongue in a mix of flavors: honey, cinnamon, ginger, cloves, and something else that is both bitter and sweet. Nutmeg? I take another bite, larger than the first, and chew it, allowing myself to taste every spice that is in there and remarking at how the slivers of carrot are not too soft, nor too crunchy, but just right. My lips smack together as I lick some frosting from my fingers, enjoying the way it has just the right amount of sweetness so as not to drown the flavors of the cake itself. Two arbiters push past us; their envious glares burn holes in my cake as they watch me eat it, and I take another bite, reveling in their displeasure. Snorting, they turn away and rush out of the eatery.

"You shouldn't rub it in too much," Renal warns me.

"I never liked them anyway," I reply. Since the day I had first arrived at the manor, those two have given me a hard time, teasing me and taunting me. Let them see me enjoy food that they are forbidden to have.

"Oh-ho!" Sigal walks up to us in his usual jovial manner. "Having dessert first, are we? Are you sure you should?"

I swipe my thin bracelet against the tablet he holds in his meaty hands and my information scrolls across the screen. "Dietary restrictions temporarily removed, I see. Well then, I guess I should tell my wife to bring you another piece. As for you,"—he turns to Renal—"it will be the same fare."

"Surprise me," Renal jokes.

Sigal bounds off, and within minutes, he returns with a tray overflowing with savory foods to eat. Before Renal, he places a plate full of baked black beans, steamed broccoli, twice baked chicken breast, and a bowl of dragon fruit. In front of me, he places a plate with pulled brisket, steamed broccoli, candied apples, and baked pasta smothered in a creamy herb sauce. My stomach gurgles, encouraging me to not waste my time delving into the food.

"Dig in!" says Sigal, as he moves closer to Renal and smuggles a small roll onto his plate, and where he had that hidden stumps me. "Don't tell anyone," he whispers and hurries away.

Renal eats his contraband roll first, while I shove my fork into my pasta, marveling at how creamy the sauce is and wondering what herbs had been used to give it its savory flavor. Time passes, and as I place the last forkful of food in my mouth, the door opens, which isn't unusual, but who walks in intrigues me. Natalie. She steps inside, looking around in a manner that displays she does not want to be noticed, while wrapping a dark coat around her, holding it tight in an effort to mask her white uniform. I have never seen her here before, not that it means much, since I can only come in for a single hour each day, and she does work in the eastern sector, and Sigal's place is the highlight of this region, yet her behavior is odd. She closes the door with care and skulks in the shadows, away from the ceiling lamps, her head twisting in every direction, as she creeps to the back hallway where the restrooms are located.

"I'll be back," I tell Renal.

"Where are you going?"

"Restroom," I reply.

"Be quick."

I nod and hurry off, making my way to the back hallway, hoping to abate my curiosity about Natalie's strange behavior. Mindless chatter fills my ears, but I hear none of it as I enter the darkened corridor that leads to the restrooms and away from the bustling activity of the main dining area. No one is there. I go to the women's bathroom and push the door open, poking my head inside, finding no sign of her having been in there. I close the door.

Soft voices prickle my ears; their faint sound cause me to believe that it is an illusion, a trick of my mind based on my already suspicious thoughts. I head for them, stepping past the restrooms and further into the interior of the hallway, moving toward an area I had not noticed before, well away from prying eyes and overcurious ears. Slinking through the dim light and sticking to the shadows myself, I creep to a closed door and place my ear near it. Muffled voices spill through it. I detect Natalie's and she sounds scared. What is she afraid of? Who is she with?

Another voice filters through the wooden door: a man's, deep and baritone, filled with anger, hushed by Natalie's softer, gentler voice. They are arguing, but I cannot make out what the argument is about. A few words I do catch: time is now, we can't, we must, and if they. From what I do make out, it sounds as though they are planning to try and escape, but not just them alone—they have friends they wish to bring with them. Or are they smuggling people out of Arel? Leaving the city is forbidden. Everyone knows this, but it does not stop some from attempting to flee.

Shuffling and the scraping of chairs against the floor fill the area, warning me that they have finished their discussion and are preparing to leave. I sneak away, not wanting to get caught. Just as I reach the middle of the hallway, a sharp voice stops me.

"What are you doing?"

I whirl around, startled, my mind racing to come up with an excuse for my wandering, thinking that it is Renal who has found me, but instead, I find Sigal. His harsh tone unnerves me and seems odd when compared to the jovial behavior I am used to seeing.

"I'm sorry," I say, deciding it best to pretend to be lost and act like the newbie most treat me as, "but I was looking for you."

"Me?" His surprised tone tells me that he did not expect that answer.

Wringing my hands to give the impression that I am about to break a rule I know I shouldn't, I look toward the dining area so that he believes I do not want anyone to overhear us, and Sigal's expression softens. "I wanted to ask you… was wondering if perhaps I could have three extra pieces of that carrot cake?"

"That's a lot for one person," he says, now curious as to why I want them.

"They're not for me"—I guide him toward the wall and glance at the dining area again—"but for some friends of mine, who…"

"Wait right here." Sigal hurries away and I hope that he has forgotten about my sneaking around. The seconds pass like hours as I wait for him to return, knowing that Renal will have begun to wonder if I have grown ill again, but before I can worry too much, Sigal returns with a brown package, small enough to be concealed under clothing. "Next time," he says as he hands it to me, "just go up to the counter, but don't make a habit of it."

"Yes, sir," I reply in a sweet voice, smiling at him and using my youth to my advantage.

I hurry away, sticking the bundle in the pouch I have strapped to my waist, which holds some of my arbiter belongings, glad that he bought my story, though in the back of my mind, I wonder if Sigal played a part, like I had.

Renal waits for me by the door. "It took you long enough," he says, arching his eyebrow.

"Sorry, sir," I reply. "There is no excuse, sir."

Renal chuckles. "I am not Commander Vye."

We turn down the street and a woman hurries out of our way, an act I have become accustomed to. As we walk with our feet clomping on the broken and cracked pavement in tune with one another, my thoughts turn back to the when I had challenged Molers over his treatment of Sheila, reminding myself that there will be no escaping his fury. A question enters my mind: why did Renal stop him? I want to ask. My mouth begs to form the words, but each time I start to, my mind clamps it shut, scolding it that such an act could be construed as questionable. Rebelling, my mouth opens once more and a sentence squeaks out before my mind can stop it.

"Sir..." I begin.

"You can call me Renal when we're not around the commander."

"Yes, si—Renal"—I pause for a moment, wetting my lips and forcing saliva to coat my cotton tongue—"that day Molers chose to reprimand me, you stopped him. Why?"

Renal stops and faces me, a bewildered and concerned expression clouds his features, wondering why I bothered asking such a ridiculous question. "Reprimanding you? He was going to kill you."

Maybe Renal doesn't think my inquiry ludicrous. I know that Molers had intended to kill me that day, but I dare not say it, in case others agreed with him, and I had been on the receiving end of Molers' anger before. His methods have always been cruel.

In my 12th year as a recruit, during a training session in which the recruit learned to throw knives, my aim had been off. It was my first time throwing such a large knife. I had thrown smaller ones, the size of my index finger, but this one had a bully handle that weighed my hand down and the blade was twice the length of the handle, setting the balance of the knife off-center. When I chucked it at the target, it bounced off the side and almost struck Molers in the shoulder. His quick reflexes prevented him from being stabbed, though why he stood so close to the target is something I never learned.

I had tried to apologize, but apologies make one look weak,

and it infuriated Molers even more. He dragged me outside into the courtyard where a single pole stands, the one we use to hoist the flag of Arel, and tied me to it, stripping off my jacket and outer shirt, forcing me to face the cold in my underclothes. As though to make his point, he snatched a bucket of water that had been used to catch the drips that fell through a small hole in the entrance to the building and tossed it on me, soaking me, causing my already chilled skin to turn to ice. Winter had come early that year, and throughout that night, I stood there with my back against the icy pole and my arms tied behind me, with the falling sleet as my only companion.

Mandi saved me. Before the sun had a chance to peek over the horizon, she rushed out with the commandant and his second in command, screaming at the guards of the facility to let me go, her hoarse voice filled my ears with comfort, and I realized that she must have spent hours convincing the commandant's second in command of the unjustness of Molers' punishment. The commandant had been away that day, but Mandi must have somehow gotten a hold of him and forced him to return. I remember the ties around my chafed and soar wrists falling away and falling into outstretched arms that comforted me and carried me to the medical wing amidst an array of angry shouts, dominated by Molers' and the commandant's voices.

I spent a week in the hospital wing and lost the tip of my right pinky due to severe frostbite, lucky that it was the only thing I lost. No one saw Molers for five months after that, and the commandant's second in command had been reassigned to an outpost.

Without thinking, I look at my maimed pinky, one of the lasting scars left to me by Molers, and Renal breaks through my musing. "What you did wasn't smart, but it did not warrant his reaction."

"I should not have interfered," I concede.

"He did break Arelian law, even if it is one that most people and arbiters ignore, but be smart about it next time, Noni."

I glance up into Renal's eyes, remembering how his actions had forced Molers to let me go, and had silenced everyone within the manor, seeing a look in his eyes I had never seen before and the opposite of what he shows me now: loathing. I think back to how Molers released me, refusing to challenge him, something that goes against his character. Could Renal be…

Renal's wristband beeps and flashes red, jolting me out of my internal musings and back to the present. He taps it, turning off the annoying, high-pitched sound. Finding the nearest information booth, he scans his palm on the monitor and a message appears on the screen, and judging by the frown on his face, it is not a good one.

"I have to go," he says. "You should report back to the manor."

"I can carry out the rest of my duties," I say, not wanting to go back to the manor where I will be forced to take it easy.

He gives me a doubtful look.

"I'm more than capable and… please don't make me go back there, where they will force me to stay in my room on bedrest. I can't take staring at those walls anymore." I hope I do not sound too whiny, but what I say is the truth. Staring at the walls of my room for the last week has driven me crazy. "If anything happens, I know what to do, and the other arbiters on patrol are not far away."

"Fine," Renal concedes, "but at the first sign of trouble, radio for help. I'll meet you back at the manor at the end of your patrol. No deviations."

"Yes, sir."

A panel opens in the information booth, the same one used for detainees, but Renal's orders must have conveyed how quick he needed to be somewhere else, and he steps in, disappearing behind the wall as it closes.

Left alone on the street, I look around, catching a few stares that avert themselves when they notice me watching. A familiar shape, sneaking out of the alley that backs onto Sigal's restaurant catches my attention. Natalie. I hurry to the walk, keeping my distance as she darts down the street, pushing her way past people, while still trying to hide her uniform under the jacket she wears. She glances around with the same disposition she had in the eatery—she does not want to be noticed. I stay back, not wanting her to see me. She darts down a narrow path, avoiding the moving walkway, past two buildings squeezed close together—I have to walk sideways just to keep her in sight—and out the other side, blending in with a crowd of people wearing a jacket similar to hers and heading for the plebeian quarters.

I have never been to the plebeian quarters, and every region has an area designated for them. The plebeians who reside there are ones not assigned to a specific residence or business, but belong to the sector itself, doing menial tasks or laborious jobs that need doing. In the eastern sector, those jobs consist of repairing the wall, cleaning the streets, waste removal, building repair—when we receive the funds for it—and sewage maintenance. The quarters themselves are just a block that is sectioned off from the public where the plebeians are crammed in. Arbiters assigned to the area patrol it day and night, and to my knowledge, there is only one way in and out.

My mind races, wondering why Natalie would be heading there, as I follow her, before stopping. Eyes watch me, taking in my every move, flickering away the moment I look at them. I look around at my surroundings, noticing that the closer we get to the plebeian quarters, the fewer arbiters there are, unless they are the ones assigned to the area, but their uniforms are different from mine; they are thicker, tougher, and contain body armor. I need to blend in. Sticking to the far side of the walk, while still trying to keep Natalie within sight, I look for anything I can use to conceal my uniform, understanding why Natalie hides the white of her medical uniform. I spot some clothes hanging on a line between two crumpling brick buildings. Making certain that no one watches, I jump up and snatch a tattered shawl, wrapping it around myself and keep my head down, mimicking those around me.

Natalie turns left. I do the same. She sprints down a narrow causeway, draped in the shadow of a two-story building missing the majority of its roof, avoiding the holes within the concrete pavement as she skips over them with ease, aware of where each one is, while my feet stumble into every one of them. Splashing surrounds me, and I almost fall over when my left foot stumbles into one of the potholes. She turns around and I jump into a corner, squeezing myself against a wall riddled with bullet holes, hoping that she does not see me. I wait a few seconds before daring to peek around the edge of the wall I hide behind. She's gone.

Fearing I lost her, I run down the causeway, not caring if my feet make any noise, finding myself in another hidden alleyway. Unsure of which way to go, I pick a direction and go to my right, knowing that I have a 50 percent chance of being right. I propel myself forward, wishing that I had not been ill, as my lungs rebel and refuse to take in the amount of air they need. An opening lies ahead. I quicken my pace. Once I reach it, I stop and duck back into the alleyway, hiding. I have reached the plebeian quarters.

A stone wall similar to the one protecting Arel wraps around the area, trapping those inside, with guards patrolling the perimeter accompanied by dogs, but it has suffered damage from the constant outside attacks on the city; gaping holes filled in with barbed wire make up much of it. As for the dogs, these ones are not kept in a starved state like the ones in between the outer and inner parts of the wall that encloses Arel, but they are bred to be mean, snarling and growling at any who venture too close. A few people stroll past at a hurried pace, not wanting to be so close to the plebeian quarters for longer than necessary. I spot a gate. Studying it, it is clear that this is meant to be the only way in or out, as more guards hover around it, checking the wristbands of the plebeians wishing to leave, making certain that they have permission to do so. I watch the despondent, pallid faces as they form a line, not daring to look their darker-skinned masters in the eye.

Movement catches my attention. Natalie. Glad to have found her, I spring away from my hiding place and hurry after her, wrapping the shawl over my head and tight around my neck, keeping my face down. A guard strolls past me. My heart beats three times its normal rate when the dog sniffs my shoe before moving its inquisitive nose to the pouch that holds the pieces of cake Sigal had given me, and I curse myself. My shoes are standard issue and will give me away if anyone cares to take a closer look at them. When the guard yanks the canine's leash, I hurry away, thankful that he seems more interested in finishing his patrol instead of my attire. I look up, but Natalie is gone.

Knowing that I have wasted too much time, I think of a way back to the central part of the eastern sector. I need to get back there before anyone notices my absence. Not only do I not have permission to be near the plebeian quarters, but I have abandoned my post and have nothing to show for it, except suspicion. If caught, nothing will save me from the tribunal's wrath.

Barking catches my attention. Another dog and its owner heads for me. I turn and head in a different direction, but see another guard heading my way. Shit! The first one must have noticed the shoes, and maybe even the pants. I head in a third direction, doing my best to keep my pace normal, debating whether I should reveal myself or not, but knowing full well what will happen if I do. I have no proof that my suspicions of Natalie are correct, and without it, I have nothing to bargain with, leaving me with a single destination if I do not get away. I hear the bell of the trolley and spot a group of people making their way toward it. Falling in behind, I follow them while glancing behind me, hoping that the guards fall for the ruse. They don't. Why do they not just grab me?

I glace at the neck of the person in front of me and receive my answer. Her number begins with a one, meaning that she and the others with her are from the executive district—why they are here is a mystery—but it explains the reason for the guards staying back: they don't want to cause an incident that puts them in a bad situation. I stay close to them, but not close enough to garner any questions. If I can get on the trolley with them, I will be safe.

We pass a small gap in the buildings we stroll by just as someone pulling a cart crosses between me and the guards following me. Hands seize my shoulders, yanking me into the gap, pushing me along, not giving me a chance to speak or grasp what is happening. I try to talk, my desire to know what is going on outweighing my common sense. In response, the same hands pull me back toward a door, shoving me through it and shutting it behind us. A hand clamps over my mouth, stopping me from speaking. I reach up to remove it, when a familiar voice whispers in my ear, "Stop!"

Chase?

He allows me to turn so that I can see him, and my eyes focus on his grungy face as he holds a finger over his lips, pleading with me to remain silent. I obey. We listen as the guards wander outside, conversing amongst themselves, disappointed that I managed to evade them, but refusing to tell their superior. Failure means the same in Arel regardless of who you are: death or severe punishment. A dog sniffs around the door and my heart sinks, but just when I think we are about to be discovered, a whistle sounds and someone yells about seeing us go in a different direction, and the guards sprint away.

"What are you doing here?" Chase demands.

"What are you doing here?" I reply. Like me, he is not supposed to be in the plebeian quarters.

Chase refuses to answer.

"I need to go."

He holds me back. "You can't leave yet. They will spend the next ten minutes searching for us. After that, they will give up."

"How do you know?"

Again, Chase refuses to answer me.

"How often have you been coming here?"

He averts his eyes. "Sometimes," he says in quiet voice, "your commander sends me on an errand. If I have time, I sneak in here."

"Why?" One look at his face and I know the answer. "You know people here."

He hangs his head.

"You shouldn't worry about them. The plebeians are given all that they need," I say, regurgitating what I have been taught since birth, but in this abandoned building, my words sound hollow, even to me.

"You know nothing about the plebeian quarters, do you?"

Awkward silence fills the empty space between us, and I remember that I still have the cake in my pouch. Since we were to be trapped here for a while, I pull it out, unwrapping the pieces and discovering four instead of three. Good old Sigal. Bribing me with cake.

"Here," I hand one to Chase.

"What..."

"I managed to sneak some pieces of cake at lunch for you, Gwen, and Sheila."

"And yourself it seems."

"Do you want it or not?"

Chase takes a piece and shoves half of it in his mouth, gulping it down without bothering to chew. "What are you doing here?" he asks again.

I glance away, not sure how to tell him my real reason for being where I do not belong. "I was doing my job."

He glares at me, aware that I have left out most of the story.

"I was following someone."

"Doing your job," he spits. "Your job gets people killed."

"I am an arbiter, Chase. What do you expect me to do?"

"You're right." He finishes his cake. "It is your job to do the bidding of Arel by keeping us all in chains."

"We protect Arel," I say. "When the attacks on the wall happen, who do you think puts their lives on the line? It's not you."

"All right. I'll give you that one, but what about the other things you arbiters do? You dispose of anyone participating in unlawful activity."

"We hand them over to the Ministry of Justice."

"And what do you think happens to people there?"

"You don't understand," I say, taking the last bite of my cake. "It's my job to root out suspicious activity and keep the citizens of Arel safe, including plebeians. Failure means death. That's not just a slogan, but life." I stop talking, realizing for the first time that the very mantra of Arel that I have been programmed to say, and said along with all the other arbiters at the training facility, was more than something we spouted, but reality, but not in the sense that I have always believed.

"You're right," says Chase. "I have spent my entire life hating your kind that I never considered that you would suffer the same fate as a plebeian for failing to carry out your duties."

Silence follows. A change comes over him, similar to the change I witnessed while we both tried to survive in the wild outside the wall. The hatred that always filled his eyes has disappeared, replaced with pity.

"Suspicious?" Chase asks me, breaking the silence. "What suspicious activity?"

"Well, what would you call someone from medical personnel being here disguised as somebody else?"

Recognition flashes in his eyes and the feeling that he knows who I am referring to wafts over me, but before I can say anything, Chase beats me to it. "Probably the exact word I would use for an arbiter doing the same."

"I..."

"You should go. It's been over ten minutes and you need to get back."

Refusing to argue, and knowing that he is right—I have to get back—I stand up and hand him the package with the remaining two pieces of cake. "Here. Will you see to it that your sister and Sheila get these?"

He takes the bundle. "Go straight down this alley and over the wall. Make a right, take the first left, and keep going straight. That should take you back to the central area."

"You should come with me."

"It's best if we go separately."

"What were you doing here?" I ask again.

"Meet me in my room tonight after lights out."

I open the door and peer outside, seeing no sign of any guards or citizens wandering about. "Tonight, then," I tell Chase as I dart outside and run for the wall at the end of the alley. The soft thud of the door closing fills my ears, drowning out the thudding of my heart.

When I reach the wall, I study it, spotting an iron bar poking out of the stone where bits of it has fallen away. I take a few steps back and ditch the shawl. I bolt for the wall, running as fast as I can and leap at the last second, grasping the iron bar and hauling myself up, until I reach the top of the wall, my muscles straining as I heave myself over. I drop down on the other side. Following Chase's directions, I head to my right, taking the first left that I find. I hurry down the narrow alleyway, rejoicing as the sounds of the central part of the eastern sector grow louder. Before I reach the end, I slow down, steadying my breathing and wiping the sweat from my forehead.

People stroll past me, unaware of my presence. Taking a deep breath, I step out onto the main road and mingle with the crowd, heading for a stairwell that leads up to the moving walkways. The ring of a trolley pierces the air. Smiling, I wait for it to draw near and jump on, clinging to its rear bumper, much like I did my first day within the eastern sector as I hurried to report for duty. A few odd glances come my way, but I ignore them, relishing the breeze that blows over me as the wind whistles over my ears. Once we near the manor, I jump off and wave good-bye at the people aboard the trolley. One waves back.

I race up the driveway and to the front door of the house, slowing down the closer I get, so that people will not think I am tardy again. Just as I reach the door, a voice calls out.

"It appears that I am the one who is late." Renal hurries to the door with a huge smile, but worry fills his eyes.

"Is everything all right?" I ask, concerned.

"We should go inside and fill out our reports," he replies, evading my question.

I let the matter drop and follow him inside, counting down the hours until I get some answers from Chase.

Chapter 27

A Night's Excursion

The cracked door to Chase's room creaks as I open it after having snuck down to the plebeian quarters the moment Commander Vye called lights out. All arbiters within the manor are to be in bed. The only ones allowed up are those assigned to night patrol, and if you are caught out of bed when you have no reason to be up, the punishment is severe. I slip inside, closing the door until it clicks, and spin around to be met by two pairs of eyes staring at me in the musky darkness, illuminated by a single lamp situated in the far corner of the room.

Gwen lies in the only bed in the room; the color has returned to her pale cheeks and her gray eyes stare at me, wide open and bright, taking in everything around her and allowing me to see the intelligence contained within them.

"Put these on," Chase says, tossing me a pair of grungy and tattered pants, along with a soiled shirt and a hooded jacket that smells as though it had been washed in a toilette.

I remove my arbiter uniform, glad that I had decided to leave my wristband tucked underneath the mattress of my bed, and dress in the clothes he gives me, unconcerned about being half-naked in front of him, and secure the jacket's hood around my face in an effort to conceal it. Once done, I place my folded uniform—the arbiter within me detesting the thought of a wrinkle showing up, knowing what will happen if I allow it to become creased—on the bed with a mental note to get it back before sunrise.

"You have to promise to do as I say," Chase says.

"Understood."

"Are you sure you want to do this?" he asks me, giving me one last chance to back out.

My hardened eyes stare back at him in response. I want to know the truth of why he was in the plebeian sector and why Natalie might have been there as well.

Chase heads for the door, but stops when Gwen calls his name.

"Don't go," she pleads, hugging her bony knees.

Chase runs to her, comforting her. "I have to. I promised Noni that I would."

A tear wells up in her eyes as a frightened expression crosses her face, worried that he might not return.

"I'll be back," he reassures her, holding her close before kissing her on the tip of her pointed nose. "I love you more than the horizon."

"And I love you more than the sky," she replies in a soft whisper, wrapping her slender and short arms around him.

I watch the pair of them as they comfort one another in an effort to ease the worry each has for the other, my heart pulled in several directions. I have never known the love of a mother, father, brother, sister, or even a lover. I have never known love; and here, in a stygian room with cockroaches and rats' feces for company, are a brother and a sister telling the other that they love them, in case they never see each other again, reminding me that if I am to die, no one will miss me because I am loved by no one. I have never thought about it, until now, until this moment.

"Ready?" Chase says to me, yanking me from my moment of self-pity, a wasteful activity that arbiters are not supposed to participate in because it leads to mistakes and distracts us from our duties.

"Yes," I reply, masking the choking feeling that grips my throat as warm tears try to form, shoving the tender moment between him and Gwen far from my mind. I must remain focused.

Chase waves me through the door, and I follow him into the inky darkness, listening for the sounds of people who might not be asleep, but the silence within the corridor puts my anxiety to rest. He turns and heads further down the hallway, away from the stairwell that leads to the main floor.

"Where are you going?" I whisper.

He shushes me and I clamp my lips together, annoyed at being reminded that I had promised to do as he says, a notion that goes against everything I have been taught. I swallow my pride and fall into the role of subordination, allowing him to issue me commands. He turns a corner and heads for a dead end. My mind wishes to demand to know what he is thinking, and my tongue rushes to carry out my mind's wish, when I bite the end of it, forcing myself to remain silent. A rush of water flows through the pipes we tread under, meaning that someone has just finished using a toilette, one of the few reasons an arbiter may be allowed out of bed at night. The further we go, the darker the area becomes.

Chase stops. I almost ask him why he has stopped when I notice a small window, just big enough for someone of slender build to squeeze through. He opens it, being careful not to make a sound, and motions for me to crawl through. I place my hands on the uneven edge of the windowsill, ignoring the sharp points that dig into my skin, and hoist myself up, forcing my way through the window, releasing the breath I have been holding so that my chest will fit through, grimacing when the metal frame of the window scrapes some skin off my left breast as though I had no shirt or jacket on at all. Moist grass greets me when my feet exit the window. I jump into a sitting position and hug the exterior wall of the manor; my heart beats so fast I think that it will burst from my chest. Chase slithers through the window and closes it before urging me onward.

We dart across the grass to the fence that surrounds the manor. Again, I question his plan, since I know that neither of us can squeeze through the bars, but he crouches behind a hedge and grabs one of the iron bars, shifting it some, showing me that it has loosened and its repair has been neglected, assuming Commander Vye even knows about it. I crawl through the space with him right behind me. Before I have time to reconsider my actions, Chase taps my right shoulder and motions for me to follow him. We charge down the street to a nearest alleyway and duck down it. No sounds greet us as we move through the eastern sector, enveloping us in an eerie atmosphere of the unknown. We head for the moving walkway. I reach out to stop him, knowing that there are cameras there. Granted, some have been damaged from previous attacks, but enough of them still work.

Chase stops underneath a set of stairs that lead to the lower level of the jumble of moving walkways. He starts to jump at a low hanging bar, but stops. I hear it too. Steady, rhythmic footsteps approach us. I seize his shoulder and jerk him away from the sidewalk, deep into the dark shadows that fill the empty space beneath the stairway, watching and listening. An arbiter on patrol strolls past, twirling his baton in a bored fashion. He stops, turns a couple of times, before continuing on, tossing his baton into the air and catching it, as he disappears down the street. Once he is gone, I motion for Chase to continue.

He steps out, looks at the low hanging bar, and jumps for it. As I watch Chase climb upward, stepping from one iron bar to another until he reaches the narrow causeway that stretches underneath the moving walkway, an area for the maintenance crew to conduct repairs, I notice, for the first time, that the network of iron rungs underneath the stairwell form a haphazard ladder that one can climb. Chase hisses at me to hurry up.

Following his movements, I leap for the first rung, gripping it and hauling myself up, straddling the bar as I reach for the second one. Heaving myself upward, I hang onto the back of one of the steps, steadying myself as I stand. I spot the third iron bar. Taking a deep breath, I bend my knees and jump, clinging to the third bar, pulling myself up and balancing on it. Bar four, five, and six are easy to climb, but the seventh one lies just out of reach.

I gauge the distance, calculating the amount of force I will need to reach it, preparing myself while Chase waits above me, his impatience showing more and more as time ticks by. Once again, I balance myself on the bar I stand on, bend my knees, and propel myself into the air with all of the force my legs can muster. I grasp the seventh rung, but my left hand slips and I hang in the air, willing my other hand to remain firm in its grip. I look downward and the ravine in my stomach grows, knowing that at any moment, I can fall. I swing my free hand up and grab the bar, heaving myself on it just as Chase reaches down and grabs me under the shoulder, helping me onto the maintenance access walk.

We make our way down the access walk, hurrying down the narrow path that is just wide enough for a single person to amble down. Concealed in darkness, we have a good view of Arel's eastern sector. I glance at the wall and the beams of light spilling from the towers, shrouding it in white light, which fades the further down it goes, until a curtain of black overtakes it. My hands reach out for the rail on each side of me, steadying me, as my quick steps try to keep up with Chase. Vibrations riddle through my body from the constant hum of the causeway above us, the roar of its motor drowning every other external noise, until my mind hums in tune with the conveyor belt.

We reach the end and climb downward, jumping from iron beam to iron beam until our feet touch the ground. Chase pushes me down another alley and toward a brick wall, the same wall I had climbed when escaping from the plebeian quarters earlier this afternoon. I go first, taking a running jump at the wall and grip the top, my muscles burning as they pull me up. Keeping my body flat, I roll over and drop down on the other side, feeling a slight twinge in my right ankle as I land. A soft plop sounds next to me as Chase appears by my side.

He hurries down the dim alleyway and I follow after him, stopping when he holds his arm out. I watch his face, remarking at the concentration upon it, and realize that he is counting. Glancing to the side, I see a guard patrolling the outside perimeter. Chase watches him too. He pauses to investigate a spot on the cracked pavement before rounding a corner and fading from sight.

"We have fifteen seconds until the next guard appears from the other side," says Chase. "Go!"

He runs across the open space and I charge after him, stretching my legs, allowing them to carry me to the wall surrounding the plebeian quarters. Chase stops at a hole with barbed wire filling it in a shoddy attempt at patching it and bends the wires so that I can squeeze through. I do not wait to be told to go, but ram my way through the barbed wire, cringing when one of the barbs rips my jacket. Turning back, I do the same for him, holding the wires so that he can also crawl through. Chase grabs my arm and pulls me away from the opening just as the second guard on patrol strolls past, swinging his arms in a tired fashion before stifling a yawn.

"Here." Chase hands me a tattered cloth napkin.

I take the tiny bundle, cupping my hands beneath it so as not to drop the contents within as they shift. I unfold it, revealing an orange, a pear, a chunk of bread, and four nuggets of cheese. Studying the remnants of food, I realize that he must have been stashing some of his rations away just for this purpose, and not so that I would blend in.

"Let's go," Chase says, holding a similar bundle of food.

I snatch his hand and hold him back. "What if they give me away?"

"They won't." He stands up and creeps in the shadows, staying out of the moonlight, and I follow him, keeping in the darkness myself.

I search around for any guards, but the only ones I spot are on the wall itself with their heads turn toward the city outside, ignoring the people who live within its confines. We steal through the murkiness, stepping over discarded rods and boards, as bits of paper drift past us, scraping across the broken pavement before getting caught in the cracks. Eyes devoid of every emotion, except fear, watch us. I turn toward them, gasping at the spectral faces staring back at me, their pale skin turned zombielike by the pale moonlight. A slight breeze brushes us, swinging the loose strands of blonde hair around one woman's face as she crouches with a child cradled in her arms, encased in the darkness, while the silver light of the moon shines upon her cheeks and nose, transforming her sorrowful demeanor into that of an apparition.

"Here," Chase says, holding a loose board up.

I crawl through it and into a building. Bulbs, encrusted with layers of black dust and abandoned webs, shed yellow light on the morose atmosphere within. Frightened faces gape at me as my hood falls, revealing my dark-skinned face, and those nearest me jump back. Sunken eyes and protruding cheekbones surround me, a striking contrast to the plebeians I have always seen in Arel. As I glance at the sallow faces surrounding me, shrouded by a translucent veil of dust waltzing in the amber glow above us, something stirs within me, a feeling I have never experienced for anyone: pity.

"What is this place?" I ask.

"A tomb," answers Chase.

When I give him a questioning look, he continues.

"About half of the plebeians are kept here, especially those who are deemed too weak to work in public. The strong are sent to do the menial tasks that need doing. The lucky ones, if you can call them that, are sent to houses or businesses to work where they will be fed and kept relatively healthy, but if you get a horrible master, your life can be more hellish than this place. These people have been declared unfit, and so are left here until they die. Every week, guards come through with another group of plebeians to cart the bodies away for disposal."

By disposal, I'm sure Chase means that they are sent to the crematoriums.

"But, why keep them here if they are too ill to work?"

Chase gives me a harsh look, but his expression softens as he remembers that I have spent my life thinking of people like him as nothing more than servants, property to be dealt with as I saw fit.

"People die in the medical centers every day. Someone needs to sort through the clothes of the deceased, discarding what is deemed irreparable, and cleaning those that are kept and redistributed. Who better to do it than the ones who are already dying? What you see before you is one of Arel's many secrets."

A claw-like hand reaches for the orange in my own and I jerk away, startled, unused to seeing something that resembles the spokes of a cultivator more than a hand. The hand snaps back. My eyes follow it, finding the teenage boy it belongs to, but his physique is nothing like Chase's. Chase is strong and healthy, but this one resembles a skeleton. His wide eyes study me as he shrinks away, afraid that I might retaliate due to his overzealous reach for the fruit. I place the orange in his hand and wrap his bony fingers around it.

"There are so many children here," I say.

"Most of their parental units are dead, or have been assigned to a place that did not want them,"—he points at the children before us—"so they are sent here. The strong ones survive and are reassigned somewhere. The weak ones are given other tasks."

"Other tasks?"

"Suicide missions."

I scrunch my eyebrows together, unsure of what Chase means.

"One example is the mines. If a new shaft needs to be built, or there is an area too small for an adult to fit into, one of them"—Chase points at three pallid children huddled together—"will probably be sent with an explosive charge that detonates the moment you set it."

I understand his meaning now. It makes sense, in a morbid way, but as I study the people around me, a part of me, the portion that has been beaten into silence since I was a child, believes that such things are wrong.

"Mines?"

"Where do you think some of the resources for your weapons come from?"

I had never thought about it. The training facility always gave me what I needed to survive, and even now, my needs are provided for at the manor.

We wander through the mass of stretched-out hands, each begging for some semblance of mercy, and the fear that had crippled so many of them when they first saw me vanishes. Refusing to focus on which hand gets something, I dole out the few pieces of food that I have crammed in mine own, dismayed when it is gone so soon. Is this what Natalie has been doing? But why? As I glance around at the dead-like bodies surrounding me, I understand the reasoning: she feels empathy for others, no matter who they are.

"Did you ever spend time in a place like this?" I ask Chase.

"Yes."

"Tell me."

"Gwen and I were not born in a maternity ward, like so many within Arel," says Chase. "Our parents happened to have been assigned to the same outpost. They managed to hide my mother's first pregnancy and keep me a secret until I was old enough to pass as one of the newly assigned plebeians to the outpost that are sent there every few months. I was never allowed to call them mother or father."

That makes sense. The outposts use water that they get from their own wells and do not share water from Arel's reservoir.

"But, she had two children."

"They were unable to hide my sister. The commander found out, and when I intervened to stop his punishment of my parents, he realized why I looked so similar to them. He executed them both, but kept Gwen and me alive. We were both healthy and would make fine additions to

Arel. Though, I think he just wanted me to suffer, as I watched my infant sister die before my eyes, unable to feed her or care for her."

"What makes you say that?"

"We were sent here. A guard shoved me through the gates, leaving me alone with strangers and with nothing but a newborn infant in my arms. What food I got, I had to scrounge for, often times stealing it from another in this place. Gwen would have died if it wasn't for our mistress. She came here, looking for a strong plebeian to do the heavy work around her home and she took us both. She saw to it that Gwen was cared for and that we were both treated well, until she died and we came to your manor."

I picture Chase as a child of about eight or nine, walking alone in this dismal place with a screaming Gwen in his arms, understanding why he is so protective of her. There are few siblings in Arel. Some manage to be born, but it is rare. I open my mouth to speak, thinking that it is something I should do, but before I can utter a single word, the harsh yells of the guards pierce the air, forcing us to hide. Chase grabs my arm and pulls me away toward the hole we had crawled through, but before we can reach it, the door bursts open and guards storm inside. We duck behind some tattered blankets that had been hung up to provide someone a sense of privacy. I peek through a hole in the soiled blanket and watch as a plebeian crumples to the floorboards the moment he tries to stand, his legs unable to support his weight. A guard hauls him up and tosses him to another, muttering something about taking him to disposal, but instead of fear on the boy's face, all I see is contentment.

"Line up!" the guards yell, shoving those huddled within out the door and into the rain.

I start to stand up for a better look, but Chase yanks me back down, forcing me to look through the tiny hole as people shuffle outside, forming a single line, while keeping their eyes to the ground, ignoring the rain that drenches their clothes and tangled hair, providing the only bath that they will get. The last guard stalks outside, but remains close to the open door as it swings in the wind, its hinges creaking with every movement, giving me a glimpse of what is happening. Mud squishes beneath the boots of a man with steady strides as he paces in front of the plebeians being offered to him, his sour expression conveying how unimpressed he is with the offering. A gold sash stretches from his left shoulder to his right hip, standing out against the emerald shirt he wears, a nice contrast against his dark skin, with Arel's insignia embroidered in silver in the middle, catching the moonlight with every turn, displaying his importance.

I gasp. This man is from the executive district, maybe even from the council chambers itself. "That one," he says, pointing at a teenage girl whose muscles have not atrophied yet. Guards seize the plebeian, shoving her to a nearby transport, and the man stalks away, waving his dismissal of everyone.

Chase grabs my wrist and motions me to the hole in the wall, and I follow him, wanting to get out of here before we are caught. I crawl through the hole and cringe when my jacket rips as it snags on an exposed nail. We hurry through the encampment, hiding in the shadows, taking advantage of the distraction that the night's visitor provides. Chase reaches the opening in the fence and lifts the barbed wire, waving me through, and I crawl through head first, before holding the wires up for him. Hugging the wall, we check the street, thankful that no one is there, and dash across to the alley right across from us, disappearing into the darkness, allowing the rain to provide cover.

I reach the wall at the end of the alley first and jump, placing my left foot on the exposed tie rod and grabbing the ledge, hauling myself up, but stop, remembering Chase. Straddling the wall, I lean down and hold my arm out. He jumps, grabs my arm, and I pull him up, dropping down to the other side with him landing next to me. The barking of a dog fills the cold, night air, and we race away from the wall toward the center of the eastern sector, avoiding the streetlamps and arbiters on patrol.

One hundred yards away from the moving walkways, we stop

and jump back into the shadows as an arbiter on patrol strolls past. He ambles down the sidewalk before turning around and walking back, passing us once again. Frowning, I urge Chase to go first, knowing that we will have to dart across the street one at a time, but he shakes his head.

"You have to or he'll catch us," I tell him.

His lips press into a firm line, but he darts across the street, slipping into the darkened conclave underneath the causeway just as the arbiter turns.

Waiting, I control my breathing, sinking into the shadows even more as he stalks past, unaware of my presence. I reposition myself, ready to sprint the moment the arbiter is gone, but stop. A low whine, the same sound I have heard most of my life, pierces my ears, warning me of an approaching drone. Panic rises in me when I spot it hovering over to where Chase has disappeared. I have to do something. I must do something, or it will find him. I snatch a pebble form the ground and chuck it at the drone, striking its cylindrical, metallic siding with a soft—clink!—causing it to stop. My heart beats against my ribcage, threatening to burst through as I wait with bated breath for the drone's next act. It moves toward me just as the arbiter blows his whistle.

I run.

No longer caring about remaining unseen, I charge down the walk and dart through an alley, squeezing through a hole in a fence from a loose board that had fallen away and to another walkway. The drone's whine remains on my tail and more shouts and whistles fill the night. Water vapor forms before me in rapid succession as I hurry through the eastern sector, watching as lights fill darkened windows with the occupants not daring to poke their heads out to witness another dissenter receive their just punishment.

I turn a corner, skidding to a halt when I spot another arbiter heading toward me. Turning, I race across a square to another alley. It splits into two. Not sure which way to go, I veer left, cursing the moment I do as a dead end blocks my path. Spinning around, I hurry to the other path, but am met by the pounding of boots on pavement, all drawing nearer, sealing my doom. I turn in circles, unable to think of a way to escape. Backing further into the alley, I hit a wall and take five deep breaths to steady my pulse as I wait for the inevitable, when strong hands seize my arms, yanking me off my feet and through a door.

I stumble and fall to a rug, rolling across the floor. Instinct takes over, telling me to fight, and I swing my fists, striking a cheek before being stopped by a single word.

"Silence!" hisses a harsh voice, and I obey, laying on my side as the rough fibers of the rug scratch the skin of my face as we both wait, frozen, listening to the voices outside discussing where I might have gone and what to do next.

Harsh fists pound the door, and the man in the room with me places a table with a cloth draping over both sides in front of me, hiding me from view. The hinges of the door creak when he opens it.

"Yes?" he says in a calm manner.

"Have you seen anything suspicious tonight?" asks an arbiter.

"No, I haven't."

"Anyone else in here with you?"

"No," replies the man in the same calm demeanor, "but you are welcome to have a look, if you like." He opens the door wider and steps aside.

"That won't be necessary."

"I insist."

"If you see anything unusual, report it immediately. Have a good night." The arbiter leaves and the door closes.

The man moves the table back to where it had been, placing the feet in the same holes left by it in the rug. "Mora, I'm sorry..." He stops. "You are not Mora."

I sit up, rising to my full height, standing erect and proud like any arbiter would. Seconds tick by while we stare at one another, measuring the other, wondering who will act first. Freckles surround his nose, but none of that compares to his eyes, brown like his skin, which reveal the sharp mind behind them. Reaching up, I realize that my hood has fallen away, revealing my face and the fear that he will call the arbiters back that I try to mask.

"No, I am not," I say.

"Where is she?"

"I do not know." Though I have no idea who this Mora is, I can only guess that she is either his wife, or adopted daughter, and is also out past curfew.

The man touches the bruise on his cheek, left there by my fist, and walks around me, taking in my posture, squared shoulders, and my obdurate eyes, muttering to himself.

"The erect stance, toned muscles, and"—he puts his face near mine, our noses almost touching—"deadly."

Bracing myself, I envision grabbing his arm and throwing him to the floor, disposing of him, if need be, for me to survive.

"Oh, yes," he says, backing away, "very deadly. A perfect soldier. Trained to kill without remorse. You're thinking of it right now— how to get rid of me, should I prove to be a problem. And who would question my death after they search this place?"

For the first time, I notice the book on the table that he had placed in front of me to hide me from view moments before. It looks like a normal book, the kind found in Arel, but, upon closer inspection, something about it seems off. I pick it up and open it. Instead of finding a screen that mimics a single page, I find pages themselves with printed words. Flipping through them, I read some of the words, but have no idea what they mean.

"It's called a book."

"I know what it is," I snap.

"But you've never seen one like this before, have you?" says the man.

I put the book back on the table.

"What are you doing out of bed, I wonder," the man says to himself, but loud enough for me to hear.

"I do not have to answer you."

"Perhaps not, but I can always call the others back. Oh, but you don't want me to."

My eyes turn to slits.

"There it is! The killer. Whatever humanity you had in you has been beaten out of you, to where all you have left is the desire to destroy anything that goes against Arel, a void where a soul once resided. And yet, here you are, out at night, afraid that your fellow arbiters will find you... and without your wristband."

I grab my wrist, pulling the sleeve of my jacket further down, glaring at him.

"There it is again," he says, "that look in your eyes as you debate whether you should kill me or not. A true arbiter would not hesitate, but you do. Why?"

I remain silent.

"You've witnessed something. Something that has made you start to question the world around you."

"You know nothing about me," I whisper.

"I've seen people like you before. The arbiter who is no longer certain of the laws she has sworn to uphold."

A distant whistle sounds, its faded tone almost inaudible.

"Sounds like your friends have given up," says the man. He grabs me by the shoulder and shoves me toward the door, opening it, but I twist around and seize his wrist, removing his hand.

"You may think you have me trapped, but I can still arrest you in the morning," I hiss.

"Then, I suggest you decide quickly what it is you will do." He pushes me outside and slams the door in my face, leaving me alone on the cracked and puddle ridden pavement of an abandoned alley, wondering what he plans to do as he holds my fate in his hands, for the moment.

Rain is in the air. Knowing there is nothing I can do now, I run off, making my way back to the manor, hoping that Chase has made it there and is safe with Gwen.

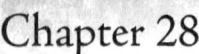

Chapter 28

Black Fire

I zip up my jacket, preparing to leave for the wall, as I listen to the clinking of forks on plates, wishing that I could eat before reporting for duty, but succumb to the idea of not having supper. I will just have to eat a huge breakfast tomorrow.

"Ready?" says Trix as she walks up to me. We are assigned to the wall tonight.

"You're late," I say to her, repeating the first words that Commander Vye had said to me, staring past her and at Chase—pleased that he had made it back to the manor when we had gotten separated after sneaking out four nights ago—who gives me a nod as he pulls Gwen into view, letting me know of her recovery. The only comfort I can give him is a slight smile in return.

The door slides open as I step outside into the orange glow of the evening sun, the hairs on my skin standing up from the goosebumps that form due to the chilled air, informing me of the change in the season. Has it been almost eight months since I have first reported here? The weather says it has. Soon, recruits will run the gauntlet and new arbiters will be brought to the manor. Trix's hurried footsteps tap the pavement behind me, but I do not pause and continue down the drive to the street, remembering what Sheila had told me about her.

Once we reach the wall, we both head for the room where the body armor and weapons are kept, scanning our wristbands. The side of a wall opens, revealing a plethora of armaments for us to choose from. "At least we'll be well-dressed," Trix jokes, snatching a helmet.

Ignoring her, I take off my jacket, placing it in a locker, and grab a Kevlar vest, strapping it on and securing it so that it fits snug, before putting on arm and leg guards.

"You don't like me, do you?" Trix says to me when I pick up a helmet.

"I have no reason to," I say, remaining cold toward her.

"You have no reason to hate me," she says.

"I dislike your tastes in extracurricular activities," I say, facing her, holding my helmet by my side, "which gives me no reason to like you."

Trix laughs. "I had a feeling you knew. I saw the way you glared at me when you caught me with that plebeian girl that one day. And the way you stopped the Master Arbiter from harming her, I would have sworn it was because you wanted her for yourself."

"My tastes are more mature."

"I like mine young and innocent—fresh, if you will." She saunters up to me, swaying her hips in a suggestive manner, until I am backed against a wall with her breasts pressed against mine. "And I love it when they are unable to fight."

"You disgust me."

Trix releases a sultry laugh as she holds my gaze. "Maybe you should let me change that opinion of yours. I could be persuaded to like someone older and more mature, as you put it."

I shove her aside and head for the exit.

"I will have that little bitch when we get back."

I stop, whirling around, doing my best to control my desire to plant my fist into her face.

"And when I get done with her, she'll just be another poor plebeian who passed in the night, unable to handle the harshness of her duties."

I start for her, but another arbiter storms inside. "You two! What is taking so long?"

"Nothing, sir," Trix and I both respond.

He gives us a disbelieving look, but continues with the reason for his presence. "Arbiter Trix, you will be in the center of the wall by the main tower. Arbiter Noni, you'll be on the south side of the wall at station six." The man leaves.

"The law states that we are not supposed to..." I begin.

"The law?" Trix says, cutting me off. "No one cares about the law, Noni. Wake up! Everyone does it, including the commander."

Before I can respond, the guard yells into the room, reminding us of where we are supposed to be. "Now!"

I put my helmet on and leave the armory, snatching a weapon from the wall as I pass through the door and into the ever-softening glow of the sun, heading for the stairwell and receiving a reprimanding glare from the guard. Once at the top, I step across a walkway to the outer wall, glancing down at the snarling dogs below salivating for a meal, and make my way to station six, relieving one of the guards already on duty there.

"Oh, look, they sent us fresh meat," jokes one of the others. "Why don't you relieve me, princess?" he asks, pointing at his crotch.

I respond with a rude gesture.

"Enough!" another guard yells at him. "Get back to your post!"

"Sure thing, sergeant." The rude man stalks off.

Wishing I was somewhere else, I stare out at the open plain before us, remarking at its calm beauty, before roaming my eyes up and down the length of the wall as it stretches up the eastern side of Arel, the point of the W sticking out like an oddity that does not belong. Lights turn on, filling windows up and down the city, from the uppermost level down to the forgotten streets of the eastern sector, golden bows on a pristine package that conceals a dark secret.

The mountain Arel nestles into stretches above us all, and my eyes are drawn to the steel door, shining gold in the sinking sun, where our aircraft are kept. Arel's planes are limited in number and are used only when necessary so as not to waste resources. A part of me wonders what my life would be like if I had been chosen as a pilot, but I shake it off. Only those with the highest scores are given that honor, and they spend their lives in a bunker, never allowed outside, except when needed. I turn back to the open field and stop as I almost rub against a smooth, shiny black mark on the wall.

"Be careful there," says the guard who defended me moments before. "That spot has been touched by…"

"Black fire," I finish for him, wondering why his voice sounds familiar.

"You might want to keep this"—he pulls out a small container of gel from his pocket—"in case you…"

I hold my own container out, having kept it with me since the day it was given to me.

"So, you remembered."

I grin, not that it matters, since my helmet prevents anyone from seeing my face,

"Well, stay alert. And I'll be just over here if you need anything."

"Yes, sir," I reply, surveying the others on the wall with me, all of whom stand yards apart.

I stare out at the open plain in the fading sunlight as it dips below the bumpy horizon, allowing the golden violet crowns of the trees to conceal it from view, laying it to rest until it returns tomorrow. Memories of my time spent in the wildlands struggling to survive flood my mind as I cough, as though I were in the river again almost drowning. I glance at my leg, remembering how it had been broken, and if it weren't for Chase, I would not be here now? Chase. Why didn't he leave me to die out there? Why didn't I leave those who had fallen behind in the gauntlet to die?

I shake my head, tossing the questions and memories aside, no longer wanting them to clog my mind, which needs to be clear as I stand here at the wall: one of the many reasons I hate being left here to stand guard—you're alone with your thoughts and your thoughts can betray you. Once again, my mind wanders and Chase's ecstatic face at seeing his sister well again fills my mind. My debt to him is now paid.

Crows caw as a flock flies overhead, disappearing in the darkening distance. My mind sharpens. The cries of the crows cease, but not the gradual fading that is normal as they fly farther and farther away, but sudden, as though someone ended their migration. Gripping my weapon tighter, I peer out into the distance, trying to focus beyond the growing shadows of twilight as it's bluish-gray glow settles upon the land, obscuring my view, and the hairs on the back of my neck stand up, accompanied by the feeling of not being alone.

Something whistles past me. The guard nearest me falls. Another projectile soars past me, striking another guard before glass shatters as something strikes the tower, killing whomever is in there.

"SNIPER!" I scream, ducking behind the protection of the wall, wondering where the barbarians managed to find one, much less learn the skill or acquire the necessary weapon.

Another on the wall drops over the side with a hole in the front of his helmet, followed by a series of yells that rise up, echoing off the side of the mountain, instilling fear into any who hear it. The alarm! Why has it not sounded yet? I glance over at where one of the controls for it is and find the guard nearest it slumped over the edge of the wall. Crawling, I inch my way closer, moving over dead bodies, doing my best not to think about how they were once alive. A high-pitched whistle strikes my ears. I curl into a ball, covering my head just as a mortar shell sails over the wall and strikes the streets below, exploding on impact, its roar thundering its way through my chest as dirt and bits of stone rain down around me, pelting me and covering my body.

When the last pebble hits my back, I scramble to my feet and run for the control to the alarm, reaching it just as a flash appears in the distance. The whistle of another mortar shell fills my ears and I pull the alarm, releasing the blaring bells on Arel's loudspeakers, warning everyone of the attack. A mortar shell strikes the earth just before the wall, creating a crater, and the explosion lifts me off my feet, propelling me backward until I slam into the side of a tower covered in rubble. Dazed, I try to look around me, but my cracked helmet impedes my ability to see what is happening. I tear it off.

The cries of a crazed man fill the air. I look up. A barbarian races for me, his knife glinting in the firelight. I raise my helmet and his blade bounces off it. He swings again. Ducking, I lean to the side as sparks fly from where his blade strikes the side of the tower and swing my helmet, hitting the man in the side of the head. Before he has time to recover, I shove the rubble off my lap and squirm out from under it, jumping to my feet just in time to block another attack, using my helmet as a shield. He goes for my leg, but I ram my helmet into his head again and again, until he falters, allowing me to snatch his knife and ram it between his ribs as warm blood oozes over my gloved hand.

Another pop sounds in the distance and I duck just as a shell detonates against the other end of the wall. Its flames form bulbous circles, growing larger by the second, until fizzling out, leaving only black smoke and the agonized cries of the wounded behind. Shots fire above me. Jerking my head upward, I watch as one of the guards in another tower fires upon the field of grass below us and I follow the projectory of his bullets. Faint movement scurries through the grass. I concentrate my focus, doing my best to make out the activity below in the faint light. People with packs strapped to their backs run for the wall. A few fall from the guard's fire, but not enough.

"Below us!" I yell to the arbiters nearest me, pointing at the barbarians.

Dropping my helmet, I snatch a rifle from the ground and aim at the barbarians, wondering why they run up to the wall, and fire, striking two. More come.

"Get down!" yells the same man who had defended me earlier, pulling the pin from a grenade.

I hunker behind the wall, covering my head just as he throws the grenade into the mass of people below, and close my eyes when it detonates, sending dirt and body parts into the air. As I start to stand up, another explosion rocks the wall below me and the ground crumbles away beneath my feet, disappearing; and I drop downward with the rubble, unable to catch myself. Fear mixed with a cold calmness strikes me, but before I can accept my impending death, a hand seizes my left wrist and I jerk to a halt, feeling a sharp pain grip my shoulder. I look up. The same arbiter has saved me once again. I swing my right hand up and grasp his as he yanks me to safety.

"Black fire," he says to me.

Clapping his shoulder as a way to say thank you, I scramble to my feet and hurry to one of the flame throwers still standing along what is left of the wall. Rubble crashes around me. I swerve to avoid it, jumping over bricks and stone fragments of the wall and dodging the other arbiters between me and the flamethrower. A barbarian climbs over the top of the wall. He spots me. With a monstrous yell, he charges me with a long gun, which has a blade attached to the end of the barrel, forming a bayonet. Refusing to stop, I drop to the ground, somersaulting beneath his swing and kick him in the back of the knee, forcing him to stumble and lose his stance. I ram my heel into his knee again, feeling it bend backward. Ignoring his anguished cries, I spiral around and grab his bayonet, twisting it, and fling him into the air, forcing him to lose his hold on it. He slams onto his back, but before he can recover, I stab him with his bayonet and a shocked expression crosses his face before his head lulls to the side, and he stops moving.

Another barbarian reaches the top of the wall and races for me. I aim the long gun at him and pull the trigger. Nothing. Dammit! That explains the home-fashioned bayonet. The barbarian nears, swinging a combat knife in each hand. I meet his attack, using the bayonet like a staff and raising it in front of me, blocking the strike from one knife, while jumping back to avoid a blow from the second. He strikes. Again, I block with the bayonet, slicing the man's knuckles, forcing him to drop his knife. Infuriated, he lunges. I spin around, jabbing the butt of the gun into his stomach, but before I can finish him, another explosion rocks the ground, causing me to stumble and allowing him to seize me from behind.

Another barbarian sees us and raises his weapon. Before he can fire, I jerk my head back, ramming it into the face of the one who holds me. I feel his grip slacken. Seizing my chance, I break free, wrenching his arm as I twist around and stand behind him, using him as shield just as the other barbarian pulls the trigger. I snatch the knives and run for the third man, dropping to my knees and stabbing him in the thigh, before plunging the second knife into his stomach.

A sword strikes the ground beside me. I roll to the side out of the way and face my new attacker. He lunges. I cross the blades of the knives in front of me, blocking his attack. He raises his sword, but before he can strike me, I tackle him, dropping him to the ground, and slice his throat with both knives, almost severing his head, not caring about his suffering as he struggles to breathe, while blood spurts from the mortal wound I delivered him. I pick up his weapon and spot a familiar crest on it: Kition. Taking a closer look at the man I have just killed, my mind races with questions, trying to answer an unknown puzzle, while I realize that this barbarian's face appears to have just been shaved and shows no signs of having lived outside of civilization.

"Black fire," I whisper to myself when a flamethrower on the other side of the wall spews its unforgiving wrath on those below it, reminding me of what I must do.

Jumping to my feet, I charge through the fray, ignoring those around me and killing any intruder who tries to stop me. A body drops in front of me. I leap over it and plunge my knives into the back of a barbarian who has an arbiter in a choke hold. Refusing to stop, I rip my blades from the corpse and continue to race for the nearest flamethrower. Another explosion strikes the earth just short of the wall, and I bring my arms up, shielding my face from the clumps of soil that fly my way while still running, reminding myself that the people within Arel depend on me—on all of us succeeding.

Once I reach the flamethrower, I drop the knives and disengage the safety, aiming at the invaders below. I pull the trigger. Black fire bursts from the nozzle, raining down upon those below it, drenching them in its never-ending fury as I swing it side to side to increase the damage done. Agonized screams fill my ears as those covered run amok, not caring what direction they go in, attempting to get away from the black flames that burn their flesh from their bones while its smoke sears their lungs. Some crash into the wall. Others run into their comrades. Most drop to the ground and writhe in pain before going still. I release the trigger and stare out at the inferno I have unleashed, refusing to display any recoil at the stench of burning flesh as it saturates my nostrils, while the notion that I should be repulsed at the sight ebbs at the corners of my mind. The whine of a drone jerks me from my lingering thoughts. I turn toward it and watch as the soft-ball sized thing hovers beside me. It flies away.

A fist plows into my cheek and I fall to the ground. A bit stunned, I glance up at the invader who has punched me, the anger on his face at what I have done to his friends evident, visible to the world. He takes a step for me. I get on all fours, ready to pounce when he moves.

The man springs for me. I dodge out of the way, flinging myself to the flamethrower, and swing myself over the wall, gambling that it will support my weight, and circle around, lifting my feet as I cross over the edge of the wall the second time, and kick him in the face. I let go, landing on my feet. Before he can regain his senses, I snatch his right arm, stretching it out, and plunge my fist into the back of his elbow, breaking it. He screams, but I am not finished. Stepping around him, I grab him by the back of the head with both hands and ram his face into the sharp edge of the wall until his face caves in and the gray stone is colored red from his blood. I release the body and notice the same drone hovering nearby. It had seen everything.

A horn sounds in the distance and the barbarians that are left flee, running for the trees, and disappear behind the protection of their trunks and broad leaves. I glance at the drone again, but it has left, much to my relief, as I have never liked the way those things appear without warning sometimes and capture every move one makes. Bowing my head, I rub the sweat from my face and catch an interesting pattern on the dead man's tanned forearm and kneel down, picking it up and pulling his sleeve away from it. He's been branded, but I know this mark. It is the mark a plebeian receives when they have tried to run away, but got caught. It's meant as a warning to others and to us, the citizens of Arel, as well. Dangerous thoughts race through my mind as I put the arm back down, knowing that there is only one reason for him to have it.

Scuffling sounds put me on full alert as I whirl around, ready to defend myself from the next threat. Trix lies on the edge of the wall, near the space between the inner and outer portions, trying to use the broken railing to haul herself to her feet.

"Noni," she says, spotting me, "help me."

I refuse to move.

"Come on, you bitch," she yells. "I think my ankle is broken." She clutches her side and blood drips between her fingers as she attempts to stand up, but her ankle gives out, forcing her to drop back down in danger of falling over the edge and to the wild dogs below, whose incessant barking gives me a headache.

I take two steps toward her.

She glares at me. "Well don't just stand there!"

"An arbiter who cannot walk has no business being an arbiter," I say, repeating a line taught to us countless times at the training facility.

"Are you still mad about earlier?"

I show her my back, but before I get far, Trix stops me.

"You know what I'm going to do when I get back? I'm going to take care of that little brat and then I'll take care of you."

Something inside me takes over: a fury I have never known to exist before. I face Trix and stalk over to her, my face unreadable and devoid of any emotion. Shouts echo over us as more arbiters arrive at the wall through the underground tunnels that spread throughout the city, and Trix and I both know they will reach us soon.

A devious smile spreads across her lips. "You'll regret this and—"

I take another step toward her.

"—there is nothing you can do about it. She'll suffer, you know, and you will be the cause of it."

I stand a foot away from her, scowling at her.

Trix laughs and red bubbles squirt from her bloodied lips. "What are going to do now?"

I raise my foot and kick her in the chest, knocking her backward over the edge of the wall and to the hungry dogs below, not bothering to watch as her screams echo around me, while their sharp teeth rip into her flesh, tearing it from her bones as they devour her alive. Turning, I walk away, silhouetted by the fires that still burn, refusing to look back or acknowledge the emptiness that fills me after my rage toward Trix dissipates.

"Noni!" Faya's voice calls out to me when I reach the top of one of the stairwells. She rushes for me, overjoyed at seeing me alive and unhurt, and plows into me, giving me a giant hug, releasing me as she realizes that people surround us, witnessing this display of emotion. "I'm so glad that you're okay."

"How did you…" I begin, noticing her dust-covered armor, and stop when I remember that when the alarm sounded, the majority of the city's arbiters would have been called to the wall to defend it. "Are you okay?"

"I'm fine. It's you I was worried about."

"I'm okay. Not even a scratch."

Relief washes over Faya, and I imagine the worry she must have felt knowing that her one friend from the training facility was stationed where the attack took place.

Medical transports arrive, flooding the area with their lights and sirens and people in white uniforms jump out, adding a harsh contrast to us arbiters and our black armor in the dancing light of the fires.

"Come on," Faya says to me. "They're going to need our help."

Faya rushes to the wounded and follows the orders given to her by medical personnel, while I take one last glance at the raging flames in the open field beyond, from where I had sprayed the black fire, before trailing after her to deal with the aftermath of this latest attack.

Chapter 29

Another Day

A dull, throbbing ache in my right shoulder pulls me from my uneasy slumber, insisting that I wake up and get ready for what the new day has to offer. Moaning, I roll over onto my left side, wishing that the pain would subside and leave me alone, or at least allow me a few more minutes of sleep, but sleep was not on the roster, as a knock sounds on my door: soft at first and more forceful when I refuse to answer. I sit up, rubbing my bruised shoulder. Two days have passed since the attack on the wall, but the purplish-black mark the size of my fist remains, unable to camouflage itself in my black skin. I touch it with my fingertips and wince from the ache. This will take over a week to heal. The door rattles as whomever insists on disturbing me pounds it with their fist.

I get up and open it. Shelia's hair spills through the gap and guilt rises within me, making me wish that I had answered her earlier.

"Is anything wrong?" I ask her, pulling her inside, worried that something may have happened, since she never shows up at my door unannounced like this.

430

"No," she replies. "Commander Vye sent me to get you up, even though you are not on rotation today."

Did someone fall ill and I need to take their place?

"You have an incoming call. She has had it sent to your room and sent me to tell you."

My face lights up and random names of people roll through my head as my mind grapples with the unexpected call, wondering who would be contacting me.

"Thank you," I tell her.

"Hey, brat!" Anan strolls by my room and stops to taunt Sheila. She shrinks under his gaze.

"See that dull color,"—he grabs her head and forces her to look at his pointed boots—"why are they like that?"

"Because I forgot to shine them yesterday," replies Sheila, keeping her eyes downward and her voice low.

"I want to see my face in them when I get off duty." He shoves her back until she hits the wall.

"Shine your own boots," I say to him.

Annoyed, Anan glares at me. "What did you say?"

"You heard me," I reply, a dangerous edge to my voice, and the same anger I had allowed to overtake me when I kicked Trix off the wall and to the dogs below threatens to expose itself.

"Getting a little big for your breeches, don't you think?"

"She's doing work for me."

"So now that the competition is out of the way, you want the little brat for yourself," he sneers.

I remain silent.

Anan closes the distance between us as he reaches up and brushes my hair with his fingertips. "You know, if it's company you want, I will gladly provide it."

I grab his wrist and yank his arm downward, squeezing it so tight that his ebony fingers start to turn purple. "Not interested."

"Anan!" Commander Vye's sharp voice echoes through the hallway. "Why aren't you on duty?"

"No reason, ma'am," he replies, jerking his arm free of my grasp.

Commander Vye's scowl could curdle milk. "Just for that, you will be pulling a double rotation today with no break," she says, placing emphasis on the word no.

Taking one last glare at me, Anan stalks away and stomps down the steps.

"And why aren't you dressed?" Commander Vye demands of me.

"I have no excuse, ma'am," I reply, standing at attention.

"Hurry up and get downstairs. For your tardiness, you will not be allowed breakfast."

"Yes, ma'am."

"I know that the loss of fellow arbiters can affect a person for a while, but you mustn't allow it to hold you for long. An arbiter who fails to perform her duty is of no use to Arel."

"Understood."

"And for goodness sake, answer that message!" Commander Vye walks away and disappears down the stairs.

"You can wash my beddings," I tell Sheila in a soft voice. "That should keep you busy for a while and away from Anan."

Once she has grabbed my bedding and left the room, I turn on the monitor, answering the message that has been sent to my room, receiving a pleasant surprise.

"Noni!" Faya's face appears on the screen, and I am taken aback, since I did not expect her to call me.

"Faya," I say, unable to contain my surprise, "what… is something wrong?"

"No, silly. I wanted to make sure you are okay."

"A little bruised, but nothing that won't heal. I don't mean to be rude, but I do have to report for duty." I say as I pull my pants up and put on my shirt.

"I won't take long. I just wanted to be one of the first to congratulate you."

"Congratulate me?" I face Faya, wondering what she is talking about, and her overexcited smile and jittery demeanor tells me that she knows something I do not. "For what?"

"I don't want to ruin the surprise."

My curiosity piqued to the point where I want to beat the secret out of her, I stand in front of the monitor with my hands on my hips, my expression nonplussed.

"Oh, don't go giving me that droopy face."

"What are you talking about? You know I don't like secrets."

"Joel made me promise not to ruin the surprise, but I wanted talk to you before anyone else does."

"Don't make me come to the economic sector and strangle it out of you," I joke.

Faya laughs. She knows I detest secrets like this, but it is her way.

"So how is Joel?" I ask, changing the subject.

"Excellent," she replies with a wink.

"You're terrible."

"We should all get together sometime."

"I'll see if I can get some leave." I grab a jacket and put it on, making certain that it is straight and the collar isn't turned up, and zip it close.

"Your commander will have to give you some now that you're— Oh! I almost ruined the surprise."

My brows furrow. It almost worked.

"I have to go," Faya says, "but you take care of yourself and I'll see you soon."

"You too," I tell her.

She waves and clicks off her monitor, allowing mine to go black, and I turn it off before leaving the room. A minute later, I reach the bottom of the stairs and stand outside the dining area, waiting for my instructions from Commander Vye, who sits at the head of the table with a glass raised.

"Trix was a good arbiter and proved her worth in the latest attack on the wall. She will be missed, but never forgotten," Commander Vye says. "To our fallen comrades!"

"Strength in our kind!" the others chant. "Strength in numbers! Strength over weakness! Weakness is failure! Failure is death!"

I repeat the mantra of Arel with the rest of them, saying it under my breath and without the gusto that they possess, watching as they each sip from their water glasses. Once they have finished, they each file out of the room, and Gwen and one other plebeian hurry in to clear the dishes. I catch her eye, wanting to ask her how she feels and about Chase, since I have not had a chance to speak to him since the night we had snuck out, but before I can wander over to her, Commander Vye calls my name.

"Noni!"

"Yes, ma'am," I reply, standing at attention.

"I have you on day patrol today."

There goes my day off.

"Who will be with me today?" I ask. In the past, either she or another arbiter had accompanied me while I was on patrol, to ensure that I carried out my duties in accordance with the law.

"No one."

I raise my eyebrows.

"You will be one your own today," says Commander Vye, her tone indicating that something more is at play here. "Consider this a test to ensure that you are capable of carrying out your duties."

"Is everything all right?" I ask.

"Why wouldn't it be?" she snaps.

"Sorry, ma'am," I apologize for assuming that she is under some sort of duress. "I just did not expect to be given this honor so soon."

"Consider it a test."

Everything is a test. "Yes, ma'am," I reply and salute her. Some of the arbiters within the manor give me a few odd glances and turn away the moment I look at them, making me wonder what they know that I do not. Not wanting to remain the object of their attention, I storm out the front door and into the gray light outside, not bothering to look at the overcast sky.

Soon, I find myself strolling near the plaza, not caring where my feet take me, as my mind lingers on the wall and the latest attack. Two plebeians weighed down with overflowing sacks of goods stroll by, giving me a passing glance as they hurry along. The exposed brand on the bare forearm of one catches my attention and my mind races back to the invader that had attacked me on the wall and how he bore the same mark. An escaped plebeian attacking us and wearing Kition clothing? I think back to the attack on the wall soon after my arrival here in the eastern sector, remembering my puzzlement at seeing Kition weapons in the hands of the barbarian invaders.

The plebeians hurry away, looking back at me in nervous agitation. I have been following them without realizing it as my mind had taken me to a different time, forcing me to focus on questions I had filed away, hoping to forget about them. I slow down and am about to turn away when I pause. Why are they afraid of me following them? This is a crowded city. People are bound to walk in the same direction, and though I am used to people giving me a wide berth, the reaction of these plebeians seems more agitated than most.

Slowing my pace, I slack off and allow them to get a little further ahead of me, believing that I have lost interest in them, while still keeping them within sight. Their nerves ease a little as they continue onward, still clutching their bundles, refusing to let them go. They cruise down the crowded walkway, moving between groups of people, keeping their heads low, but their eyes alert, while I maintain a steady pace behind them, using the unobservant crowd as cover to mask my presence. The further we walk, the more I wonder where they are headed. They turn, taking a shortcut to the plaza and trek across it, heading straight for Sigal's. I pause. Why are they going there?

Not wanting to lose them, I run across the street and burst through the door to the café, becoming swamped by the jubilant sounds and mindless chatter that his place is known for. A few people glance in my direction, but turn away when they decide that I am of no interest. My eyes roam the darkened interior, but find no sign of the two plebeians who seem to have disappeared without a trace. Deciding that there is no reason for me to stay, I turn to leave, but Sigal's boisterous voice stops me.

"Come for an early lunch?" he asks, taking my arm and dragging me inside.

"No, I…" I start to say, but never get a chance to finish before he guides me to a table and has me sit down.

"You do look a little peckish," Sigal says to me, concerned, and I am helpless against his insistence that I sit. "I'll go get you something to eat."

He saunters off, taking a moment to shake hands with another arbiter on the way to the kitchen. In the few spare moments I have, I look around the eatery, searching for the two plebeians that I saw come in here, but they are nowhere to be found. Thinking that they might have gone to the back like I had seen Natalie do before, I start to stand up, but Sigal bursts from the kitchen before I can get very far, so I sit back down.

"Here you go," he says, placing four bowls in front of me. "Steamed carrots with garlic sauce and an almond nut crust. Sweet potato hash browns. One steak cooked to medium well. And eggs benedict with hollandaise sauce, minus the muffin, of course."

I stare at the four heaping helpings of food, wanting to dig into it, but I do not have much of an appetite.

"Is the food not to your liking?" asks Sigal, his voice calm yet troubled.

The back of my throat seizes up and my eyes begin to water and a single tear escapes, something that has not happened since I was a child.

In an instant, Sigal sits in the chair across from me and gives me a napkin to wipe my face. "Looks like the wife put a little too much pepper in that sauce," he laughs as a couple of arbiters pass by us, but his eyes hold no joy.

"What is it, dear?" he asks, leaning closer. He senses my hesitation and snaps his fingers. Within moments, his daughter stands in the middle of the room with a jubilant smile on her face, yelling, "Who wants to hear a song?"

Cheers rise up as everyone turns toward her.

"All right then," she yells across the room, her curly hair bobbing up and down with each movement. "In honor of our latest victory against those who attacked us, I dedicate this song to our arbiters and, of course, our presidents Kumi and Tapiwa!"

A few people pull out pocket instruments that they carried with them at all times and start playing a tune, while Sigal's daughter sings a song that she makes up on the spot, her alto voice carrying throughout the room, surprising some, including me.

"Now,"—Sigal turns toward me—"what is troubling you?"

"Have you…" I begin, but have trouble getting the words out, not knowing if this is a trick or not, but something in Sigal's demeanor tells me that his concern is sincere. "Have you ever wondered if everything you've been raised to believe… that maybe something is missing?"

"It is natural to questions things," says Sigal.

"But, here…"

"What has brought about this change?"

I think back on the last eight months. So much has happened: the riots, the woman with the baby, the barbarian whom Commandant Paq murdered, the one who saved mine and Chase's life, and this latest attack on the wall. "I was given an assignment outside the wall some time ago. While there, the convoy was attacked and I managed to escape with a plebeian. My leg was broken, and without his help, I never would have made it, but there was this outsider. He helped us and did not act at all like the ones who attacked us. Is there…"

"Be careful what you question," Sigal warns me, "and do not let your doubts show."

I clamp my mouth shut and regret confiding in him.

"You are young," he continues, easing my fears, "and I have seen so many like you through the decades. Bright, happy, ready to do your duty for Arel, but the world has a way of changing our outlook on life. Most find a way to accept it, or to at least pretend that they are like everyone else so as not to draw suspicion. Others, never find a way, and they are never seen again. You are going to have to decide which one you will be."

"Should I just forget everything?"

"No. You should remember it. Underneath the glamour of every peaceful city lies a darkness, and you are just beginning to scratch the surface of Arel's. You are about to receive an award for your actions and you will need to smile and act like you did when you first came here."

"Award?"

"You don't know?"

I frown, scolding myself for being the last one to know something as important as an award ceremony, which is to take place in Arel. My mind has been so consumed with recent events that I have not paid attention to the latest news broadcast.

"You and four others are to receive an award tomorrow for your heroics on the wall." Sigal glances at his daughter. Her song is almost finished, and despite her talent, she cannot sing forever. "Now, eat, be happy, and make sure you cheer."

Sigal leaves just as the song finishes and I clap my hands, joining the euphoric crowd, doing as he has advised me to do.

I finish my meal, responding to any who talk to me as they stroll pass and leave. Once outside, I spot the same two plebeians I had followed here walking down the street, carrying different bags and chuckle to myself. Well played, Sigal. His semblance of caring about my depressed state distracted me from my original curiosity, yet a part of me cannot help but believe that the café owner does care, since his comforting words hold some truth in them.

Chapter 30

A Ceremony

The warm sun bears down upon me as I stand outside with Renal, Commander Vye, the four other arbiters who are to be awarded alongside me, and two commanding officers whom I do not know, dressed in my dress uniform: black like my other ones, but with silver bands stretching lengthwise up the sleeves. My fingers twitch from nerves as a white car, longer than any of the transports I had been in before, bearing the presidential flags, pulls into the drive, heading straight for us. It rolls to a stop, and a plebeian, adorned in white satin pants and a red satin shirt, jumps out, opening the back door for all of us. My ears pick up the snapping of shears as they trim the hedges in a rapid fashion. Glancing in their direction, but being careful to not attract attention, I spot Chase standing next to one of the front hedges just so I can see him. He gives me an encouraging smile. I grin back.

One by one, we each get into the vehicle, while I hang back, making sure I am the last one in so that I will be seated by the window. The plebeian shuts the door and jumps back into his place at the front, and as we drive away, I glance out the window, taking one last look at Chase, even though I know that he cannot see me through the tinted windows. His words from the night before roll through my head and I focus on them in an effort to calm my anxiety.

"Arbiter Noni?"

"Sir?" I whirl around, unaware that someone was trying to talk to me, noticing the luxurious interior of the vehicle for the first time.

Plush, white leather seats with maroon and emerald embroidery lining the tops form a horseshoe within the presidential transport with armrests that fold down, should someone wish to use them. The warm glow spilling from the recessed interior lights of the vehicle turns my black dress uniform into more of a golden color, accentuating the silver stripes, but none of that compares to the mirrored interior that makes it look as though there is six of me. I shift a little, pushing the purple shag rug on the floor with the tips of my boots.

"A bit nervous, sir," I say, hoping that it answers whatever question he had asked me. The man smiles and a few others in the car chuckle.

I fold my sweaty palms into my lap, staring out the window once more, watching the people zip past as they jumped out of our way and pretend to not care that the presidential car is in their sector. The charred sides of a building missing an entire wall, which forms a pile of ash where it once stood, catch my eye, but that is not what causes me to stare. A man huddles next to the ashen remains, comforting his wife, and their forlorn faces explain their situation: they have lost their home and have no hope of it being repaired.

We leave the eastern sector and cross into the northern sector, heading for the economic district. The difference between them and the eastern sector is apparent when the transport ceases to bounce and rock from every pit in the road and glides over the smooth, glassy surface that paves the northern sector. The dull charcoal and slate colors fade, replaced by buildings of vibrant colors, rivaling any rainbow. Bay windows fill every floor of the multistory structures, each with a planter brimming with daisies, petunias, and marigolds, while the glass panes reflect the city of Arel. A railcar passes overhead, but the soundproof interior of the transport muffles its long-winded whine. People hurry out of our way, but unlike those in the eastern sector, they stare at us, curious as to who we are and where we are headed. Even the plebeians watch and have a certain spring to their step, though they remain careful to not intrude too much or anger their masters.

We pass into the economic district and the homes and shops vanish, transforming into spiraling towers of glass and metal that change colors depending on the time of day. I picture Faya carrying out her duties, strolling through the skyscrapers on paved walks and streets that do not have a single crack or pit in them. We drive past a café and I remember the time I had met her at one, marveling at the sleek designs of the buildings, wondering what goes on within them and what the planners are dreaming up.

The transport stops. Leaning forward, I look through the glass separating us from the driver and his passenger, wondering why we have stopped. A copper gate holds the answer. We have reached the executive district, the seat of Arelian power. No one is allowed to enter the executive district without permission. Even the railcars do not come here, but stop a block away, forcing any venturing there to walk the rest of the way.

The plebeian and the driver both roll down their windows when two arbiters guarding the gate walk up, weapons raised.

"State your business," demands one.

The plebeian holds out a translucent card, which he had strapped around his neck, with a barcode on it. The arbiter scans it.

"You may pass," says the arbiter and he and his partner wave us through.

I look at the others within the transport, wondering why we were not searched or why we all were not asked for our identities.

As though reading my mind, one of the commanders within the vehicle answers me. "We are here at the invitation of presidents Kumi and Tapiwa. Because of that, they do not dare search us, but do not try to get past the gate without such an invitation."

His warning does not go unnoticed.

Once on the other side of the gate, I gasp, unable to peel my eyes from the exorbitance that lies ahead of me. Hexagonal columns made of ivory surround us, each attached to a tremendous structure with rows and rows of marble steps leading up to the 20-foot high doors, made of copper-lined steel, that bear the insignia of Arel. To my right, lies the council chambers—I recognize it from the pictures I have seen—its square front glows orange despite the overcast sky. An abundance of trees stand to my left; their trunks spiral upwards as though they have been hand-carved instead of formed by nature, overburdened by the wide, oval-shaped leaves whose Persian-green color dulls the jade grass engulfing them. Vines hang from the branches, swinging in the wind, twisting together to form hammocks. As I study them, I see bits of sandstone and guess that there must be an atrium there.

Central to the entire arrangement is the auriferous dome building in front of us, nestled between the wildlife and the council chambers. An array of hexagonal plates, made from pure gold, construct the dome as it arcs downward, melding into panels of glass, embedded in stone that allow light through. I stare at it. Commander Vye notices my widening eyes and chuckles, understanding my awe, but clears her throat, reminding me of the professionalism I am expected to display. I straighten up and stare straight ahead, looking at the building through the windshield, absorbing every detail of the auric structure looming before us.

The driver guides our transport to the triangular, front steps of the domed structure, and the moment he stops, the plebeian jumps out to open the back door. "Madam," he says to me in a polite tone, holding his hand out for me.

Perplexed, since no one has ever helped me out of a car before, as arbiters are expected to stand on their own, I do not take it. The man gives me a cheerful smile, masking any disappointment he might have had at my perceived rudeness, but my guilt for not allowing him to assist me dissipates the moment Commander Vye gets out, having refused his hand as well. A bit of sunlight pokes through the clouds and reflects off her shaven head, illuminating her sharp features and strong chin, reminding me that I had wanted to be just like her when I first met her.

"Welcome," greets a boisterous man, walking down the steps. The legs of his coal-colored pants brush against each other, creating *pish-pish* sounds, while the tails of his marigold tunic, with crimson and blue cords stitched in a way so that they coil down the sides, flap behind him. The clothing's bright color contrasts with his night-colored skin, making it stand out even more against the marble backdrop. "We are pleased to have you all here."

I follow Commander Vye's example and stand erect, trying not to gawk at the copper sandals that the man wears.

"You may call me Kaleb. I am the Minister of Affairs here. If you need anything, just ask." He motions for us to follow him and we each hike up the steps, leading into the central building, passing underneath the copper-lined, arch doorway and into the domed area. Unable to contain myself, I crane my neck backward, taking in the magnitude of the dome itself, admiring the paintings that adorn its underside, each depicting a glorious moment in Arelian history, and how it appears to be as bright inside as it is outside.

"The dome is a masterpiece, is it not?" Kaleb says, appreciating my wonderment. "Please, take the time to admire it. It is one of the finer pieces of Arelian art."

"Kaleb," says a strong voice, and we all glance up a flight of broad stairs to find Tapiwa standing at the top, adorned in white, "you aren't going to keep our heroes all day, are you?"

"My apologies, Madam President." Kaleb ushers us up the stairs and I place my hand on the smooth rail, remarking at its cool touch, wondering how it had been constructed, as I climb the shallow steps to the second floor, where two more staircases branch off, ascending to opposite sections of the mansion.

"Impressive, isn't it?" Kaleb asks in a boastful manner.

"Yes, sir," I reply.

"Lala palm. The wood has been bleached to give it this color, but the plebe—citizen who built it had quite a unique skill when it came to woodworking. Hurry now. They do not tolerate tardiness."

I quicken my pace. We all follow Kaleb down a walkway on the second floor, passing underneath a mirrored ceiling, and I glance up to watch our reflections, until we reach a triangular beam of light spilling through a ten-foot wide doorway with statues of our presidents on either side, each looking bold and noble, ready to defend their city. The statues' gazes follow us, unnerving me. Kaleb beckons us outside, his broad smile exposing his pearl teeth, and we obey. Cheers bombard me as I step into the sunlight and I stop, unused to being greeted in such a manner.

Commander Vye's firm hand presses the edge of my right shoulder as she whispers into my ear. "Take a deep breath and put one foot in front of the other."

I inhale, filling my lungs past capacity, and step onto a balcony overlooking a massive crowd that have been allowed to gather underneath us. Arbiters patrol the perimeter and meander amongst the people, each armed and ready to act should someone be foolish enough to interrupt this momentous occasion by attempting an assassination. Tapiwa and Kumi stand in front of a microphone placed near the waist high railing with carvings of laurel leaves and eucalyptus flowers weaving their way along it, brushing the oval-shaped supports. I take my place with the other four arbiters, while Commander Vye stands with the other commanders; her erect and proud posture reminds me of how I must carry myself. Arms by my side, I stare out at the exuberant crowd and notice the cameras placed at even intervals, so as to capture every moment of this ceremony and broadcast it live throughout Arel.

"Thank you! Thank you!" says Kumi into the microphone, waving his silky hands at the crowd with a warm smile, looking just as immaculate in his ivory outfit as Tapiwa appears in hers. "As you are aware, Arel has once again suffered an attack by the barbarians that live outside the wall, but they did not act alone. They were assisted by the war mongers in Kition!"

Boos rise within the crowd at the mention of our oldest enemy. Tapiwa and Kumi look pleased.

"But we will not allow them to dampen our spirits," Tapiwa takes over. "We shall rise up, stronger and more determined than before. We are Arel! Strong and proud! Strength in—"

"—our kind!" the crowd finishes, along with those of us on the balcony. "Strength in numbers! Strength over weakness! Weakness is failure! Failure is death!"

"These five arbiters—" Kumi steps back, allowing the cameras to pan over us and I stare straight ahead, keeping my face impassive—"have demonstrated courage far beyond what any of us could ask for. They are a testament to their training and to their commanders, having bravely defended you—the citizens of Arel!"

A huge screen behind us flashes to life and footage of our exploits from the last attack are displayed, showcasing each of us and our moments of triumph, focusing on one before switching to another. Across from us is another building-sized screen playing the same footage captured by the drones. Like everyone else, I watch each scene, but take a sharp breath when my face appears. The drone that had followed me captured all my best moments—if you can call them that—from when I defended myself against the barbarians that had made it over the wall, to my desperate desire to reach the flamethrower. My face falls as I watch myself engage the flamethrower, spewing black fire upon the invaders below. The flames from the burning bodies cast dark shadows upon my stony face as my dead eyes stare out at the damage I had created, unfeeling, uncompassionate, just robotic—a drone myself: cold and calculating, and almost enjoying their misery.

I do not regret defending the people within Arel's walls, but why is it I felt nothing? The people set aflame felt pain. They felt agony. Did they deserve the fate I bestowed upon them even if they did bring it on themselves?

Remembering where I am, I swallow the saliva building within my dry mouth and continue to keep my face stolid, matching the reticent expressions of the four arbiters standing next to me.

"They are the ones deserving of your praise!" Tapiwa says when the footage finishes playing. "They are the ones who have saved us all! Their commanders should be proud!"

The commanders standing to one side of the balcony straighten their postures and stick their chins out to demonstrate their pride, bringing credence to Tapiwa's words.

"And so," Tapiwa continues, "we present to each of them the Arelian Medal of Honor."

One by one, Kumi calls our names, and I watch as the four before me march up to receive their honor, saluting the presidents and remaining stoic, though beneath the surface each one beams with pride.

"Arbiter Noni," Kumi calls my name and I am reminded of the banquet and the day I received my commission.

The man who had assisted me on the wall gives me an encouraging smile as I walk up to the presidents.

I manage a grin in return as sweat pools underneath the collar of my jacket and the hairs on my arms stand on end in response to my throbbing pulse, overshadowing the roars of the crowd. When I reach them, I salute the two presidents, standing erect, and Tapiwa pins a medal—a pair of eagle's wings with Arel's symbol of an A with three S's attached to it—on the left breast of my jacket. She and Kumi both shake my sweaty hands and I salute them once more before returning to my place with the others, taking a quick glance at Commander Vye's beaming face. I have not only made her proud, but cemented her leadership within Arel.

"To the heroes of Arel!" both Tapiwa and Kumi say, clapping

their hands, and the crowd below follows their lead, sending up a thunderous applause to our heroics.

Once the cheers fade, arbiters usher the crowd out of the gathering area, and Kaleb urges us back inside, following Kumi's and Tapiwa's departure.

"That was momentous," he says, "was it not?"

None of us respond.

"There is a dinner to be held in your honor," says Kaleb. "Your commanding officers will be there along with some of our most distinguished arbiters and, of course, the presidents themselves. This way! This way!"

His enthusiastic steps echo in front of us as his shoes stamp the LuxTouch floor, with each embedded diamond and pearl dazzling my eyes as they glint in the glowing lights of the chandeliers. We follow after him, each of us doing our best to not show our awe at such a breathtaking set of tiles. Even Commander Vye's eyes wander to the jade molding on the ceiling and the sapphires sparkling from within it. A maze of corridors branch off from the one we trek down and I wonder where they all lead.

"Hurry! Hurry!" Kaleb's voice stops my curiosity, and I speed up, matching his quick steps.

Oil paintings of past presidents line the wall, each entombed in a gold, hand-carved frame, starting from the first and ending with the portraits of both Kumi and Tapiwa on opposing sides so that they not only stared at each other, but anyone unfortunate to be standing between them as well. I take a moment to study them, noting the erect stance, each with their arms crossed, as they look down upon any who dare to traipse through the halls of their home. Their stern expressions bleed through the canvas, making the images appear so lifelike that I forget I am staring at two paintings.

Kaleb's voice springs me from my musings and I continue onward, catching up to the others just as they turn a corner. I stop. A glass encased room, its walls and ceiling separated by aspen molding, looms before us at the bottom of a small, wide set of steps, and judging by the plants and the courtyard that lie just outside, I surmise that the dining area is within the garden itself, separated by the panels of blue-tinted, crystalline glass. Following after Kaleb, we amble down the four marble stairs and onto the carpeted floor below; a sunset orange color gives the room an inviting appeal. The translucent ceiling allows us to glimpse the dull clouds above us, but their gloominess is displaced with the glow of the amber, elephant-shaped lamps in the upper corners of the room, each facing the center of the dining area with their trunks raised.

"Take your seats," Kaleb says.

I find the one with my nametag and sit down, sinking into the velvet cushion of the chair, as I admire the embroidered tablecloth bearing the crest of Arel. Footsteps reach my ears and in walk Tapiwa, Kumi, three members of the council, and a man I recognize, but had hoped I would never see again: the same man from the plebeian quarters Chase had snuck me into. If I think his presence is shocking enough, nothing prepares me for the person who enters after him: Molers.

I summon every ounce of willpower to remain where I am instead of fleeing from the room. His cold eyes find me and I meet his gaze, refusing to back down, as he finds his seat and we await the first course of our meal.

"Welcome, all of you," says Kumi. "Now, don't be shy. There is no reason to stand on ceremony here. This is your dinner and this is all in your honor," he finishes, looking at the five of us who have been given medals.

"Please," says Tapiwa, "feel free to converse. We are all friends here." Something tells me that the opposite is true.

"I must say that I am surprised to find you here, Master Arbiter," says Commander Vye in a faux sweet tone, inquiring about his presence, something I want to do.

Molers grins. There is no joy behind it, but something more

sinister. "I must say that I am surprised to be here, but sometimes surprises can be rewarding."

"Senior Arbiter Kyles suggested that since he helped train our five honored guests, he deserves to share in the celebration," Tapiwa says, breaking some of the tension between Molers and Commander Vye, introducing the arbiter I saw at the plebeian quarters the night I had snuck out. She turns toward him to finish her statement. "Though, you will have to return to the munitions factory when we are finished."

"Of course, Madam President," Molers replies. "I am honored to be here."

"How much time do you have left on your sentence?" asks a member of the council.

"Three weeks."

"And how is it you managed to be sent there?"

Plebeians enter the dining area, carrying silver trays filled with bowls. Their shaved heads reflect the light within the room as they place porcelain bowls, with gold leaflets etched into the rim forming semicircles, in front of each of us, not spilling a single drop of the cheddar bisque. Something seems familiar about my server. Upon closer examination, I realize that she is the plebeian girl that Senior Arbiter Kyles had taken from the ghetto. Despite the shaved head, scrubbed skin, and sea-blue outfit she wears, there is no mistaking that it is her. The fear that she might recognize me springs to my mind, but I do not remember if she even saw me that night. She places the last bowl on the table, tucks the tray under her left arm, and stalks out of the room with the other servers in silence.

"Our young arbiter over there is the reason." Molers points at me, answering the question that the council member had asked him moments before, and I wish that I am invisible as all eyes turn toward me.

"He broke the law," I say, keeping my voice even, hoping that it would not quiver and betray my uneasiness, and sip a spoonful of the bisque.

"Very ballsy of you," says Kyles.

"Now, let's not insult our youngest recipient of the medal of honor, Senior Arbiter," chides Kumi.

"Really, Kyles," says another, sloshing some of the bisque onto his shirt, "there is no need to make her uncomfortable."

"I meant no disrespect, Mr. President," Kyles says. "It was a compliment. After all, I remember when Molers here ran the gaunt-let. He murdered fifteen in total to ensure that he finished first. So, your actions, my dear, are certainly braver than most."

His words seem complimentary, but his tone conveys an unspoken warning.

"Indeed," says Tapiwa. "Her performance on the wall is a testa-ment to that fact. We thank you. We thank all of you." She raises her glass in a toast and the others follow suit. "You must be very proud," she says to Commander Vye.

"I am. Noni is everything one could hope for in an arbiter, and soon she will no longer be just an apprentice, but a full arbiter."

"Then we are in good hands," says a member of the council.

Once we finish the first course, the line of servers enter the room again, picking up our bowls and replacing them with plates of lamb chops with blueberry sauce, grilled asparagus, creamed spin-ach, and sweet potato curls, all arranged in in a tidy fashion. I take a bite of the lamb chop, marveling at its tender texture and how the meat melts in my mouth.

"How are things in the eastern sector?" one of the council mem-bers asks Commander Vye, and she swallows the food in her mouth before answering.

"Well. This latest attack has been a setback, but we are managing."

"Things could be better," I mutter under my breath, not realiz-ing that everyone can hear me.

"What was that, Noni?" Molers asks, enjoying my little mess up.

Heads turn in my direction, and I simmer under their gaze as they wait for me to elaborate on my statement, while I scold myself for not keeping my thoughts private. "Many of the buildings within the eastern sector have not been repaired."

"The wall requires our attention first," says another member of the council.

"As it should, but after the wall is repaired, what then?" I take a deep breath, preparing my next statement, hoping that I do not end up being carted away for overstepping my bounds. "Many of the buildings within the eastern sector were in a state of disrepair when I first arrived there, made this way from previous attacks. Since I have been there, we have suffered from two more attacks: the first one happened soon after my arrival, and the second one... well... we all know when that happened. Not once did the council send resources to repair the shops or people's homes, which is why there is a lot of anger."

"Are you insinuating..."

"You are all partly responsible for the unrest within Arel," I say.

"How dare you!" A council member pounds his fist on the table, but Tapiwa's harsh voice drowns him out.

"Stop! I want to hear what she has to say."

"If you have a home, food, and live relatively safe, you have no reason to be unhappy. People in the eastern sector have seen their homes destroyed all because they are unfortunate enough to live where all the attacks on the city happen, and no one at this table does anything about it." I scan some of the angered faces surrounding me and know that I have made a few more enemies. Commander Vye's face remains unreadable.

"You are right," says Tapiwa, much to my surprise, since my statement was a critique of her as well.

"Madam President..."

Tapiwa holds up her hand, silencing whomever had spoken. "We have neglected the eastern sector. Tomorrow, I propose that an initiative be passed, allocating resources to the eastern sector to repair the homes of its residents. What do you think, brother?"

Kumi winks at his sister and I am reminded of their rumored re-lationship. "As always, your wisdom knows no bounds. I have to agree."

"Madam President, you cannot just insist…" the council mem-ber who had started to speak, stops, rethinking his words, and changes his tone. "Of course, I am sure that the council will do as you wish."

"The people will thank you," says Kyles.

"Tell them to thank Noni," Tapiwa replies. "It was her idea."

I shove the last bite of food on my plate into my mouth, hoping that I am not asked to speak again. Something tells me that I am being watched and I raise my head, meeting Molers' piercing glare, and I know that the last few minutes did not go as he had planned. I avert my eyes, but I needn't have bothered.

"I'm afraid it is time for you to return, Master Arbiter," Kumi says to Molers, summoning a guard.

Molers wipes his mouth with his napkin and places it on the table beside his half-eaten plate, bowing his head at both Tapiwa and Kumi before uttering his good-byes and leaving with the guard.

"Dessert, anyone?" asks Kumi.

A series of agreements emanate around the room as the servers enter once again to cart our plates away, depositing parfaits in front of us, and I find myself mesmerized by the delicate patterns on the slender dishes. I dip my spoon into it and take a bite. Pudding! I haven't had pudding since the banquet, and now that I taste it again, I remember that I quite enjoy it.

"Is the dessert not to your liking?" Tapiwa asks Commander Vye.

"Not at all. It's just… we do have strict dietary guidelines."

"I think they have been temporarily waived. At least for tonight."

Under Tapiwa's unwavering gaze, Commander Vye takes a small bite of her vanilla pudding and swallows; her mouth twitches, telling me that she must not like pudding at all.

"If you really don't like it," says Tapiwa with a chuckle, "I'm sure your protégé won't mind finishing it for you."

Commander Vye gives me a sharp glare and I realize that not only have I eaten my entire dessert, but vanilla pudding eases its way down the side of my chin. I wipe my mouth and pretend to not be embarrassed, but it fools no one.

"Mr. President," says one of the council members after a couple had excused themselves, "I notice that you have a new plebeian."

"Is it that obvious?" jokes Kumi. "We do, yes. One of our plebeians wished to serve elsewhere. So we allowed him and got a new one."

"Are you sure he didn't just leave the city?" laughs another, who had drunk a little too much wine, and Kumi's and Tapiwa's eyes narrow.

"Leave?" asks a third.

"Yes," continues the inebriated one. "You don't know? A group of three plebeians were caught trying to sneak out of the city. It's ridiculous! Where did they think they would go? But that isn't the best part. The best part is that one of our own teachers tried to smuggle them out."

"A teacher?" says the third.

"Yes! I think she said her name was Mora, or something, when she was brought before the Ministry of Justice."

Mora! I know that name. That's the name the man who helped me escape the drones the night I had snuck out had called me.

"It's a shame, really," continues the man.

"I'm sure she has been dealt with," I say, doing my best to sound as cold as Molers would if he had asked about the woman's fate.

"Let's just say that the dogs were a little less hungry afterwards."

The news hits me hard. It shouldn't. I never knew this woman, but I feel as though an anchor has been set in my stomach, and I think of that man still waiting for his daughter to return and lying awake at night wondering what happened to her.

"I think you've had enough to drink," Kumi says, his voice even and tight.

"Oh, now…" The man stops, noticing the dark expression on Kumi's and Tapiwa's face. "Perhaps, you're right."

"I don't mean to be rude," says Commander Vye, navigating the terse silence with care, "but it is late and we do have rotations tomorrow."

The tense mood in the room calms, and both Tapiwa and Kumi resume their smiles as though nothing had happened and stand up.

"We wish to thank all of you," says Kumi to the five of us honorees, "for honoring us with your presence. Arel owes you all a debt of gratitude."

"Thank you, sir," we all say in unison.

Tapiwa approaches Commander Vye and pulls us both aside. "You have a bold one there."

"A little too bold sometimes," replies the commander.

"Perhaps not," says Tapiwa. She looks at me. "I'm going to keep my eye on you."

I don't know what to say and salute her, unsure if I should be flattered or worried.

"This way!" says Kaleb, appearing from nowhere and ushering us all out of the dining area and to the front entrance, where the presidential transport waits to take us all back to the eastern sector.

We file inside and I sit by the window again, watching the immaculate buildings disappear behind the gate as we leave.

Chapter 31

A Choice

Three weeks have passed since the ceremony, but I have not noticed the passage of time. It could have been three days or three months. Commander Vye has kept us all busy with double rotations. Something has changed. I sense it, but cannot figure out what it is, and it cannot all be blamed on the last attack on the wall. Rumors have slithered throughout Arel, whispering about how we have caught one of the leaders who helped smuggle people out of the city.

Dusk hovers over the land as the sun slips behind the wall, dipping lower to the ground, threatening to leave us all in darkness forever. I stand in front of the mirror in my room, cast in the shadow of the wall, ever reaching, always overbearing. Once, I looked upon it as a source of protection from the cruelty of the outside world, but such notions have faded, withering away the same way the flowers die every fall. A somber face stares back at me, full of confusion, full of uncertainty. Bony cheeks, brown, oval eyes, walnut-colored skin—all components that tell my mind it is my face that stares back at me. But where is the certainty? Where is the wonder?

"Noni?" whispers Shelia's voice through the door.

I open it, allowing her inside.

"Commander Vye is looking for you. It is almost time for your rotation."

"I'll be down in a moment."

"You're not even dressed!" Shelia stares at me in my under-clothes. "Here." She hands me a small bowl of steamed carrots that she had hidden under her shirt, and I take them, marveling at how she is looking out for me, when it should be the other way around.

"Thank you," I tell her. "Now, you best go before you are missed. And…"

"Don't worry," Sheila smiles at me. "I have found a way to re-main busy and avoid Anan."

She leaves, and I am left alone, kneeling on the floor, holding a bowl of steamed carrots. My room grows dimmer. Knowing I haven't much time to report for duty, I cram half the carrots in my mouth and swallow, not bothering to chew them before rushing to my clos-et and snatching a pair of pants and a shirt. Once dressed, I stand in front of the mirror again, observing the way my uniform hugs every curvature of my body, but the strands of hair floating in front of my face thrust me back to the night I first saw Gwen—her hair covered her face, allowing only her gray eyes to stare back at me, filled not with fear, but resolution. Why are mine filled with confusion?

Reaching up, I pull the individual strands away from my face, twisting my hair into a tightknit bun, securing it with bobby pins, before grabbing my jacket and zipping it up. Now, I look every bit the part of an arbiter. I rush out the door and stop. Chase waits for me. Before I can utter a single word, he pulls me aside, away from the lights.

"Be careful tonight, Noni," he says.

"Chase, what's…"

"Just be careful," he says again. "People are on edge, and after this latest attack… please, promise me that you'll be careful."

Something bothers him, I can feel it, but there isn't time for me to coax it out of him. "Chase, what…"

"Just promise me!"

I wish he would tell me what troubles him. "I'm an arbiter," I say to him. "I'll do what I must to protect Arel and its people. All of them."

Chase looks at me and releases a long sigh. "I know you will."

I glance at Shelia as she dusts the window panes at the other end of the corridor. "Look after her for me."

"I will."

Leaving him alone in the hallway, I hurry down the stairs and find Commander Vye waiting at the bottom, wearing her usual disgruntled expression.

"Cutting it close," she warns me.

"Sorry, ma'am." I take my place in line with the other arbiters scheduled to go out tonight. Most days, we just leave the manor and report to our assigned station, but tonight, Commander Vye thinks it necessary to say something to us first.

"I want you all to be extra vigilant tonight. The wall, though under repair, still has a few weak spots that have yet to be fixed. We do not know what the outsiders are planning, but they may try to take advantage of our weakness. But the dangers that lie outside the wall are not our only adversary. We must watch for the threats that are within. The latest attack has caused some old discontentment to rise to the surface once more, and President Kumi is addressing the city tonight. Stay alert. Dismissed."

We all file out of the manor.

"So, it is you and me again," greets Renal when I step outside into the night air.

"Sir," I say to him.

"Come on. We are assigned to the central region of the eastern sector, near Sigal's place."

I say nothing and follow him down the drive and through the open gate.

Eerie silence looms as we walk to our assigned area, permeating the very atmosphere and delving deep within our bones. Not even a hint of a breeze closing a shutter that hangs ajar is heard. Ahead of us is the center of Arel, bright and lit up for all the world to see as people in those sectors gather to hear President Kumi's speech, while Renal and I remain shrouded in darkness on this moonless night, with sparse lamps spread throughout to give us some semblance of comfort. Cheers rise from within the executive district, filling my ears with their jubilance, and I picture the stage where President Kumi stands, staring out at the crowd in a regal stance, waiting for the perfect moment to deliver the first word of his speech.

The speakers in the city sputter to life just as Renal and I reach the plaza area, lit up by the central screen within it, allowing us to see our president as he speaks to us, though the bottom corners are blacked out, making President Kumi appear to be disembodied. I look at it just as a drone hovers past, disappearing down a side street.

"Citizens of Arel!" President Kumi's voice booms over the loud-speakers, but I ignore most of his words, aware that I must stay alert.

Renal and I split up, patrolling opposite ends of the plaza. My steps clack on the pavement, sending distinct sounds into the air, penetrating the uneasy silence that envelops me as my mind wonders why it is so quiet. No one is outside, which is normal at night, since curfew dictates that only the arbiters on duty are allowed to wander the streets after sunset, but I cannot shake the nagging feeling that something is off. The more I walk, the more I feel the humidity increase around me, causing my clothes to become damp from sweat, and I know that it will rain again. I reach the end of the plaza, turn, and begin my trek across it again, surveying the darkness around me without moving my head. Renal looks at me from his end and we both nod at one another, while Kumi's speech reverberates around us.

I hear a low whistle. At first, I am unsure if I had heard it, or if my ears and heightened awareness are fooling with my mind. Stopping, I turn my head in its direction, trying to peer into the night and make out what could have caused it, but all I see is darkness. Renal stops, too, having noticed my wariness. Before either of us can say anything, a rock crashes into one of the speakers above us, releasing a tremendous clang that echoes off the walls of the buildings around us. Running footsteps grab our attention and we both take off after them.

"Stop!" yells Renal.

A shadow sprints down an alley with us both behind it. It veers to the left, rounding a corner. Renal and I follow suit. Our boots pound the pavement as we chase after the mysterious man, but he jolts to the right, jumping on a low-hanging ladder, and climbs up it to the balcony above. Renal pursues him, but I pause. The man climbs to the balcony above him and to a third one, until he reaches the roof with Renal scrambling after him. He jumps to the roof next to him. Thinking of a plan, I sprint down the narrow street, keeping my eye on the man as he leaps from rooftop to rooftop of the housing complexes, nothing but a dark silhouette in the city lights. He turns. I change my direction, matching his, and spot another ladder, guessing that it is his destination.

I race for it. Just as I reach the ladder, feet spill over the edge of the roof and the man lowers himself onto it. I pull out my handgun, waiting. Just one more step, I think to myself, as I stand poised beneath the ladder, concealed in the darkness, waiting. When he is halfway down, I fire at the bolts connecting the ladder to the brick wall of the building, and it falls to the ground, discarding its occupant, who crashes into the pavement with a groan. Before he can move, I pounce on him, flipping him onto his stomach, jamming my knee into his back, and wrenching his hands behind him. Renal runs up from behind, having found another way off the roof, as I bind the man's hands together.

"What are you doing out here?" demands Renal, but the man's brown eyes glare at us in defiance. He is no plebeian, but it is clear that he has no love for arbiters either. "Answer me!" Renal says again.

Nothing.

A can skips across the pavements the next street over, and a second later, my wristband flashes red, the same as Renal's.

"A drone has spotted something," says Renal, touching his wristband, letting the drone know that he is on his way. "Take him to the detainment box while I check this out."

"Shouldn't we go together?" I ask.

"It might be nothing."

"Yes, sir."

Renal runs off.

The man makes a desperate attempt to get away, but I elbow him in the jaw, stunning him, while I drag him to an information booth, glad that there is one nearby, surrounded by the words of Kumi's speech; his loquaciousness is well-known. Once at the booth, the monitor screen flashes to life, and I scan my bracelet, giving my name and serial number and the reason for this man's detainment—vandalism, out after curfew, resisting arrest—and shove him into the detainment box when it opens. He spits in my face. Angered, I push him hard until his head strikes the side of the box.

"You arbiters are all the same," he says.

For a brief moment, I consider letting him go as my mind dwells on what will happen to him once he reaches the Ministry of Justice, but I push it aside as the whine of a drone hits my ears. He did break the law, even if it was just throwing a stone at a loudspeaker during Kumi's address to the city. The rock. Something isn't adding up. Why would one man risk being caught just to vandalize a speaker, unless…

"Who are you working with?" I demand.

He spits at me again in answer.

"Tell me!" I place my arm against his neck, choking him, hoping to force him to answer my question.

"Your day of reckoning is coming," he hisses at me. "Even you arbiters won't be safe."

A diversion. The rock was nothing more than a distraction, but for what? I tap my wristband, bringing up the communications channel. "Renal? Renal, come in. It's a trap! I repeat. It's…"

The man slams into me from behind and I fall on my hands and knees, the pavement burning as it rips a layer of skin off my palms. Rolling onto my back, I kick him in the stomach. He lunges at me, but I leap to my feet and plow into him, jabbing him in the throat before slamming his head into the side of the open door of the containment box. Blood pours down the left side of his face and he goes limp, dropping back into the box just as I hit the button to closes it.

Renal.

I tap my wristband again and a small screen appears above my wrist, showing me my location in relation to Renal's. He isn't far. I race down the street, glancing at my band, making sure that I am on the right path. I turn down an alley. All the while, the small image above my wrist blinks at me, showing my position in relation to Renal's. He is the next street over. The alley veers west, but I need to head east. Skidding to a halt, I spot a narrow space between two buildings, just wide enough for me to squeeze through. Placing my back against the cold, damp exterior of one of the structures, I shuffle sideways, inching my way through, holding my already flat stomach in as I navigate my way through the cramped space, feeling a bit claustrophobic.

"Stop!" Renal's voice spills through the opening, bringing me relief that he is okay.

I reach the end of the opening.

"I said stop right there!"

Peeking around the corner, I watch as a strange scene unfolds in front of me: Renal's back faces me, but in front of him is Sigal with his wife, daughter, Ian, and two plebeians.

"Sigal?" says Renal, not believing his eyes. "What are you…"

"Please, Renal," Sigal says in a calm voice, "just let us go."

"But, you've always been a friend to us."

"Yes, and I am still yours," says Sigal. "If you want, take me in, but please, let them go."

Renal keeps his weapon pointed at them, struggling over what to do, caught in an internal battle between what he knows the law to be and what his heart asks of him, the same as me.

Staring into their eyes, I see no malice, nor hatred like the man who vandalized the loudspeaker, just resolution, the same acceptance that Gwen's had the night I had caught her stealing medicine for her bedridden mistress. Memories of the plebeian quarters that Chase had taken me to flood my brain, mixed with images from the munitions factory and the woman who chose death for her and the infant in her arms over a life of hopeless servitude, and I know what will happen to them if Renal turns them in, a fate that rips my heart from my chest. This must be why that man threw the rock and risked being arrested.

Sigal's wife spots me and I place my finger over my lips, signaling her to remain silent, as I step out of the narrow opening between the brick buildings and tiptoe to Renal, sneaking up behind him, pulling my baton free of its holster. While Sigal pleads with Renal, I creep closer, raising my baton and strike him over the head, rendering him unconscious. He collapses to the ground, and I use my foot to kick his weapon out of his hands.

Awkward silence ensues as Sigal and I stare at one another. The whine of a drone reaches my ears. "Quick!" I hiss, ushering them to the shadows, while I stand behind the protruding edge of a building, baton raised.

The drone hovers closer, floating through the air, scanning the area, but remains unaware of Renal's still form. Listening, its whine grows louder, more intense. Taking a deep breath to still my nerves, I tell myself that this is just another test, like the gauntlet, and that failure means death. It hovers inches away. I swing my baton, smashing the drone into the wall, shattering it, pleased when it's blinking light goes out.

"Go!" I hiss at them.

They hurry away, while I check Renal and place my fingers on his neck, where his pulse should be. He is still alive, but unconscious. Knowing what I must do, I take my wristband off—it's a gamble because if he wakes before I return, he will know what I have done—and place it next to him before running after Sigal and the others, catching up to them.

"This way!" I say to them, taking the lead.

At first, they hesitate, unsure of my intentions, but I show them my naked wrist. Sigal follows me first and the others copy his actions. I take them through the maze of alleys and their plethora of mud, puddles, and trash, staying clear of the moving walkways and their cameras, heading for the wall which once served as our protector, but is now our jailer. Another drone hovers past and I stop everyone, shoving them into the shadows until the softball-sized sphere disappears.

"We must always be on the lookout for any who might betray us," continues Kumi's speech. "They can be someone you know, a teacher, a doctor, or even an arbiter."

How fitting.

Waving Sigal and the others onward, we dart across an empty street to another alley. One of the plebeians bumps into a garbage can, sending it on its side. Cursing, I urge them to move faster, rounding another corner, hoping that no one heard the noise, or bothers to look. A drop of rain hits my cheek. Ignoring it, I keep going, making certain that they are close behind as I take them to a place in the wall where the repairs are not finished. We reach it. Pausing in the shadows, I look for any guards and spot one further down facing the city. He turns around. Seizing our chance, I usher everyone across the street to the wall itself, pushing them into its shadow.

There's the hole and two guards standing next to it, but the dogs are nowhere to be found, which means they are penned somewhere to prevent them from mauling the workers repairing it. I find a piece of stone, rubble still left behind from the last attack, and chuck it as far away from me as I can, hoping that the two guards will take the bait. It clatters against the pavement with sharp clacks. They turn toward the noise and one speaks into his communication device. They leave their post.

"Go!" I say to Sigal and the others.

They run to the hole in the wall. Sigal urges Ian and the plebeians through first, followed by his wife and daughter, but pauses when it is his turn.

"You should come to," he says to me.

"Where?"

"Trilya."

I think of Shelia, Chase, and Gwen. "I can't."

"Noni…"

"Go! When the guards aren't looking, hide in the tall grass and make your way to the trees." Before he can slip through the wall, I speak the question on my mind. "The man with the rock. He was to provide a distraction for you, wasn't he?"

"I don't know him," says Sigal, looking at me in confusion. "We just took advantage of his actions."

My face falls and more questions enter my mind as the man's warning repeats itself in my head.

"Noni,"—Sigal grabs my arm—"there is more going on here than just the smuggling of people out of Arel. It is no longer safe for me here, which is why we're leaving, and it's not Arel's laws or arbiters that I fear."

I stare at him with a perplexed expression on my face.

"Strange that there are only two guards here," he says before disappearing through the hole.

I watch as they wait for the guards to look away before they dart across the sand and into the tall grass, vanishing from sight, and place the wiring back where it belongs. I hope they make it.

Once it is safe, I dash away from the wall and down a side street, concealing myself in the shadows, just as the two guards return to their station. Before I can take another step, a huge explosion rocks the city, sending plumes of smoke and fire into the air, lighting up the night.

Renal!

Slack jawed, I stare at the fires that burn, watching them reach for the stars as the alarms go off, summoning all arbiters to the chaos, reminded of the man's warning and Sigal's words. There is more happening here than a few attacks and people being smuggled out of the city, and citizens and plebeians are not safe.

I make my way back to Renal, using the darkness to my advantage and staying away from the lights that fill windows, knowing what I must do.

Noni's story will continue in book 2: Ensnared.

Get the Entire Series

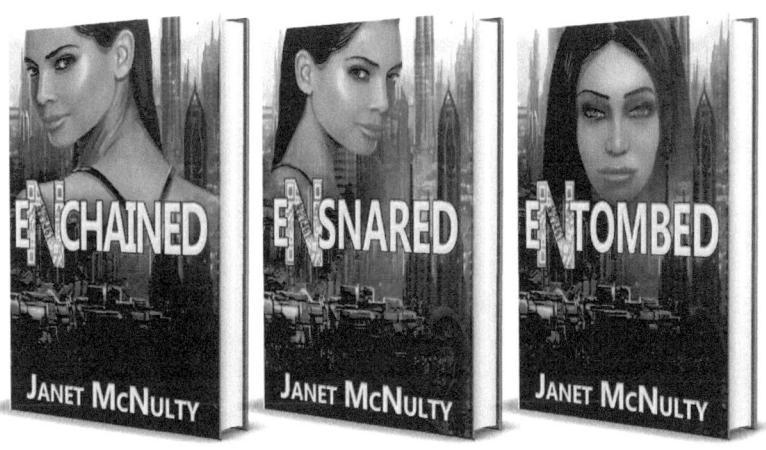

Having spent her entire life secluded in the Martial Diplomatic Corps, Noni passes the final test, achieving the coveted position as arbiter of Arel. Placed under the tutelage of a seasoned veteran, Noni will see her city for the first time and learn that not everything is as she had been taught to believe.

Available at major retailers.

About the Author

Janet McNulty is a self-published author, practicing what she calls the most expensive hobby one can engage in.

In 2011, she released Legends Lost Amborese, which was published under the pen name of Nova Rose. Ms. McNulty has since published three novels in the Legends Lost series: Tesnayr and Galdin.

Ms. McNulty has gone on to publish three more books series in the last seven years: The Mellow Summers Series, The Dystopia Trilogy, and The Solaris Saga.

Currently, Ms. McNulty is working on the next book in her new dystopian series: The Enchained Trilogy.

More books by Janet McNulty

The Solaris Saga

Solaris Seethes
Solaris Seeks
Solaris Strays
Solaris Soars

Also available in audio.

Every myth has a beginning.

After escaping the destruction of her home planet, Lanyr, with the help of the mysterious Solaris, Rynah must put her faith in an ancient legend. Never one to believe in stories and legends, she is forced to follow the ancient tales of her people: tales that also seem to predict her current situation.

Forced to unite with four unlikely heroes from an unknown planet (the philosopher, the warrior, the lover, the inventor) in order to save the Lanyran people, Rynah and Solaris embark on an adventure that will shatter everything Rynah once believed.

The Mellow Summers Series

Sugar And Spice And Not So Nice
Frogs, Snails, And A Lot Of Wails
An Apple A Day Keeps Murder Away
Three Little Ghosts
Oh Holy Ghost
Where Trouble Roams
Two Ghosts Haunt A Grove
Trick Or Treat Or Murder
Roses Are Red...He's Dead
Double, Double Nothing But Trouble
Ring Around The Rosy Not Another Ghosty
Hickory Dickory Dock The Ghost In The Clock
Violet Are Blue More Trouble Brews
Hey Diddle Diddle The Zombie In The Middle

Mellow Summers moves to Vermont to attend college, accompanied by her friend Jackie. They soon find themselves running into ghosts and one mystery after another.

Some titles also available in audio.

The Dystopia Trilogy

Dystopia (Book 1)
Tempered Steel (Book 2)
Liberty's Torch (Book 3)

**Imagine living in a world where
everything you do is controlled.**

Dana Ginary lives in a world where every aspect of her life is
controlled by the Dystopian Government. Forced to work in
Waste Management, her life becomes a nightmare with hunger
and survival is her only constant. Before she knows it, she is
caught up in a resistance movement and exiled from Dystopia,
forced to find her way in the barren wastelands. While there,
she must learn to live independently and discover how far she
is willing to go to live and achieve freedom.

The Legends Lost Series

Published under Nova Rose

Tesnayr
Amborese
Galdin

Enter the Lands of Tesnayr and join on an epic fantasy adventure that spans over 1,500 years.

Begin with Tesnayr, the first king of the five lands as he unites the against a savage foe bent on their destruction.

Next, Join Amborese as she fights reclaim the throne after her family was forced to flee from it.

Thinking peace has finally entered the land, follow Galdin as he returns to Tesnayr to find it greatly hanged. Barbarians, led by a mysterious sorcerer, burn and destroy as they go. And only Galdin can stop them if he chooses to accept his fate.

Grandpa's Stories

My grandfather grew up in Arizona during the 1920s and 1930s. One week after the attack on Pearl Harbor he joined the Navy. During the summer of 2012, my mother visited him and recorded his stories about growing up, World War II, and his time as an employee at the Pacific Bell Telephone Company. This is the history of the 20th century as he lived it. These recordings make up this book. These are his words.

Something for the Little Ones

The Dragon Who series

The Dragon Who was Afraid of the Dark
The Dragon Who Went to the Moon
The Dragon Who Found a Monster Party
The Dragon Who Found a Spider in His Shoe
The Dragon Who Explored the Sea
The Dragon Who Caught a Cold

The Fairy Who series

The Fairy Who Lost a Tooth
The Fairy Who Got Lost

The Mr. Chili series

Mr. Chili's Chili
Mr. Chili Goes To School
Mr. Chili's Halloween
Mr. Chili's Christmas

Others

Mrs. Duck and the Dragon
The Hungry Washing Machine
Rhymes-a-lot
Are You the Monster Under My Bed?
How Do You Catch An Alien